BRITTANY ELISE

Awakening the Trinity

Black Rose Writing | Texas

ISBN: 978-1-68433-126-0
PUBLISHED BY BLACK ROSE WRITING
www.blackrosewriting.com

Printed in the United States of America
Suggested Retail Price (SRP) $19.95

Awakening the Trinity is printed in Plantagenet Cherokee

This one is for those who still believe in the possibility of magic.

Acknowledgements

With all the words in the English language at my disposal, it still remains impossible that I could properly thank everyone who helped me make this book a reality. As always, I am eternally grateful for the support of my family, and for my husband, Benjamin. You always know the right thing to say. I couldn't do this without your unfailing love and encouragement. I'd like to express my gratitude to the publisher and the team behind the scenes at Black Rose Writing, and also give a special shout to Caleb J. Oakes–my writing coach, my mentor, my friend. (And all the other titles that go along with keeping a writer sane.) Thank you for challenging me, and thank you for all the work you put in with my cover art. I'd also like to thank Wolf Creek Habitat out of Indiana for donating the picture of Onyx for my cover. You guys rock!

Awakening
the Trinity

Chapter One
The Stranger

He smelled like pine.

Not that synthetic chemical garbage that comes in household cleaners or scented candles. This scent was tangible; like the forest right outside the café windows, heady and thick like the earth. It was the first thing I noticed right before my Supernatural senses kicked into high gear and I could *feel* him. His presence caused the hair on the back of my neck to stand on end, and a shiver descended the length of my spine. That's how it always started, radiating outward in a slow caress until it felt like someone was pulling the strings on an invisible corset that choked the air from my lungs. That's how I knew he was different–like me.

I reached up, cupping the back of my head that was still tingling. The sensation should have worn off by now–I'd made a connection with the guy, so what was the hold up? It was like I was hyperaware of whatever he was, which made his presence impossible to ignore. I gazed at the back of his head from my position in line, wondering if he could sense me. It was different for all magical beings. Witches in particular could sense one another, but that wasn't always the case with the rest of the Supernatural kind.

Aside from my mother and me, Silver Mountain was void of other Supernatural beings. The town itself was just a small black dot on the map en route to bigger cities on the Eastern Seaboard. Population: twenty-five hundred and declining. Our town wasn't exactly the kind of place that people chose to visit on purpose; in fact, most people rolled right through town before realizing they had. Not that it was a bad place to live or anything, because it wasn't. It was just a very rustic, very secluded place that didn't have a lot of modern draw. Silver Mountain contained two kinds of people; the ones who were native born, and the ones that moved away but missed the ambiance so much they ended up coming back. Kind of like that song–Hotel California–you could check out if you wanted, but you could never really leave. Silver Mountain had a way of grabbing hold and getting in your bloodstream. It made me wonder what could have drawn this guy in, or what it was about his presence that was wreaking havoc on my Supernatural alert-system.

The mysterious newcomer paid for his order and then moved out of line. He chose a lone corner table (my favorite) in the back of the café, sitting next to a big window beneath a replica painting of *Starry Night* by Vincent van Gough.

"What can I get you, Quinny?" Torrance grinned from behind the counter. The overhead lights glinted off the studded jewelry that pierced her nose and lip and when she smiled, her lateral incisor jutted out slightly over her front tooth.

"Better make it a double this morning," I said, drumming my plum fingernails across the counter as I studied the menu above. "I'll take a caramel macchiato, and a vanilla cappuccino, please."

"I take it Annabelle is running late again?" Torrance giggled, tapping a few buttons on the register in front of her.

"Have you ever known her to be on time?" I asked.

"It's her quirk," Torrance said. "Everyone has something." She tossed her long, wavy blonde hair over one of her shoulders with a shrug.

I lifted an eyebrow, waiting for her to tell me what my "quirk" was but she just laughed and spouted off the price of my coffee. I suspected Torrance had her own opinions about me but didn't want to voice them. I reached into my faded, multi-colored messenger bag to retrieve some money. Annabelle referred to it as my "hippie bag" because it was made from different fabrics that had been put together in patchwork-type patterns. At its center, a silhouette of a wolf sat howling up at a yellow moon. It was the last gift my mother had given me before she died.

I collected our drinks from the end of the counter and picked my way through the maze of tables, settling for a small table wedged between a support beam and a window that had a lovely view of the front parking lot. I sighed, sinking down into the chair. At least I could still see Silver Mountain Forest from across the street, and the silver-blue of the mountain peak poking over the backdrop of giant evergreens. I shot the new guy a look; knowing my expression portrayed a serious case of table-envy. It didn't matter though. He had his back to me and he was bent over the table; head slightly tilted over paperwork. I watched the pen moving in his hand in a slow rhythm, almost as if he were distracted. Judging by the set of his shoulders and the way he was seated in the chair, it was like he was both relaxed and ready to bolt at the same time if he had to.

Stop staring, Quinn, you have homework to do, I mentally reprimanded myself. I concentrated on building a mental block against the Supe and pulled my history book from my "hippie bag." Just then, the little brass bell above the door jingled. I looked up, spotting Annabelle's small frame as she picked her way through the congested space of towering bodies. She was easy to miss if you weren't looking down. "Excuse me," she muttered in annoyance. She pushed outward with her hands; a gesture like Moses parting the Red Sea before she managed to break through. "Must be Saturday," she said with a bitter tone. "I hate that this is the only coffee joint in town." She pulled a chair out from the table; the wooden legs scraping against the linoleum tile.

"I ordered for you already." I pushed her cappuccino across the table.

"Thanks," she said, picking it up, "double shot of espresso?"

"You actually think I'd forget?"

"You're the best," she told me. "Sorry I was late. Caitlyn was monopolizing the bathroom for a job interview. Unfortunately for me, that falls under category one section A of our bathroom treaty and gives her the rite of dominion over the mirror for ungodly lengths of time. Like seriously, how is it possible that one human being can be in there for hours at a time–what are you even doing?"

"Yet another reason why I'm happy to be an only child." I cracked a half smile.

"You don't know how lucky you are," Annabelle said. She scanned the room until her gaze fell upon the new guy who had taken up our usual table. "Who's the table thief?" She tipped her chin in his direction and lowered her voice so he wouldn't overhear. Not that he would anyway; the coffee shop was buzzing with sounds of mingled voices and bluegrass that was spilling from the overhead speakers.

I glanced up, taking in his dark hair and matching leather jacket. It was well worn but fit him nicely across his broad shoulders and narrowed with his waist. He was of slender build, but I sensed he had a bit more muscle definition hidden beneath his autumn attire. Most Supernaturals tended to run on the fit side.

"Uh, I don't know," I replied with a frown. I wasn't sure why I didn't just tell her he was different. Annabelle was the only human aside from my immediate family that knew the truth about what I was. I could trust her with my life. But there hadn't been another Supernatural in Silver Mountain in eons, and I suspected this one wasn't staying long. Besides, we Supernaturals had an unspoken code of concealment. Being a witch meant that I had an unfair advantage in knowing he was different, and considering I didn't actually know what he was, I thought it best to just keep my mouth shut—even if he was frying my mental wires.

"Maybe he's a transfer?" Annabelle wondered aloud.

"From where," I countered, "and *why*?"

"How should I know?" Annabelle retorted. "I'm not the one with the abilities. Can't you do a little witchy-woo and figure it out?"

I shot her a look, and she held up her hands in mock defense. Witch or not, I didn't tamper with magic unless it was a necessity. All magic was given at a price. There were rules, and if broken, the consequences could be severe. You couldn't just go around casting spells to make acne disappear or add a cup size to your breasts because you felt like it. You couldn't cast any spells for the sake of vanity for that matter, nor could you tap into a person's brain and get the four-one-one on them—unless of course you were me. I possessed a natural power that allowed me to see into people's minds and get a glimpse of someone's past or future. It was fairly complex to tap into, and not at all as simple as tuning in and just "listening" to a person's mind, either. As if the "gift" wasn't already awkward enough, I could only do it if I came into contact with blood.

It didn't have to be a monumental amount, just a pinprick would do. If I touched it, a flash of images shimmered through my brain; at first appearing like the inkblot smears of a Rorschach test. The images shifted until they took shape, and I was thrown smack into the middle of the scene. Seeing a glimpse of someone's past was like being transported through another place in time. It scrambled my center, making me feel as though gravity were a relative concept that no longer applied to me. I didn't physically go anywhere when it happened, but the spinning sensation always left me reeling as though I had.

Seeing someone's future was like watching a movie. I stood apart from it, observing from a distance, but this was by far the most painful experience. When it happened, I felt like I was being swallowed by the ocean, dragged beneath the waves and the crushing weight of it squeezed the air from my lungs. When you tapped into that sort of magic, you were watching something that hadn't yet come to pass, and in doing so meant you had the knowledge and capability to change an event before it could happen. Tampering with something like that could alter everything; disrupting the natural course of events, and maybe for worse. Regardless of what I did with that knowledge, I still had to pay a price for tapping into the ability. The divine elements would punish me by leaving me weakened. Nose bleeds accompanied by teeth-gritting pain would circulate through my entire body immediately after a vision. I guess it was nature's way of finding balance–damage control, if you will. And it wasn't pretty.

"Earth to Quinn," Annabelle said, snapping her fingers in my face. "Zone out much?" She rolled her eyes.

"Sorry," I said. My senses were overstimulated. The Supe in the corner might as well have been wearing a flashing neon sign bright enough to induce a migraine.

"What's with you this morning?" she asked.

"I'm just having trouble staying focused," I said, rolling my neck from side to side in hopes of easing the building tension. "I probably just need to recharge."

Annabelle's dark eyes widened, her doll-like face shifting into an expression of understanding. "We can take a hike if you want? We have the whole week to finish this report. I could use some fresh air."

"Yeah?"

"Of course," she answered. "Let me just use the facilities, and then I'll meet you outside."

I nodded gratefully and began stuffing my books inside my bag with haste. I wound through the obstacle course of people and scattered chairs and deposited our empty coffee mugs on the counter.

"Thanks Q, see ya' Monday," Torrance said.

"Thanks for the caffeine fix." I tapped my goodbye on the counter and turned away. My shoulder bounced off a solid object, and I found myself looking up into the face of the Supe. For a moment, time seemed to stop all together. He had midsummer night eyes, I thought, voltaic; reminiscent of slow-rolling heat lightning on long, lazy summer nights. I blinked a couple of times, working my way out of the trance.

"Sorry," he said in a low tone that sounded more like a rumble, "I didn't see you there." He started to smile, and I noticed a smirk seemed to take its place naturally, accentuating the small dimples on either side of his lips.

I meant to speak. I felt my lips parting, but for some odd sort of reason, the words just wouldn't form. Instead of fading, the pulsing of my awareness only heightened in his immediate presence.

He strolled past me then, stirring the air with scents of earth and pine as he headed for the door. He moved with a vigilant awareness of his surroundings; every motion calculated. He'd bumped into me on purpose, I decided. And as I watched him climb behind the wheel of an old, black Pontiac Firebird, I wondered just what sort of game he was playing.

"Homecoming is next weekend," Annabelle said behind me. She'd tried for a nonchalant approach to the subject, but I couldn't help hearing an influx of interest in her tone.

"So it is," I replied. My calves were filled with the delicious ache from climbing through the forest. There were plenty of hiking trails mapped out through the park, but I knew the forest by heart, and preferred the adventure of hacking through uncharted land. I couldn't say the same for Annabelle, though she tolerated my escapades without complaint.

"So," she continued, "I was thinking that since we're seniors this year maybe we should go–you know, for the sake of high school tradition."

I wrinkled up my nose. "Since when do you care about high school traditions?"

"I don't really. It's just that years from now I want to be able to look back on my life and know that I didn't miss out on anything. I don't want to have any regrets."

I stopped abruptly and felt her smack into my spine. I spun on my heel to face her. "Okay, who are you and what did you do with my best friend? Do I need to perform an exorcism spell, because the Annabelle I know doesn't give a flying rats ass about 'high school traditions'–in fact, I'm pretty sure she'd tell me they're overrated."

Annabelle rolled her dark eyes skyward, reaching back and looping her long black hair into a ponytail. "You're not funny, Quinn."

"I can't be both comedian and witch–it's against the rules of the universe." I continued to tease her. She sighed deeply and moved in front of me, stomping off through the wilderness. "Anna, wait," I said, catching up to her. "I'm just playing with you. I honestly didn't mean any offense–but I do know you, and I know you wouldn't want to go to this dance unless you had a very specific reason."

She wheeled on me and blurted, "Shawn asked me to go with him."

"Shawn *Fletcher*?" My eyes widened owlishly. "When?"

"Last week." She shrugged, studying my expression. "He asked me after AP chem. I didn't tell you because I was sure you'd try to talk me out of it."

"I wouldn't do that!" I said defensively.

Annabelle lifted a perfectly manicured eyebrow and just glared at me.

"Well what about Huck's anti-homecoming party? We already

agreed to go." (As had most of our cross-country team.) Huck was the boys' team captain, and his parents were conveniently going to be out of town for their anniversary that weekend.

"I guess you'll just have to go without me."

"But you love Huck's parties."

"I don't like the party aspect of it so much as I just like hanging out with all our friends," she told me. "It's just this one time."

"Do you even like Shawn?"

Annabelle laughed, the sound of disbelief carrying high into the treetops. "Shall I hand you a shovel now? It's looking pretty deep in there."

"All right, I'm sorry," I told her. "You've just never mentioned him before." Book-smart and driven to succeed, Annabelle rarely mentioned boys or crushes. I could count the number of dates she'd been on with one of my hands and still have a few fingers to spare. It wasn't that she didn't get asked out, because she did. It was just that she was always so practical–wise beyond her years. Most of the boys at our school were leagues beneath what she called an "acceptable maturity level."

"Shawn's nice," Annabelle said. We'd reached one of my favorite hideaways in the serene forest. Ducking beneath the low branches of the surrounding pines, we found ourselves in what I'd christened, The Hollow.

The opened area was nearly a perfect circle surrounded by towering rows of ancient pines, where the dense greenery and rubble of the earth rose up to meet the sun. Thousands of russet colored needles coated the forest floor, and several moss-covered boulders jutted forth from the earth; some taller than six feet, and just as wide. Annabelle slung her pack from her shoulders, letting it drop at the base of a boulder and climbed up so that her feet were dangling above the ground.

"He is nice," I agreed. Shawn had a mop of brown shaggy hair that curled over his shirt collar. His glasses were too big for his face–he was always pushing them up the bridge of his nose whenever he looked down. He was clumsy too, tripping over shoelaces and dropping school books down the stairwell on a semi-regular basis. He was, however, undoubtedly wicked smart. He was valedictorian, sitting at the top of our graduating class with a perfect GPA.

"And if you don't mind his scruffy hair and baggy clothes, he's kind of cute," she added, bouncing her heels off the boulder.

"Hey if you like him, that's all that matters." I sat down at the base of her boulder, resting my back against the moss-padded surface. The sun filtered down through the branches, casting rays of slanted golden light through the Hollow. The Earth's power was strong here. I pressed my fingertips through the orange needles and into the top layer of dirt below. I inhaled deeply, practically tasting pine. The image of the Supe's amber eyes flashed across my inner vision; the scent sparking a memory. The back of my neck tingled, so I pressed my fingertips deeper into the ground and concentrated on letting the Earth element rejuvenate my senses.

"You could come with us–to the dance I mean," Annabelle suggested a moment later, and I snorted.

"Tempting, but I think I'll pass on the third-wheel portion of the program."

"What about Jamie? I see the way he looks at you at practice. I'll bet he'd be more than happy to escort you to the dance."

Jamie was cute, and on very rare occasions he could be charming. Mostly he was an arrogant goofball. I'd had a huge crush on him my sophomore year, but neither of us had been brave enough to take a step past flirting. "I'm going to Huck's party," I said. "It'll be fun."

"Yeah, but we always do everything together," Annabelle added. "I just don't want you to be upset with me for going to the dance."

"I'm not upset," I told her, forcing what I hoped was a tone of enthusiasm into my voice. "I hope you have a lot of fun at the dance, honestly. And if for some reason you guys want to duck out early, you know where to find me."

"Yeah, okay," she said. "Are you feeling any better?"

"A little." A witch's magic source is derived from the earth itself. Since our abilities are intricately linked with the elements, being outside in nature makes us stronger. It was like nature provided a charge and I could use it to replenish my rundown battery. It was harder to do from inside a building, or in places like a city. From what I understood, I could only draw energy from things that were alive.

"You always seem a little off in the magical department this time of year." She'd said it innocently enough, but I knew she was thinking of the real reason behind my magic-blockage.

Autumn had always been the season I looked most forward to. In the mountains, nature put on a spectacular display of fall foliage as leaves and shrubbery erupted in brilliant hues of rich color. The air was crisp and sweetly scented, and the town put on the annual Autumn Apple Festival to celebrate the change. But for magical beings, particularly witches, autumn meant something more powerful. It brought on the harvest moon, and the autumnal equinox. It was a time for light and dark to find balance, as day and night stood equal in time. The equinox brought on regeneration and restoration; a time for giving thanks.

My mother and I used to celebrate the autumnal equinox–or Mabon–together. We would climb deep into the Hollow and cast a protective circle, lighting candles that represented each of the five elements to start our ritual. We'd arrange an alter honoring the Earth Mother and reflect on the past year and talk about what we were grateful for–not so different from the Christian celebration of Thanksgiving. It was a time where my mother and I celebrated what we were, and in doing so, I'd never felt freer, or more alive.

That was before she got sick, and cancer took her from us.

I hadn't celebrated the equinox since.

There were still so many unanswered questions about who I was and what I could do–still so much I needed her for.

The wind picked up, carrying the scents of the forest in a blustery breeze. Sometimes, I could still smell her perfume; a vanilla musk that was out of place among the trees.

Chapter Two
Skin Contact

"Have you seen my boots?" My father's voice boomed down the hallway along with sound of the kitchen door that led into the garage; echoing, as it whined angrily on its rusted hinges.

"You left them on the deck," I called to him.

The hinges squealed again as the door closed behind him. "Oh. That's right."

"What would you do without me?" I said, my voice returning to a normal octave as I stepped into the kitchen.

"Well I'd be barefoot, for one thing." He squeezed my shoulder as he walked by, heading toward the sliding door that opened to our wooden patio. The patio hovered high above the ground, showcasing the grass field below before disappearing into the base of the forest. A dirt path cut through the field, lining the makeshift driveway to my father's workshop about two hundred yards out. He was a carpenter, skilled in the art of woodcraft. We had an inside joke about that being his magical power. I watched as he shook out his boots, and then brought them inside so he could slip them on at the kitchen table.

I might have my mother's fern green eyes and small frame, but I had my father's thick mane of dark hair. He kept his short and brushed back while mine fell in unruly waves well below my shoulder blades.

He rose from the table, stretching and yawning as he reached for the ceiling. At forty-eight, he stood tall and dignified, but his body had become a weathered canvas that painted the story of his life. His hands were scarred from years of onerous labor; the pearl-like flesh mapping out the battles he'd lost against the machinery in the workshop. I knew them all, but the bruise beneath the thumbnail on his left hand stuck out to me the most. It marked an old injury he'd gotten while building my rocking horse. He'd missed the nail, whacking his thumb with the iron hammer instead. He'd shed blood for my happiness and told me that my smile had been well worth the pain. That was Emmett Callaghan in a nutshell: benevolent, selfless.

He'd always been strong, but after my mother passed, those sinewy edges of his frame only hardened. There are nights that I lay awake, consumed by aching rawness of missing her, and I knew that my father must be sharing in that silent pain. We didn't talk about it much, but there was proof in our faces; the dark half-moons underlining his even darker eyes. Her absence left a hole in our lives that could never be filled, but we still had each other, and we were getting by.

"What's on the agenda today?" I asked him, pulling a midnight-blue thermos down from the cupboard. It had silver stars mapping one of my favorite zodiac constellations: Virgo.

"I'm still working on the pergola structure for Josephine's new outdoor dining area." He rolled his eyes, reaching for the plain silver thermos above me. "If she keeps changing her mind on the design, I'm likely not to finish in this century."

"What's she asking for now?"

"She wants a lattice constructed into it so she can weave 'enchanting vines and flowers through it.' Her words. Not mine." Dad waved this off, but I could hear the irritation in his voice. He liked building things with purpose. Decorative plant-life was not in his area of expertise.

"I'm sure it will look great."

Dad ran his palms over his jeans, patting his pockets to make sure his wallet and keys were in place. "All right, I'm off. See you after school, Q." He bent to place a kiss on my cheek, scooped his coffee thermos from the counter, and headed for the front door. "Oh, I almost forgot. Come by Jo's after practice, we'll get dinner out tonight."

"Sure, sounds good. I want to see all your progress."

"Don't hold your breath." He winked and then closed the door behind him. After dad's truck had left the drive, I picked up my things and headed out into the cool, late September morning. Autumn was a moody season. Once the sun crested the tops of the trees, the day would hold its warmth until the cloak of night would sweep it away again.

I jiggled the doorknob to make sure it locked in place before heading down the lane. Like most homes in the mountains, ours shared a drive with three other homes that were tucked into various parts of the property. Ours had the best view. A stream cut across the mountainside, winding its way along the edge of the forest and dipped across our property. Dad built a footbridge that crossed the stream, and just on the other side, tucked beneath the branches of a weeping willow was our gazebo. He'd constructed it for Mom. Her special hideaway now turned memory.

Silver Mountain High was only a few blocks away, sitting within the lower valley. From the end of the drive, I could see the arc of the aluminum roof glinting in the morning sun. The ramshackle school building was one of the oldest structures in town. It was built of brick with very little insulation. We suffered through the muggy, stale air in the summers and half froze to death in the winter when the old radiators hissed and moaned; unable to generate enough heat. The tiles were warped in places and peeling up from the floors, and the janitors couldn't keep up with the constant clogged pipes in the restrooms. We might not have the best-looking school in the state, but there was something about the old flaws that I liked. It was hard to explain, but I had a soft-spot for things that held history. I could feel it in the walls— all the stories they'd absorbed over the years left them humming with energy. Thanks to my powers, I could always feel it in the old things.

A burst of movement caught my eye up ahead—a school bus was heading in my direction. I had about two inches between the side of the road and the natural cliff wall that lined it. I'd have to cut across the road if I wanted to avoid being squashed. I glanced over my shoulder and jogged across the road, heading for the yellow line in the center when I heard something strange.

At first I couldn't place it. It sounded distant, yet at the same time echoed from the cliff walls like it was all around me. Then I saw it. There was a dark car coming around the bend from the opposite side, and the driver was speeding. Adrenaline swelled in my chest as the school bus laid on its horn–blasting my eardrums. I knew I'd never make it across the road in time. I planted myself on the middle line, and squeezed my eyes shut as both vehicles whirled by in a black and yellow blur. The wind between them swirled my hair around my face and stole the breath from my lungs. The black car swerved away from me, hugging tightly to the edge of the road before finally zooming out of view.

I recognized the gold bird emblazoned across the Pontiac's hood, and knew that the erratic driver was in fact the mysterious stranger from the coffee shop. What was he in such a hurry to get away from? My heart thudded rapidly, and my knees felt as though they could slip out from under me. I raked my fingers through my hair and forced myself to take a step forward. *Get off the road, Quinn, just keep moving*.

My heart returned to its regular rhythm by the time I entered the school building, though my shoulders were tensed and knotted. Annabelle was waiting for me by my locker. She was dressed in a long black skirt with a white T-shirt tucked into the waistband. "You're late," she stated.

"You're one to talk, Miss I'm-always-late-for-everything. I'm four minutes early," I replied, checking the screen of my cell phone.

"You said you'd be here twenty minutes early to go over French notes." She cocked her head sharply, eyes widening as she waited for the realization to sink in.

"Crap." I sighed and leaned back against my locker. "I'm sorry, I completely blanked."

"It's fine," Annabelle waved a hand in the air, "we'll just have to cram at lunch to make up for it."

I twisted the combination dial on my locker, listening for the pop as it gave way. The inside door was covered in pictures of my friends and I, a few cross-country ribbons, and a schedule of our upcoming races. I pushed a couple of granola wrappers out of the way and switched out my books for first period class.

"God, your locker is such a mess."

"An organized mess," I corrected.

"As if there is such a thing." She reached in, snatching the wrappers and a few empty water bottles before walking them to the recycle bin near the end of the hall. She twitched when she walked, and I noticed her hands were balled into fists.

"Okay, what's wrong with you?"

"Nothing, I'm fine."

"I know you, Anna. There's no sense in trying to avoid it." I caught her wrist and gently pulled her near the wall. "Spill."

"I told my mom about the dance last night."

"And..."

"And I think she's planning my wedding."

I snorted, and she shot me a pointed look. "Sorry." I cleared my throat, forcing myself to remain composed. "Not funny."

"You know my mother can be a little overbearing at times, I'm just worried she's going to scare Shawn off. He's already skittish as a cat; the last thing I need to worry about is the added torment of him meeting my mother."

"You really like him, huh?"

"Well yeah, Q, I do." She looked up at me then, her features softening.

"Don't worry about your mom. I'll keep her distracted."

"You will?"

"We're family, Anna. Of course I will. You have nothing to worry about, just trust me." The first bell rang, signaling for us to get to our homeroom classes. "Did you show her the dress you picked from Snow Lily's?" The pale blue reminded me of Cinderella's ball gown, only Anna's wasn't quite that puffy.

"Yeah, she liked it. She's shortening the hemline much to her dismay. I told her Shawn would trip on the extra fabric if she didn't."

I laughed, and the motion sent a sharp pain ricocheting through my shoulders. I reached up, working my knuckles into a knot in the curve of my neck.

"You okay?" Annabelle asked.

"Do you remember that guy we saw at the coffee shop on Saturday?"

I asked, "The one with the old Pontiac Firebird."

"You mean our table thief?"

"That's the one," I said. "He about ran me off the road this morning. His car flew around the bend at the same time I was trying to avoid getting hit by a school bus. Between the two of them, I was almost flattened into road pizza."

"You're kidding," she said. Her fingertips brushed against my arm as she absorbed the shock. "You're lucky you didn't get hurt."

"I suppose a stiff neck isn't much to complain about in the grand scheme of things." We walked through the door of our homeroom as the second bell rang.

Mr. Anderson took roll call as the morning announcements crackled in and out over the intercom and Principal Keller's broken voice vibrated through the old speaker. "Seniors be sure to... vote... Friday will... court winners... presented... homecoming game... rival Wildcats."

Mr. Anderson walked over to the corner of the room, picked up a broom, and tapped the handle against the speaker a few times–as if that alone could fix the problem. What was about malfunctioning equipment that made people think banging on it was a surefire solution to making it work again? The intercom snapped and crackled, releasing a spray of dust and other unidentifiable debris that drifted down in a foul-smelling cloud. I coughed, batting the dust as I walked into the hallway. "Sorry, everyone," Mr. Anderson mumbled as we exited his classroom.

"Translation...?" Annabelle bumped my arm as we started down the hall to our first period class.

"The senior class needs to cast their votes for homecoming court so the nominees can be announced at the game against the Wildcats on Friday," I said.

Her eyebrows lifted to her hairline. "I'm impressed."

"It's an acquired skill." I giggled as we slipped through the doorway of our English class and took our seats in the back of the classroom next to the big row of windows. I dropped my bag at my feet, bending to pull out my Lit book when a familiar tingling sensation started expanding across my skin. It diffused down my spine, sending out vibrations that tightened across my sternum. I lifted my gaze to the doorway as the Supe from the coffee shop strolled in. He made his way to the front of the classroom, pausing in front of Miss Lane's desk as he handed her a folded piece of paper. She scanned it briefly before greeting him with a smile.

"Welcome to English class Mr. Whelan. Why don't you grab a book from the shelf there, and then take your seat in front of Miss Callaghan." She pointed in my direction, and as our eyes met, something in his expression shifted–ever so slightly. That cocksure demeanor of his slipped; his dark brow lifted in a flash, the corner of his mouth pulling into a smirk. He recognized me, I realized, and he didn't look at all surprised to see me as I felt to see him.

A rush of heat flooded my chest. I watched him grab a book from the shelf, and then glide to his seat in front of me. The piney scent of his clothes drifted across the small space that separated our desks, heightening the ringing in my ears. I wanted to bolt from the classroom. I wanted to lean forward an inhale the smell of him. I wanted to… to…

"All right, class," Miss Lane addressed us, "please take out your textbooks and flip to page one sixty-three. Yesterday, we had just begun reading from Mary Shelley's '*Frankenstein*.' I'd like us to get through a few more chapters before we start a discussion board. As we read, please keep in mind that we are looking for themes to help us develop a strong thesis."

Miss Lane rose from her desk; her long violet skirt flowing like delicate flower petals around her ankles as she bent to adjust the volume on the stereo. The enthusiastic voice of the British woman from the CD filled the air while we followed along in our textbooks, swallowing the sounds of pages being turned, and aluminum chair legs scuffing against the linoleum tile. I only hoped that it also hid the sound of my heart hammering beneath my rib cage.

The Whelan boy leaned forward in his chair, resting his elbows on the desk. The movement caused the fabric of his navy T-shirt to cling tightly to the contour of his back. Lean muscle stretched across his shoulders and down either side of his spine. Beside me, Annabelle knocked her notebook off the desk and it crash-landed against my right boot. Miss Lane glanced up from behind her plastic-rimmed glasses at the sound of the ruckus, but just as quickly went back to the papers she appeared to be grading. I leaned over, fingertips grazing the thin cardboard cover. I picked it up and slipped the top piece of paper out of the binding before handing it back to Annabelle.

Oh my god, she'd written, *is that the guy?*

I nodded, and folded the piece of paper in half, tucking it into the back of the literature book. I didn't want to risk passing a note back to her. With eyes like a hawk, Miss Lane was quick to notice any sign of unusual movement.

The girl sitting in front of Annabelle, Courtney Davis–captain of the cheer squad (or the Zombie Squad, as we'd affectionately labeled) was twisting a strand of long honey-blonde hair around her index finger. Her chin was cocked to the side; a devious smile lifting the corners of her mouth as she openly gazed at the new guy in front of me. She'd zeroed in on him like a cat about to pounce on his dinner. Fitting, I thought, considering I always thought she had rather cat-like shaped eyes. They were the lightest of brown, piercing, and sharp at the corners.

From what I could tell, his eyes remained fixed on his textbook. He sat like a statue, completely still–though entirely relaxed in his environment. My brain was buzzing. I wanted so badly to find out what he was. I continued to gaze at the back of his head, spotting a thin, black cord poking from beneath the collar of his T-shirt. His skin was tanned, and now that he was in near proximity, I wondered if he had some Native American heritage.

The class hour seemed to last infinitely. I rubbed the back of my neck, forcing my attention on the text while trying to ignore the throbbing sensation that covered every inch of my skin. When the bell finally rang, I could feel Annabelle's eyes on me. I leaned over, deflated from concentrating, and gathered my bag from the floor. The guy in front of me rose swiftly, stirring the air with his woodsy aroma.

"Welcome to Silver Mountain High, new guy." Courtney reached across the aisle, resting a red manicured hand on his bicep. "I'm

Courtney."

"Hi," he returned. His voice was a deep beguiling rumble. "I'm Wren."

"Well, Wren, I'm at the head of the welcoming committee and student body president, so if there's anything you need, I'm your girl," Courtney purred. I watched her cat-like claws curling into his bicep.

I rolled my eyes, doing my best to ignore them as I walked by. His hand shot out with lightning speed and wrapped around my upper arm, trapping me in a gentle grip. The moment his palm contacted my skin, the tingling sensation that was short-circuiting my brain stopped abruptly. As if someone had simply flipped the off switch.

"I owe you an apology," he said.

For a moment, all I could do was gaze up into his peculiar midsummer night eyes. Looking into them was like falling backwards through a mirror; I recognized something perpetual. I had an odd feeling that I knew those eyes–like maybe this wasn't the first time I'd really looked into them and felt a timeless sort of pull.

Okay, hold up. *Did I really just use words like perpetual and timeless?* I blinked rapidly, coming back to my senses. I could feel the rush of blood coming to my cheeks and managed (after what seemed like an eternity of awkward silence) to gather enough sense to speak. "You really shouldn't drive that fast," I said. Oh *goddess*–was I the traffic police now?! He'd let go of my arm, and I could still feel the impression of his fingertips–light as feathers on my skin.

The corner of his mouth twitched at my remark. He straightened the strap of his bag over his shoulder, peering down at me through a thick veil of long, dark lashes. "It isn't in my nature to go slow," he said, enunciating each word deliberately. The muscle in his jaw tightened over the bone, as if he were fighting back a smile. He didn't blink once as he gazed down at me; eyes shining with mischief.

I was aware that Courtney was gawking from the other side, and Annabelle was waiting for me. "I should go," I managed to say. I stepped around him, meeting Annabelle at the front of the classroom before slipping out into the hall. I'd never been more grateful to suck in a gulp of muggy air.

Annabelle peered over her shoulder, looking back to make sure we weren't in range of being overheard. "Okay, what was that about?" she asked. "The way he was looking at you was intense."

"Intense is one word for it," I said, rubbing the trail of goosebumps that had risen on my arms.

"What was he saying? I couldn't hear."

"He apologized for almost ending my life this morning," I said.

"Well that was valiant of him." She snorted.

"I guess." I shrugged.

"You should have seen the look Courtney was giving you–talk about pointing daggers. You're lucky that girl doesn't have laser-vision, or you would've been toast. I sense she's not too thrilled about having competition."

"It was just a conversation."

"Yeah but you know as well as I do that the Queen Bee doesn't like anyone else standing in her spotlight. She's been that way since kindergarten."

"She'll get over it," I said. "Just give it a couple of weeks before the newness wears off, then she'll be on the hunt for her next victim."

"I don't know, Q, he's pretty hot."

My eyes widened at the use of her selected terminology. I don't think I'd ever heard her use the word "hot" when describing anyone other than her favorite actor. As we moved through the door of our next class, I couldn't shake the image of his–of Wren's–distinct eyes from my mind. I was even more curious about his touch, and how it had stopped the humming sensation from crawling over my skin. Maybe this was a new magical development. My mother told me that as I aged, my powers would grow with me. I made a mental note to check out the Magic Shoppe later for research purposes. If this was something new, I wanted to learn how to control it so it wouldn't distract me in the future.

Chapter Three
The Kings of the Forest

Wren showed up to cross-country practice. Late. We were already spread out in a circle, stretching our muscles after completing our mile warm-up. Annabelle elbowed me in the ribs, jerking her chin towards the scene. He was talking to our coach, Mr. Walker. Coach Walker was probably in his late forties, short and stocky, always wearing a ball cap and a pair of mirrored sunglasses that hid his gray-blue eyes. I tilted my head, trying my best to listen in on the conversation all the while blocking out Huck's boisterous laughter to my right.

"We don't normally let transfers on the team after the start of the season, but it looks like you have a pretty good record," Coach was saying as he scanned the white slip in his hands. Coach nodded, stroking his goatee.

"Do you think he wants to join the team?" Annabelle whispered.

"Why else would he be here?"

"We're already three weeks in. Coach would never let anyone else join."

"How much do you wanna' bet that paper in his hand is a list of Wren's PR's?" I said. "Guarantee he'll let him run if he's fast enough."

"Get changed and meet us back here quickly," Coach told him. "Lucky you decided to join us on mile repeat day."

The rest of us groaned audibly as Wren dashed back to the school. He returned in four minutes flat, just as the rest of us were finishing with our stretches.

"I've selected two team leaders to guide our waves based on last week's race time improvements," Coach said. "Jamie Long took five seconds off his PR so he'll be leading the first wave." The rest of us clapped and cheered as Jamie went up to stand by Coach, and Annabelle pinched my upper arm. "Quinn Callaghan took four-and-a-half seconds off her PR so she'll be leading the second wave." Again, the team cheered as I made my way to stand beside Coach.

"We'll be practicing on the track today," Coach said. "The first wave will be sent out, and after completing an eight hundred, I'll send the second wave out. You'll need to be careful and watch your surroundings since you'll all be running at once. The rest of you will need to match your pace as best you can with your team leader. If you feel you can move faster than your team leader, I'll expect you not to fall behind. And no puking on my track," he added.

After Coach divided us into two groups, we lined up on the track with the afternoon sun beaming down our necks. Already, I could feel beads of sweat forming on the surface of my skin. Coach blew his whistle, signaling the first wave of runners. Jamie darted out in front of the pack, setting a nice strong pace for his team to follow. His bronze colored hair flopped across his forehead, his right hand swatting the air a little more fervently than necessary. Wren worked his way to Jamie's side, nodding once to acknowledge him as he matched his pace with total effortlessness. I couldn't help but notice his incredible form. He had a physique that looked as though the gods had sculpted it with the intent and purpose of running in mind.

"Second wave get ready," Coach called out.

"He's pretty good," Annabelle noted, kneeling in the starting block on my right side.

"Who, Wren?" I pretended not to notice.

"I bet he's faster than Huck."

Definitely, I thought. Coach blew his whistle and the sound of it caused a spike of adrenaline to slam through my body. I pushed out of the starting blocks, feeling the welcoming wind against my face as I approached our first one hundred yards. I glanced back at the pack around me, choosing a pace that was slow enough so that I wouldn't leave any stragglers behind, but also quick enough to push those who were really trying to knock a few seconds off their PR.

I stayed light on my feet, rolling from heel to toe, working the calf muscles in my legs. A few of my teammates started breathing heavy as we finished our first half mile. "In through the nose, out through the mouth," I called over my shoulder, hoping to encourage the smallest boy who was holding his right side. He was a freshman, thin and blond. His features twisted in pain. I wished I could cast a small spell of encouragement to send his way, but I knew better. Instead, I did what I probably shouldn't have, and slowed my pace as we finished the first mile.

The boy was doubled over now, hands on his knees as sweat dripped down the bridge of his nose. I wasn't sure that he'd be able to make it another mile, but he met us on the starting line as Coach signaled for our second wave.

The first wave darted out across the track, working on their third mile. A sophomore girl groaned when Coach told us to line back up after our third completed mile. "How much longer are we going to do this?" she asked.

"You'll go until I tell you to stop," Coach answered. "Let's go, let's go." Coach clapped his hands together, urging us to get a move on.

I carried us back onto the track and picked a nice even pace to start our fourth mile. The team was intermingled now; scattered through all the lanes. Hunter had slowed to a light jog about fifty yards in front of me. The boy had determination, to say the least, but the color was rapidly draining from his face. He was drenched in sweat; his hair plastered to either sides of his face. He was practically green from the pain I knew he must have been feeling. *Uh-oh*, I thought, I knew that look. I kicked it up a couple of notches to catch him at the half mile marker, but as I came around the bend, Hunter stopped dead in the lane. The freshman girl that had been running behind him smacked into his back, and when he collapsed in front of her she let out a blood-curdling scream.

"Get Coach over here now!" I called over my shoulder and knelt in front of Hunter's listless body. He'd hit the track like a sack of potatoes, lying on his side with his right arm tucked beneath his body. I didn't want to move him in case he'd broken something, but I inspected him carefully. "Hunter," I said, gently reaching out to brush his hair back from his face. His skin was pasty white, and cool from sweat. Within a matter of seconds, Coach was beside me.

"What happened?"

"He collapsed," I said.

"Hunter, can you hear me son?" Coach reached out and gently shook Hunter's shoulder. He stirred then, squinting against the intensity of the sunlight. "Welcome back," Coach said. "Are you hurt?"

"I don't know." He coughed a little and struggled to get himself in an upright sitting position. "I'm a little dizzy."

"Take it easy," Coach instructed. "I think we'll call it a day. Let's get you inside and get some water in you."

I reached for Hunter's arm on instinct to help steady him. I didn't even think. Annabelle saw it before I even had time to react. "Quinn, no!"

I heard her voice behind me, but it was too late. My hand wrapped around his shoulder, and I felt the warm stickiness of his blood against my fingertips. My body was yanked away by a rip current. I knew I must have fallen back on the track, but somewhere in my subconscious the waves dragged me under the saltwater and flattened me into the bed of sand. Everything shifted into darkness.

I saw Hunter walking through the woods. He was with a girl, but I didn't recognize her. I noted the color of her top: pink, eyelet lace. The vision shimmered, like ripples on a mirrored lake, and all the colors washed away. There was fear in Hunter's eyes; a cold sense of desperation. His hand shot out protectively in front of the girl, and he was yelling for her to run.

In the path in front of them stood a large, gray wolf with eyes that shined like the harvest moon. Its lips were pulled back over sharp, glistening white fangs; its muzzle twisted into a lethal snarl. I could smell the blood on its breath, the sharp metallic stink of it permeating the air. The wolf leaped with flawless grace, and I opened my eyes, only to find a pair of amber colored spheres hovering inches above my face.

"Are you all right?" Wren asked.

Funny. I hadn't remembered him being close to me when I went down. Annabelle was kneeling beside him, chewing on her bottom lip as concern spread across her features. She reached out, cupping her hand over my wrist.

My head was pounding, and I could already feel the blood streaming down my nose and across my lip. Wren tore a piece of cloth from the hem of his T-shirt, and handed it to me, helping me into a sitting position. "Thanks," I finally managed to say. "Where's Hunter?"

"Coach and some of the other guys are taking him inside to call his mom," Annabelle said. "You really gave us a scare."

"Blood make you queasy?" Wren asked.

"I told them you must have seen the blood on Hunter's arm and passed out," Annabelle explained–quick as ever with a diversion.

"Right," I said, pressing the fabric tightly to my nose to stanch the bleeding. "I have an issue with seeing other people's blood." This of course, was not the first time I'd had a "magical" incident involving blood in front of my friends.

"Um, Wren, maybe you could grab Quinn's water bottle?" Annabelle suggested.

"Yeah, sure," he said, pushing to his feet.

"I left it by the bleachers. It's the blue thermos with silver stars."

Annabelle glanced over her shoulder, and then lowered her voice so that only I could hear, "So, what did you see?" she asked.

I shook my head, trying to clear the fog. "I'm not really sure. Hunter was walking in the woods with a girl; she might have been younger–maybe his sister? I couldn't tell exactly where they were or *when*, but, I saw a wolf trying to attack them. I came to just before it happened." Goose bumps appeared on my arms despite the surrounding warmth.

"A wolf?" Annabelle repeated.

"Yeah, but, it couldn't have been, right? There haven't been wolves here for years. At least, not in vast quantities."

"I don't know," she paused, brows furrowing. "You sure it wasn't a coyote?"

I thought of those clear, yellow tinted eyes and their vibrant intensity. There was no mistaking the size and shape of its body for anything else. "It was a wolf, I'm positive."

"And you had no indication of where or when it might happen?" Annabelle asked.

"None," I said, "well, maybe. The girl that was with him–I saw her wearing a pink shirt. Her hair was in braids." There was something else, too. Something so wholly distinctive, yet entirely deceiving at the same time. The color had drained out of my vision, leaving the moving canvas a perfect black and white concept while only certain colors filtered through. "It was dark," I decided. The clouds were obstructing the silver moon. "It might have been a full moon."

"Okay, that's a start at least."

Wren was making his way back with my thermos. He'd torn the hemline of his shirt in a way so that a tiny sliver of skin was peeking above his hip bone. I felt my cheeks flush and looked away as he bent to hand over the thermos.

"Thanks," I said, unscrewing the lid. "I guess I owe you a new shirt."

"It was old anyway," he said.

Jamie and Huck were making their way from the school, heading in our direction. I tried rolling myself forward, but my head was still spinning from the vision. It took me a while to get my bearings; I felt like a beehive had taken up residency in place of my brain. I couldn't seem to get the buzzing to wear off.

"Are you doing okay, Quinn?" Jamie asked.

"How is it that the one person who can't stand the sight of blood always seems to end up right in the mix of it?" Huck said teasingly. "You're like a magnet for disastrous accidents."

"Trust me," I said, "if I could avoid it, I would."

Annabelle snorted, rising to her feet to join the others, and placed her hands on her hips. Wren stayed silently beside me; I could feel the intensity of his eyes on me, but I was too afraid to meet them–afraid of what I might see.

"Nice running by the way," Huck said, jamming a playful punch into Wren's bicep. "Where did you transfer from anyway?"

"West Coast," he answered. "Small town outside of Seattle, you wouldn't know the place."

"Well we're glad to have you," Jamie said. "We've got one of the fastest teams in the state, but all anyone cares about around here is the lousy football team. It doesn't matter how many trophies we bring home, we'll never hold a candle in comparison."

Wren lifted an eyebrow; a signature move I was realizing. I doubted he even knew he was doing it.

"What's your PR for a five-K?" Huck asked him.

"Just under sixteen minutes," Wren replied with a shrug. My neck snapped in his direction as I scanned his face for any sign that he might just be yanking our chains. Wren's face was as sculpted and still as stone.

"You're joking?" Jamie said.

"That's nearly three consecutive five-minute miles." Huck stated.

"AKA nearly impossible," Annabelle added.

"What's your PR?" Wren asked.

"Sixteen forty-three," Huck replied flatly. He reached up, scratching at the gelled spikes of his blond hair.

"You trying for a scholarship?" Jamie asked.

"Nah. I've moved around too much for that. I just like to run," Wren said.

Huck snorted, the sound of disbelief catching in his throat. "Well damn," he muttered, now rubbing the stubble on his jaw. "I'm impressed."

"I should probably get going," I said, "I'm supposed to meet my dad at Jo's."

"You might want to get cleaned up first." Huck pointed to my face, wrinkling his nose at the mess.

I squeezed my eyes shut, determined not to let my appearance embarrass me any further. I rolled myself to my knees and felt the world tilt on its axis. I used my arm for balance and was surprised to feel the warmth of Wren's palm enclosing around my upper arm. His other hand closed around my hip as he helped me into an upright walking position. He was looking down at me, but again, I couldn't make myself look up into those knowing eyes of his.

"I'll take it from here," Annabelle said, slipping an arm around my waist and looping one of my arms around her neck. "You good to walk?" she asked.

"Are you offering to carry me?" I forced a smirk and let her guide me off the track while the boys stayed behind to talk about records and running courses.

"You need some protein," Wren called after us.

"Thanks, I'll take care of it," Annabelle said, moving us through the field.

When we entered the school, the florescent lights cast a bright glare against the tile, and I squinted against it. The steps down into the locker room were a little tricky, but Annabelle helped me ease down onto the bench before whirling for my locker.

"You know," she said, "there's got to be some sort of spell or something you can cast to help protect yourself against the aftermath of these visions. It's not like you asked for the damn curse."

"I wish there was," I agreed.

Annabelle dropped my bag on the bench. "All right, you get cleaned up and I'll see if I can find something in the vending machine to hold you over until we get to Jo's. With any luck, they might have a sun-dried granola bar."

"You don't have to do this," I said.

"I know," Annabelle said. "Someone has to look out for you though."

"I just don't want you to feel like it's your responsibility."

Annabelle pressed her lips into a soft smile, tucking a strand of flyaway hair behind her ear. "I just like to think of myself as the Chloe Sullivan to your Superman-like abilities. Everyone knows she's the brain behind the operation. And besides, what else would I do?" She shrugged and then disappeared through the doorway. I listened to her tennis shoes squeaking down the hall.

I'd first told Annabelle what I was when we were nine. My mom was always drilling in the importance of keeping my secret, but it was nearly impossible to hide what I was all the time–especially at that age. I wasn't always in control of my powers, and my emotions were psychological triggers.

I remembered being particularly excited on that day because our parents had finally agreed to let us have our first sleepover. Annabelle and I were outside, sitting patiently by the bonfire pit while my mom went inside for more chocolate bars. Dad had been on edge–recently let go from his job at the Lumber Mill, and our finances were a little tight. I listened to my dad's agitated voice carry through the screen of the opened kitchen window.

"What's this purchase on the billing statement for fifty-four dollars?" Dad asked as Mom entered the kitchen.

"Let me see," Mom said, reaching for the bill statement. "Oh, I bought Quinn a new pair of running shoes. She's growing like crazy."

"Which means in another six months, she's going to be in another size anyway. Couldn't you have bought a cheaper pair?" My dad asked. "She's not even on the school team yet."

"They'll start training in the summer, Emmett." My mother sounded tired.

"Vivian, we can't be spending this kind of money right now. You know that." Dad's voice was pinched, like he was fighting to keep it level, but he was failing.

I had never really heard my parents argue before over anything, and the fact that this argument had stemmed because of *me* made it even worse. I had been so adamant about getting a pair of ASICS and my mom–not wanting to disappoint me–had given in. I knew things were tight financially, but my mom assured me that we would be able to swing it. Everyone else had ASICS, and I was convinced the right pair of shoes would help me with tryouts. I wanted to make an impression–to be noticed for something. I'd had to hide so much of who I was, and running was a chance for me to really shine. My mom wanted that for me, too.

The bickering continued, and the more they argued the more nervous I became. I felt like a wave of anxiety was washing over me. I was staring into the yellow flickering flames, wishing so hard that I could get Mom and Dad to shut up. The next thing I knew, the red-hot flames shot out six-feet high; like dragon's breath billowing toward the indigo painted sky. Electric sparks shot into the air, raining down like sharp stinging crystals. A blast of balmy air surrounded us, and Dad shot through the back door, grabbing me off the stump I was sitting on. His arms circled my waist, causing me to blink out of my trance, and the flames returned to normal.

Annabelle was staring at me. She'd dropped the package of marshmallows that she'd been holding and was looking at me with wide, penetrating eyes. Her mouth parted, a slow smile tugging at the corners. "I knew it," she breathed. "What are you?"

"I'm a witch," I blurted. I couldn't believe how unbelievably relieved I felt to say it out loud to my best friend and have her looking at me in awe instead of bolting for the hills in terror.

I supposed I could have made something up–blamed a freak gust of wind on the fire blast–but there wasn't a single part of me that could stand lying any longer. I remember the look on my mom's face–the worry that creased her brow. She sat Annabelle down with my father hovering and pacing anxiously behind us while she talked about the importance of keeping my secret.

"I swear I'll never tell a soul." Ever the comic book loving geek, she'd said, "This is just like when Pete Ross found out that his best friend Clark Kent was an alien from Krypton and had superhuman strength and powers. I know it won't be easy," Annabelle said adamantly, "but I know I'll have to protect you. Always."

Chapter Four
What Dreams Are Made Of

"It's times like these I wish one of us had a car," Annabelle said as we exited the locker room. Josephine's was only a few blocks away. The downside being that we'd have to climb a steep hill and descend another before getting there, and my premonition had rendered my limbs gelatinous.

With my defenses weakened, the afternoon sun scorched my eyes when we exited the building. I saw Hunter climbing into the front seat of his mother's SUV. When he saw me, he paused between the seat and the car door. "Hey Quinn, I'm really sorry about what happened."

"You don't need to apologize," I said. "Are you all right?" Healthy color had returned to his skin and he didn't appear all the worse for wear. There was a minor scrape on his shoulder resembling a rug-burn, (probably the source my fingers had contacted.) A thin red line traced the curve of his cheekbone, and a shadow of dried blood congealed in the contour of his nose.

"I'm a little banged up, but I'll be okay." He grinned. "See you tomorrow."

"Take it easy," I said. As they pulled away, I caught a flash of a girl in the backseat, the tinted windows shrouding her features. The girl in my vision was middle-school age, eleven–maybe twelve years old. It was impossible to determine with the shade of the windows whether in fact it was the girl I saw. Still, my stomach seemed to lurch at her sight.

"Do you think?" Annabelle asked.

"I don't know."

"Come on," Annabelle said, "we better get going or we'll never make it there before nightfall."

"Don't remind me," I grunted. We'd just made it to the edge of the school property when Wren's Pontiac pulled up beside us; the engine purring like a satisfied lioness. I didn't know much about cars, but I knew his was an early eighties model and looked brand new. He must baby the thing.

He leaned out the window with his elbow propped over the edge. "Do you need a ride?" he asked, pushing his hair back from his eyes. My stomach did a strange little flop. He looked at me like he knew all my secrets and I was desperate to find out how.

Beside me, Annabelle straightened. "We wouldn't want to put you out."

"I don't have anywhere to be," he answered. His alluring voice made him sound years older than he was. In fact, everything about him was atypical of the average high school male. The way he held himself–so still and confident. It was like every move he made was a well thought out strategy–like life was a chess board and the rest of us were just pawns.

"Sure." Annabelle looked at me and shrugged.

Wren was out of the car before I could blink, lifting the seat so we could climb in. I slid in first, and the scent of pine hit me all over again, working its way through my nostrils and lingering. I bit the inner corner of my lip, trying not to let those appealing fumes get to my head.

"Going to Jo's right?" he asked, sliding back into the driver's seat.

"Do you know where it is?" I asked.

The corner of his mouth twitched. "Yeah, I know where it is. I'm from Silver Mountain, actually."

"You are?" I felt my eyebrows shifting.

"My parents split when I was four," he explained, "I moved to Washington with my mom, but I still came back to visit my dad in the summers."

"Why have we never seen you before?" Annabelle asked.

"I'm not much of a socialite."

"Yeah, but how did you manage to stay off the radar? Silver Mountain has a small-town reputation for a reason," she added incredulously.

"I only came out at night." He was smirking, but the impish set to his mouth made me wonder if he was joking.

"So why *did* you come back?" Annabelle asked.

Wren visibly tensed in the driver's seat; his skin stretching white across the knuckles. "I needed a change. My mother got remarried and then came along a couple of babies and I felt like I was in the way, so I bounced."

"Senior year is an odd time to relocate yourself," Annabelle commented.

"You're quite outspoken for such a small person," he countered.

A bubble of laughter escaped me. Wren's eyes flashed to mine in the rearview mirror; their amber color darkening in the fading light. He had eyes like a predator, I decided–nothing got past him.

"I'm just curious," Annabelle said.

"Well, you know what they say about curiosity…"

"Lucky I'm not a cat." Annabelle grimaced, fixing her eyes on his in the mirror.

Wren pulled the Pontiac into the diner's parking lot, slowing as he approached the sidewalk. He clicked out of his seat belt in one smooth motion, hopped out of the car, and pulled the seat forward to let us out. He offered his hand to the both of us, and when it was my turn his fingertips seemed to linger on my inner wrist.

I reached up and tucked a strand of hair behind my left ear. "Thanks for the ride," I said.

"Anytime," he replied, climbing back behind the wheel of his car. He added, "Stay out of trouble, *Cat.*" He revved the engine, and then he was gone.

"You know," Annabelle said, staring after his taillights, "I don't think I like him."

"Why not?" I asked.

"He comes across awfully arrogant."

"I'm not sure he can help it," I said.

Annabelle looked at me, scrunching up her features as she tried to decipher my expression. "You can't honestly tell me you're making an excuse for the guy who almost ran you over with his car this morning?"

"Oh come on, Anna. He apologized. It's not like he did it on purpose, and he's tried to make up for it. You're just mad he got after you for being nosy. *Cat.*" I shoved her shoulder playfully.

"It's as bad as I feared; his startling good looks and running skills have gotten to you, haven't they?"

I laughed. "I just think he's fascinating."

"*Sure,*" Annabelle said, drawing out the syllable in a tone of disbelief.

We turned up the sidewalk, passing a couple of hay bales and scarecrow decorations that were propped against the side of the red-brick building. We pushed through the glass doors, swatting against some low-hanging Halloween decorations that were swinging down from the ceiling in glittery spirals. A display of small pumpkins and mums decorated the center of each table, complementing the deep mountain charm of the usual rustic decor. Vintage metal lanterns swept down from the rafters along with old canoe paddles, fishing poles, and other various camping equipment. As usual, the old jukebox in the corner was playing bluegrass.

"Hey girls, y'all want a table?" Nadine asked. She was Josephine's best server. With short, curly dark hair, cornflower blue eyes, and long legs– she was easily the most gorgeous woman in Silver Mountain. She'd modeled as a teenager and even did a few commercials for camping safety and sunscreen ads. She was a prime example of sticking to your roots. She gotten out for a while, but she returned to help take care of her family.

"In a bit, but, I'm looking for my dad," I said.

"Emmett is out back." Nadine grinned, revealing a perfect set of pearly white teeth. "Poor guy has been working hard all day. Tell him I said he needs to take a break." She winked, rolled on her hip, and strutted away.

"She's so perfect it's annoying," Annabelle said.

I led us through the maze of dining tables and out the back door to the new patio. Its grand opening was set for the weekend of the Autumn Festival, and my dad had solely been responsible for the construction. There was an access ramp for wheelchairs on the outside of the building, and tree-trunk stepping stones that lined a walking path from the parking lot to the deck. Twinkling globes wound up each of the support beams and were draped through the lattice work that covered the top of the patio. Forest shrubbery concealed the deck, erupting in various shades of green. I spotted my dad fussing with the pergola at the side entrance. His eyes were squinted on a piece of the framework that looked to be bowing ever so slightly.

"Hey Dad," I said.

He looked up, and the lines around his eyes softened. "Well if it isn't my favorite daughter, and her best friend, Quinn," he teased.

"I'm flattered," Annabelle said, hugging him briefly.

Dad wrapped his arms around me and pressed his lips to the top of my head. The smell of sawdust and earth enveloped me. "It looks great out here," I said.

"You should see it with the lights on," said a female voice from behind. I turned, and spotted Josephine standing in the doorway. She was wearing a quarter-sleeved brown and green asymmetrical flowing top, and a pair of brown slacks. Bangles of silver jewelry decorated each of her wrists, matching the big silver loops hanging from her earlobes. Her strawberry red hair was pulled up at the sides and spilled down her back in loose ringlets. The years may have changed, but Josephine had permanently rooted herself in the hippy era. The only thing missing from her ensemble was the peace-sign and rose-tinted sunglasses.

"Hi Jo," I said. "You're a visionary." I gestured around the patio. "The place looks great, really."

"I may have been the visionary, but your dad really brought this place to life." She walked over, touching the pergola with a smile of adoration.

Dad said nothing, but I could have sworn I saw his cheeks start to flush with color. He smoothed his hand over the piece he'd been fussing with and hammered a tiny nail in place to secure it.

"You must be hungry," Jo said. "What can I get you to eat? It's on the house tonight."

"That isn't necessary, Jo." My father started to protest.

"Oh, for Pete's sake–It's the least I can do for all that you've done around here," she said. "Just let me show my appreciation, will ya'?"

"Well," Dad reached up, scratching the corner of his mustache, "okay, sure."

"Fantastic!" Josephine beamed. "Let me grab a couple of menus. You'll be the first ones to test out the atmosphere for me." Jo turned on her heel and practically skipped to the doors.

"I gotta' go," Annabelle said. "My parents are making lasagna tonight and I promised I'd be home for dinner."

"Do you need a ride?" Dad asked.

"No thanks Mr. C but I appreciate the offer. See you tomorrow Quinn, try and get some rest tonight." Her expression softened as she glanced my way.

"Kay," I muttered, watching her go.

Dad's eyes were on mine; the worry creasing his brow seemed to drain the light out of their color. "Did something happen today?"

"Sort of," I admitted. Dad abandoned his tools and led me over to a nearby table where we sank down across from one another. "One of the freshman boys passed out on the track today, and when I went to see if he was okay…" I let my voice trail off, careful not to mention anything involving my secret too loudly.

Dad nodded, stroking his mustache. "Did you see something unsettling?"

"You could say that," I said.

Josephine burst through the back doors with a couple of menus and a tray with colorful looking glasses that sported little festive umbrellas. "Don't worry," Jo said, placing the drinks in front of us, "I made yours a virgin." She winked at me.

"Thanks," I said, examining the blue liquid and the maraschino cherry floating on the top layer of the shaved ice.

"I'll have Nadine come out in a few minutes to take your order. Let me know if I can get you anything special." Jo squeezed my dad's shoulder suggestively, and he glanced up, giving her a half-tilted smile.

After the doors had closed behind her, I let out a small chuckle. "Your lack of flirting skill is truly remarkable."

"I'm not flirting," he said defensively.

"Well that's obvious." I cocked my head to the side. "Jo clearly likes you, and you have zero game."

"I think we can save this discussion for another time. Or *never* would suit me just as fine," Dad said, reaching for his drink for the sake of having something to distract himself with. He hadn't dated anyone after my mother passed, but I had been watching Josephine flirt hopelessly for the last two years to try and win his attention. Sure she was a bit eccentric, but she had a humungous heart.

"Sure, okay Dad." I grinned.

"So, what did you see?" My father prompted after taking a sip of his fruity concoction. He made a face, shooting a suspicious look into his cup before placing it back on the table.

I lowered my voice and checked my surroundings before telling my father about my vision involving Hunter. When I finished, Dad leaned back in his chair, crossing his arms over his chest. Contemplating, he ran his index finger back and forth over the plane of his bottom lip.

"Dad?"

"There have been other rumors about wolves being spotted in the area recently."

"Really?" I felt the patch of skin between my eyebrows furrowing.

"Patty Elmer claimed she saw a wolf rummaging through the dumpster down at Mo's Butcher Shop last week, and Kendra thinks she saw one in the back of Serendipity's when she was locking up the other night. I didn't give it much thought since we haven't had wolves in this area in a number of years, but, if what you saw is true, then we need to be careful. Listen, I don't want you getting involved in this. I know it's in your nature to help, but this could be dangerous. I don't want to take any chances."

"But, Dad–" I started to say.

"–I'll have a talk with the game warden about it, but until the coast is clear, I don't want you going back into the forest by yourself."

"I have to," my words left in a desperate whisper, "you know I have to."

"You're going to have to recharge at home, and that's final."

I sighed heavily, wrapping the toes of my shoes around the chair legs stubbornly, as if planting myself in silent rebellion.

Dad was overreacting. He always overreacted when I had a magical accident. I tried to keep in mind that he responded the way he did because he could never fully understand what I was going through. My abilities scared him–maybe even more than they scared me, and this was the only way he knew how to control what was happening. I knew that he was only concerned and wanted to protect me, but there would soon come a day when he could no longer play that role. I thought about reminding him that I was almost eighteen, but I didn't want to be cruel. I was all he had left, and I didn't want to push him away.

I couldn't just sit back and wait for the game warden to handle things, either. I was the only one who knew what was going to happen; it was a question of when, and I couldn't knowingly wait in the corner while someone's life was at risk. I didn't want to lie to my father, but he wasn't giving me another option.

"Just–lay low for me," he said, "can you do that?"

I looked my father straight in the eye as I nodded.

And I lied.

That night, I dreamed of Nathan Reed and how because of me, he was fated to spend the rest of his life in a wheelchair.

Nathan was a year older than me, Silver Mountain's star basketball player and all-around golden boy. From having scouting recruits come to almost all his games senior year, to dating the prettiest girl in school, Nathan had everything going for him. But he wasn't just this star athlete, too-good-to-talk-to-us-regular-people type, Nathan was kind. Genuine. We had the same gym period, and he'd wait for me at the door of my biology classroom so we could walk together and talk strategy. He liked the idea of running cross-country just as much as I liked basketball, but that didn't stop us from bonding over our mutual need for competition. With Nathan there, gym class was always a riot and my favorite part of the day.

But something different happened that day.

He was leaning against the lockers, his face pressed against the cool metal when I came out of the classroom and saw him. My smile faltered. "Hey, Nate, are you feeling okay? You don't look so good." His skin was ghostly pale, and a fine layer of perspiration broke over the surface of his forehead.

"I think I'm coming down with something," he admitted. "The big game against the Cougars is tonight, and I can't miss it."

"You can't play sick either," I said, reaching out to put my hand on his arm. "You should go home, get some rest."

"I appreciate the concern Q, but I can't miss this game. I'm probably just a little dehydrated." We'd reached the end of the hall, and he stopped in front of the drinking fountain. He bent at the waist, but before I could react, his face hit the metal spigot. His body collapsed in front of me, blood spurting from his nose and busted lip.

"I need some help over here!" I yelled over my shoulder and lowered myself on the ground next to him. There was so much blood pouring from his nose and lip, I don't think I could have avoided it if I tried. Power sliced through me like a swift flowing ocean current, jostling me along for the ride. I saw Nathan driving his girlfriend to the homecoming dance, and I watched as his red car wrapped itself around a tree after smashing into a guardrail on a foggy mountain pass. Glass glittered off the pavement; the moon reflected in the broken surface.

I woke up in the nurse's office. My head was pounding, ears ringing so loudly I had to reach up to see if something was covering them. I struggled to get myself into an upright position and squinted hard against the too-bright walls and lights.

"Hey there, Quinn." Nurse Mary poked her head around the door frame and folded her hands around something small as she walked in. "Feeling all right?"

"Where's Nathan?" I asked.

"We sent him home honey, here," she handed me a small paper cup of clear amber liquid, "drink this, it'll make you feel better." I sniffed the contents, and the apple smell fizzed up my nostrils. "It's just apple juice. You need the sugar."

I tossed back the juice. "Is Nathan all right?"

"He's probably going to need stitches, but he'll live. His mom picked him up about five minutes ago, you just missed him." Nurse Mary sat down in a faded swivel chair and scooted herself up to my cot. She reached out, patting my forearm. "We had to call your dad to let him know you passed out, he's on his way but if you think you're feeling well enough to continue classes, we can try to reach him on his cell."

I grumbled and rolled my neck from side to side. Exhaustion radiated through my limbs, but I needed to talk to Annabelle. "I just need a few minutes and then I can head back to class," I said. Just then, my own nose started dripping. I watched the scarlet droplets splatter the surface of my jeans and closed my eyes as Nurse Mary handed me a wad of tissues.

"Tilt your head back," she instructed. "You're not going to faint on us again, are you?" I could feel her heavy hand on my shoulder.

"No," I said, "I just can't handle the sight of other people's blood."

"Okay," she moved her hand in comforting circles. "Sit tight, I'll call your father." I heard the chair squeak as she stood, but I didn't want to open my eyes. My eyelids were playing the scene of Nathan's crash on a loop. I recognized the bridge, knew where it would happen beneath the underpass. Homecoming was less than a week away, but it gave me enough time to develop a plan. I couldn't exactly go up to Nathan and tell him what I'd seen without exploiting my own identity. It was a risk I couldn't take, but I knew I couldn't just let him get into a car accident, either.

I called my dad later to tell him what happened. There were a lot of pauses followed by sharp inhales and deep exhales–his way of showing panic. "You shouldn't involve yourself," Dad said moments later. "It's much too dangerous."

"I saw this for a reason, Dad. I can't let something bad happen to him. He's a friend, maybe if I just tell him he'll under–"

"–No," Dad cut me off. "Absolutely not. You know the rules."

I clamped down on my tongue, biting on the pain to keep from saying something I shouldn't. He was simply scared, I told myself. The things I could do weren't normal–not even by Supernatural standards. I knew better than anyone that fear had a funny way of shaping a person, molding their resolve into something even they didn't recognize. I knew his silence was filled with the images of my mother because I saw her too. Something so human had taken her from us and no amount of magic had been able to save her. Magic wasn't a gift. It was a curse.

"Do I make myself clear, Quinn?"

"Yes," I said quietly.

"Too dangerous," he murmured this last part before hanging up the phone. I listened to the dial tone, letting it swallow the sounds of chattering in the courtyard behind me. A lump had risen in my throat, constricting my airways.

I slid the phone back into my pocket and leaned up against the gritty brick of the school building. Life wasn't fair. I squeezed my hands into fists, feeling my nails biting into the flesh of my palms; my lips parted from the pain. I couldn't just do nothing. I didn't have to tell Nathan the truth, but I could do something to keep him from going to that dance. I had to.

Chapter Five
The Spell Song

When I woke, I felt restless; my muscles sluggish and sore. I was in desperate need to recharge, but Dad had taken it upon himself to hover over me like an eagle on the horizon; just waiting for an opportune moment to strike its prey. He kept peeking out through the blinds, making sure I wouldn't slink away to the woods. I'd curled up in the patio chair, counting constellations while calling on the elements to strengthen me. It helped a little, but it was nothing like having access to the heart of the forest; soaking the energy directly from the earth in the Hollow.

I couldn't stop thinking about Nathan.

Dreams were peculiar demons. They possessed the ability to show you things you could only imagine, fill you with a sense of happiness– *or*–they had the ability to flood your subconscious with absolute misery. Today, I wore the melancholy of it like a cloak, allowing it to rest heavily on my shoulders. That vision, along with Nathan's eyes never stopped haunting me.

"Quit stressing," Annabelle said to me the night of homecoming. She'd accompanied me on my mission to unhook the battery from Nathan's car. We were dressed in black, parked across the street in a car that belonged to Annabelle's grandmother. We'd chosen it in hopes that it wouldn't be recognized and otherwise give us away. I'd already unhooked his battery, though I wasn't sure what good that would do once they discovered the quick fix. I thought about slashing his tires, but I was a good kid and I wasn't about to sully a flawless record.

"Get down," I hissed. "They're coming out." Nathan and Myra were dressed in their homecoming attire. Myra had on a bubblegum pink dress that amplified her curves, and Nathan had on a matching pink satin tie and a small rose boutonniere. Their parents filed out onto the front lawn, snapping obligatory pictures to mark the occasion; the women taking turns to gush over Myra's gown and glittery hairstyle. They looked nice–if you were a fan of bubblegum pink–which, I was not. I felt my lungs constricting; breath halting entirely as Nathan climbed into the driver's seat of his red sports car. The keys fumbled in the ignition. My heart sank to my stomach and stopped beating.

"What's wrong, son?" I heard his father ask.

"I don't know. It just won't start," Nathan said, obviously miffed.

"Is there gas in it?" his dad asked.

"I just filled it up this morning."

"Pop the hood," his dad instructed.

I felt Annabelle's fingernails sinking into the flesh of my upper arm–even through the black cotton fabric of the long sleeves. "What do we do?" she whispered.

"Just wait," I said.

Perhaps my tampering with the battery was enough to set the course of events off track. Sometimes a stall was all that was needed to completely disrupt the process. And sometimes, it wasn't... It took his dad all of ten minutes to get the battery reconnected. They exchanged some inaudible words, and then Nathan and Myra were headed off to the dance.

"I should have let the air out of the tires," I whispered to Annabelle, disappointed that this revelation hadn't occurred sooner.

"That would have been a quick fix, too. Should we follow?" Annabelle asked.

"Let's wait until his parents are back inside. It was obvious that his vehicle was tampered with, I don't want to throw us under the bus just yet."

"It's for a good cause," Annabelle said with a shrug.

Approximately three minutes later–which felt like an eternity–Nathan's family had retreated indoors. Annabelle started up the car, and we followed the familiar winding road that would lead us through the mountain on our way to school. It was a foggy night, not at all unusual for the elevation we were at in the mountains. Her headlights cut across the road, catching the smoky tendrils that snaked across the hood of the car as we drove. We were both silent. Annabelle clutched my hand in hers as we disappeared beneath the mouth of the mountain. Up ahead, a vibrant display of color stretched out before the headlights. Pieces of shiny red metal lay scattered across the pavement, mixed with the debris of broken moonlit glass.

I swallowed hard against the rising lump in my throat and unbuckled my seatbelt. "Call an ambulance," I said to Annabelle, thrusting my phone in her unblinking direction.

As I made my way across the road and looked at my bloodstained classmates and the car that was twisted around the trunk of the tree, I knew then with a feeling of absolute realization that I resented my powers. I was furious with myself for not doing more–for not taking a bigger risk and exposing my true nature. So what if I became the laughingstock of the whole town? It wasn't like the sixteen-hundreds anymore where witches were burned at the stake. What's the worst that could happen?

And then I heard my mother's voice in my head; the memory of her velvet tone bringing tears to my eyes. "The world is cruel," she said when I first asked her about my powers. "People aren't always capable of understanding. You're different, Quinn, and being different can scare people. It's dangerous for you and for all the other Supernatural kind, too. Do you understand? You must always keep your abilities a secret. There will always be a greater evil keeping close watch if you don't."

I had always thought the part about "great evil lurking around" was just an added ploy to keep me quiet, but even so, she was right. Knowing what I was, and what I could do *was* dangerous. I knew the old stories about monster hunts and torture chambers for creatures that defied the laws of human capability. I didn't want to end up a science experiment but sacrificing a friend wasn't worth keeping myself protected. After the accident, Myra walked away with minimal injuries and Nathan kissed his scholarship goodbye.

And I had to live with the knowledge–the awful, gut-raking knowledge–that I could have done something more to stop it.

I was not a hero.

I forced the lingering thoughts of Nathan to the back of my mind, and headed down the lane. I sucked in a big gulp of the chilly morning air and hoped the cold would invigorate my senses on my walk to school. When I reached the bottom of the lane, I froze. Idling in the drive sat Wren in his car. He had the window rolled down, patiently waiting.

"Morning," he called to me.

"Hi," I said, stupefied, "what are you doing here?"

"I just thought you might like a ride. Consider it as my serving penance for almost running you over yesterday."

"You don't need to do that," I said, pausing. "How did you know where I lived, anyway?" I narrowed my eyes.

"Lucky guess." He shrugged.

I bit my bottom lip in contemplation, and the pupils of his eyes seemed to dilate. He watched me in a way that made me feel self-conscious. Things that I had never questioned in the past started to drift to the surface in self-doubt. Was there something on my face–was my eyeliner smeared in the corners? Was my deodorant working? Was my burgundy shirt too tight? I shifted nervously on my feet, adjusting the strap of my backpack on my shoulder.

"Relax," he said, "I don't bite."

I didn't like that he could read me so clearly. I remembered that I wanted to pick his brain, and this opportunity may not come knocking twice, so I swallowed my pride and walked toward the passenger's side of his car. He leaned across the seat, pushing the door open for me before I slid in.

"Do you want the heat on? I tend to run a little hot myself, but I can suffer through it if you're cold," he said.

"I'm fine," I replied. My nerves were sending a flush of heat and color to the surface of my skin. I pulled the seatbelt across my chest and buckled myself in. As we pulled out of the drive, Wren started humming a couple of bars from a song that seemed familiar, yet I couldn't quite identify where I had heard it before. The deep tone of his voice gave the song a melancholy edge, and for a second, I found myself wishing I could listen to him sing the lyrics.

I shook my head, trying to clear the mental fog that was clouding my once rational functioning brain. "So," I began, "you must live around here?"

"Just up and around the corner," he replied. "You can't see it from the road. My dad has a nice chunk of land up in the forest. His father built the cabin we live in."

"Who's your father?"

"Niall Whelan," Wren answered. "You probably wouldn't know him. He lives off the land and avoids most human contact. He's a bit of a recluse."

"That sounds lonely."

"It's just his way." Wren gave a small shrug.

I wanted to ask him so much more, but I couldn't quite make the words form. Besides, how was one supposed to come out and ask the sort of questions that were formulating on the edge of my tongue? *So, I know you're some kind of Supernatural based on my own Supernatural instincts, and I was just wondering what you were exactly?* Right. Not going to happen. I ran my palms across the thighs of my pant legs until they warmed from friction.

"You've lived here all your life?" Wren asked me.

"Yep. Born and raised."

"That must be comforting, knowing you have somewhere to belong, or, something that belongs to you." He glanced over at me briefly, and I noted the sadness in his tawny eyes; the thick of it in the sound of his voice.

"You don't have that?" I asked softly.

Wren snickered, the corner of his mouth lifting into a sardonic smile. He didn't exactly answer me, but we were pulling into the school's senior parking lot, located next to the football stadium. Because we'd driven, we'd gotten to school fifteen minutes early, and my heart began to race at the thought of those unmarred minutes and the possibility of what they could hold. I unbuckled my seatbelt, but Wren made no move to join me in getting out of the car.

"Thanks for the ride," I managed.

"You're on the way to and from school," he said, "I'd be happy to keep giving you a ride."

"Oh, well, consider your sins atoned for." I forced a smile and watched as his features lit up in amusement.

"I'd still like to give you a ride," he said in that dazzling low tone of his. I could practically feel the vibration of it through the seat.

"We'll see," I said. I reached for my bag, tossing it over my shoulder as I pulled myself out of his car. I breathed in the fresh, crisp air, and welcomed the cool feel of it against my skin.

When I turned, Wren was beside me–merely an inch separated our bodies. If I faced him, I realized my mouth was in perfect alignment with his collarbone, and that small, prominent hollow at the base of his throat. I crossed my arms over my chest and folded my hands over my biceps to keep my hands from trembling.

"Cold?" Wren rumbled.

"A little," I lied.

"I've got a jacket in the car, hold on a sec." Before I could say anything, he'd turned back for his car, and was pulling his leather jacket from the back seat. It was the one I'd seen him wearing at the coffee shop, and as he handed it to me, I breathed in the heady aroma of the earth that was clinging to it.

"Thanks." I slipped my arms through the sleeves, pulling my hair from underneath the back of the collar.

"It looks good on you." He was grinning down at me, not a full smile, but the closest glimpse of one I'd seen yet.

"It's a little big," I said.

"Well I should hope so." Wren looped his thumbs in the waistband of his jeans as we walked. The ordinary gesture almost made him seem casual, but there was something about him–something unidentifiable– that made him stand apart from the rest of the high school population. It wasn't that he stood out so much as perhaps the rest of us just didn't belong in his realm.

We entered the building, and the warmth of the air surrounded us. The school always smelled a little musty, like old newspaper and the inside of an art supply box.

"We're still a little early," Wren commented, "wanna' swing by the cafeteria and pick up a cup of coffee?"

"I have my thermos," I said, patting my backpack.

"Oh." Wren's eyes shifted to the side, an evident look of disappointment corrupting his features.

"I could probably top it off though." After a night of vision-pressed dreams, goddess knows it would take a lethal amount of caffeine to get me through the day.

We headed for the cafeteria and passed the school secretary on our way. She glimpsed at us briefly–*well*–she glimpsed at Wren briefly. Her eyes had skipped over me all together. Wren, however, didn't appear to notice this. Miss Foster was pretty, I thought, a fresh graduate from Silver Mountain University and single. If Wren could ignore the look of her slim legs in the navy-blue pencil skirt she was wearing, I was dying to see his reaction to Nadine.

We turned into the cafeteria and made our way to the cappuccino machine. I pulled the thermos from my bag, and unscrewed the lid while Wren filled his Styrofoam cup with the vanilla flavored option.

"Virgo, right?"

"What?" I reached up, brushing the hair back from my face.

"The constellation on your thermos, I noticed it yesterday after practice."

"Oh, yeah, that's right," I said. "You know your stars?"

"Probably not as well as you." His eyebrow lifted reflexively. "My dad is big into legends and old wives-tales. I guess you could say a lot of my upbringing was determined by what was written in the stars."

If it had been possible for me to spontaneously burst into flames from heightened curiosity, I would have been ablaze with fire. I had to bite my lower lip to keep from asking about these mysterious star legends he knew of. I wanted to know so badly what he was. I could feel it circling through my gut like the way adrenaline swam through my veins at the starting line before a race. There was so much excitement in face of discovery, so much possibility.

"What are you thinking about?" Wren was staring at me in that knowing way of his. His eyes flickered to my lower lip.

"I'm just really into the stars," I said.

"Tell me then, what makes the Virgo constellation so special?"

"There are a few reasons," I admitted. "My mother was a Virgo. It's also the second largest constellation in the sky, and I like the mythology behind it."

"Hades kidnaps the goddess Persephone while she's out picking flowers, but her mother, Demeter, retaliated by stopping the growth of all green plant life until Hades agreed to return Persephone to the heavens. Then there was something about pomegranate seeds and since she ate them she could only return with the penance of staying in the underworld for three months out of the year," he finished. "That's not exactly a cozy bedtime story." His eyebrow flicked upward again.

"No, but it's symbolic of the beginning of autumn, and the cycle of all life forms; the death and rebirth of all things. The constellation also happens to have a shared point with Libra which represents the autumnal equinox." My mouth went dry, and I wondered if by saying this I had given too much away about my own identity. It was understood among the Supernatural realm that the autumnal equinox was a powerful and meaningful time for witches.

His eyes danced back and forth between either of mine, and a slow smile pulled at the corners of his lips.

I didn't think I could come out and say it, but, if he guessed what I was, I wasn't sure I could deny it. A wave of dread rushed through my being at the thought of another person learning my secret, but there was also something thrilling in it, too. I didn't know him, but I sensed that I could trust him somehow... After all, he'd been living with a supernatural secret of his own. I waited for him to say something–to say anything, but he just stood there; his gaze unraveling my twisted insides.

A moment later, a group of giggling underclassman girls walked into the cafeteria, breaking whatever trance Wren seemed to have over me.

"I should get to homeroom," I said, gesturing over my shoulder.

"See you in English."

I left the cafeteria then, clinging to my thermos and let the warmth of it seep into my fingertips. I risked a glance over my shoulder, releasing the breath of air that had been trapped inside my lungs since Wren picked me up this morning. He hadn't followed me out of the cafeteria. I wasn't sure where his homeroom was located, but I was relieved to know it wasn't in the same direction as mine. I needed a few minutes of clarity to refocus.

I had only ever come across other witches in passing, but I knew there were other Supernaturals out there that I knew nothing about. Wren knew a little about the stars and mythology that surrounded them, but that didn't exactly give me a helpful lead. Plenty of Supernatural-types relied on star-magic. Perhaps he was some kind of celestial being, or demi-god.

"There you are," Annabelle said as she appeared around the corner. "I was beginning to–*what* are you wearing?" Her eyes narrowed into thin slits as she came to an abrupt stop in front of me. Her shoes even scuffed the tile.

"Uh," I muttered, "Wren's jacket."

"Okay," Annabelle said slowly, "explain please."

"He was waiting in my driveway this morning. He offered me a ride."

"*And* his jacket?"

"It was cold out." I shrugged.

"Quinn, as your best friend, I feel that it's my duty to tell you that I'm a little concerned about this Wren guy's intentions. I saw the way he was looking at you yesterday. He watches you. Like, more than just a guy with a crush on a girl should. There's something off about him. I don't know what it is exactly, but he definitely has a few screws loose."

"He doesn't." I started shaking my head.

"Then what is it, because it's not normal."

"Keep your voice down," I said, grabbing her arm and yanking her into the ladies' room. I checked beneath each stall door to make sure that we were alone. "If I tell you something, you have to promise not to breathe a word of it."

"I think that goes without saying, obviously." A dark shadow crossed over her eyes, pulling her features together in look of hurt. If only she knew that I was just trying to keep her safe.

"What I'm about to tell you goes against the Supernatural code of conduct and puts you in the line of danger–yet again."

"Stop worrying about me. I can handle it." She gripped my forearms tightly.

"You know how my abilities allow me to sense when another Supernatural being is near?"

"Yeah." She shrugged.

"Well…" I grit my teeth together, waving my hands like a magician who had just pulled a rabbit from a hat.

"Hold on." Wide-eyed, she flattened her hand in the air between us. "You don't seriously mean what I think you mean."

"I do," I said meekly. "There's something different about him, Anna. Usually when my senses activate, all I have to do is just make a mental connection with the Supe in question and then it stops. But that didn't happen with him. He had my senses in overdrive. I felt like my mind was screaming at me, and it didn't actually stop until he grabbed my arm yesterday after English class. I don't know why, but it's almost like I was being called to him somehow," I finished.

Annabelle blinked, giving her head a quick little shake. "First of all, that's creepy. Second of all, why didn't you tell me about it the minute you knew he was different?"

"Anna, I didn't think I should. You know it could be dangerous."

"Yeah–dangerous for *you*," she said. "You don't know anything about him. I mean, what if he knows what you are?" She whispered this last part.

"Well, that's what I'm trying to find out," I said, tugging on the zipper of Wren's jacket. "As subtly as possible."

Annabelle mulled this over, her lips visibly puckered while she chewed on the inside corner of her cheek. "You sure he's not a warlock or a sorcerer?"

"He couldn't be," I shook my head, "I would have recognized that."

"Well, we should know exactly what we're dealing with."

"I don't disagree," I told her, "I just need to be smart about the way I find out."

"Fine." She crossed her arms, flipping a lock of hair out of her eyes. "You should know that while you've been playing undercover witch detective, I also did a little digging of my own. Social media is good for more than just self-indulgence. I happened to find out that Hunter does have a younger sister. Her name is Amanda and she's in the eighth-grade."

"About that..." I'd nearly forgotten about the false promise I'd made to my dad about staying out of the woods until the wolf thing was resolved. I filled Anna in on what happened after she'd left us at the diner last night.

Anna waved a hand through the air. "Minor hiccup. We can work around it, but, maybe you should start limiting yourself about what details you discuss with your dad. I know he means well, and, he has a point, but you have a destiny that you can't ignore, and he can't keep you from it."

"Oh, Annabelle," I sighed, leaning against the cinderblock wall. "You give me far too much credit."

"You'll see," she said, leading us out into the hall as the homeroom bell rang. We scurried into the classroom and sat in the last two open seats as Mr. Anderson started taking roll. We listened while the announcements clanged through the broken speaker, but Mr. Anderson only fixed the intercom with a menacing glower. Clearly, he'd decided that giving it a good whack with the broom handle had been a poor decision on his part.

Wren was already seated when we walked in to Miss Lane's classroom. His literature book lay open on the desk while he leaned over the text, following the printed black ink with the tip of his index finger. I hadn't noticed before, but he had strong looking hands; long fingers. My eyes fixed on a scar on the back of his right hand; it curved with the shape of a jagged half-moon, tracing from the knuckle of his small finger to the joint of his thumb.

I sat down behind him and slipped his jacket from my arms. The room felt cooler without it, but I leaned forward in the chair and tapped him on the shoulder. When he turned, I swore his eyes had taken on an unusual color and shape. There was something almost animalistic–primal even–about the change. I blinked rapidly, gazing back at his unusual amber colored irises. The change must have only been a figment of my imagination. I wanted to believe so badly that he was something more, so my mind was making those beliefs into reality.

"Thank you," I said, shaking off the momentary mental shock, and extended his jacket across the small distance that separated our desks.

He took it wordlessly, acknowledging me with a slight smile and a nod of his head before turning back to his textbook.

We picked up where we'd left off yesterday, listening to the book on tape until the class hour ticked by. As the class started packing up their belongings, Miss Lane stood in front of the blackboard. "Tomorrow, I'd like to start a discussion based on the contemporary issues we see with science, and whether or not we believe that Frankenstein is playing God by creating life. Just because we have the knowledge and power to do so, does it mean that we should?"

The bell rang then, and Wren gathered his things in one swift movement and glided out of the room with ease. I was still stuffing my notebook into my bag, but I was all too aware of Courtney's piercing gaze out of my peripheral. I looked up, meeting her honey-brown glare.

"You seem to be getting awfully friendly with Wren," she commented. She tried for indifference but failed to keep the indignation out of her voice. Courtney had never been gifted at the art of feigning anything–other than the unnatural color of her blonde hair.

"He's nice," I said, and then added, (as if I needed an excuse to be friendly with him. Really, it wasn't any of her business.) "He joined the cross-country team."

"*Really*," she purred, her glossy bottom lip curling around the vowels. "I took him for more of a football player with his height and build."

I reminded myself that she knew nothing about runners before I snapped a snarky reply. Instead, I worked my lips into the shape of a grin. I gathered up my bag and started up the aisle.

"You know, I wonder if he has any plans for homecoming." She crossed her arms, cradling them in a thoughtful way as she gingerly tapped the corner of her mouth with an index finger. "It's probably too last minute. He doesn't strike me as the type of guy that just happens to have a tux lying around anyway." This was Courtney's not so subtle way of letting me know she was into him–as if the entire world wasn't already aware.

"You can always ask him," I said encouragingly. I wanted to make it clear that this was in no way a competition.

She snickered, the high-pitched sound catching in her nasal passages. I pushed past her and met Annabelle in the doorway.

"Well that wasn't awkward at all," Annabelle said.

"Typical Courtney," I muttered. We started down the hall, and I caught a glimpse of Wren disappearing behind the door to Mr. Knoll's trigonometry room. He was whistling a couple of bars from the song he was humming this morning, and I was struck again with the familiarization of the tune. It was starting to bother me that I couldn't place its origin. I knew I'd heard it before, but I couldn't remember where.

Hunter was finishing his last mile around the track. He looked stronger today, more confident. If it weren't for the slight bruising around his cheekbone, you wouldn't even guess he'd taken such a tumble on the track yesterday.

The football team was practicing on the field; the sound of their helmets and pads crashing together echoed in the air, but was swallowed behind the sounds of their pained grunts and growls. The vexing chants of the Zombie Squad carried through the wind in my direction, and as I bent to stretch out my sore shins, I spotted Courtney. She was standing front and center of the pack as she led the squad in one of their robotic dance routines. She was looking this way, I realized, and as I followed her line of vision, I wasn't at all surprised to see Wren chatting with Huck and Jamie just a few yards behind me.

I looked down at my shins, running my finger along the bone-sharp edges of my right leg and felt the tiny bumps that started to develop and grimaced. Shin splints were the last thing I needed right now. I wished Coach would stop running us on the track. I needed to be back in the woods, working through the mountain terrain. Conditioning was long since over, and I wondered why he hadn't been taking us through our usual trails in the forest.

Wren appeared in front of me in a flash, kneeling so that our eyes were level with one another. I startled slightly, a small wave of fear passing through my chest at his sudden presence. He possessed an uncanny ability to move in utter silence. Maybe he was part ghost?

"Sorry," he breathed, a smirk tugging the corner of his lip. His right hand wrapped around my ankle while his left pressed into the sides of my knee. My leg jumped at his touch, like he'd hit me with one of those reflex hammers at a doctor's office. His thumbs squeezed either side of my kneecap gently. He pulled my foot forward, toes pointed toward the grass, and the bunched muscles in my shin and calf began to sing with the sweet release of pain.

"Where did you learn how to do that?" I asked, tipping my face to the sun.

"Can't give all my secrets away," he replied. He ran his thumb along the contour of my right shin, igniting a trail of flames in its wake. At that moment, I would have settled for just one secret. I kept my eyes on his deft, skilled hands that were working a magic of their own. He pushed my foot the opposite way, stretching the muscle in my calf. I murmured a sigh of relief.

"You should ice your shins when you get home."

"Plan to," I said.

"You ran well today."

"Thanks. I just wish Coach would let us back on the mountain trails, he doesn't usually keep us practicing on the track after conditioning is over."

"He's probably just trying to keep everyone safe."

"Safe?" My brows shifted together in a frown.

"Ah. So you haven't heard." He shifted my leg again, pulling my foot so that my toes were pointing toward the grass.

"Heard what?"

"The rumor about the rouge pack of wolves," Wren said.

"Pack?" I heard myself repeat. The vision I had of Hunter snapped across my eyes, causing a slight painful sensation to zap through my temples. I swallowed over the lump rising in my throat, and added, "I didn't think wolves were really a danger to humans."

"They're not supposed to be." Wren was watching me again, his eyes unblinking and poised on my face. There was something in his expression that underlined the caution in his words. *They weren't supposed to be dangerous*, he'd said, but his eyes were telling me that they could.

Chapter Six
The Blaire Witch

The crystals hanging above the glass doors chimed as I walked into the Magic Shoppe. Penny Francis, the owner, looked up from beneath her wire framed glasses and marked the place she was reading in her book with a slender metal crescent moon.

"Well hello, Quinn." Penny beamed. She pushed back from her wooden chair and walked across the rickety old floor to embrace me. She smelled like patchouli and moth balls, but the scent–as overwhelming as it was–could be overlooked. Though Penny was not a *real* witch, she played the part well in her nineteenth century garb. Her tight black ringlets were streaked with gray; they framed her face like an untamed mountain shrub.

"It's good to see you, Penny." I grinned.

"Haven't seen you in a while, but I'm glad you're here. Tell me. What can I help you with?" Penny smoothed the creases in her long skirts.

"I was just hoping to browse your book selection," I said, "school project."

"I had no idea that Silver Mountain was so proactive with its teachings of the supernatural. You seem to have a lot of school projects broaching the subject." Surprise and delight raised her voice an octave.

"This one is for extra credit," I said in a rush. "Mrs. McCarthy wanted to do a little side project in celebration of the upcoming autumn festival."

"Fascinating indeed," Penny said. "Well help yourself dear, I've just gotten a new order of gemstones in, and I've got to organize the lot. If you need anything just yell." In the far corner of the shop, Penny had hundreds of different stones and crystals on display in tiny, square-shaped wooden dividers. Each holder possessed about ten of the same stone, with a small placard to indicate what each stone was, and a small description of what they were used for. I watched as she turned for the storage room, and then I headed for the book cases.

Penny had gotten most of her books from antique sales, old libraries, and second-hand used book stores. The old, leather-bound books lined the top shelves, their spines were cracked and torn; the metallic lettering scratched and faded. A thick smattering of dust cloaked their true colors. Still, the smell of their frail pages lingered in the air like a memory–refusing to be forgotten.

I ran my index finger along the spines, sifting through the titles. There had to be something I missed; something that might be able to help balance my visions, or something that would block them all together. If only I could find a way to stop them, I wouldn't have to spend the rest of my life walking on eggshells or wishing I could change things I had no control over.

My fingernail snagged on the spine of a book that read *Gemstone Energy and their Magical Properties*. I pulled it from its resting place, but before I could remove it from the shelf, the hair on the back of my neck prickled. A light breeze caused the crystals above the door to chime, and my skin began to pulse. I reached up, cupping a hand over the back of my neck and spun on my heel.

There was a girl behind me; she stood about my height and similar build, with spirals of long, raven-black hair. A hint of a smile turned the corners of her full mouth upward as her sharp, black eyes anchored mine. "Hello," she breathed, her head tilting slightly. Her eyes didn't move. They pointed straight ahead, fixating on me with a steady magnetic pull.

"You're..."

"As are you," she answered in a thick Irish accent. She didn't seem at all surprised–as if meeting another witch were an everyday occurrence for her.

"Who are you?" I asked.

"Blaire Alderdice, I'm Penny's niece. It's a pleasure to make your acquaintance...?"

"Quinn," I said, "Quinn Callaghan."

"I see we share a common thread–other than the obvious magics," she said with a wink. "What part of Ireland does your family hail from?"

"Um, I don't know, actually."

"That's curious," Blaire commented, her eyes narrowing. "The Callaghan's are known for a long bloodline strong in powerful magics."

I shook my head. "My mother wasn't a Callaghan by birth. I mean, I inherited my abilities from her."

"You can say *witch* you know," Blaire giggled, "no one is going to hang you for practicing the craft in here. You're quite safe."

"Does Penny know what you are?" I asked.

"She does. I'll wager she doesn't know about you, though."

Blaire hadn't phrased her speculation as a question, but I felt compelled to answer anyway. "No, and, I'd like to keep it that way."

"You needn't worry, I won't tell a soul." She mimicked drawing a line across her lips and threw away the invisible key.

Just short of about a thousand questions started taking shape in my mind. Here I stood face to face with an actual witch–a girl–who didn't appear much older than me, openly seeming interested in my Supernatural heritage. My heart sped up, spiked with curiosity. What if this girl could help me?

My mother's voice rang in the back of my mind; her constant warning signals weighting me down and paralyzing me in a familiar state of fear. My hesitation rooted me in self-preservation. *Caution, caution, caution.*

"You have a very strong presence, Quinn, but I've never seen such a clouded aura in my entire existence."

"What?"

"I'm an empath," Blaire attempted to explain. "I can read emotional energy. Every person has an energy field that represents their state of mind, but yours..." she trailed off, moving forward as she circled me–

examining things that I couldn't see. Her features shifted thoughtfully; her movements languid and preoccupied. "It's like you're fighting against your own nature," she observed. "You're so tired of hiding who you are, but you don't like your gift. Why do you not like your gift?"

My head snapped up to meet her eyes, and she was frowning at me. "It's more of a curse," I whispered.

Blaire was shaking her head. "Tell me what you mean."

I took a step backward mechanically.

"You're safe in this place," Blaire said, her hands wrapping around my wrist gently. Her grip was feather-light but reassuring and solid. The room started to warm with a soothing sense of calm. For a second, I thought I could smell something floral–jasmine, perhaps? And lavender.

"Are you doing that?" I marveled.

"Part of my gift," she said with a smile. "I have an Earth affinity which allows me to encourage environmental settings if I'm touching a person's skin."

"You mean you can manipulate people into giving you what you want if the mood is right?" I snickered. "Now *that* is a handy gift."

Blaire let go of my wrist. "I only meant to help."

"It's okay," I said, sensing somehow that she really was just trying to help me. I'd come here looking for answers, I just hadn't expected to find them in Supernatural human form. Caution be damned. After all, what did I really have to lose? "I can see things," I told her, "*visions.*" I paused, gauging her expression but her features stayed neutral. She nodded her head, gesturing for me to continue. "I can only see things if I come into contact with a person's blood–"

"–Blood magic," Blaire interrupted, eyes brightening. "That is an extremely rare and powerful gift indeed. Nigh only about a hundred witches across the world have ever been gifted that power since the beginning of time."

I swallowed hard, continuing to stare at her.

"Have you any idea how special your gift is?" She said in awe. I was all too aware that she was looking at me like she'd just discovered an invaluable artifact, dug up from an ancient burial site.

"I know it's extremely painful," I said.

"Painful?" Blaire's eyebrows furrowed.

"Yeah. I get nose bleeds and splitting pain after the visions happen. Fatigue and strength loss also occur," I said, ticking the side effects off my fingers as I named them. "It's like I'm being punished."

Blaire was shaking her head. "You've got it all wrong, lass. The Mother goddess would never punish you for using a given gift. It's only so painful to you because you don't practice. You shouldn't fight against it. When it happens next, you should concentrate on going with the current."

I was sure my mouth parted, but I didn't know what to say. I thought I had been going along with the current. I didn't feel like I had any control over the visions whatsoever. I was a slave to the journey they brought me on.

"What charms do you carry?" Blaire asked me.

"Charms?"

"Oh for goddess sake, don't you know anything about being a witch?" Her accent grew thicker as she scolded me.

"Well, my mother died before I came into my clairvoyant powers and I don't know any other witches," I said defensively. "Silver Mountain isn't exactly crawling with Supernaturals."

"Come along then, I best show you about." Blaire took hold of my wrist and half dragged me to the gemstone display. "Let's get you a little something to strengthen your aura. Now. Hold out your hand over the stones and close your eyes," she instructed.

"Why?"

"Because I want you to sense what stone you need," she said. "Your magical instincts will guide you. You just need to have trust."

With a sigh, I extended my right hand over the gemstone display and closed my eyes. I let my palm hover over the stones, not sure what to expect as I did. I moved my hand lower over the stones, waving it in a slow, semicircular motion. As I reached the upper right corner of the display, my palm began to burn as if I'd been holding it over a candle flame. I winced, opening my eyes and clenching my fist.

"It's as I expected," Blaire said, reaching into the small bin and retrieving a deep violet-blue colored stone. She dropped it in my palm, and I noticed as I shifted it in the light, the stone seemed to mimic a deep, night sky with flecks of lighter colored fragments that almost looked like stars.

"What is it?" I asked.

"That," Blaire pointed with a deep red fingernail, "is called iolite, also known as the 'Vikings' Compass' or 'Water Sapphire.' Iolite is a great stone for healing and balancing your energy. When you wear the stone, it helps to awaken any psychic abilities that you haven't tapped into, and encourages deeper, vivid details for people who experience psychic visions."

"I don't know if I want that," I said hesitantly. "I already feel like the visions leave me spinning out of control, I don't think I can handle a more vivid vision."

"Bollocks," she chided. "The stone will help balance the effects so you won't feel like you're spinning off to Never-Never Land. This is also a dream talisman, so you'll have to be careful when wearing it to bed. They say Iolite can cast glimpses into other worlds. I haven't tried it myself, but I've heard it can be quite confusing." Blaire picked the stone out of my palm and carried it to the counter where a row of silver pendants was hanging from a jewelry rack. She rifled through the contents, and then plucked an amulet free of its resting place.

She was holding a beautiful filigree crescent moon, and from the upper tip hung a pentagram with a hollowed center. She fit the stone into the center and rummaged through the drawer until she brought forth a coil of silver wire. I watched her work, expertly wrapping the wire around the stone in the pentagram as she fixed it in place.

"Tell me you at least know what the pentagram represents?" Blaire challenged.

"Yes," I said with a derisive edge. "The five points of the star represent each of the elements. I pointed to the apex of the star and said, "Spirit," I moved right with my finger and pointed to the next, "Water," then, "Fire, Earth, and Air."

"Yes," Blaire said, "and what does the circle around it represent?"

"Protection."

"Very good." Blaire grinned. "Every witch needs to wear a talisman or amulet for protection. This, combined with the magical elements of your crystal, should help you along." She reached across the counter and handed me the necklace. "Until you learn how to manifest your powers on your own, the stone will help."

"Thank you," I said, feeling the cool metal of the crescent moon. "How much do I owe you for this?"

"This one's on the house," Blaire said. "Like I said, every witch needs an amulet, and yours is long overdue."

"But, what about Penny?"

"You're not to worry about my aunt. She won't even know its missing."

I nodded appreciatively. "Don't take this the wrong way," I said, "but, why are you helping me?"

Blaire snickered. "You act as if it were a crime or something."

"Sorry, it's just that I've never even met another witch before. My dad..." I trailed off, deciding how best to phrase this. "Well let's just say that what I can do scares him. Since my mom died, he kind of resents the magical world."

"Can't pretend to know what that must be like. My family openly practiced among one another while I grew up. We have a coven back in Ireland." She pressed her lips together in sympathy. "Look, I'm staying here with Penny for a while. I'm on holiday, but I was considering attending the States for post-secondary education, so I'll be around if you think you might want to learn more."

"Yeah?"

"It could be fun. I could show you loads of great spells." She smiled.

I nodded, toying with the silver chain in my hands.

"What's the matter lass?"

"It's just that... for so long, I thought that I was being punished for seeing the future. Learning what I can from the visions is dangerous. I don't like the burden it places on me if something goes wrong. I've always felt responsible for what I see, like it's my duty to fix what happens, and, I haven't always been successful."

Blaire nodded, "I can understand why you'd feel that way. A gift like that is very *special*," she carefully decided on the word, "but the Mother wouldn't place it upon you if she didn't think you couldn't handle it. You're meant to do great things, Quinn Callaghan. You've a greater purpose yet."

I swallowed hard, feeling the strings of saliva sticking to the sides of my throat. "So, just to clarify, I am meant to change what I see? Isn't that a little too close to playing with fire?"

"What's wrong with playing with a bit of fire?" Blaire asked. Her eyes sparkled as if they were made of embers. "We're protectors of the innocent. Helping people is the very reason for our existence." She shrugged. "We are the beacon of light in a world full of darkness."

Goose bumps prickled my skin at her words, but I continued to gaze at her coal black eyes. There was a glow there; a steady strength that radiated with warmth. I wanted to ask her more, but the crystals chimed behind me, and a couple of customers walked in. "I should go," I said, "but thank you for this." I held up the amulet.

"Come see me some time," Blaire said, "we'll talk more."

I left the shop then, slightly addled by Blaire's willingness to discuss witchcraft. I couldn't pinpoint why I felt so compelled to share my background with her, but something about her seemed so familiar to me; like I had known her from another life. It was strange really, but I felt like I could trust her. I slipped the pendant over my head, and as it fell into place just above my heart, I felt stronger somehow. Like I didn't have to be afraid of what I could do. I had spent too much time resenting my gift; living with the knowledge that it was a punishment.

And I had been wrong.

The forest floor was cool beneath my paws–no, not *my* paws–but I could feel what the wolf was experiencing. I could smell things that were undetectable to the human nose and hear things that the human ear couldn't. The wolf lifted its head into the wind, sampling. About a mile away, the sharp, putrid odor of an animal corpse lay rotting in the underbrush. I could smell the decay of its body, and the acrid stench that told me the decomposing animal was in fact a skunk. The odor drifted through the breeze, fusing with the scents of the rich earth, the bark on the trees, and the rapidly changing autumn leaves. Everything was so distinct I could almost taste it.

The wolf drifted through the forest soundlessly. It was heading toward the riverbank where red and yellow leaves had begun to fall, decorating the rocky terrain. The wolf walked out into the stream, bending to drink from the icy creek. When it lifted its head, I caught a glimpse of its reflection. Its features danced within the glittering water, shifting with the slow-moving current. Its fur was so black it appeared blue in the moonlight. There was something oddly familiar about its eyes–the shape and color, a deep, clear yellow with a predatory gaze. The wolf was staring at its own reflection, looking past the water, and through the mirror of its awareness. It recognized me, and the shock of that realization shot through me and left me gasping for air.

I sat up in bed, clutching a hand to my heart and the pendant that lay nestled in the curve of my breasts. The sheets were tangled around me, half sticking to my sweat-covered body. Air ballooned in my lungs as my heart struggled to regain its regular rhythm.

"Quinn?" There was a knock on my bedroom door, and my dad's concerned voice muffled behind it. "You okay?"

"Yeah, Dad, I'm fine," I called.

"Bad dream?"

"No. Just, extremely vivid." I twisted the pendant in my hands, rubbing a thumb over the inky violet colored stone at the center. I'd forgotten Blaire's warning about sleeping with it on.

"All right, I'm heading to Jo's for the final touches."

"Bye, love you."

"Love you too, kiddo."

I listened as his footsteps creaked across the wooden floorboards in the hall until he was descending the stairs. I pushed my matted hair back from my forehead and dragged myself out of bed. The cool wood beneath the soles of my feet reminded me of the smooth rocks at the bottom of the creek bed. My skin ached, like I'd spent too much time out of my own body, and my tendons had been rearranged in all the wrong places. I thought of those luminous yellow eyes, gazing back at me in the reflection of the water, and had an overwhelming realization that I had been eavesdropping into a life that didn't belong to me.

The dream had mimicked one of my visions; but unlike my visions, my presence was made known to the host. Perhaps that was a side effect of the magical properties in the stone. I made a mental note to ask Blaire about it later.

I'd told Annabelle about meeting Blaire the next day at school. She'd tried, with minimal success, to keep her expression neutral. Annabelle had a tell–her eyes narrowing into thin slits whenever she became disgruntled. Annabelle wasn't the jealous-friend type, but I knew a part of her liked being the only one that knew my secret. "And, you trust this Blaire character?" she asked me after I finished telling the story of our peculiar meeting.

"She doesn't have any reason to lie to me," I replied with a shrug, "and besides, everything she said made perfect sense."

"So I assume you'll want to start practicing your *gift*?"

"It's worth a shot," I said. "If I can learn to control it, I can learn how to help people more sufficiently."

Annabelle lifted her foot to the trunk of the tree we were huddling around, bending to retie her tennis shoe. "You can practice on me," she said assertively, "but I don't think I want to know anything about my future."

"Annabelle, I would never ask that of you." I started to shake my head in protest.

"I know you wouldn't, which is why I'm offering."

We argued about it the whole way to Jo's and while we ate dinner on the new patio and worked on our history project. As she bit into her double burger, a glob of mustard fell from the opposite end of her bun and splattered her notebook. She wiped it away with a napkin, leaving a yellow smear in the upper left-hand margin.

"Do you think Mrs. McCarthy will notice?"

"I think you'll probably get points deducted if you don't rewrite it." I made a face, pressing my lips together in sympathy.

"I'll re-write it if you agree to practice on me."

I fixed her with my best scowl.

"Oh come on," she said. "You don't really have another option."

"I could ask Blaire," I countered.

"But I'm *volunteering*."

"Annabelle, you even said that you don't want to know your own future, what makes you think that I want to know something that you don't? If something were going to happen to you…"

"You'd find a way to stop it." She looked me straight in the eyes as she said this, all traces of concern wiped free. "I believe in you."

I never gave her a reply.

I finished showering and changed into a pair of jeans and a plain, white T-shirt. Thanks to my trance-like dream, I was now running ten minutes behind. I scrambled through the kitchen to throw a quick lunch together, and swept my thermos off the counter as I rushed for the living room. A wave of shock electrified my spine when I opened the front door. The thermos exploded at my feet, dousing the floor and splattering hot liquid up my pant legs. For a moment I just stood there, arms suspended at my sides as I gazed up into a smirking face.

"I was going to knock," Wren said, sidestepping around me.

"Sure, just come right in." My tone flattened with irritation, but my pulse betrayed me, racing as he walked inside. He found his way into the kitchen and tore some paper towels from the rack beside the sink and returned to start mopping up the mess. I grabbed a wet rag from the counter and bent beside him to assist with the cleanup.

"I'm sorry that I startled you," he said.

"You seem to have a knack for that."

"Maybe you're just jumpy." He glanced up at me from the side, a simpering grin tugging at the corner of his lip.

"Why weren't you at school yesterday?" I asked him.

"Did you miss me?"

I shot him a pointed look, ignoring the way my pulse quickened in my ears.

"Some family showed up unexpectedly," he said, rocking back onto his knees.

I nodded, tucking a strand of hair behind my ear. "Coach was concerned his star runner had already deserted the team." I extended my palm, and he handed me the soiled paper towels. "Thanks," I said, looking down at my speckled jeans. "I should probably get changed."

"I can wait for you outside, if you want?"

"I'll just be a minute. You're fine." I left him at the bottom of the stairs and wondered if he was watching after me.

When I returned to the living room, I found Wren standing in front of the fireplace, looking at the pictures that were propped up on the mantel. "Was this your mom?" he asked without turning to look at me.

"Yeah," I answered softly. My dad had taken the photo at Grandma and Grandpa Callaghan's fortieth wedding anniversary party. Mom and I were both dressed up for the occasion, our hair pulled back from our faces. Our eyes matched in shape and color, the only difference being the faint lines, crinkling the corners of her eyes when she smiled. It was the last picture my mother and I would ever take together. Though I'd permanently be frozen as a twelve-year-old beside her, I'd never stop cherishing that single, perfect moment. It wasn't a week later that we found out about her terminal illness.

"You look like her," he said. "She was beautiful."

I didn't want to ruin the compliment, so I didn't say anything. He turned slightly, eyes scanning the layout of the room. They swept over the coffee and end tables that had been hand-crafted by my father, accents for the leather couch and recliner. My mother's touch remained in the decorations–the moss colored walls, the lace table runners, and rustic country charms. "You have a nice home," he said.

"Thank you."

"No pets though?"

"My dad is allergic." My tone was laced with resentment. I'd always wanted a dog and begged my dad to take allergy shots, but the answer had remained a steady no. Wren snickered–as if allergies were somehow humorous. "How is that funny?" My eyebrows furrowed.

"Inside joke," he said, waving it off. "You ready?"

"Sure." I scooped my bag up from the floor and followed Wren out into the cool morning air. The clouds were hanging low today, suppressing the sunlight. Wren opened the passenger's side door for me as I slid in.

"Interesting bag," Wren commented as he twisted the key in the ignition.

"My mom gave it to me." I spread my fingers over the worn fabric, picking at a stray piece of thread that was hanging from the wolf's tail. "Annabelle calls it my hippie bag." I looked up at him, grinning.

"It's nice," he paused, "what did I miss in English yesterday?"

"Only the discussion of man playing God by creating monsters," I said.

"Is that what you think Frankenstein did?" He glanced over at me briefly before turning his attention back to the road that spiraled in front of us.

"I think that's what the author was implying," I said plainly. "Man shouldn't tamper with creation. There's consequences."

"Makes you feel kind of bad for the monster, huh?"

"What do you mean?" I asked skeptically. "Frankenstein's monster was a brutal killer."

"The monster resented Frankenstein for creating him, I think. He was angry and in pain. All he wanted was to fit into society–to be accepted, but the humans turned away in fear and revulsion. They would never see him for anything but a beast."

"So, you think he should be excused for murdering innocent people just because he didn't *ask* to be created or loathed by the human race?"

"I'm just saying that it's not entirely as black and white as it seems." Wren was rounding the corner for the senior lot, giving me an opportunity to study the contours of his face without the intensity of his eyes searing through mine. Wren, the Supernatural that possessed a soft side for monsters.

"New hardware?" he asked, turning to look at me after we pulled into a parking space and he'd cut the engine.

"What?" I felt my eyebrows knitting together.

"Your necklace," he stated.

"Oh." My fingers instinctively reached up to wrap around the sleek curve of the crescent moon. The iolite stone felt warm to the touch. "A friend gave it to me," I said.

"Silver?" he asked.

"I think so."

He made a noise, something like disgruntlement catching in his throat. At that exact moment, Courtney tapped on the driver's side window. Wren turned and rolled it down. "Courtney," he greeted her.

"Good morning Wren!" She beamed. "I know this is extremely last minute, but I was wondering if you had plans for homecoming?"

I felt my eyes widen in amusement. She couldn't even wait until he was out of the car. "I do, actually," he replied. "I'm going to Huck's anti-homecoming party."

"You are?" I asked.

"Oh." The look on Courtney's face was priceless. It surpassed disappointment, leaving her standing there–resembling a small child whose candy had been yanked out of their grip. Her cat-like eyes shifted to me, narrowing into slits; like somehow this was my fault.

"Maybe next time," Wren said, diffusing the situation by giving her (what I expected was) false hope.

"I guess I'll just have to talk to Huck. His anti-homecoming bash has certainly gained a reputation. It's taking away all my potential dates, and believe me, the list isn't very long. You should know you're at the top of it." She grinned, her glossy lips parting to reveal a perfect set of white teeth. Nausea rolled in my gut.

"I'm flattered," Wren said.

"See you in English." She wiggled her fingers into a sort of wave, and then spun on her heel as she twitched toward the building.

"Wow," I breathed. "You've only been here four days and you're already breaking hearts," I said. He arched his eyebrow sharply, unbuckling his seatbelt before sliding out of the car.

"Are you going to the football game tomorrow night?" he asked me.

"I am," I said. "Are you?"

"I haven't decided yet. I'm not a huge fan of the sport."

"Neither am I, but it's tradition." I shrugged. "The cross-country team usually hangs out in the student section on the far side of the bleachers." I pointed as we walked by on our way up the sidewalk. "The concession stand makes killer hot chocolate. The nachos are pretty good too."

"That doesn't sound like an appealing combination." Wren pulled the door open, gesturing for me to walk inside.

"Don't knock it until you try it."

Once we were inside the building, Wren paused in the middle of the lobby. This is where I would go right, and he would go left. He prolonged the parting, gazing at me with a curious look in his eyes. "You're very peculiar, Quinn." *I'm the peculiar one?* I thought. "See you in English." He turned then, humming the chorus to the song I still couldn't place as he went.

The door closed behind her stepping onto the sidewalk. "We're fine," she said open, pausing her to walk down.

Out the window side he looked out. When passed through the moving, the figure resting only to his own the sliding door and the moving away from him as though it did not keep my watch over that and after in the would vanish in an empty height as though kept that looked rather to he when doing of it all lighted place as he went.

Chapter Seven
Under the Friday Night Lunar Lights

I cast a circle of protection, placing a white pillar candle at each of the five points of the invisible star on my bedroom floor. As I lit them, I named each of the elements, and asked for strength and guidance with my task. Annabelle sat in the center of the circle with her legs crossed. When I finished lighting the candles, I joined her on the floor with an athame blade in my shaky hands.

"You can still back out you know," I said for the hundredth time–hoping that she would give into fear and change her mind. Talking about it had been one thing, but now that the circle was cast and the steel athame gleamed in the candlelight, I couldn't ignore the hollow feeling twisting my gut. I was afraid of what I might see–afraid that I wouldn't be able to save my best friend from whatever nightmarish event that could plague my vision. I couldn't handle the thought of losing her if I failed. I swallowed hard, begging her with my eyes to back out.

The flickering flame of shadows danced on my bedroom walls, and my ears grew red-hot. I imagined steam rolling from the pounding in my eardrums, adding more smoke to the thick atmosphere that was making it difficult to breathe.

"I'm fine," she said calmly. "Just, get it over with." She held out her left hand, palm facing up. I cupped the bottom of her hand in mine and held the athame over the translucent flesh of her upturned palm. I spotted the blue of her vein there, the snaking river mapping out the flow of blood. On a fluttering inhale, I pressed the tip of the blade against her flesh. She winced but held her hand perfectly still as I placed the ceremonial knife back into its holder.

"Okay," I said, "this is it."

Annabelle nodded once, her eyes level with mine. I wondered–not for the first time–if she knew how brave she was for doing this. A crimson bead was growing over her skin, pooling to the center of her palm. I lifted my index and middle fingers, pressing them to the sticky warmth.

Go with the current, Blaire had told me. The familiar pull of the deep ocean grabbed hold of my body and threatened to drag me under. Consciously, I gripped the stone in my pendant, and let the waves roll over me. The surface of the water began to shimmer, fusing with the sky and the autumn sunlight filtering down through the golden leaves. I reached for the surface, digging my nails into the dirt at the base of a large oak. Annabelle was there, sitting on the opposite side with her back pressed against the trunk. She was older–maybe in her thirties with a man at her side and two small children–a boy and a girl–chasing each other in dizzying circles. The smiles on their faces were contagious; the laughter in their voices echoing into the foreground of the air, louder, like they'd sound in a movie. The sunlight caught the diamond on Annabelle's left hand, casting rainbow flecks that shimmered in the afternoon light.

I wanted to see more, but I knew I couldn't stay. The other side was already pulling me back. A sense of peace and contentment flooded my being and left me feeling weightless as I landed back into my body. I blinked a couple of times, opening my eyes as the air rushed through my lungs.

"Quinn?" Annabelle was watching me carefully.

"Hi," I said breathlessly.

"You didn't pass out," she said. "How do you feel?"

"Tired, but I'm not in pain."

"Good." Annabelle was nodding her head slowly, but I could tell she was worried by the set of her jaw and the crease of her brow. "I know I said I didn't want to know anything, but I'm sort of freaking out right now."

I smiled, releasing a half cry of relief. "You were so happy," I said, "I think you have a beautiful journey ahead of you."

"Tell me–no, wait–*don't* tell me." She held up her hand. "I don't want to know. If it's good, then I don't want to ruin it by anticipating its arrival. That's how the future gets screwed up."

I giggled, and Annabelle joined in until our laughter intermingled as one. I was still giddy from the rush of adrenaline, and the uplifting feeling of relief I was sure the Spirit element was responsible for. It felt beyond amazing to have gone through a vision and not come out all the worse for wear. I had controlled it–or at least, I was learning to control it with the aid of the elements.

I wished I had known that it could be like this. As my heart hummed behind my rib cage, I thought of my mother, and wondered if she was looking down on me now, able to feel the happiness coursing through my soul. I wondered if she would be proud of me for embracing my gift, or if she was worried–like she'd always been whenever she'd see that my powers were growing. I made a promise to her to be careful, but I was no longer afraid of where my gifts would take me.

I walked across the track under the flooding of synthetic stadium lighting as the sun sank below the silver mountains in the background. Hundreds of bugs swarmed around the lampposts; in the harsh contrast, their fluttering could be mistaken for the flurry of snow.

I pushed through the sea of silver and black as fellow students and parents huddled in groups on the track, catching up from the week before. I spotted Annabelle in the bleachers along with half of our cross-country team all wearing our matching hoodies: Black, with the outline and lettering of the Silver Mountain Foxes logo. Our last names were composed in block lettering across the back of our shoulders.

"There you are," Annabelle said, placing a string of silver beads over my head. "What took you so long?"

I reached up to adjust the strand, pulling my hair free from the entanglement. "I had to help Dad with a lumber shipment."

"Is he still cool with you staying the weekend?" she asked me.

"Yep. I put my bag in the locker room, so remind me to get it after the game." I looked around. "Is Hunter here?"

"He's sitting with the group of freshmen a few rows in the back." Annabelle gestured over her shoulder with a pointed thumb. "I don't think you need to worry about him tonight. I highly doubt he's going near the woods."

"I still want to keep an eye on him," I said, though now I felt better for having logged him into my mental data base. "What have I missed so far?"

"Nothing important," Annabelle said, "homecoming court is lining up, though." She jerked her chin in the direction of the sports cars that were rumbling near the back gate of the stadium, ready to escort the homecoming court nominees onto the track for introduction. If Coach were here, he'd be working up an aneurysm just watching all those tires touching his precious turf.

"Is that Wren's car?" Annabelle pointed to the last car pulling up in line. I recognized the gold bird emblem splayed out across the hood of his car, and felt my heart anxiously leaping into my throat.

"It sure is," I said, instantaneously spotting Courtney's blonde head bobbing animatedly in the passenger's side window. She was probably droning on about her cheerleading uniform and whatever else rolled around in the vapid space between her perfectly perfect little ears.

Static crackled over the intercom as the volunteer announcer cleared her throat. The static pulsed into a sharp, high-pitched whine before finally leveling out. "Welcome to the home of the Silver Mountain Foxes! Please rise and join me in facing the flag as senior Tanya Williams sings our national anthem."

The sound of shuffling rattled the aluminum bleachers as the crowd stood to face the flag at the end of the field. The sea of people fell silent as Tanya's voice boomed through the air. I tried to keep my eyes on the waving American flag, but I kept sneaking glances to the line of cars just below.

When Tanya finished, the crowd cheered and sank back into their seats as the announcer took control of the microphone. She went through the line of cars, naming the driver of each vehicle, and the homecoming court nominees. The cars circled the track as the court members waved and smiled out at their adoring crowd. Proud parents rushed to the front row of the bleachers so they could photograph their offspring climbing out of the cars, and standing atop the makeshift stage that had been constructed specifically for this event. It was a glorified table from the cafeteria with bands of colorful streamers taped from the sides.

"Check out Megan's dress," Annabelle said, bumping me in the shoulder as Megan climbed out of the baby blue vintage Mustang. It was skintight, white, and just barely managed to cover her ass. "My mother would have a heart attack if she saw me wearing something like that. How did that even pass dress code?"

Next was Shayleene Mathews. Her dad owned a maintenance garage on the far end of town, and I envied her for the vintage maroon Stingray she was climbing out of. Shayleene was the salutatorian of our senior class and worked with the local Habitat for Humanity branch. She also volunteered at the animal shelter on the weekends. I was positive there wasn't a single selfish bone in her body.

"And last, but certainly not least, please welcome Courtney Davis. Courtney is a senior this year, student body president, and captain of the cheerleading squad," said the announcer in an entirely too cheerful tone.

"Zombie Squad," Annabelle and I corrected in unison. We gave each other a look and then started laughing.

Wren, sporting his worn leather jacket, climbed from the driver's side door, and gracefully helped her from the front seat. Courtney was wearing a similar version of Megan's dress, only she'd chosen to go with fire-engine red–complete with a matching pair of stilettos.

"Do you think she realizes she's a walking cliché?" Annabelle asked.

"You know it wouldn't even matter if she didn't lord her status over everyone like she does," I said. "Courtney was nice for about a millisecond and then her daddy became a doctor and gave her everything she ever wanted."

"And then she broke all of your colored pencils in the third grade and we've hated her ever since." Annabelle laughed.

"Hate is a strong word," I said, watching as Wren took Courtney's hand and helped her onto the stage. A general annoyance was a more accurate description for how I felt about Courtney.

"Yeah, well, it looks like she managed to sink her claws into Wren after all," Annabelle said beside me.

"Please," I replied with a snort. "He's not her date."

"My, don't we sound possessive." Annabelle was smirking, eyeing me in a way that made it entirely obvious that I wasn't being as stealthy with my fascination towards Wren as I thought.

Just then, a pair of hands slammed down on my shoulders, nearly knocking me off the bleachers. I turned abruptly, throwing a punch into Huck's bicep for good measure.

"Gotcha!" Huck laughed, and fist-bumped Jamie who was standing beside him.

"Where have you two obnoxious morons been?" I asked.

"Waiting on Meyer's brother to show up with the forbidden fruits." Jamie opened his jacket, revealing a glimpse of the silver flask tucked within the inner pocket of his Letterman.

"Easy with the peep show, bro." Huck covered the flask with a large hand.

"You better take it easy in general." I warned, "We have a meet tomorrow, remember?"

"Relax, don't be so uptight," Huck said.

"Yeah, nobody likes a Debbie Downer," Jamie inserted.

"It's your funeral," I said, and turned back to face the football field. The homecoming court had been escorted from the field and the football players were taking their positions on the line of scrimmage.

I spotted Shawn making his way up the bleachers and bumped Annabelle's side with my elbow to get her attention. "Your date is here," I teased her. She deserved it after the "possessive" comment she'd made about Wren. Annabelle shot me a look, but eagerly waved Shawn over to join us. And goddess love him if he didn't trip on his shoestrings on his way up the stairs, catching himself on the railing at the last second.

Somehow, his clumsiness was endearing. I leaned back as he entered our row, giving him plenty of room as he shuffled past. He planted a soft kiss on Annabelle's cheek, and a scarlet blush flooded her porcelain skin. Shawn, I noticed, had even tried to dress up a little. He'd traded in his short-sleeve button-up for a nice V-neck sweater and a black jacket. I wasn't entirely sure, but I think he'd even gotten a hair cut–and, was that cologne I smelled?

The whistle blew, and the football went sailing through the air as the crowd pushed up from the bleachers and immediately began screaming. Our team parents were known to get a little rowdy, which is why the principal gave the student body their own section–if anything went awry, he'd know exactly who to blame.

I watched as our quarterback, Pete Saunders, tossed the ball into the end zone where a freshman player threw himself into the air, arching his body at an impossible angle and caught the ball, scoring the first six of points. The crowd clapped and cheered as popcorn went sailing through the air, raining over us like fallen, fluffy yellow stars. I clapped along with my fellow classmates, grinning at the lucky play.

"I thought you didn't get into this stuff?" Wren materialized beside me, but I only jumped a little this time. He grinned and pulled a piece of popcorn out of the hood of my sweater.

"It must be contagious."

"I'll take your word for it," he said.

"I don't think you need to. Judging by the act of school spirit you performed this evening, I'd say you're already in as deep as it gets."

His features shifted, and I knew instantly he understood what I was referring to. "She stopped me in the parking lot, I couldn't exactly say no."

"Right, and I'm sure that dress she was wearing didn't help to sway your decision, either." I made a face.

"Well, I am a guy." He grinned playfully; his amber colored eyes were alight with amusement. He was standing close enough so that our shoulders were brushing–or rather, my shoulder was brushing against his bicep. I bit down on my lower lip.

"We're going to the concession, you want anything?" Annabelle asked me. "Oh, hey Wren." She added a small smile in acknowledgment.

"Cat." He smirked.

"No, that's okay–" I started to say, but Wren interrupted me.

"–I think we'll join you. I heard there's killer hot chocolate, and I'm just dying to try some. No pun intended."

"Sure," Annabelle said, stretching out the syllables in apprehension.

"After you," Wren said, letting Annabelle, Shawn, and myself pass before he followed us down the steps and across the track. There was a lengthy line at the concession stand, but the temperature had dropped significantly since the start of the game, and everyone was awaiting the warmth from a cup of hot chocolate.

Annabelle and Shawn were deep in conversation in front of us, but I couldn't hear what they were saying over the howling wind. Wren looked entirely unfazed by the temperature; he stood relaxed as though he were made for the cold. I buried my hands deep within the pockets of my hoodie and hunched my shoulders forward in response. Wren noticed this, shifting in front of me and using his body as a human barricade against the wind. He was slipping out of his jacket before I could protest.

"I'm okay," I said.

"Don't be stubborn." He took a step forward, cradling the jacket around me like a cape. The heat from his body was miraculously trapped inside the fabric folds.

"Thank you," I said, slipping my arms through the sleeves.

"I don't really get cold, so don't feel guilty about wearing it."

I nodded, and my mouth slipped into an involuntary grin. When it was our turn in line, Annabelle and Shawn waited off to the side while Wren ordered two cups of hot chocolate and a tray of nachos. I slipped a five from my pocket, but Wren's hand folded over the top of mine as he handed the cash to the woman behind the counter with his free hand. I was starting to gather that Wren wasn't the type to make a scene or cause a fuss about anything. If he didn't agree with something, he didn't waste time talking about it–he just simply diffused the situation by taking action. I found this trait both admirable and irritating.

"You want marshmallows hon?" the woman behind the counter

asked. Wren glanced in my direction, his left brow arched in its signature way.

"Please," I said.

She nodded and set to work behind the counter.

"Looks like it's a full moon tonight," Annabelle said, gesturing toward the tumescent orange orb cresting the highest mountain peak. A quiver passed through my stomach, my eyes scanning the student section of the bleachers to make sure Hunter was still in his seat. He was.

"First phase." Wren barely gave the harvest moon a glance, his tone matter of fact. He gathered our order and handed me a cup of hot cocoa. Annabelle's eyes swept over him with suspicion. She glanced at me, and then her gaze slowly traveled back to his; waiting. "I like astronomy," he said.

"Oh, well, you two should get along famously then." Annabelle turned, starting back to the bleachers with Shawn at her side.

"I don't think Cat likes me very much," Wren decided.

"She just doesn't know you."

"Neither do you," he countered.

"Yeah, well, I like a good mystery." I regretted admitting that the instant the words left my mouth. I didn't want him to know that I thought of him in terms of a puzzle–and one that I was eager to solve. I slid in front of him on my way up the bleachers, deciding it was in my best interest to keep my eyes averted from his face. I could practically feel the look he was giving me, and it felt as though he were burning holes through the fabric of his jacket. Or that was just the temperature of my skin–elevating from my own embarrassment.

We shuffled back into our row, and Huck and Jamie, seeing Wren for the first time, clapped him on the back. "Hey man," Jamie slurred, "you want some fireball?"

"I'm good, thanks."

"Don't say no because of Quinn," Jamie said, and leaned forward to whisper, "because she's a prude."

"Jamie!" Annabelle turned around and jammed a frog-punch in his gut. He lurched forward, coughing in pain which caused Huck to burst out in laughter.

"You deserved that one, buddy." Huck helped Jamie into a sitting position and slapped him in the middle of the back.

I suppressed a chuckle and took a sip of my cocoa. I could feel the slow burn of Wren's gaze from the side, and knew he was watching me. He seemed to always be watching me, and I wondered what thoughts were circling in that pretty head of his. I looked up at him demurely. "What?"

"Nothing."

"You're watching me," I stated.

"Do I make you uncomfortable?" He shifted toward me, hovering.

"I haven't decided yet." For now, this seemed like a safe enough answer. "So. What's the verdict?" I held up my cup of cocoa, shook it a little.

"It's good, but, I make a better cup."

"Oh really?"

"Secret ingredient."

"Let me guess." I ran my index finger over the rim of my cup. "You'd tell me, but then you'd have to kill me?"

"Something like that."

"Of course."

"It's just I have to be sure I can trust you with such paramount information." He squinted his eyes slightly. "Maybe you couldn't handle the truth."

I waited a moment, and then said, "We are still talking about baking components, right?"

His mouth twitched but his midsummer night eyes never left mine. I could feel the weight of that look–knew that if I let it, his eyes would be my undoing. He stood there, so apart from everyone else, like he was the sun keeping the earth in its gravitational orbit. It was like that first day in English class all over again. When our eyes met, I felt like I recognized some unspoken thing. Could he feel it, too? I cleared my throat, blinking out from under his gaze and settled on his hands instead.

"What happened here?" I reached out, boldly tracing my fingers over the jagged crescent moon shaped scar on the back of his right hand. The pale skin felt deceivingly smooth against my fingertips.

"You don't want to know," he said darkly, his tone deepening into a rumble that prickled the hair on the back of my neck.

"*O-kay*," I breathed out, taking a sip from my cocoa for the sake of having something else to focus on.

"I'm sorry," his voice softened, "it's just not something I like to talk about."

I nodded, keeping my eyes on the players running on the field in front of me. His mood could change so easily, it was almost hard to keep up with.

"I am sorry," he said again, this time with a sense of desperation. I looked up into his eyes then, wondering how it was possible that one person could conjure so many emotions from me in such a short amount of time. I felt like I was a scale, and a single word, or look from him could tip the balance in his favor.

"We all have sensitive areas," I said. "No need to apologize."

He leaned forward, bending to place his empty cup at his feet. Something silver slipped from the collar of his shirt, hanging by a black cord. He reached up, noticing me staring, and tucked the coin underneath his collar.

"Four minutes until halftime!" Huck shouted behind me and pulled the hoodie he was wearing over the top of his head. His chest had a giant 'S' painted in black.

"*Oh no*," I breathed, reaching up to cover my eyes.

"What's going on?" Wren asked, looking back as several of the other members of our team started stripping off their hoodies. The 'I' and 'L' were in my immediate line of vision.

"There's this halftime cheer," I started to explain, but Huck was yelling loudly behind me. "The guys have been crashing it at all the home games, dancing around when the cheer squad calls their letters."

"Where's my V?" Huck shouted. "Oh *shit*, I lost my V!"

"Probably not something you want to be yelling out loud, man," Wren told him, chuckling a little.

"Hilarious." Huck pointed at him, and then continued to search through the crowd for the guy with a painted 'V' on his chest. "Dude, where's Aaron?"

"He's not here, bro." Jamie answered. "He had a date or something."

"Caroline, do you still have the body paint?" Huck turned and asked one of the sophomore girls on our team. She bent forward to retrieve her purse, her sunshine curls bouncing as she began digging through the contents.

"Here ya' go." She tossed the tube to Huck and he caught it one-handed.

"Wren, you gotta' be my V, man." Huck leaned over him with desperate, wide blue eyes. He was already unscrewing the cap on the tube of body paint.

"I don't think so man."

"Don't make me beg. Come on, for the sake of team spirit."

Wren looked at me, searching my face for an answer.

"Come on Wren, show us your team spirit," Annabelle said in a demeaning sort of tone. She reached over, snatching a nacho from our tray and scooped it into her mouth with a teasing leer.

"You asked for it, *Cat*." He rose to his feet, and effortlessly pulled his T-shirt over his head; my throat went as dry as the Atacama Desert. He looked like art; like he'd been cleaved from a block of marble.

Huck began to paint the letter across Wren's chest in haste, and I managed to tear my eyes away from his abdomen for half a heartbeat as Wren tossed me his T-shirt. I caught it, hoping my expression was veiled better than the beat of my pulse.

"*Jesus...*" Annabelle started in a breath of air, watching as the group of guys made their way down the stairs as the halftime whistle blew. "Did you know?"

"How would I?"

"Well I don't suppose you've gotten any closer to unraveling the big mystery–I mean, *what* is he?"

"A god?" I blurted out before I could stop myself.

"Okay, are you two, like, speaking in a secret girl code or something?" Shawn piped up, curiously observing our behavior. Annabelle and I rarely had to guess what the other was thinking. We operated on our own wavelength.

"Sorry, Shawn." Annabelle turned her attention back to him, offering up her best smile. That put him at ease. I, on the other hand, sat twisting Wren's shirt in my grasp as I struggled to regain my composure.

The guys had lined up behind the cheerleaders in correct-spelling formation. The squad started their halftime chant, and the crowd responded by standing up in the bleachers, shouting the letters that spelled out the word 'silver' and each of the guys hooted and hurrahed as the letter on their chest was shouted out.

Under the stadium lights, Wren's skin took on an ethereal quality. The light should have washed out the color of his skin like it had done to the others, but instead it made him glow–blue, I thought, like he was the living shadow of the moon.

The cheer was ending, and Huck led the group of boys around the track, pumping up the crowd before the third quarter of the game. The sound of their footsteps thumped up the bleachers as they returned to their seats. Wren moved back into the row beside me, reaching for his shirt. I let go with some reluctance, wishing I could just keep staring at his body with the way the moonlight played over his skin.

"I should go," Wren said, tugging at the hem of his T.

"Don't tell me you have a curfew," Annabelle said smugly.

He glanced in her direction, and I felt goosebumps rising across my arms. The phrase "if looks could kill" flitted through my mind, and the washed-out expression on Annabelle's face told me she'd felt it too. I started to take off his jacket, but his palm covered my hand. "Tomorrow," he said, "stay warm."

"Thank you," I breathed.

"Later, Cat," he said to Annabelle, and then started down the bleachers.

"*God*," Annabelle hissed, "he's so... so..."

"Unconventional?" I offered up.

"I was going to say he has a serious superiority complex, but I suppose your way of thinking is kinder."

"You really don't like him, do you?"

Annabelle took a deep breath, blowing out slowly. "I don't know,

Quinn. There's just something about him that seems–*dangerous*. We already know he's a Supe," she whispered. "I just want you to be careful, that's all."

"I am being careful." At least, I thought I was. Annabelle shrugged and turned her attention back to the game and back to Shawn as she looped her arm through his, leaning against his shoulder. I suddenly felt like the lone, third-wheel and leaned forward, propping my elbows on my knees.

Maybe Annabelle was right. Maybe Wren *was* dangerous, but there was something inside of me that kind of liked the thought of that. For my whole life I had been taught to be careful, and I had never done anything but obeyed and respected the rules my parents had set for me. Caution was my middle name. But there was also a part of me that desperately wanted to break free of those chains–to test the water, and to see what all life had to offer.

I dipped my chin into Wren's jacket, blocking out the breeze that cut through the bleachers and stung my face with cold. I took a deep breath, inhaling the scents of earth and pine that sent a rush of fluttering through my stomach. Wren might be dangerous, but I decided that I wasn't afraid of him.

Chapter Eight
Silver Has It

"Breakfast." I tossed a banana to Annabelle who was still sitting up in bed with her legs dangling over the edge of the wooden frame. Her hair was matted, sticking to one side of her face, while the other frizzed up above her crown.

"I don't understand how you can function with so much energy this early on a Saturday." Annabelle took the banana, and fell back against the pillows, slowly peeling back the layers of the fruit.

"I'm always ready to roll on meet days," I said, bending to straighten the blankets and pillows I had used on the air mattress. It was pushed up against the lavender wall opposite her bed, where I had a perfect view of an old Hello Kitty poster that she refused to take down. Other posters of various Japanese anime were taped around the room, as well as a couple vintage posters of The Smiths and The Cranberries.

"How long have you been awake?" she asked me.

"Only for about twenty minutes."

"I didn't sleep so well," she said, rolling her neck from side to side.

"I know. You spent most of the night tossing and turning. How old is that mattress, by the way? I'm pretty sure those box springs are rusted."

"Shut it." Annabelle tossed a pillow at my head, but her aim was off by about six inches, and the pillow smacked into the wall behind me, bouncing off the Hello Kitty poster. The bottom corner ripped free of the push pin. "Great," she muttered, "look what you made me do."

"It's a sign from God," I joked, "it's time to take it down."

Annabelle narrowed her eyes at me, hopping off the bed to retrieve the pillow. "Seriously though, weren't you even the slightest bit creeped out last night? All those branches snapping in the woods on our walk home, I just know there was something out there. It felt like we were being watched." She shuddered. "Not to mention the howling wind against the windowpane. I felt like we were secretly starring in a horror movie, and Jason was out there scratching on the window all night long."

"Freddy Krueger," I corrected.

"Huh?"

"Jason is the one with the hockey mask," I said. "Freddie has the claw hand thingy." I waggled my fingertips for reference sake.

"Whatever," she waved this off.

I bent to pull my running shoes out of my bag, purposely not answering the question regarding her fears. The truth was that I had sensed something out there, and as much as I wanted to believe it was just a herd of deer, the Supernatural part of my brain indicated otherwise. I'd felt the ribbon tugging at my spine and wrapping tightly around my chest. Whatever it was hadn't made itself known, so I chose to stay quiet about it. There was no point inducing fear when I had a more important mission to concentrate on–and that–was keeping Hunter and his sister safe.

"Great," Annabelle said, holding up her phone and the weather map that was opened on her screen. "It's a full moon and partly cloudy tonight."

"Sounds like my vision," I said.

"Maybe I shouldn't go to the dance." Annabelle's voice teetered on the edge of uncertainty. Instinct would tell her to help and protect, but I could see the conflicted lines tugging at the corners of her mouth.

"Oh no you don't," I said, adamantly shaking my head. "You did not spend sixty dollars on that gown *not* to wear it tonight. You are going to that dance, Annabelle Carter."

"Sixty-five, actually." Her eyebrows laced together, drawing a worry line in the crease between her eyes. "But what if you need me?"

"I'll call you." I shrugged. "Hunter is going to Huck's tonight, so all I have to do is keep an eye on him and make sure he doesn't go outside. How hard can it be?"

"You shouldn't have asked that." Annabelle sighed.

"And why not?"

"You probably jinxed yourself."

"Supernaturals can't jinx themselves." I winked.

"You're making it worse," Annabelle said, slowly shaking her head.

"Come on. We can talk about this later. As usual, you're going to make us late. We have a bus to catch, and you, my dear, have a much-needed date with your hairbrush." I grabbed her by the shoulders and gave her a gentle push through the door toward her bathroom.

After she'd left the room, I turned toward her window, gazing out at the forest less than a hundred yards away. The underbrush was thick there; too thick to even get through to find a path for walking. Still, I pictured a wolf in my mind, standing at the base of the trees just watching me; those arctic yellow eyes piercing through, causing the blood in my veins to run cold. I cradled my arms, hoping to chase away the chill, all the while praying that I had the strength to look after Hunter. I had a sinking feeling in my gut that whatever was looming in the ominous forest would show itself tonight. I reached up, squeezing my pendant for courage.

Annabelle and I turned up the sidewalk as the bus, smelling strongly of diesel and exhaust fumes, pulled in front of the school. Coach was waiting on the sidewalk in front of the building with a clipboard in his hands, checking attendance as the team filed onto the big, yellow tank. I shifted the strap of my cross bag up my shoulder, squeezing Wren's jacket in my hands as I scanned the parking lot for his car.

"Could you be more obvious?" Annabelle asked, pursing her lips together.

"What?"

"He's over there." She tilted her head toward the senior parking lot.

I followed her gaze and spotted Wren climbing out of his car. "You wanna' sit with him?"

"Don't be silly," I said.

"I was being serious," she said, "if tonight is what we think it is, then you should probably try to solve the puzzle that we know is Wren. We need to find out if he's on our side, or if he's doing the devil's bidding."

"He's not evil, Annabelle."

"How do you know?" Her voice was thick with apprehension.

"I just know," I said, "I can't explain it."

"I think that's called 'wishful thinking.'"

"And I think you should cut him some slack."

"Whatever, we both have work to do. You sit with Wren, do some digging. I'm going to sit near Hunter and do some investigative work of my own, see what his plans are for tonight. Maybe I'll overhear something helpful."

I rolled my eyes, splitting from her as we headed for different sides of the bus. I met Wren around the back, doing my best to ignore the sensation that was pooling heat toward the center of my abdomen.

"Morning," I called out. When he reached me, I noticed the violet half-moons that colored the hollows of his eyes. There were a few minor scratches above his left eye, angled with the arch of his brow. "Rough night?" I asked.

"Oh this," he pointed to the scratches. "It's nothing." He sounded like he'd swallowed a mouthful of gravel.

"Um, here," I said, extending his jacket.

He took it, raising the corner of his mouth into a small smile. He motioned for me to walk in front of him as we headed toward the front of the bus. "Where's your friend *Cat* this morning?"

"She's already on the bus," I said. "She's sitting with a friend to work on a project." It wasn't exactly a lie, which made me feel less guilty for having said it. "And, maybe if you called her by her name she wouldn't find you half as irritating."

This declaration caused what I thought sounded like a laugh to catch in Wren's throat. I couldn't be sure though, as every sound he made seemed more like a growl or grumble rather than anything human.

"If it will please you, I'll make more of an effort to be friendly with her," he said, following me onto the bus. I started down the aisle slowly, heading for the back which was naturally reserved for the seniors. I chose a seat second to the last and slid in toward the window, holding my breath as Wren slid in beside me.

"Why would you care if it pleased me?" I asked, my tone low enough so that only he could hear.

"Because I care what you think."

This statement perplexed me. I looked up at his face, feeling the heat circulating in the small space that separated us. I was sure my heart was beating loud enough to hear, but the ringing in my ears was displacing the sound of my heartbeat. I so desperately wanted to close the distance between us–to touch his face, to trace the shape of his lips with my fingertips. I didn't trust my hands, so I tried to fold them beneath my thighs. I almost sighed in relief when the engine roared to life, jolting us forward as we pulled out of the parking lot.

"So, what happened last night?" I asked, looking again at the scratches above his brow.

"Don't ask that question," he said softly.

A wave of heat flooded to the surface of my skin. His evasiveness was vexing. "Fine," I said coolly. "Where did you get this scar?" I reached for his hand, but before I could touch it, he was wrapping his fingers through mine, gently lacing them together and making no effort to let go. Heat surged forcefully in my stomach.

"Perhaps I should have called *you*, Cat," he said, grinning wryly.

"So secretive," I hissed.

"So curious," he countered, running his thumb over the back of my hand. His touch was electric, and I felt my resolve melting into a puddle before him. I hated that he could do this to me. I didn't understand how I could be so hopelessly captivated, and exasperated by him at the same time.

"What are you?" I breathed.

He laughed again, the deep rumble vibrating through his chest. The question could have been innocent, but I was tired of playing games.

Surely he could sense that I knew he was different. I sighed, leaning my head back against the seat.

"How about this," I said, "what can I ask?"

"Anything." He shrugged.

I narrowed my eyes. "What can you answer?"

"I don't want to scare you." He looked at me hard. I could see the warning pulsating behind his irises, but his voice betrayed him. There was something else; hope, that maybe he would?

"I'm not afraid."

He chuckled darkly, looking down at our entwined hands. With his free hand, he slid his fingertips across my inner arm. The fluttering in my stomach intensified, and I fought against the urge to close my eyes, to relax into his touch.

"How about this," he said quietly. "All I ask is that you give me this one day, to just act on whatever impulses we're feeling. To just be human."

"And tomorrow?"

"I'll tell you anything you want to know," he said. His eyes were level with mine, but there was a deep sadness there, creeping in from the back like a shadow of grief. He was afraid to be honest with me; afraid that whatever he had to say would push me away. I didn't know if he was right, but I could already feel something inside of me give–a nameless something–that only heightened whatever it was I was already feeling for him. I knew it wasn't rational, but it went deeper than basic attraction, rising from somewhere deep within my being; an ancient knowledge.

There was a small part of me that wanted to keep pushing for Hunter's sake, but I knew–somehow–that Wren was on the good side.

"Deal," I said finally.

He grinned, and reached up to cup his hand under the back of my head, pushing gently so that my head was resting against his shoulder. He rested his cheek against the top of my head, and squeezed my hand.

"Thank you," he said, and I felt him relax beside me.

"Tell me you're closer to uncovering something, because I literally got nowhere with Hunter and his merry band of freshman goons." Annabelle moved her arm into a shoulder stretch. "All they could talk about was some dumb video game and a map that takes place on the deck of a battle ship."

"Battleship War Gods."

"Irrelevant." She scowled, as if this was the biggest waste of a breath of air. What did you find out about Wren?"

"Annabelle, I think you're just going to have to trust me with this one, okay? I can feel it in my gut. Wren is one of the good ones."

At this, she rolled her eyes. "For Hunter's sake, I hope you're right."

"I am." We finished stretching, and hurried over to the starting line so we could watch the boys take off in the first wave. It rained the night before, softening the terrain. I liked a good challenge, but at least a mile of the course was up-hill and my muscles were already screaming from the warm-up.

"What box are we in?" Annabelle asked.

"Seven," I said, pointing to the square where the silver from our black uniforms was catching the morning sunlight.

"Remind me to thank the person responsible for creating our uniform shorts," Annabelle said, lifting her eyebrows as the group of guys lined up in starting position.

The starting official was making his way onto the field, climbing up on a stool that was about fifty yards out from the starting line. Coach and the others joined Annabelle and I on the sidelines, and the world fell silent as the official raised his orange flag and starting pistol high in the air above him.

I loved this single, heart-stopping moment. When I was the one on the starting line, adrenaline slammed through my body, awaking every cell in a way that brought me to a new sense of life. Most people hated that feeling; eyes on the official, watching as those slow pulses ticked by what felt like hours instead of seconds. But not me, I lived for that moment and the way my blood seemed to sing inside my veins. Now, I watched as the official lowered the flag, and the gunshot rang out through the atmosphere, echoing high in the treetops. The boys burst forth from the starting line; the colors of their uniforms blurring together in a thick rainbow-colored sea. Within seconds, Wren, Huck, and Jamie shot to the front of the pack.

"All right, Foxes!" I yelled, clapping my hands.

"Think we can make it to the first mile marker?" Annabelle asked.

"We can try," I said, jogging with the rest of the crowd, taking shortcuts through the course to try and make it to the first mile marker before the runners did. I looked down at my watch. A minute and a half had passed. It took us about two more minutes to reach the marker, and by the time my watch was flashing four fifty-seven, Wren came flying around the bend.

"Holy crap," Annabelle gasped, clapping her hands. "Way to go, Wren!"

"Four fifty-nine," I called out his time, feeling the wind stir around us as he flashed by. He was still breathing through his nose and had barely broken a sweat.

"He's going to win this thing," Annabelle said.

"We'll skip the second mile marker, and just head for the chute after the rest of the team comes by," I said.

"Good idea."

We took turns calling out times, clapping for Hunter as he passed by the first mile marker with a time of seven minutes and fifty-two seconds. "Stay strong Hunter, you're doing great!" He had a look of determination on his face, squaring his shoulders as he barreled around the bend.

"Finish line," Annabelle said, grabbing my arm as we headed for the chute. It took us about three minutes to get to the roped off area of the finish line, and spotted the big, red digital clock hovering just above the chute.

"Whoa, where's the fire?" a familiar voice called from my right. I turned, and found my dad in the crowd. He was wearing his team jacket– the same jacket he'd bought my freshman year and worn to every single one of my races since. Needless to say, the Foxes insignia had faded badly, but he swore up and down that it was a good luck charm.

"Oh, hey Dad," I said, quickly throwing my arms around his waist. As usual, he smelled a little like saw dust.

"You two better slow down or you'll run all your energy out before the race." He chuckled, squeezing both of my shoulders.

"We're just really excited," I said. "Our team is looking really good today."

"First runner, number twenty-three," the announcer called over the intercom, "Wren Whelan of Silver Mountain High."

We all turned our attention to the tree line, watching as Wren emerged from the dense underbrush of the forest canopy. My dad was squinting, hands on his hips as the rest of the crowd began to cheer.

"Come on Wren!" Annabelle and I clapped and cheered as he sprinted to the finish line, disappearing through the chute with a time of sixteen oh-two.

"Wow," my dad said, staring up at the clock. "That guy goes to your school?"

"He's new," I said.

"Yeah, and your daughter has a thing for–" I elbowed Annabelle sharply in the ribs, cutting off her sentence. "–Oof."

Luckily my dad was too distracted to pay close attention to what she was saying. He was still focused on the time clock, watching as a few others, including Huck and Jamie, had started sprinting for the finish line.

"Hey, look who's here," I said, pointing to Annabelle's parents. They were making their way over a hill behind us, and Shawn was with them. He was wearing a pair of jeans with a light-weight wind breaker practically zipped to his chin. The beanie he was wearing caused his floppy hair to curl under his ears. "Did you know he was coming, Annabelle?" I asked.

A light blush crept up over Annabelle's cheeks. "No," she said, grinning. "I should go say hi."

"Annabelle has a boyfriend?" my dad asked, watching her give Shawn a big hug. His expression was pensive, as though he couldn't fathom missing the status change since last week's meet.

"It's in the early stages," I said, patting his arm sympathetically.

"Hey," Wren said, nodding in my direction. He'd appeared, as per usual, without a sound. His hair was incredibly windblown, fluffed in the front, and slightly matted with sweat. This look could have been gross, and on anyone else it might have been, but on him... it was working. I swallowed hard, channeling the Earth element to help me stay grounded.

"Hey, Wren, congratulations. You were incredible." I smiled up at him, and placed my hands on my hips, resisting the urge to run up and give him a hug. "Dad, this is Wren," I said, remembering to introduce them.

"Nice to meet you, sir," Wren said politely, extending his hand in greeting. My dad took it, firmly shaking once. Wren had about an inch height-wise on my dad, but Dad, I could tell, was pretending not to notice.

"Please," he said, "call me Emmett. That was some nice running, son. Quinn tells me that you've recently transferred."

"Thank you, and yes, just moved back from Washington," he said.

"Moved back?" Dad asked, studying him.

"My dad lives here," Wren explained.

"Oh really, who's your father? I probably know–"

"Callaghan!" Coach shouted, "Get your butt in gear, race starts in five."

"That's my cue," I said, backing up slowly.

"Good luck, see you at the first mile marker," Dad said, wrapping me up in a quick hug.

"Be careful at the second mile marker," Wren said. "You'll want to swing wide around the bend. There's a pretty big mud pit, and I imagine it's only gotten worse."

"Thanks," I said. "See ya' in the chute." I dashed over the hill toward the starting box, finding Annabelle and the others stretching. I checked my shoestrings, making sure that they were double-knotted and secured.

"Here, I've got your number," Harper, one of the other seniors said. I turned so that she could fasten the number onto the back of my uniform. "Okay, all set," she said. "You nervous?"

"Nah, are you?"

"A little." She shrugged, and reached up to tighten the elastic band around her thick mass of brunette hair.

"You'll do great," I said encouragingly.

Coach pulled us into a huddle after that, and we all knelt as he said a prayer. "Okay, hands in everyone, hands in," Coach said. "On three, Foxes. One! Two! Three!"

"Foxes!" we all shouted, and just like that, the familiar flow of adrenaline began rising in my blood. We jogged back to the starting line, and took our places as the official made his way across the field.

"Quinn, your necklace," Annabelle reminded me. Jewelry wasn't permitted during a race, and if you were caught wearing it–consider yourself disqualified.

"Shit," I muttered breathlessly. I quickly pulled my pendant over my head, and scanned the crowd in search of my dad. It took me all of two seconds to spot him, as he was standing next to Wren.

I stopped a couple of yards in front of my dad, shouting his name to catch his attention and tossed the necklace. The silver chain caught high in the sunlight, rippling through the air like incandescent liquid. It hung in suspension, passing through the threads of time at an impossibly slow tempo.

A clammy sweat broke over the back of my neck as my throat constricted with panic. Had I somehow been responsible for this? I glanced around, but no one else seemed to be aware of the change.

The amulet continued its stagnant trajectory; both Wren and my dad reached for the chain; reflexively, like the way your body tells you to do something before your brain catches up, but Wren got there first. The moment his fingertips made contact, I heard a sizzling snap, like a vat of bacon hitting the grease in a frying pan. A wisp of silver smoke rose up from his injured fingers as he let go, pulling his hand back with lightning speed.

It burned him.

My necklace had physically burned him, and I felt my brows creasing–my lips parting, and the breath catching in my lungs. The world returned to its regular rhythm, and my necklace lay gleaming in the grass.

"You almost had it," Dad said to Wren who was holding his wounded hand into a tight fist. My dad hadn't seen what happened, I realized. He'd been too focused on catching my necklace.

As I looked up into Wren's face, terror flashed across his bright, neon yellow irises. He squeezed his eyes shut, and when he opened them, they returned to their original tawny hue.

He wasn't human. I'd known this since the beginning, but my mind wouldn't turn over the truth of what I'd seen.

"You better get a move on." Dad chuckled, and without hesitating I turned and jogged back to the starting box.

"Everything okay?" Annabelle asked me.

"I'm fine," I answered. But the rush of adrenaline did not come as the starting official raised his gun in the air.

I crossed the finish line with a time of twenty minutes and seven seconds. Decent, but I hadn't beaten my PR. My muscles still felt limber; it was my mind that was numb. The image of Wren recoiling in fear when he touched my necklace seared itself into my brain. It was all I could see. He'd been with the others at each mile marker cheering me on, but he wouldn't meet my eyes. I didn't know what he was, but I needed him to know that I wasn't afraid.

"Great job, Quinny," Dad said as I exited the chute with a top placing ribbon. "I'm so proud of you." He scooped me up into a hug, planting a kiss on the top of my head before placing me back on the ground.

"Thanks, Dad." I grinned. I could have finished dead last and he'd still act as though I'd won the first-place trophy.

"Oh, before I forget," Dad said, reaching into his jacket pocket. He pulled my necklace from the temporary resting place, and I leaned forward as he placed it over my head. It suddenly bore the weight of a thousand pounds.

"Thanks for coming out, Dad. It means a lot to me."

"I'd never miss a meet." He tugged on the hem of his sports jacket.

Annabelle skipped over, proudly waving her ribbon as Shawn and her family followed not far behind. "I broke my PR!"

"That makes one of us," I said, giving her a sweaty hug. "Congratulations."

"You seemed distracted at the starting line," she lowered her voice while our parents exchanged pleasantries, "everything okay?"

"I'll explain later."

She pursed her lips, but nodded once. "See you on the bus?"

"Yeah."

We said our goodbyes, and she and her family parted ways. Dad gently pulled me to the side, glancing over his shoulder to make sure no one was eavesdropping. "I wanted to tell you that I talked with the game warden. It's been confirmed that a pack of wolves moved into the area. They can't seem to pinpoint where the den is, but they're working to keep things under control and out of the public eye."

"Why?" I frowned.

"They just don't want to frighten anyone, or cause unnecessary panic. They're hoping they can eradicate the problem before word gets out."

"Eradicate?" I blinked rapidly. "They're going to wipe them out?"

"If it comes to that, yes."

I started shaking my head involuntarily. "Wolves aren't a threat to humans."

"Maybe not, but if they become a nuisance the warden won't have any choice. They're trying to deter them from settling in the area, but I wanted you to be aware. Your visions have never been wrong, Quinn, so we need to be careful. I don't want you or anyone else at Huck's party going out into the woods tonight."

"I know, Dad. I'll be careful."

"Good girl." He hugged me once more. "I'll see you tomorrow."

"Bye, Dad."

When I reached the bus, Wren and the other boys were already sitting in the back. Relief flowed through my chest; I didn't know what to say to him after what happened with my amulet. I knew there were all sorts of mythological legends and folklore with prophecies regarding silver and its use to ward off evil entities and creatures. I had watched the metal burn him with my own eyes; watched as his irises changed color, beaming like the electric yellow light of the sun. But what I knew as fact didn't correlate with what I felt for him, and I trusted my instincts far more than I trusted what I'd known to be said from old folklore and legends. I wouldn't accept the idea of him being a monster. I trusted him, and he'd promised me tomorrow.

"Looks like you're not going to celebrate with your boy," Annabelle teased, patting the open space on the seat beside her.

"I'll see him tonight," I said.

"I may not be a top supporting member of his fan club," Annabelle said, "but that boy can seriously run."

"Yes," I agreed, "he can."

But he can't hide… at least not forever, I thought.

Chapter Nine
Dressed to Kill

Caitlyn, Annabelle's older sister, was home from college this weekend, which, wasn't entirely out of the realm of normalcy. She was a bit of a homebody–spoiled, too, and just a little on the entitled side. Currently, she was sitting in the arm chair, legs tucked beneath her as she flipped through the pages of the latest Cosmo magazine. Caitlyn had a thick coat of makeup on, a fresh mulberry glaze across her long fingernails, and her hair pulled back into a French braid. The platelets were perfectly even, not a strand of hair out of place. She sucked in a deep breath of air through her nose, expelling it into the piece of gum she was chewing until the bubble snapped over her matte stained lips.

Between the sound of the grandfather clock ticking off the slow passing seconds, and the sound of Caitlyn continuously cracking her gum, I was beginning to feel the shards of my sanity slipping away.

"Annabelle, your date is pulling up." Mrs. Carter–or as I liked to call her–mama Akari said as she peered through the blinds in the living room window.

Annabelle poked her head out of the bathroom door, her face slightly flushed from standing under the light, and having a curling iron so close to her face for the last hour. "Quinn," she breathed, "can you tell him I just need five more minutes please?"

"Sure," I said, happy to have an assignment. If I had to listen to Caitlyn smack her gum for another minute, I was going to pull out my hair.

"You look fine, Annabelle," Caitlyn said exasperatedly, rolling her eyes. Caitlyn, being two and a half years older, rarely wanted anything to do with us when we were growing up. Of course Caitlyn was about the opposite of everything we represented. She grew up taking dance and ballerina classes while Annabelle and I were into soccer and roller-skating. She'd even entered junior pageants, and held the student body president position all through high school. She'd graduated with honors, and enrolled in a hospitality management program at SMU. I didn't fully understand the specifics of the career, but I knew she hosted a lot of events that required her to look as though she'd just stepped off the fashion runway.

It wasn't that Caitlyn had ever been particularly cruel to either Annabelle or myself–it was more like we just didn't exist in the same universe let alone the same room. Which was why I was surprised to find her helping Annabelle get ready for homecoming. I'd pushed open the bathroom door to check on her, only to find that Caitlyn was fixing Annabelle's lipstick, wiping away the excess with one of her manicured fingernails. I was sure I blinked a couple of times–hoping my mouth hadn't been hanging open in utter disbelief.

"Save it," Annabelle hissed, pointing an index finger in my direction. I immediately tossed my hands up in surrender.

"Okay, I'm thinking you should wear your hair up," Caitlyn said a moment later. "It'll complement the detail on the back of your gown."

"Okay," she replied nervously.

"I'm pretty sure I have a clip that will match the color of your dress– here, Quinn, I need you to hold this–" She indicated to the strip of hair that she was currently holding. I walked over, and took Annabelle's hair as Caitlyn's fingers slipped away. She ducked out of the bathroom.

"Okay, what just happened?" I whispered.

"I don't know," she breathed. "But I'm definitely not going to complain about it. Do you see what she did to my eyebrows?"

"Think she can fix mine next?" I grinned.

"I wouldn't push your luck."

I giggled. Caitlyn returned a moment later with a slender, pearl beaded clip that she'd used as an accent piece to hold a single curl beside Annabelle's bun. I looked in the mirror at both their reflections, studying the similarities. They had the same, teardrop shaped face with smooth porcelain skin. They shared the same color of deep, hazelnut brown eyes. Small noses, full mouth. With her makeup done, Annabelle looked even more like her sister than I realized.

Their mother was full-blooded Japanese, but their father, Jeremiah, was born and raised in the southernmost point of North Carolina. They'd met on a cruise, fell in love, and decided to get married all within a year of having known one another. Some would say they just got lucky, but, the hopeless romantic in me wanted to believe that their love was written by divine intervention.

"Hey Shawn," I said, pulling open the door. He was dressed in a slim-fitted black tux with a baby blue tie that matched the color of Annabelle's gown. His hair–which he had combed–was slicked back with gel. In place of shiny black shoes, he'd chosen to wear his beat up pair of black and white Converse. I grinned, waving him into the foyer. "Annabelle just needs a few minutes."

"Sure, no problem. My girl is habitually late. It's one of the many things I admire about her," he said with a nervous grin. He ran his hands over his pant legs, drying the sweat. "Oh. I left the flower thingy in my car."

"Corsage," I said.

"Right. Corsage." He snapped his fingers, turning, and half tripping over the transition piece that was nailed at the bottom of the doorway.

"That boy is a serious train wreck," Caitlyn said under her breath, looking up from her magazine.

"A cute train wreck," I added.

"Okay," Annabelle appeared a moment later, "I'm ready."

With her hair and makeup done up that way, she looked years older than seventeen. Still shorter than me, even in heels, but I thought she looked like a princess. "You look amazing," I told her. My words, however, were no match for the way Shawn was looking at her as he stopped short of the doorway.

"Oh, there you are Shawn–come in, come in!" Mama Akari beckoned with a waving hand. "My! Don't you look handsome–you clean up well."

"Thank you, Mrs. Carter." Shawn beamed.

"Mom, we're going to be late," Annabelle said, quickly wrapping her hands around Shawn's arm, and nudging him out the door.

"But I wanted a picture." Akari's face melted, the lines visibly pulling the corners of her mouth and eyes into a frown.

"Come on, Anna, for Mom," Caitlyn added.

"Fine." She rolled her eyes toward the ceiling, as if surrendering for the picture would break her. I surmised her display of annoyance was probably all for show, seeing as how Annabelle and I had always made fun of the traditional homecoming school pictures that were featured in a special section of the year book. I bit my lip, feeling guilty for ever taking part.

"You'll be glad you did," I said. "For the sake of memories."

"Out in front of the burning bush, I think." Akari ushered the pair out the front door, making them stand in front of the house where the burning bush had turned a beautiful, crimson red. "Stand closer." Akari gave a demonstration with her hands, pushing two invisible objects together until her hands were touching. "There. Now smile!" She held up her digital camera, adjusting the focus.

"All done?" Annabelle asked impatiently after the shutter snapped the first couple of frames.

"Your father will be so upset he missed this."

"Highly doubtful," Caitlyn said, "Dad was never too fond of any of my high school dates, so consider yourself lucky, Shawn."

Shawn's face must have burned three shades deeper in color. Annabelle grabbed his hand, hauling him toward the car before further verbal damage could be done. Shawn helped her into the passenger's side seat, carefully closing the door before turning and waving to the three of us.

"Remember to call if you need anything," Annabelle said to me from the rolled down window.

"Have fun," I shouted back. We waited until they had pulled away before going back inside.

"She looked beautiful," Caitlyn commented, again, striking me with surprise. Part of me wondered if Caitlyn had just been waiting for an opportunity to arise–to find something that she and Annabelle could bond over. Goddess knows it wouldn't have been over sports or Annabelle's taste in music.

"She's growing up." Akari sniffled, tears brimmed her eyes.

"Oh don't cry, Mother," Caitlyn said. Her tone was a little snide, but she wrapped her arm around Akari, pulling her into a side hug. Something inside of me quivered then. Perhaps it was the tender mother-daughter moment, and the cold fact that I'd never get to experience that again. Akari had always been a second mother figure to me, treating me as through I were one of her own–even before my mother got sick. Still, a parent was irreplaceable–especially a gentle, loving spirit like my mom. Not a day passed that I didn't think of her, or miss her.

"What do you feel like having for dinner?" Akari asked, breaking my momentary trance.

"Let's order a pizza," Caitlyn suggested, pulling open the drawer at the island counter that contained the town's takeout menus. We might have been the tiniest dot on the map, but Mountainside Pizzeria had *the best* pizza in the world, I was sure.

"That sounds good," Akari agreed, "Quinn, honey, what toppings would you like?" She looked up at me, a warm smile on her face.

"Unfortunately, I have to pass on dinner. I've got Huck's party to get to."

"Oh that's right, I almost forgot."

"Huck Tillerman?" Caitlyn asked.

"The one and only," I replied, surprised that she even knew who he was. Being that Caitlyn was two grades ahead of us, we did share the same hallways for two years. However, I had been under the impression that Caitlyn never glanced outside her immediate circle of posh friends. I just assumed that the rest of us had never been a blip on her radar of acknowledgment.

"Is he still the fastest boy in school?" she asked with mild curiosity, flipping through the pages of the Pizzeria's menu.

"Not anymore. We have a new transfer–he actually finished the race in first place today. He's pretty incredible."

"Sounds like it." Caitlyn flicked her eyebrow upward, which only reminded me of Wren.

I stood there a second longer, watching Caitlyn. I was quite sure this was the most she had talked to me since–well, ever, really. I was tempted to keep the conversation going, but I didn't know what to say. I felt like a deer caught in the headlights. "So," I cleared my throat, "you wouldn't be interested in going to the party, would you?"

"Huck's?" She snorted. "No."

So much for the brief opened door policy, I thought. I tapped my fingertips across the counter, and then headed to Annabelle's room to change.

"Quinn," Caitlyn called. I stopped short, turning to face her. "Thanks for the offer though." She grinned.

"Sure." I smiled back.

There were only about twenty-five homes in the Pines–nicer homes, all two-story vinyl-sided with attached two and three car garages. Huck's was at the end of the cul-de-sac; his back yard was part of the Silver Mountain Forest–so close that pine tree branches swept onto his deck.

Music thumped from the garage as I walked up the driveway; I sucked in a breath, exhaling slowly as I twisted the knob on the front door. Huck's living room was packed. An L-shaped sectional stretched along the length of the wall and not a single space was available. The group consisted mostly of underclassman boys who appeared to be taking turns playing Guitar Hero. I moved through the living room, already feeling the temperature rising from all the body heat. When I entered the kitchen, the stench of alcohol hit me like a roiling wave.

"Quinn!" Huck shouted. He was standing in the middle of the kitchen wearing nothing but boxers, and a pair of black knee socks. A red tie was wrapped around his head, hanging down the side of his face like a long lopsided ponytail. Glassy-eyed, his face was already flushed from the alcohol he'd consumed.

"It's not even nine yet," I stated, shaking my head as he rushed over and picked me up, spinning in a circle.

"Yeah well it's my house, my rules."

"We pregamed," Jamie informed me, appearing from the hall. He had a red Solo cup in his hand, held it up in mock toast.

Huck sat me down. "What can I get you–beer, vodka, wine cooler? I think Torrance made some sort of spiced cider."

"I'll have that," I said. I followed Huck over to the fridge, where he bent to get a better look at the many contents stuffed within the shelves. He staggered a little. I reached over the top of him, grasping the handle of a pitcher with cider-looking liquid. I smelled it, nodded my head.

"I'll take that," Torrance said. She'd come around the side of the fridge, closed the door as she took the pitcher out of my hands and spun toward the counter as she set to work, grabbing spices out of the baking cabinet.

"You can take the girl out of the coffee shop…" I teased.

"Haven't heard that one before." She laughed, reaching into the cupboard for an actual glass. I watched her pour the cider mixture into the glass along with some crushed ice. She reached for an apple in the fruit bowl, sliced it expertly, added some whipped cream and a dash of cinnamon before dropping in an apple slice. "I trust you can handle this," she said, handing the glass to me with a wink.

"Thank you," I said, taking a sip. It tasted incredible. "Wow, what is that?"

"Maple bourbon," she said. "You like it?"

"Oh yeah. Two thumbs up."

Torrance smiled. "Be careful though, the bourbon has been known to sneak up on you." She patted my shoulder. "Be sure and grab something to eat."

"Are you suggesting that I'm a lightweight?" I grinned.

"I happen to know for a fact that you are. Remember last Halloween?"

"I prefer not to," I said sourly.

"Oh yeah," Jamie laughed, "didn't you like, spend all night in the bathroom?"

I decided not to answer, pressing my lips into a tight line, rocking innocently to my tippy-toes. Last Halloween had not been one of my prouder moments. Jamie had challenged me to a game of beer pong, and my competitive nature kicked into high gear. I relented to give up, as I was only losing by a couple points.

"I told her to eat something," Torrance said.

"Hey, at least she managed to vomit in the toilet, unlike someone else," Huck said, jamming a light punch in Jamie's gut.

"I cleaned up after myself," Jamie said, and then turned to me, "What do you say we have a rematch. It's long overdue." Jamie grinned his boyish smile, flipping his bronze hair back from his eyes. When he smiled, it was easy to remember why I'd had such a crush on him, but those feelings had long since dissipated.

"I don't think so Jamie," I said. "Better that history doesn't repeat itself."

"Burn!" Huck shouted. "That's a shutdown, in case you were wondering."

"Yeah, I got that." Jamie scowled.

"I'm just trying to be more responsible," I added, hoping to take off the edge. It seemed to help a little.

"No fun in that," Huck said.

"Lay off," Torrance warned, wrapping her arm through the crook of my elbow. "No one is allowed to pick on my Quinny."

"She doesn't swing that way, Tor." Huck and Jamie both burst into a fit of laughter, high-fiving one another on top of their lame joke.

"Neither do I, ass-hat!" She leaned forward, smacking Huck up the back side of his head. He picked her up, throwing her over his shoulder as he ran off down the hall. Torrance was laughing and screaming at him to put her down.

Aside from a few stragglers talking in the corner, this left Jamie and I alone. I took another sip of my drink, feeling it warm my throat on the way down. He was staring, and I could sense the desire in his eye, no doubt fueled by the amount of alcohol he'd already consumed.

"Just how early did you and Huck start drinking?" I asked.

"Around five I think. Torrance came over early to help us mix drinks."

I nodded. "Have you seen Hunter?"

Jamie's expression shifted into something like confusion. "The freshman?"

"Yeah."

"I'm pretty sure that's statutory rape."

"And I'm pretty sure you're a dumbass," I snapped, shooting him a look that conveyed my immediate annoyance. "I'm not into him," I added, in case I needed to clarify.

"Chill, I'm just teasing," he said, reaching up to push his hair back from his eyes. At that moment, I would have liked nothing more than to run a pair of clippers through his long locks.

"Think I saw him out in the garage earlier. He brought a chick."

"Pink shirt?"

"Yeah," Jamie frowned, "how did you know?"

"Lucky guess." My stomach felt hollow, like I'd gulped down too much air. "I'm going to use the bathroom," I said, giving myself an excuse to disappear for a while. I slipped into the bathroom off the hall, checking my reflection in the mirror, and gripping my amulet. The iolite stone caught the light from the bulbs above the sink, glinting off the glass. My hands were shaking.

I squeezed my eyes shut, and I saw Nathan Reed's glacial eyes looking up at me from the wheelchair. And just like that I was back in the hospital lounge with Myra and her parents. Annabelle's parents had taken her home hours ago, but my dad was in the cafeteria getting the others coffee. Myra sat across from me, picking at the pink threads that had split from the hemline of her dress. Her eyes, red and watery, never looked up from the black scuff mark on the tile between us.

The doctors came out an hour later, informing us that surgery had gone well, but the nerves in Nathan's spine had been permanently damaged. A sea of rolling waves shook the contents in my stomach. Nathan's mother began to cry, folding herself into her husband's arms. I remembered the sound she made, and the way it reverberated through my eardrums until it was all I could hear.

"Your son is lucky," the doctor said, "he probably wouldn't have made it if his friends hadn't found him when they did. He lost a lot of blood."

Dad put his arm around me, silently pulling me to his side. Those words should have comforted me, but they didn't. I may have saved his life, but I'd drastically reduced the quality by not stopping him from going to that dance all together. I carried the pain of that mistake with me every day; dragging it through life like it was an anvil strapped to my ankle. I couldn't make a mistake like that again.

I should have thought of a better plan to keep Hunter and his sister safe. If I couldn't keep them from venturing into the forest tonight, I didn't know how I was supposed to protect them. I didn't even bring a weapon. I glanced up at the mirror, staring at my green eyes and the smoky tones outlining them. My dark hair spilled below my shoulder blades, softening my appearance. I saw my mother staring back at me, and my heart sputtered in my chest. Heat flickered across my palms. The Earth element was with me now, surrounding me with courage and strength.

I didn't need a weapon. I was a weapon.

I poked my head through the opening, making sure Jamie wasn't still hovering in the kitchen. He wasn't. I moved through the kitchen with purpose, yanking on the door that would lead to the garage. I stepped down onto the cement floor of the garage as the crowd erupted in cheer. I looked up across the makeshift table as two guys from the football team raced each other at the keg. Hunter and his sister were sitting off to the side with a few of the other freshman, huddled around a small TV playing video games. *Battleship War Gods,* I thought, feeling relieved. I physically melted against the wall I was standing by. And that's when I saw Wren.

He was leaning against the door frame that led out onto the deck, half in, half out. His arms were crossed over his chest, causing the muscle of his biceps to protrude just enough to make me glad he hadn't seen me yet. I followed his gaze, which seemed to be glued to the small TV screen. He was watching the freshman intently, his brows furrowed like he was deep in thought. I was studying the outline of his face so closely that it took me a second to realize he'd turned to face me, his summer eyes softening.

One look, and my heart was beating fast enough to give a hummingbird a run for its money. I remembered the way he looked at me at the meet, but the fear that had contorted his features was gone now. He titled his head, gesturing for me to join him.

I maneuvered through the rows of coolers and stopped short in front of him, tucking my hands into my back pockets because I didn't trust them not to develop a mind of their own. I didn't understand how he had the ability to put me at ease, and wake me up in one fell swoop.

"Hi," Wren breathed in that captivating deep tone of his.

"Hi," I replied. Again, my mind flashed back to the image of him catching my necklace, the silver burning his hand. I couldn't help myself, I reached for his right hand with both of mine, turning his over in my palm. My fingertips found the scar on the back of his hand, but my necklace hadn't caused any damage. I frowned.

A sound–mimicking a growl of annoyance–escaped Wren's throat, and I looked up in time to see him rolling his eyes. He pulled his hand free, and I recoiled from his abrupt dismissal. "You promised," he said quietly.

"That was before–"

"Please," he begged, "don't."

Now it was my turn to roll my eyes. I shifted, rolling my weight to one hip as my eyes glanced up at his. I realized that nothing I could say would change his mind.

On a sigh, I glanced over to check on Hunter.

Wren took me by the elbow, gently tugging me out onto the deck. There was a stone fire pit in the center, and a group of people gathered round in mismatching lawn chairs, laughing and roasting marshmallows. Out here, the breeze was cooler on my skin, and I shivered despite my layers as Wren led me to the furthermost corner of the deck. The scent of pine was thick in the night air, mingling with the rich aroma of burning firewood. A Coldplay song, "Green Eyes" was drifting from the outdoor speaker system.

"You can't honestly be cold?" Wren asked, guiding me to the railing.

"I don't understand how you're out here in nothing but a T-shirt," I said.

"I told you, I tend to run on the warm side." He reached for my waist, tentatively, pulling me against his body. Careful to keep my amulet from touching his skin, I tucked my forearms against his chest as he pulled me closer. Heat pooled to the center of my abdomen, and I momentarily forgot all about the outside temperature. I wanted to forget everything else, too, explore the way his chest felt beneath my fingertips. I bit down on my lower lip.

"I wish you wouldn't do that," he said, lifting my chin towards his face.

"What's that?"

"Bite your lip that way."

"Why?"

"Because," he whispered darkly, "It's torture. I don't think I can stand another minute of not touching you–of not kissing you."

I was sure I hadn't heard him correctly. I gazed up into his face, absently watching the way the wind was swirling through his hair. If he hadn't been holding me up, I was positive I would have melted on the floor in front of him. His mouth was inches from mine, but I suddenly couldn't remember how to breathe.

He'd asked me for this one day, to just act on our feelings–to throw our inhibitions to the wind. I wanted to. I really did. But there were so many questions pulsing through my mind, so many things I didn't know about him. I tried to find reasons to say no, but something inside of me– something that I'd never recognized before–wouldn't allow me to step away.

My blood was humming through my veins, and as I reached up to loop my arms around his neck, he pressed his lips against mine, and I remembered how to breathe. He'd awakened something inside me that I hadn't known was there. I named it desire, and pressed my body as tightly to his as I could. His fingertips slipped beneath the hem of my shirt, pressing into the bare skin of my back, and the sensation parted my lips. I tasted him, the sweet heady aroma burning in my lungs. I felt his teeth close around my lower lip, gently tugging.

My fingers slipped into the back of his hair, my left hand tracing the strong contour of his jaw. I could feel the stubble beneath my fingertips–

could feel the passion igniting deep inside my core–*intensifying*.

Someone screamed from behind us, and the sharp cry caused us to break apart. From behind, the fire pit was blazing–flames dancing twelve feet high into the air, sending sparks and ashes raining down over the people who were scurrying back from the lawn chairs as they raced away from the flames.

"Shit," I whispered, bringing a palm to my forehead. I closed my eyes, invoking the element of Air and asking it to calm the fire. I grasped my amulet, helping to center my focus as the fire returned to a normal, low burning flicker.

"Did you see that?" someone gasped, pointing at the flames.

"Freak burst of wind, I'll bet," another said. The two girls were huddled together, gazing into the embers as if they were at risk for going up in flame that very moment.

"That happened to me a few years ago on a camping trip," a third said, launching into the tale as they straightened their chairs back around the fire pit.

One thing that I'd learned over the years was that people tended to come up with an explanation in the face of the inexplicable–or in this case, in the face of the supernatural. They needed something logical they could wrap their minds around, something humanly perceivable.

I knew I wasn't going to get that lucky with Wren. I turned slowly to face him, anticipating his reaction. He was leaning against the railing, a look of satisfaction twisting his lips into a smug grin. I resisted the urge to pull his mouth to mine, and started to bite down on my lower lip. Thought better of it; tucked my hair behind my ears instead, rocking back on my heels.

He gave me a knowing look.

"Say something," I pleaded.

He reached for me, taking hold of me at the waist and pulled me back into his arms. "I'd rather kiss you again." I felt his breath against my lips, felt myself giving in and knowing that it wasn't safe while we stood this close to the fire. He made me lose myself, and while the feeling was completely intoxicating, I knew I couldn't risk it. Reluctantly, I pushed against his chest, stopping his embrace.

"Not here," I managed to say.

"Where, then?" He tipped his forehead against mine, bending to nuzzle my ear.

"Wren, you saw what happened."

"Freak burst of wind," he repeated the phrase that the others had concluded. I knew he was only saying this to appease me. He knew what I was. I know he did. He'd known since that first encounter in the coffee shop–I had only speculated before, but now I was certain. His lack of reaction matched with the look on his face was all the proof I needed.

"Wren..."

I heard him sigh, felt the vibration of it through his chest. He'd loosened his grip around my waist, deciding to cling to my elbows instead. He lowered his face to mine, pressing his lips against my forehead. We stayed that way for several seconds, just clinging to one another. I didn't know what this meant, but for now, it was enough.

Wren slid his hand down my arm until his fingers laced with mine. His hand was so warm. I held on tightly as he led us away from the deck, and through the garage where I quickly glanced at Hunter. Wren was reaching for the garage door, but I squeezed his hand to stop him. He turned to look at me, brows furrowing.

"I'm–" I licked my lips, searching for a way to explain what I was doing here. I tried again. "–I'm keeping an eye on Hunter."

"I know," he said simply.

I looked up at him, feeling the crease deepening between my eyes.

"Do you trust me?" he whispered.

My whole life I had viewed trust as something that had to be earned. Because of what I was, because of that dreaded "C" word that ruled every move I'd ever made, I'd never just given my trust away so freely. But as I looked up into Wren's amber colored eyes, the force in which he was looking at me; intently, like this answer would determine the fate of our destiny. I knew I could only say one thing. But even as I answered, I knew it was true.

"Yes," I said. "I trust you."

Chapter Ten
Something Wicked
This Way Comes

"And so I told the guy there was no way I was making him an Americano–it's like, so disgusting. I mean it's literally just a shot or two of espresso combined with a few ounces of hot water. No taste." Torrance visibly shuddered at the thought. She'd been telling us coffee shop horror stories from her summer spent in New York with her grandmother. She lived in Brooklyn, in a loft apartment above an art gallery. Torrance went for the New York experience, but decided to learn the tricks of the coffee trade, taking a job at a cute little corner cafe. "I mean, I hate to agree with the New Yorker stereotype, but it's there for a reason."

"But not everyone was a jerk, right?" Harper asked. She placed her drink on the carpet beside her, shuffling through the cards in her hand. She examined them carefully, and then tapped her knuckles against the coffee table.

"Not everyone." Torrance smiled, running her fingertips across the rim of her glass as she recalled silent memories.

"No one wants to hear about your summer romance." Huck, who was now dressed in full clothing, rolled his eyes. He tossed the football he was holding up in the air on a spin and caught it.

Torrance eyed him with a coy grin. I sensed something hidden there, though it appeared to be developing in the very beginning stages. I looked over at Wren who was sitting beside me, close enough so that I could feel the heat rolling from his skin whenever he leaned forward, pushing his betting chips around the coffee table.

Torrance had found us standing in the garage shortly after I'd sworn over my trust. She'd all but yanked us inside and made us agree to play a round of Texas HoldEm. When Wren entered the living room, she caught my elbow, pulling me aside. "I saw you sneak out the back door with him." She giggled, opening the fridge and retrieving me a beer. "Well played, Quinn, he's quite a catch."

"Thank you," I said dubiously, popping the cap off the bottle.

She laughed, leading the way into the living room where we now sat around the coffee table–most of us on the carpet.

"Your turn," Jamie said, jerking his chin in my direction. I looked at the cards in my hand hopelessly. I'd never had enough patience to learn the rules of Texas HoldEm–never played frequently enough to commit anything to memory. I sighed, glancing up at the cards lying face up at the center of the table, looked back at the cards in my hand.

Wren leaned over, pressing his mouth against my ear, "I'd fold," he said. I tried to ignore the rush of butterflies circling my stomach. His breath was warm, sending a shiver down my neck that only caused the fluttering to intensify.

"No cheating," Jamie said, pointing an accusing finger in Wren's direction. He lifted his hands, as if to innocently say, "*She's losing anyway.*"

"Fold," I decided, lying my cards down on the table. Torrance just giggled, biting the rim of her glass. She folded on the last round.

"Wren, your turn."

Wren pushed up on one elbow, shoving all of his chips to the center of the table. "All in," he replied.

"I'm out," Huck said, leaning back against the couch cushion.

"Me too," Harper said.

"Yeah, well I think he's bluffing," Jamie said, propping his elbows on the coffee table. "All in." He slid his pile towards the center of the table.

A deep rumble shook from Wren's chest, catching in his throat in a sort of snort. He sat up, placing his cards face up on the table. I was a total rookie, but I was pretty sure that Wren's Straight Flush beat Jamie's Full House. Jamie let out a sigh of frustration, leaning back against the arm chair he was propped up against.

"Should have folded bro," Huck said, bouncing the football off the side of his head. The rest of us just laughed.

"You got lucky," Jamie said bitterly.

"Don't be a sore loser," Torrance added. "We all knew you were doomed from the start."

"How so?" he challenged.

"You fidget when you're nervous," Huck said. "You can't sit still."

"Wren had an unfair advantage," Torrance continued, "the rest of us have pretty much grown up with one another. We know each other's tells. But Wren? Well he's just a mystery." She looked up from her glass, giggling. When Torrance consumed alcohol, we'd jokingly called it giggle-juice. The more alcohol she drank, the funnier everything around her seemed to be.

"What's my tell?" Huck asked, spinning the football high in the air.

"You," she started, "cross your arms over your chest and take about a million deep breaths and exhale really loudly. You," she pointed to Harper, "blink your eyelids all fast like you've been sprayed with pepper spray–"

"Do not!" Harper gasped.

"–And you," she turned her pointed finger on me, "start chewing on the inside corner of your mouth, and you have since we were in grade school."

I wasn't going to deny it. I felt Wren studying me from the side, wondering if his gaze was lingering on my lower lip.

"So tell us about yourself, Wren. We know you're wicked fast and you have a killer poker face, but if I had to guess, I'd say we're just barely scratching the surface," Torrance said. I all but snorted.

"What do you wanna' know?" he asked.

"What do you want to do with your life?" Torrance asked. "You know, like after graduation."

He gave a half chuckle, shifting his gaze toward the carpet before glancing back up to meet her eyes. "Probably something with my hands," he replied. "Something that keeps me active."

As he said this, I tried to imagine Wren in an office environment. I pictured him wearing khaki pants, a buttoned shirt tucked beneath the waistline, and a pair of black, plastic framed glasses. (Did my imagination just turn him into Clark Kent?) It wasn't a bad look, per se, but he didn't fit the environment. I just couldn't see him stuffed inside a cubicle, hacking away at a keyboard behind the screen of a computer trapped inside some stuffy office. To me, it seemed like he belonged outside–out in the open somewhere under a big, vast sky.

"Nice," Huck said, "I'm going into the police academy."

"I just want to get out of Silver Mountain," Harper said, tipping her Solo cup to her lips. "Maybe head for the city."

"The city is nice, but I was definitely homesick by the end of the summer. I think I've conformed to small town life," Torrance said. "What about you, Quinn?"

"I don't know." I picked at the label on my beer bottle. "After I tackle college, maybe I'll open up a little natural's shop like the one my mom used to run. I still have all her instruction books." I shrugged. It was the closest I'd get to keep her memory alive.

"She made the best honey-almond body scrub," Torrance said.

"Jamie?" Harper asked, bumping her shoulder into his.

"I think I'd like to manage something." As he said this, Huck tossed the ball at his head, but Jamie managed to deflect it with his forearms, thus sending the ball sailing directly into my beer bottle. I tried to save it, but only made it worse by fumbling the ball. Somehow, I'd managed to knock it into the wall behind me, ricocheting towards the crystal vase up on the mantle. Wren's arm shot out and plucked the football out of the air with lightning reflexes. My beer, however, was now soaking into the beige carpet.

"Good one, butter fingers," Huck said to me.

"Nice catch, Wren, is there anything you can't do?" Torrance giggled again. I didn't stick around to hear his answer. I jumped up, ran to the kitchen and grabbed a towel that was draped over the edge of the sink, but when I turned, I practically smacked right into Wren's chest. *Superhuman speed*, I thought to myself, checking it off the list of abilities Wren seemed to possess.

"Easy there," he breathed.

"Beer soaking into the carpet as we speak," I said, trying to step around him. He sidestepped, blocking me as he reached for the towel in my hands. A breeze drifted through the screen window then, ruffling the hair that was falling across Wren's forehead. Abruptly, his neck snapped toward the window, and his body went completely motionless.

"Wren?" His nostrils flared like he was smelling something in the air, and then he bolted around me, dashing through the garage door before I could even blink.

"You okay in there Quinny?" Torrance called from the living room.

I picked up the rag that Wren had dropped to the floor, balled it up, and tossed it in her direction. "Here," I said.

"Don't be gone too long," I heard her laugh as I slipped through the opened garage door. The crowd had thinned, but I frantically searched for Wren's face among the remaining group. My eyes scanned the empty beanbag chairs in front of the television screen, and my stomach dropped.

Hunter was gone.

White-hot adrenaline slammed through my body, igniting in my veins with panic. I cursed, dodging the people who were blocking the exit, and fought my way out onto the deck. I jumped the steps, feeling a sharp pain ricochet up my shins as I landed in the grass. I winced, ignoring the pain as I shot into the forest.

"Hunter!" I called out, hearing my voice echo with a cry through the treetops. I swore again as I struggled through the thick underbrush. I was mentally kicking myself for not staying put in the garage, and keeping a close personal watch over Hunter. Somehow, Wren had known what I was there to do, asked me to trust him, and foolishly, I had. Now, all I could think of were Nathan's eyes staring back at me. I couldn't let this be another failed attempt to do the right thing.

I glanced up through the trees, following the thin splotches of light from the full moon filtering down through the branches. The sky was still too obscured by clouds to give off much lighting. My foot caught the root of a tree, sending me flying through the air. I landed on my forearms hard, feeling the skin being ripped away by the forest floor as I collided with the earth. I slammed a fist into the dirt, transmitting my pain and anger into ground. *Concentrate, Quinn. Develop a game plan,* my inner voice reprimanded. I closed my eyes and clutched my pendant. What did I remember from my vision? There had been a path–wide enough for two people to walk on; a large, jagged boulder where the gray wolf had appeared.

"I call upon the elements to guide me," I said the ancient words that my mother had taught me, reaching out to invoke the elements. I rose to my feet, extending my arms as I silently called upon Air to strengthen the power of my mind. "*Glacaim ar na cumhachtaí ársa.*" The elements answered my call, sending a spark of warmth that surrounded me, and Spirit became my light in the darkness.

The elements led me through the forest as the canopy swallowed the light from up above. "Hunter!" I called again, praying that he would hear my voice. I must have been four-hundred yards deep into the forest by now. I broke through the last of the underbrush, finding my way to a clearing on the path. At least I was heading in the right direction. "Hunter!" I tried again.

"Who's there?" a fragile, female voice answered me.

"Amanda?" A small figure stepped out from behind a large oak; her limbs were visibly shaking and she was gasping for air. "Are you hurt?" I asked, gripping both of her arms in my hands. The light was just bright enough to see her face; dirt and blood smeared her right cheek.

"I fell but I'm f-fine," she murmured, "Are you from the party?" She looked up at me, her eyebrows slanted heavily.

"Yes, I'm a friend of your brother's. My name is Quinn," I told her. "What are you doing out here?"

"N-nothing, it was just a stupid dare," she said, crossing her arms over her chest. She dropped her gaze, casting it to the side.

"You can trust me Amanda, I'm here to help."

She looked up at me again, her forehead crinkling. Her lips parted like she wanted to say something, and then closed again before she swallowed. "Tim Ramsey was telling ghost stories about a man named Marcus Frey that hung himself in an old hunting cabin not far from here. He said at midnight you can see the shadow of a rope swinging from the rafters, and then Marcus' body appears. Tim dared us to spend thirty minutes at the cabin–said we couldn't make it until midnight without seeing the ghost of Marcus Frey. I didn't believe him but Hunter wanted to check it out–so a few of us decided to hike to the Bluff's." Amanda rubbed the goosebumps that were trailing her arms.

"Here," I said, peeling off my jacket and handing it to her. "What happened after that?"

"We didn't make it to the cabin," she said. "We were at the bridge getting ready to cross the river when we heard growling on the other side. I couldn't see what it was but it sounded big–like a bear or something. I-I think there were two of them, it sounded like they were fighting. We didn't stick around to find out. I started running and then I found you."

"Who was with you?"

"Just Owen and Hunter," she said. "I thought they were right behind me but we must have gotten separated." She cast a nervous glance over her shoulder and her whole body began to tremble again. "I-I should g-go back for them."

"No!" I said a bit too abruptly. She startled. I worked on smoothing my expression into something that resembled calm assurance. "No," I repeated, "I'll go after them. Do you remember how to get back to Huck's from here?" I didn't want her anywhere near the woods with wolves on the loose.

She nodded. "Just follow the trail."

"Good, I need you to do that for me. When you get back to the house just stay inside and wait for us to get back. I'm going to find your brother."

"Should I call someone?"

"No, everything will be okay. You probably just heard a bunch of raccoons playing in the underbrush. Your mind can make you believe funny things when you're afraid. I'm sure the others are safe. They're probably just out looking for you." I forced a smile and gave her shoulder a squeeze, hoping to reassure her.

"Yeah you're probably right. Okay, thanks, Quinn."

"Stay on the trail," I told her, watching her turn up the path. I asked the elements to accompany her, keeping her safe and warm as she made her way back to the house. Something was changing. In my earliest vision, I'd seen Hunter protecting his sister from the wolf that leapt in their path. Something must have happened to shake the timeline and alter the course of events. I thought of Wren and the way he'd bolted out of the house. Was he out here somewhere–could he have something to do with the change of events?

I started jogging for the river. The moon was still tucked beneath the clouds, hidden behind the thick branches above. I called on Spirit to keep lighting my way. Invisible to the human eye, the element responded by pushing out a pale, blueish-purple glow that surrounded me in a halo of soft light. The river wasn't far now. I could hear the rush of water–the soft gurgle of it cutting around the rocks and grooves in the riverbed. Yellow leaves littered the bank. I slowed my pace, and came to a stop. The black water stretched wide, its surface like a mirror.

I knew this place.

I recognized it from my dreams. It was the same place where I'd seen the black wolf drinking from the stream, and I remembered its yellow eyes gazing back at me from the water. A clammy sweat broke over the surface of my chest. Had my dream been some sort of premonition?

A twig snapped to my right. I jerked my head in the direction of the noise and spotted a shape silhouetted among the fallen leaves on the riverbank. At first glance I thought it might have been a log or a boulder, but as I grew closer I could see that the shape was more human. I stopped thinking after that.

I ran forward, falling to my knees in front of the figure lying face down on the path. The glow from Spirit spread out in front of me, shining its indigo colored light on Hunter. His arms were stretched out in front of him, his face tilted to the side; mouth open. I reached out, shaking his shoulder. "Please wake up," I said aloud. I gave him a solid once over, searching for blood or any sign of a broken limb but he seemed to be fine. "Hunter, please."

He stirred, and I released the breath I was holding. He blinked a couple of times as he came to, and I helped him up in a sitting position.

"Easy," I said, "go slowly."

"Ow." He winced, reaching up to cradle the back of his head.

"Do you remember what happened?"

"Quinn? What are you doing out here?" He rubbed at the back of his head, looking around as if he couldn't remember where he was.

"I ran into your sister," I said. "She told me you and Owen were out here."

"Is she okay?"

"Yes, I sent her back to the house. Are *you* okay?"

"I think so," he replied, giving his head a quick shake. "There's something out here though." He looked around frantically as his senses came back. "I heard a bunch of animals fighting or something. I started running back and I must have tripped and hit my head. Have you seen Owen?"

My stomach coiled. "Not yet. Can you walk?"

"Yeah," he said. I reached forward to help him up from the ground, and as we rose, something began to change within the forest.

At first it was subtle, like the way a slow-moving cloud crosses the sun, painting the ground in shadow. It crept slowly, but as we headed back over the path, I felt an icy cold pressing in from all directions. An inky darkness was snaking its way through the forest, gliding over the earth with black tendrils; poisoning. It came in the fog, rising to our knees, and lapping around us like tongues hungrily tasting. Hunter, I realized, couldn't see it. I heard the dark whisper, a foul, seductive breath looming on the air. She wanted me. She wanted me to give in to the pull; the slow and steady lull of Darkness that was crawling over my skin, biting, touching, tasting.

Letting go of Hunter, I clamped down on my forearms, digging my nails into the flesh. The Darkness was embedding itself into my skin–I was sure if I looked down, I would see minuscule threads of black vapor burrowing in. But I was too afraid to look.

"Quinn?" Hunter stopped to look at me as concern washed over his features.

"I'm not feeling so well. Listen, I need you to head up the path and get to Huck's. Owen is probably waiting for you back at the house."

"I'm not going to leave you Quinn." His eyebrows furrowed.

The Darkness tightened its hold on me. I could feel pinpricks all over my skin. "Please Hunter, just get out of here!" I yelled at him. "Go!"

I watched a shudder shake his body, and then he was taking off down the path. "I'll get help," he called over his shoulder.

I searched the night for a face, knowing somehow that I wouldn't find one. Whatever magic was at work here wasn't of solid body. "Shield me, Earth, I ask of thee." My voice was weak, but I couldn't allow Hunter to come back into the woods and find me. "Keep my friends safe."

The Darkness was still caressing me, toying with me like I was her plaything and she wasn't known to take care of her toys. "I sense powerful magic in you," the voice whispered, tangling around my head like a vicious echo. "I want it."

"Show yourself," I demanded.

She chuckled darkly, and her voice lifted and filled the atmosphere as if she were everywhere at once. "You've no right to ask anything of me," she said. "You're leagues beneath me. If you won't come willingly, I have other ways of getting what I want." Her voice was electric, and I felt the sting of it snapping and sizzling down my spine as she forced me to my knees.

Out of the darkness, their snarls and growls rumbled in the underbrush. I could hear their bone-chilling cries, and when the first wolf stepped through the underbrush, my blood went still. Every hair on my body pricked as goosebumps trailed across my skin. A second and third wolf emerged from the tree line, hanging back as the gray wolf from my vision stopped about a foot in front of my face. His yellow eyes were bearing down on mine. I could smell fresh blood on his breath when he snarled at me–felt the deep rumble of his growl vibrating the earth beneath my knees.

This wolf was easily as big as a Great Dane. His long, slender limbs were as long as my legs and his head was thrice the size of my own. His white teeth glinted in the reflection of my Spirit glow, his canines easily two inches long. Saliva clung to his jowls as he licked at his lips, breathing in the scent of me.

"Last chance," the voice said. "Submit to my will, and relinquish your powers."

Fear was spiraling in my gut, squeezing my organs, but I fought against it with Spirit's help. I drew from the element and let it center me. "I call upon the ancient powers," I whispered, tightening my grip around my amulet.

"Don't let her finish that spell!" the voice slammed down through the treetops, giving the wolf permission to attack. I watched it rear back before it lunged, but I was ready for the attack as I gathered Fire in the palms of my hands. I lifted both hands in the air, rising to one knee as a large black object ascended over my left shoulder. It crashed into the gray wolf in midair and tumbled to the ground in front of me. In the dim light, I saw that the black object was in fact a fourth wolf.

The sky above seemed to open at the Moon's command. A silver-blue light filtered down through the branches, chasing the shadows from the darkest corners in the forest. I scurried backwards, using my hands to push myself away from the massive beasts until my back thumped into the trunk of a tree. In front of me, crouched low to the ground, the wolves began to circle. Their arctic yellow eyes glowed in the dark as if they were emitting their own source of light.

I swallowed, fighting to calm my ragged breaths as I planned my next move. I knew I couldn't outrun them. They'd take me down in an instant if I turned my back. I allotted myself a quick moment to look up. The tree that I was pressed up against had high branches. I'd never be able to climb. The underbrush was a thick mess of weeds and vines–the kind that would tangle around a person's ankles and drag them down if they tried to cut through. My only option was to stay and fight. I began to raise my hands, ready to call on Fire when the gray wolf broke from the circle and lunged directly at me.

I squeezed my eyes shut, bracing myself for an impact that never came. Instead, I heard what sounded like thunder, and looked up to see that the black wolf had rammed into the gray wolf's side and knocked his legs out from under him. It took me all of two seconds to realize that the sound I'd heard was bones cracking. The wolves were circling again. Low, guttural sounds ripped from the back of their throats as they snarled at one another; fangs flashing. The gray wolf tried once again to lunge in my direction, but the black wolf was quick to block the attack.

Was it protecting me? I watched in horror and fascination; momentarily stunned by the dance of the two predators in front of me. I'd never seen anything so graceful move that fast in my life, or anything as deadly. The two wolves collided once more, tangling in a ball of fur and rage that swirled in front of me. The black wolf landed just a little too close to my leg, kicking up a spray of dirt that peppered my face. I coughed, spitting out a mouthful as I wiped the debris from my eyes. As they fought, I searched for the other two who were watching from the background.

I didn't know what they were waiting for, but I decided now was my opportune moment to strike. I tried to call Fire, but the black wolf managed to knock the gray wolf to the side, sending him sliding into the prickly brambles of the underbrush.

"*No!*" the voice in the trees shouted. She lifted her voice high, chanting something in a language I didn't recognize. The two wolves that were watching from the sidelines began moving forward now. Their eyes were trained on the black wolf, watching his every move. My chest swelled with a painful heat when I realized he was their intended target. The black wolf turned his head to check on me–a terrible mistake. A wolf with dark red fur leapt in his path, sinking his fangs into his flank. He yelped and spun, ready for a defensive counter move.

Now was my chance. I rolled myself forward and sprang upright, beginning a chant of my own. I called all the elements forth, reaching deeper than I'd ever done to find the strength that was buried inside me. "I call upon the ancient powers," repeating the phrase in the Gaelic tongue that my mother taught me, "*glacaim ar na cumhachtaí ársa*. In the midnight hour, I call upon the flame of Fire, to wield against this darkened night, to beckon forth the sun and Light. Gift me now, I ask of thee, with flame of Fire Darkness shall flee."

A brilliant glow danced across my palms, igniting with a spark that blazed with violet and orange flame. To my right, another wolf shot out of the darkness and entered the fight. Now, I struggled to find the black wolf in the violent mayhem.

Their growls and snarls magnified; blood flew from opened wounds, splattering my clothing. I scrambled back against the tree. My flames grew brighter, swirling in my palms like miniature hurricanes. The wolves blurred in front of me, twisting and turning, jamming sharp blows that were met with the answer of sharper teeth. I could hear flesh ripping–see fur flying. Then, in the midst of chaos, I spotted the black wolf on the ground, and my heart sank.

The gray wolf was pinning him to the ground while another clamped its jaws around his throat. I hurled my first fireball in its direction; a burst of orange and purple light exploded against the wolf's flank. He jumped back, yelping in pain. I aimed the next at the red wolf. The fireball hit him in the face with a burst of color and ash–exploding and snapping. He yelped, pawing at his wounded eye while the black wolf lay motionless on the forest floor.

Please don't be dead. Please!

Now, the gray wolf turned his attention on me. As I conjured my next round of fireballs, something caught my eye. The black wolf had begun to Change–his form began to shift, and with it came the awful sounds of bones and sinew snapping and realigning. I watched in veritable shock–frozen in place until there, glowing in the lunar light, the shape of man took its place.

I felt myself stop breathing as I gazed at the blood soaked body on the soiled ground; his beautiful face tilted to the side as if he were only sleeping. There were countless scratches across his chest, bite marks in the flesh of his neck. A deep gouge had been inflicted just under his ribs, and the wound was seeping a thick, dark current of blood.

Wren.

The black wolf that came to my rescue was Wren.

And he was dead.

Raw agony ripped through my bones, splintering, until my knees buckled and I collapsed to the ground in front of his mangled body. There was so much blood–staining the earth below. I could feel every fiber in my muscles twitching, reacting subconsciously to the shock.

A slow ignition began to blaze in my chest until the ember became a boiling inferno. I could feel it grating up my throat, and tipped my head back and cried out into the night with all the power I had left inside me. My scream pierced the veil of Darkness, and her inky threads began to recoil–slinking back into the night. I began to lose myself then as something purer took over. She was strength, and she was fury. She sang in my blood with a confidence I had only ever imagined, awakening something from the deepest part of my soul.

Wind swirled around me with the momentum of a rising storm, stirring leaves and debris through the air. My hair lifted back in an upward vortex. I cried out, hurling my flames at the ground. White lightning exploded against the forest floor, and the ground trembled beneath me. A ring of fire formed a barrier of protection around Wren's body and me–the flames leaping six feet into the air. I banished the Darkness, pushing against it with every corner of my mind.

I was vaguely aware that the wolves were howling somewhere in the background, and their cries were met with the scream of defeat from the voice of Darkness. Somehow, I'd wounded her. She was angry, but she was retreating. I felt my body giving in to sudden exhaustion, and the fire I commanded slowly fizzled out. The ground before me was charred from the embers, a blackened mark circling us.

When the power surge left my limbs, I slumped forward over Wren's body as tears pooled in my eyes. Sobs threatened to choke me, but as I reached up to brush the hair back from his eyes, my hands made contact with his blood.

I had no energy to fight against the vision, and let it pull me under the ocean's surface. I could feel the water rushing into my lungs but I was too weak to care. I didn't struggle under the water, but found that I could breathe it as if it were oxygen. I drifted there, just beneath the surface until the waves pushed me up on the beach. My fingernails raked the pebbled shore, and somehow, I managed to pull myself up.

The image ripped, and I was surrounded by a valley of wide rolling hills. There was so much green, the meadow seemed to glitter like it was made of emerald jewels. There were no houses or buildings, or anything manmade to pollute the essence of pure nature. I had a strong sense that time had no meaning here, and I was somewhere far, far in the past.

The scene rippled again, changing into midnight darkness. I caught a glimpse of light, a flash of glacial blue eyes surrounded by a mane of thick, black hair. Her face was like an unfinished portrait; featureless–the textures rough and poorly blended. She sat upon a marbled throne, her long skirts flowing to her ankles in medieval garb. She whispered one word, "*Faoladh,*" and it echoed all around me until it was ringing in my ears.

She wore a gem around her neck; it resembled opal, emitting a strong blueish-white hue. It sat center of a silver filigree framework pattern, as large as the palm of my hand. She stroked the pendant with her index finger, and I felt the darkness of her soul begin to smile. The Darkness undulated, and I could feel the seductive pull of it, and the hot breath of it rolling over my shoulders like greedy fingertips. She relished the power of it–fed on it, until it consumed her.

In that moment, I began to understand the attraction to Darkness. It wrapped itself around me like a warm cloak, burrowing into my soul as it smothered my White Light. Shame washed over me, and I remembered that the Darkness was poisoned. No human could handle the pull of it, but luckily, I wasn't entirely human. The vision cracked like an ice covered lake, the fractured lines snapping and snaking across the frozen surface until I found myself lying across Wren's chest. Small flames still burned in thin patches around our circle.

"Are you with us, White Witch?" a voice from behind called softly.

I turned my head, peering over my shoulder and found a man–probably around my dad's age with long, salt and pepper gray hair pulled back into a ponytail. Loose strands surrounded his dirty face, and he was naked. This, by far, was not at all shocking to me after what I'd just encountered. Wren, too, lay naked on the ground, but my mind was in broken, fragmented bits. He was dead, and I was alone in the middle of the woods with a naked man that was probably a werewolf.

"Are you with us?" he asked again.

"Is he–" I couldn't make myself say the word out loud–couldn't stand for it to be true. I rested my palm against Wren's face, my thumb pressing to his lip.

"No, but we need to get him home," the man said.

"Who are you?" I breathed.

"Niall Whelan," he said, "I'm Wren's father."

Chapter Eleven
Strange & Beautiful

I followed Niall through the forest with the light of Spirit guiding our way. He was carrying Wren in his arms–effortlessly, as though he weighed no more than a small sack of potatoes. We stayed off the path, and Niall navigated through the shrubbery and underbrush like an experienced animal would–following its own trail. But then, I had to remind myself that he *was* an animal, or at least *part* animal. I hadn't quite figured out the semantics yet. I was also trying not to think too much.

We exited the woods to a narrow access road that the general public didn't use. They were typically one-lane roads that led up to private cabins, ski lodges, or wildlife stations. A beat up turquoise truck was parked off to the side, leaning over the ditch a little. At first glance, I thought it must have been abandoned there, as the paint was faded and fiercely rusted. I was surprised when Niall stopped short of the tailgate, motioning for me to lower it down. I did as I was told.

He lowered Wren into the bed of the truck, and took my hand and pressed it firmly to the gouge on Wren's side. "Keep pressure here," he instructed. I felt a wave of nausea rising in my belly at the feel of his warm, sticky blood. I did my best to ignore the bile waiting on the back of my tongue.

"He needs a hospital," I said.

"No." Niall disappeared around the driver's side of the truck, reappearing a moment later wearing jeans and a red and gray flannel. He also had a blanket in his hands. "No hospital."

"These wounds are serious, he could die."

"Our kind can't go to hospitals," he said, "our blood isn't human." He hopped into the bed of the truck, grabbed Wren underneath the arms and pulled him back across the bed. "You'll stay with him," he told me.

"What's going to happen to him?"

"He needs rest, and he'll heal."

I didn't know if I could believe him, though I had no other option. I climbed into the bed of the truck, leaving a bloody handprint across the chipped paint. I lowered myself down against the back of the cab, and Niall helped to position Wren in my arms so that I could keep pressure to the gash on his side. He covered him with the blanket and glanced up into my eyes. "You okay?" His eyes reminded me of Wren's–only darker– harder.

I nodded.

"Stay with us, White Witch," he said before hopping over the side of the bed and climbing back into the cab. I didn't know why he kept calling me that–or what it even meant, but now I didn't care. All I could think about was Wren and the condition of his body, and the feel of his blood on my hands. A normal person couldn't survive the wounds he'd received.

But he wasn't human.

While my right hand clamped firmly against his side, my left cradled his head gently under my chin. I buried my nose into his hair as the truck zoomed up the mountainside, and the cool wind played in my hair, tangling it around our faces. I closed my eyes and felt liquid leaking from the corners. In my delirious state, I remembered to thank the elements for their help against the Darkness, and asked if they could aid in healing Wren. Spirit's glow never left me, and I felt the slow warmth of it in the air that surrounded us.

A few short minutes later, the truck was bumping up an uneven dirt lane, dipping and rocking as we wound beneath the cover of dense evergreens. Niall cut the engine and immediately appeared around the side of the truck. He lifted Wren out of my arms, and I struggled to keep up as he led the way into a small wooden cabin.

The cabin smelled like sage and sweet grass–herbs my mother once used for protection and cleansing. I followed Niall's silhouette down a narrow hall and into a bedroom off to the right. He lay Wren down on a bed that was pushed up against a wall, and turned to flip on the small lamp sitting on the bedside table. I blinked against the dull light, letting my eyes adjust to the contrast.

"I'll be right back," Niall told me, stirring the wind as he brushed by. I went to Wren's side, kneeling as I brushed the hair back from his face. His dark lashes were so long they nearly rested on the hollow place beneath his eyes. There was so much blood. It dried in dark smears across his throat, leaving trails of deep scratches that snaked across the left side of his pectoral muscle. The gash below his ribs was still seeping, though it appeared to have slowed. The blanket provided a modest covering from the waist down. Still, I checked his calves and thighs to make sure there weren't any other cuts or gouges we might have missed.

Niall returned a moment later with a wooden bowl of sweet smelling liquid, a rag, and a heaping of bandages. "What can I do?" I asked as he knelt beside me.

"Do you have someone you need to call–your parents need to know where you are?" he asked.

I sucked in a breath of air, pushing a hand through my tangled mane. "Um, yeah." Annabelle was probably going out of her mind with worry by now. I had completely forgotten about where I had been tonight... Huck, Torrance, and the others thought that Wren and I ran off together, but what had Hunter and Amanda told them when they came back from the forest–had they all made it back safely?

Niall nodded. "There's a phone in the kitchen. Your cell won't get service up here, so you're welcome to use it."

"Okay, thanks." I stood slowly, watching as Niall began to wash Wren's wounds with the rag and liquid mixture.

"He'll be fine, White Witch. Go."

"Quinn," I said. "My name is Quinn."

Niall nodded once more, and I left the room. The cabin wasn't big, but the lights were on now, and I could see the kitchen from the hallway.

I drifted across the hardwood floors and found a phone sitting by the sink. I knew Annabelle's number by heart and dialed it. She'd answered before it finished the first ring.

"I swear to God you better have a damn good explanation for not answering my texts and phone calls because if you don't, I'm going to kill you."

"I have a good reason," I said. Annabelle didn't respond. She must have heard the strain in my voice so I continued, "I can't explain everything in detail right now, but I need you to cover for me."

"Cover for you! Do you even know what time it is? I've been worried sick!"

"No," I said, spinning around to find a clock. I was surrounded by an L-shaped kitchen with large, oak cabinets with black iron handles. I looked above the gas stove, but there was no clock to be seen.

"It's two in the morning," Annabelle answered for me, "I told my mother that you decided to stay at Huck's with Torrance and the other girls but I'm getting texts and phone calls from them asking what in the hell happened to you and Wren."

"Are they all safe?"

"Yeah, from what I gather–are you?"

"I'm okay, but what did you tell the others?" I asked, knowing full well that she was already a step ahead of them.

"I told them that you were here of course," she said. "So you better tell me where you are and whose phone you're using to call from." Her tone was laced with concern though she was doing her best to give me the "stern parental" voice.

"I lost track of Hunter," I told her, "my vision came true... just not in the way we thought. Wren saved him, but, he's not in good shape."

"*Who's* not in good shape?"

"Wren," I said. "I'm here–I'm at his cabin. His dad is helping."

"Helping with what?" Annabelle asked exasperatedly.

"He's hurt, Annabelle, really bad." The image of Wren's mangled flesh flashed across my mind. I felt myself swaying a little, and reached up to rub my eye as tears began to pool there. "He was attacked."

"By the wolf?" she asked, gentler now.

"By multiple wolves."

"So why aren't you at a hospital?"

"That's what I can't tell you over the phone... It has something to do with what he is. I'll explain everything tomorrow. I promise. I just... I should get back to him."

"Okay," she said calmly. "Okay."

"Tomorrow," I told her.

"Tomorrow," she agreed.

"Annabelle?"

"Yes?"

"Thank you."

"Of course," she murmured, and I hung up the phone.

For a moment I just stood at the counter, listening to the silence. After what happened in the forest, the stillness was almost unbearable. I made my way back down the hall, pausing in the doorway of Wren's bedroom, and watching as Niall gingerly wrapped a bandage around Wren's side. The cuts across his throat and chest were cleaned. I moved forward to get a better look; I could have sworn they'd been so much worse. I started to lean over, reaching out to touch his skin when Niall grabbed my arm. "Careful," he said, and nodded towards my necklace that was dangling just over Wren's body. "Don't let that touch his skin."

"Sorry." I tucked it beneath the collar of my shirt. "I thought those wounds were so much worse. He was bleeding so much."

"We heal quickly," Niall replied. "Our body falls into deep slumber when we've been critically wounded. The skin regeneration process is painful; it takes great amounts of energy because of how rapidly the change takes place."

"How long?" I asked.

"For these wounds..." Niall taped another bandage to Wren's throat, just above his collarbone. "Probably the night."

I reached for Wren's hand, traced the outline of the crescent shaped scar with my fingertip. "Will he be scarred up?" I asked.

Niall looked down at Wren's hand, and I looked up to see that his eyes had hardened. "In places," he said, "it takes serious injury to cause a scar like that."

"Do you know what happened here?" I asked.

"That's not a story for me to tell," Niall answered.

More secrets. I thought back to my vision and the word that had been whispered in the air, hanging above me like an endless echo. "What does Faoladh mean?"

Niall's hands went still. "Where did you hear that?"

"In the woods," I said quietly, but decided to leave out the explanation of "*how.*" If he was going to be vague with me, then he wasn't getting any gory details from my vision, either.

"*Faoladh* is an old Irish word for werewolf," Niall replied. "It's what we've descended from. The first line of werewolves lived in Ossory."

"Your bloodline?" I asked to clarify.

"Yes," he said, "our bloodline."

"Do you know what was out there tonight in the forest?" I asked, "Could you hear the voice in the darkness?"

"Yes... Though I'm not sure why she's returned."

"She?"

"If it's who I think it is, then she traces back to the original bloodline; to the original curse." Niall pulled the blanket up over Wren's body, glancing at him before shifting his dark eyes back to me.

He could have been handsome once, I thought, but there were hard lines that pulled the corners of his eyes down, and a permanent crease in the middle of his forehead from years of worry. Something told me that Niall had lived a hard life, and I wondered if it had something to do with his werewolf genetics. He'd rooted himself deep in the mountains for a reason, practically exiling himself from the rest of the human population. I wanted to learn why.

"In the days of old, Irish folklore speaks of a man named Abbot Natalis who placed a curse on a clan from Ossory to punish them for an ancient sin. Every seven years, a man and a woman from the clan must shed their mortal skin, exchanging it for the pelt of a wild wolf. They were meant to live in the deep forest, far away from their clan, and at the end of their seven-year penance, they would shed their wolf fur and return to their human form while two others would take their place. The curse stayed in repetition long after Natalis had died.

"Later, it was said that a descendant king from Ossory wanted to use the werewolves' supernatural powers to aid in the battles against his enemies. There was other talk about a witch–a mistress of Darkness–that was said to possess great and terrible power. The king sought her out, and she agreed to help if he promised to bind himself to her, making her his queen. She placed a new curse upon a tribe of warriors of the Faelad clan, and the wolves were forced to fight in the king's army–forever trapped in their fur, and banished from their human skins.

"This went on for many years until the king gained control of all the lands, ruling with an army of wolf slaves and his witch queen by his side. Word of their victories and conquests spread through the Celtic regions, poisoning the land with fear. But evil doing has always had a counterpart. For without Light, there can be no Darkness, and without the Darkness, there can be no Light.

"The Earth Mother awakened a new witch–the White Witch–and with her powers she sought to reverse the corruption and evil doings that the Dark Witch had done. The Earth Mother gave the White Witch a special power so she could communicate with the wolf people. She told them that she was sent to free them from their bonds of slavery. Many wished to be freed from their wolf forms, but others wanted the choice to change at free will. So, the White Witch broke the curse and cast a new spell written of the moon and the stars."

I shifted on the floor, pulling my knees to my chest as Niall continued with his tale.

"The White Witch asked the Great Moon to protect the wolf people, cloaking them with her light and shielding them from the Evil One. The Great Moon answered the witch's call, and gave the wolf people a new gift. During the three phases of the full moon, the wolf people would shed their human form and take up the pelt of the wolf to honor the Great Moon and the gift that she'd given them. During the three phases of the Moon Change, the wolves would be at their strongest, purest forms, though they could change at free will.

"When the Dark Witch learned what the White Witch had done, she grew so stricken with rage that she conjured the Battle of the Dark Ages. The freed wolves fought for the White Witch, striking down her enemies with swift and powerful blows. The Light began to flourish, and the age of Darkness was coming to an end. The White Witch gave the Dark One a chance to surrender, but she refused the Light. It was then that the White Witch vanquished her enemy, and restored peace to the lands. This of course, was the story that has been passed down through many generations of the Whelan bloodline," Niall said. "Until tonight, I believed it only to be just that."

I swallowed over the lump that had risen in my throat, constricting my airways. Goosebumps prickled my skin, chilling my flesh. "If she's returned," I heard myself say, "what is it that she wants?"

"I don't know," Niall answered. He took an audible breath, released it slowly as he spread his hands over his pant legs. "It's late, and you should get some rest. The bathroom is just across the hall–there's clean towels in the closet. I can get you some blankets, set you up on the couch."

"Um, if it's okay, I think I'll just sit with Wren."

"He's going to be fine," Niall assured me.

"I know, I just… I want to be here when he wakes up."

Niall nodded, excusing himself from the doorway. I figured he'd only consented to my staying in his room because Wren was obviously out-cold. I managed my way into the bathroom, and practically jumped at the sight of my reflection. I looked like I was wearing a Bloody Mary costume. My hair was wild from the wind; twigs and other leafy particles clung to the matted strands. Dried blood was smeared all over my clothes; flecks of Wren's blood had dried on my face–a streak of it running across my forehead.

The closet Niall mentioned was barely a foot wide, tucked within the wall opposite the sink. I helped myself to supplies and set to work scrubbing my skin, and dislodging the debris from my hair. I found a bottle of mouthwash under the sink and rinsed thoroughly before silently slipping back across the hall.

Wren hadn't budged. Lying there with his eyes closed, a peaceful expression softened his features. He looked younger somehow, and if it weren't for all the scratches and bandages, one would have thought he was just a normal teenaged-boy.

A boy that almost died trying to save me.

I sank into the desk chair beside his bed, reaching for his right hand. The heat radiating from his skin was like standing beneath the unforgiving summer sun on a cloudless day. The cuts across his chest were merely scratches now. I lifted my hand, lightly touching his skin and tracing the fading marks. Remarkable. I lifted my hand to his face, tracing his cheekbone with my thumb, then his eyebrows with my fingertips. As I sat there studying him and tracing his features, a mixture of emotions welled up inside me. I wanted to cry, but exhaustion wouldn't allow it. Instead, I watched his chest rise and fall, rise and fall. The repetition slowed my mind, easing the racing current of grief that swept through my entire body.

In life, our choices determined the outcome of the moments we were given. But moments were fleeting, and there were no guarantees. Every choice was a risk. Wren didn't have any preconceived allegiance or bond linking me to him, yet he'd been so willing to sacrifice himself to save me.

And now, I owed him my life…

I didn't want to think of what could have happened, the alternative of losing him was too much to bear. I sniffled, pushing on my eyes to keep them from burning, wondering, all the while, if he knew what he meant to me when I didn't fully understand myself.

My fingers found the coin that was fixed to the black cord around his throat. I remembered seeing it that first day at school–the cord peeking out from behind his shirt collar. It was heavy; steel, and had a picture of a cloaked man kneeling before a wolf. The wolf's paw was placed in the man's outstretched hand, and his free hand was placed over his heart. I flipped the coin over, running my thumb across the inscription on the back. "*Lord, make me an instrument of thy peace.*"

I wiped at a tear that managed to slip from the corner of my eye, and got up to find clothes that weren't covered in his blood. There was a wooden dresser beneath his window; the top drawer filled with socks and boxers. The next drawer had T-shirts practically stuffed to the brim. Most were from cross-country meets. I glanced in his direction to make sure he was still sleeping before I peeled off my blood saturated layers, and pulled one of his T-shirts over my head. The sleeves brushed against my inner elbows, the hem falling just below my hips.

I searched the third drawer for a pair of shorts, and pulled them up over my hips. I turned toward a row of shelves on the opposite wall. There were no pictures–nothing to mark his existence–save for a display of first-place medals that hung from a row of wooden pegs. My eyebrows furrowed as I studied them, noting the names of each of the meets where he'd placed. Most of them were counties in Washington that I'd never heard of, but there were a few others from different states. Four years of first-place ribbons gleamed in the light of the lamp.

There were a few books on Celtic mythology, folklore, and legends. They were old and leather-bound–books that had been passed down from his family over the years. I found another book on Greek mythology, an astronomy book, and a 'how-to' book on working a telescope. I picked up a wooden carving of a wolf, turning it over in my hands. The wolf was lithe and slender, his neck stretched out as if he were baying at the moon. I put it back on the shelf, and skimmed through a stack of musical CD's. Death Cab for Cutie, Radiohead, and The Goo Goo Dolls were a few of the bands that stuck out to me, but it was the Aqualung CD that caught my attention. I lifted the stack, quietly pulling the disk from the shelf.

The lyrics to "Strange and Beautiful" clicked in my mind. It was the song that Wren had been humming earlier in the week–the one that seemed so hauntingly familiar, yet I hadn't been able to place it. I felt myself grinning, slowly shaking my head in disbelief. I realized that the song had been Wren's way of hinting that he knew what I was from the very beginning and he was subtly trying to let me know. A new sense of understanding washed over me as I returned to Wren's side and wrapped my fingers around his hand.

I didn't know what was looming on tomorrow's horizon, but I knew that we'd face it together, and I wasn't afraid.

Chapter Twelve
Scars

I was dreaming about the Dark Witch and the legend Niall told me about when I felt something warm brushing the hair back from my face. My eyelids fluttered open, and I felt pain and stiffness radiating through my limbs. I must have fallen asleep in the chair, slumped forward somehow, and ended up lying across Wren's chest. It took me half a heartbeat to figure out that his hand was in my hair, and my cheek was pressed against his bare sternum.

I started lifting myself from his chest when he leaned forward, scooping me up as he pulled me onto the bed with him. He shifted me effortlessly, gently pinning my body to his. I felt his lips brush against my forehead, his thumb tenderly tracing the length of my jawbone. "You should take it easy," I said.

"I am," he replied. My stomach did strange little flips at the sound of his voice.

"How are you feeling?"

"I'm fine," he stressed, trying his best to persuade me with a knowing look. His amber eyes riveted to mine, trapping me under his gaze. It was good to see the color back in his face–the light–back in his eyes. I worked at the inside corner of my lip with my teeth, pushing up on my knees. I reached for the bandage on his throat, and he compliantly tilted his head so I could peel back the tape. There were faint markings there, healed to purple colored bruises. His chest still had claw marks–thin, red scratches, like the marks that were above his eyebrow the day before.

I reached for the covers, lowering the quilt so I could see how the wound on his side was healing, and his hand shot out, wrapping around my forearm as I skimmed the bandage. "I need to check it," I said. He let go of my hand, wincing when I carefully peeled back the first layer of tape, gently lifting the gauze. To my immediate dismay, the wound was still opened. His skin puckered around the opening, looking raw and inflamed. My expression hardened with trepidation.

Wren sat up, folding the bandage back across the wound. "I'm fine," he repeated, reaching for both my arms.

"You're not fine," I said to him. "You almost died last night, Wren. I almost lost you. Do you have any idea how…" I struggled to finish the sentence. Too many emotions were clouding my rational senses. I don't know why, but anger seemed to be the most dominant, fighting its way to the top of the ladder. It simmered there for half a heartbeat before mellowing into something like despair. "You put yourself in the line of danger," I said, afraid to meet his eyes. "Why… why would you do that for me?"

"Because," he said, tipping his forehead to mine, lightly gripping the nape of my neck. "You're worth the fight."

"No, I'm not." I didn't feel worthy, but my heart was constricting at his words. I reached up, resting my hand against the side of his neck. The golden light of the early morning sun was streaming through the window, causing his eyelashes to shine iridescently in a reddish-gold tint. I didn't mean for it to, but my heart sped up beneath my rib cage. I knew he could sense it–could feel the vibration of it through my betraying human skin.

He reached for my leg, sliding my thigh over the top of his so I was straddling his waist. His fingertips pressed into the small of my back, and my breathing faltered when I remembered that he was naked beneath the blankets. He kissed me then, his mouth seeking mine like he needed the warmth of me. My arms tangled around his neck as desire took over. I pressed my mouth to his, savoring the way his lips felt against mine. I couldn't comprehend how I had gone this long without realizing what it meant to feel passion for another living soul, and to have that passion returned into something that moved beyond longing.

I was about to lose all control when I suddenly remembered that I was in his father's home, and the last time I had started to lose myself I almost caught Huck's deck on fire. I pulled back, gasping for air. "Stop," I muttered breathlessly.

Wren's eyes were glowing–electric yellow–like they had when he was a wolf. His canine teeth were slightly extended; sharply pointed. I lifted his upper lip with my thumb, touching his tooth with curiosity and fascination.

He pulled back when my thumb grazed the tip of his canine. "What would happen if you bit me?" I asked.

"Werewolves cannot be made," he said. "They can only be born." He leaned forward, his eyes fixed on my lips, but I pressed my fingertip against his mouth, stopping him. He rolled his eyes.

"I don't want to catch your house on fire," I said.

"You won't." He reached for me again.

"Your dad is home," I protested.

"He's asleep."

"So what if he wakes up?" I countered.

"I'll hear him." He grinned mischievously, rolling forward as he lowered me back on the bed. He was hovering over the top of me, propped up on his hands in a way that made the definition in his triceps project. I ran my fingertips up his arms, feeling every contour and impression.

"Is that because you have superhearing abilities?"

"Yes," he answered, pressing a kiss to my lips.

"Wren," I breathed, "don't you think things are progressing just a little too fast?" I wasn't an idiot. I'd never done what I was pretty sure we were about to do–or at least, it seemed to be heading in that direction. And even though my blood was pounding in my ears, I wasn't ready. I mean, I wanted him, *badly*, but my erratic girl-brain just wouldn't shut off. I had questions. And morals. Morals that I was about to chuck out the window if he kept looking at me like that.

I pushed out from underneath his arm, hopping off the bed and chose to stand by his dresser, crossing my arms over my chest. His lip quivered, sliding into a smoldering sort of smirk that made me glad I'd chosen to get up from his mattress.

"What are you doing?" he asked huskily, deep voice rumbling from his chest.

"We need to talk, and you're distracting me," I admitted.

"I told you it wasn't in my nature to go slow," he said, grinning.

"I recall." I reached up, tucking a strand of hair behind my ear.

"I like your outfit, by the way," he said, eyes appraising. "Take it upon yourself to rummage through my drawers while I was out?"

"I didn't think you'd mind, especially since my clothes were covered in *your* blood–which brings me to my next topic of discussion. I have questions."

Wren sucked in a breath of air, exhaling slowly. "What do you want to know?"

"Well, I'd like to know how you knew that Hunter was in danger, for one thing." I pulled the desk chair away from the bed, sat down.

"I heard your conversation with Annabelle that day on the track–right after you'd had a vision," he said simply.

I raised my eyebrows. "Oh. Well, what about the other wolves–do you know who they are?" I asked. "Or how many there are?"

"Not exactly, no. We've been tracking them, but whenever we get close, their scent just disappears–we think someone is protecting them. If I passed them on the street in their human skin, I'd know their scent," he said. "But they're doing a good job of staying off the radar. I caught a brief scent the day I missed school. I told you that family had been in town, but we were trying to find them."

"Is that how you got the scratches above your eyebrow?"

"I followed the scent into a thick patch of brambles and caught a face full of thorns," he said, dragging his thumb across the slope of his eyebrow. The marks were gone now, but I wondered if he could feel the ghost of them.

"When you say *we*, I assume you mean you and your father. Are there more of your kind?" I felt weird for asking, but I wanted to know if they had a pack.

"Not here," he shook his head, "until recently it's just been Dad and

I in Silver Mountain."

"Well you're kind of a recent addition too," I pointed out. "Is your mom a werewolf?" I suddenly had a whole new plethora of questions I wanted to ask regarding his family and upbringing. Did there need to be two werewolf parents in order to have werewolf offspring? And if you can only be born a werewolf, when do you first Change into one? I tried to picture human babies turning into wolf cubs but the image didn't seem to fit.

"I think breakfast is in order," Wren said, rising from the bed with the sheet wrapped around his waist.

"But you didn't answer my question," I said, and just in case he was evading me on purpose I decided to remind him, "You promised me today, Wren."

"You're relentless," he breathed, walking over and taking either side of my face gently in his hands. "We have all day. You'll get your answers– just let me get something to eat." He kissed my forehead, and turned to grab a pair of clothes from his dresser. "Meet you in the kitchen?"

"Right," I said, quickly heading for the door. He probably wanted a moment alone to change, and I needed a minute to freshen up so I padded across the hall to the bathroom. I scrubbed my face with soap and cool water, and then rinsed my mouth again with mouthwash. I decided to pull a hairbrush through my tangles, hopelessly trying to smooth my thick mane. Not that it seemed to matter. He'd already witnessed my "just-rolled-out-of-bed" look–the look that virtually no girl wants the guy she has a major crush on to see. Still, he didn't appear to be put off by it in any sense.

In the kitchen, Wren was bent at the waist, peering into the fridge. He'd put on a charcoal T-shirt that fit snugly against his frame–only slightly less distracting than his bare chest–and a pair of holey jeans. He reached for the carton of eggs and a package of bacon.

"Coffee grounds are up in that cupboard." He nodded toward the cabinet above the stove. "I assume you want your morning fix."

A slow smile pulled at my mouth. I stood on the tips of my toes to open the cupboard and retrieved the red container and a paper filter. The coffee machine was a basic model–fill the back with water, push the start button. Wren stepped beside me, reaching for a couple of frying pans in the drawer beneath the stove.

"You want to do the honors?" he asked, gesturing toward the stove burner.

I shook my head. "Can't use magic for personal gain."

He lifted a customary eyebrow. "What happens if you do?"

"There are consequences for using magic to your personal advantage; nature would punish me in some way."

"You have to practice don't you?"

"Well sure," I said, "but there's a difference between training and personal gain. Believe me."

"That hardly sounds reasonable." He turned the knob on the stove, lighting the burner the old-fashioned way.

"There has to be a line somewhere." I shrugged. "Otherwise what's to stop me from casting spells on people who piss me off or giving myself some added enhancements?" I looked down at my bust, still wishing I were at least a full cup size bigger than what I was.

Wren caught my meaning. "There's nothing wrong with the way you look," he said firmly. I watched him spray the pan with coconut oil and then peeled a few layers of bacon from the package and set them in the pan with a sizzle. He then cracked two eggs simultaneously before dropping them in the other pan. "How do you like your eggs?" he asked me, gazing up through thick eyelashes.

"Scrambled," I said. "No spices."

"Duly noted."

"What about you?" I asked.

"Raw."

I made a face, knitting my eyebrows together in disgust.

"Wolf humor," he said. "I just wanted to see your reaction. I'm more of an eggs-in-a-basket kind of guy."

"Oh," I said. "So, do you–you know, hunt and stuff when you're a wolf?"

"Sometimes," he said.

"What's it like... being a wolf?" I wondered aloud, recalling the dream that I'd had about the wolf hovering over the river. I remembered feeling like everything was heightened–all my senses enhanced. Life had taken on a whole new meaning and my human senses seemed dull in comparison. Was it like that every time; could you remember the experiences? "Are you still... you?"

"I am," he said, "but, the more primal part of myself. I have control over what I'm doing and know why I'm doing it, but, basic instincts take over in wolf form. It gets hard sometimes–to separate the two halves."

"What do you mean?"

"Well, I can Change whenever I want, right? So, if I wanted, I could stay a wolf. My father told me stories when I was a kid about a man who had lost his wife in a house fire. He couldn't cope with reality, so he shed his human skin permanently, and chose to live the rest of his days in wolf form. The longer you wear your animal skin, the less human you become. Your mind stops functioning like a human's would, and you lose all connection to your emotions and start thinking like an animal. For some, being a wolf is predominant, and when you can't learn to separate the two lives, you start showing physical signs."

"Like what?"

"Like, maybe one of your eyes gets stuck in wolf form, and you walk around with one human, and the other glowing like a neon beacon." He grinned and poured my scrambled eggs onto a plate, and retrieved a fork from the drawer. "You want any toast?" he asked.

"Please," I said. "So how do they explain that–enhancement," I decided on the word, "to normal, non-Supernatural people?"

"They probably just say they have contacts." Wren shrugged. "But those types tend to be more reclusive and don't spend much time among humans anyway."

"Do werewolves live in packs like wolves?"

He nodded. "Most werewolves travel or live together in packs, yes," he said. The coffee machine beeped then, letting us know that it was done percolating. Wren opened the cupboard next to the sink and retrieved two mugs. "Sugar is there," he pointed to the middle canister on the counter, "and there's cream in the fridge."

"Thanks," I said, helping myself as he worked on the toast. "What's the longest you've ever stayed a wolf–you know, before..."

"I started to lose myself?" He looked at me then, his brilliant eyes piercing mine. "A couple of weeks."

"What happened?" I asked softly. He picked up our plates and carried them across the kitchen to a small, square table that sat in a sun-room type nook. The thick, mouthwatering scent of our breakfast had saturated the air, and my stomach grumbled on cue. I followed him with our coffee mugs, and sat down beside him at the table. He held up his right hand, gesturing to the crescent shaped scar.

"Because of this," he said. "It's a long story."

"I'm not going anywhere." I reached over, placing my palm on his forearm. I wanted to learn everything about him.

"What did my dad say to you last night?" he wondered aloud suddenly.

"He told me about the legend of your creation," I said, "about the witches, and how your line of werewolves came to be."

Wren nodded, biting into a strip of bacon and chewing methodically while he thought. "We used to have a pack," he said gruffly. "Niall was the Alpha Master, and my mother, Gabriella, was the Alpha female." *So she is a werewolf,* I thought. "It wasn't a large pack; there were maybe ten of us all together. My father has some Cherokee in him if you couldn't tell," he smirked at that, "so, our pack lived by the laws inherit of the land and by the Native traditions.

"Niall didn't like us to spend too much time in our wolf skin. See, my Uncle Remy was killed by a hunter. He was being careless, running through the edges of town, toying with the townsfolk. He'd always been wilder–the first to break the rules, and eventually it cost him his life.

"When we die, or become seriously injured in wolf form, our body returns to its human shape. The hunter who killed my uncle saw him Change." Wren looked at me, eyes hardening. "Niall had to clean up the mess."

I swallowed hard. "You mean..." I couldn't make myself say it.

"It was pack law back then," Wren said quietly. "We don't necessarily abide by human regulation. The pack felt that they were separate from the rules that were meant to govern humans. But, once you have human blood on your hands it kind of messes with your emotional state of mind. Niall had a tough time with my uncle's death, but I think he suffered more than any of us realized when he ended that hunter's life. After that, he banned us from Changing at will–we were restricted to the Moon Change. He was only trying to keep us safe, but there were others who didn't want to follow the pack law.

"It's extremely difficult–to not become the wolf," Wren said, picking up his coffee mug. "Your skin gets uncomfortable, like you're wearing a suit that's not tailored to your body–like an itch you're not allowed to scratch. You get grouchy. Tension arises. Inevitably, the pack started breaking the rules.

"One of the men, Reese, challenged my father for the Alpha Master position. He said that Niall was neglecting his duty as pack leader and wasn't emotionally stable to lead us anymore. An Alpha Challenge is a very serious matter in pack hierarchy; it's meant to be a fight to the death. Traditionally, you fight on the second night of the full moon, when you're at physical peak in the Moon Change.

"My mother begged Niall to renounce his title," Wren said. "She claimed that she didn't want him to risk his life. Reese was bigger– stronger–younger. And Niall *wasn't* emotionally stable. So, when the midnight hour came, my father renounced his title and conceded to the dual. My mother, however, did not renounce her title, and chose to run off with the new Alpha." There was a bitterness to his words as he said this, as if there was a bad taste in his mouth he just couldn't spit out fast enough. "I was only four then, but she took me and the rest of the pack with her. That's when we moved out West."

"I'm sorry," I said softly. "I can't imagine how difficult that must have been for both you and Niall."

"Yeah, well, even in the wolf world, females tend to pull rank. They're the masterminds and true leaders of the operation, and a strong female needs a strong male. Niall didn't fit the category anymore."

"Still," I said, "She was his mate. Doesn't loyalty mean anything to wolves?"

"It's just our way," he said indifferently.

"Is that how *you* feel?" My eyes grew wide waiting for his answer.

"No," he said, "loyalty means everything to me." He reached for me then, gently tugging me out of my chair and into his arms. "You should know that I'm attracted to the fact that you're a strong and powerful female, though."

I giggled. "Too bad I'm not a wolf."

"I wouldn't want you to be," he said softly.

My fingertips brushed across his scar, tracing the moon-like pattern. "So what happened here?" I asked again.

Wren looked away, his expression shifting into something that mirrored betrayal. "Reese was trying to teach me a lesson. He liked to frequent the local Were-bar, flaunt his alpha status. It takes a lot of alcohol to get us buzzed," he said derisively, "but he'd find a way to manage and come home fighting mad and start wailing on my mom. We have a natural tendency to be more aggressive than humans, but that's not an excuse to beat on women." Wren growled, and I could feel the vibration of it through his chest as he held me in his arms. "I've always tried to protect her. But without fail, she would side with him–or make some excuse for him. The way he behaved–he wasn't an alpha. He didn't know anything about being a good leader. Everyone was blinded by his false charms and pretenses. I couldn't stand by it anymore, so, I challenged him to an Alpha dual."

I shifted in his arms, gazing up into his caramelized eyes.

"He laughed in my face of course–told me that I'd never have what it takes to be an alpha. He was giving me this speech about how he would be the only alpha our pack would ever see, and I needed to get any notion of being Alpha Master out of my head. He shoved me, just enough to get my blood going. I could feel the Change coming on right there in the kitchen, I lunged for him, but my mom slammed into me from the side. I slid into the kitchen table, reached out to catch myself when she brought a serrated knife down on my hand. It went all the way through, pinning me to the table." He rubbed the mark on the back of his hand absently. "Maybe you can understand now why I have such high standards for loyalty."

"I don't get it…" I breathed. "Was she trying to protect you in some sadistic sort of way?"

"No," he said sternly. "She told me that a threat made against the

Alpha was a threat made against her. She twisted the knife, and abjured me from the pack."

Banished. Her own son–her own flesh and blood.

I thought of my own mother, her gentle and protective ways. She'd never lifted a hand against me, at least not in a way that would ever make me question her love for me. I didn't know Gabriella from Eve, but I knew I could never respect her for what she had done to Wren.

"So you came here," I said after a long moment.

"So I came here."

"And then *I* almost got you killed."

"You didn't," he said, tightening his arms around me. "I entered those woods by my own free will."

"Yeah, but Hunter was my responsibility. I wish you would have told me what you were sooner," I said softly, tipping my forehead to his.

"I didn't want to scare you." He lifted his hand, tucking a strand of hair behind my ear. "I should have known you were fearless."

"I wouldn't quite go that far," I snorted. "But that brings me to yet another topic of discussion… How did you know what I was?"

"Ah. *That.*" He sighed. He was looking at me like he wished I hadn't asked. If I didn't know any better, I'd say he was embarrassed, though his face didn't flush with color. "Do you really want to know?"

"I wouldn't have asked if I didn't."

"What would you say if I told you that I've known who you were for a while now?"

"I'd ask just how long 'a while' is." I looked at him suspiciously.

"For a couple of years," he answered. "I saw you and your mom celebrating the summer equinox in the woods. It was a full moon, so it wasn't like I was spying on you or anything. I was keeping my distance. It was still against pack law to be seen in our fur pelts–even to other Supernaturals. I could feel your power stretching out through the forest. I know it sounds crazy, but it felt like you were reaching for me somehow; like I was being pulled to you by some unseen force of nature. I didn't know who you were then, but I knew–even from a distance–that I had to be part of your world. Even if you'd never know me, just knowing that you existed was somehow enough for me."

He was looking at me in that knowing way of his, and I felt myself turning to putty in his hands. I wanted to say something that matched the way his words had made me feel, but they'd hit me with such a force I hadn't been prepared for. I sat there, gazing into his eyes, feeling the electric surge pulsing in steady beats between us, knowing, somehow, that I was anchored to him.

"Now I've scared you," he decided.

"Not at all," I said, "just the opposite, really." Enamored, definitely, but scared? Not in the slightest. "I have an odd sort of question to ask you."

"I'm now your open book," he said, letting me know it was safe to continue.

"That first day in the coffee shop... I could sense that you were *different*. Witches have this built-in alarm system that goes off anytime they encounter a new Supernatural. I didn't know what you were, but I knew you were different. Usually, when I make the visual connection, the alarm stops ringing, but with you it only heightened. The next day when you grabbed my arm after English class, it finally stopped going off. I was curious as to whether or not you could feel it, too?"

Wren frowned contemplatively. "It's not the same with wolves," he said. "We can sense other werewolves, but we're kept in the dark from other Supernaturals."

"Hmm," I murmured. "I wonder why it was different with you."

"That remains a mystery," he said.

I brushed my fingertips across the coin at his throat. "Who is this?" I asked.

"Saint Francis," he replied, "patron saint of animals. My grandmother gave this to me when I was a small boy, it's meant to keep me safe, or so she says." He reached up, fingertips brushing against mine as he reached for the coin.

"I didn't peg you for much of the religious type." I grinned.

"No?" He lifted an eyebrow. "I suppose I'm just full of surprises, then."

"I hope you never stop surprising me." I tightened my arms around his neck, pressing a careful kiss to the bruise on the side of his throat.

The very scent of his skin was intoxicating, spiraling through my senses in a way that made me dizzy.

"Niall is awake," Wren said, and just like that, I was surprisingly sober. I made a move to get off his lap, but he only tightened his hold, grinning deviously.

"I don't know how it is with werewolves, but on my side of the forest, I was taught to have respect for my elders. I don't want Niall thinking I'm a harlot."

Wren laughed, his chest rumbling. For the first time, I saw a full smile stretch across his face. When he smiled like that, I wondered if the sun grew envious of his rays. I hadn't thought it was possible for him to look any godlier, but I was wrong. "Relax," he told me. "Niall won't think anything of it."

"Still," I said.

"Okay, fine." Reluctantly, Wren loosened his hold on me and I slipped back into the chair beside him. He picked up his mug, sipping on his coffee–shooting me an estranged look that made me second guess where I stood with him.

"Morning," Niall said, rounding the corner into the kitchen. He was wearing a pair of black sweats and a holey Carolina Panther's football T-shirt. I was surprised to see him wearing something so... *human.*

"Morning," Wren answered dryly.

"Feeling better, son?"

"I'll live."

"Good, because we need to talk about what happened last night." Niall looked directly at me as he said this, and I felt myself go rigid in the kitchen chair.

"Dad, come on, give her a minute to digest breakfast." Wren rose from his chair and carried his plate to the kitchen sink.

"We can't just ignore what happened," Niall said gruffly–his tone matching the cool look in his eyes. The worry line between his brows deepened into a groove that was shaped like a mountain peak.

"He's right," I said meekly. It was too easy to get caught up in Wren–harder to remember that there were other important things that needed addressed from last night's events. I watched as Wren gripped the edges of the sink, the muscles in his back tightening and expanding. He lowered his head, rolling his neck from side to side before turning to look at me.

"I believe that the original Dark Witch has returned," Niall spoke clearly. "I don't believe she is strong enough to rejoin with her human body quite yet, but there's no denying that she has presence here."

The kitchen fell silent, and I was holding my breath–afraid that if I breathed, they would hear the jaggedness of it and take me for a coward.

"How," I heard myself say aloud, "how has she returned?"

"It's Black Magic," Wren answered. "You give something enough power, then that power takes shape."

"Like a summoning?" I questioned.

"More than likely, but it would take something dark... blood calling blood." Niall scratched at his chin thoughtfully. "Perhaps a direct descendant from her bloodline, and they would have to possess something of hers to call her forth."

I remembered my vision when I touched Wren's body after he'd been attacked. The vision jolted me somewhere far in the past, and I recalled the opal-like sheen from the stone I'd seen hanging from the witch's throat. "Like an amulet?"

"Could be," Niall said, "though it would be very old."

"I've seen it," I told him. I sucked in a breath of air before explaining what little detail I received in my vision. I told them about the Darkness I'd felt, and how it consumed her. I could see the amulet in my mind now, luminously clear as though I were holding a photograph of it in my hands. "I know someone who might be able to help us track down the amulet's whereabouts."

"Can this person be trusted?" Wren asked with hesitation.

"I don't know her well," I admitted, "but she's a witch, like me. She works at the Magic Shoppe with her aunt, Penny, and I've known Penny since I was a small girl. Penny can be trusted." I was willing to bet my life on it.

"It's a risk we're going to have to take," Niall said. "Just leave out as much detail as you can. We don't want the humans to start asking the wrong sort of questions."

"Which begs the question of what we're supposed to do when we find the amulet?" Wren shifted, leaning up against the counter.

"Destroy it," I said instinctively. "Vanquish her for real this time."

"Yes," Niall agreed. "I fear she'll be keeping close watch over you, White Witch. Whatever drew her in has been magnified by your powers. I think you wounded her somehow, but it won't take long for her to recover, and you'll need to be ready when she comes knocking."

"You think she's after Quinn?" Wren wheeled on his father, squaring his shoulders in a way that made him seem bigger than he was. His presence swallowed the kitchen. Or I was just getting smaller.

"I had my suspicions of her return after the wolves showed up," Niall spoke slowly. "I could feel the change in the forest–sense the Darkness creeping in. I believe that her original intentions involved the wolves alone, but something shifted last night beneath the shadows. There's something about you that's made her hungry. I don't know much about the Dark Witch apart from our legend, but I could feel the devastation she felt when you cast that fire circle and shut out the Darkness."

"Fire circle?" Wren narrowed his eyes.

"You were out," I said, waving it off.

"I'm worried that she's marked you for it," Niall said, the hard look in his eye betrayed him, for I could see the fear behind it.

I could feel the cold creeping in, draping across my shoulders like a blanket of ice that melted down my spine. I didn't want to believe it. I'd blocked the possibility from my mind, but as Niall relayed his speculations, I knew he was right. I remembered the Darkness cradling me–beckoning me to give in to her tantalizing lure. The temptation was unlike anything I'd ever felt before.

But my unequivocal need to save Wren was stronger.

Chapter Thirteen
Frankenstein

Niall and Wren decided that I needed around-the-clock "supervision" until we knew more about what the Dark Witch was truly after; Wren valiantly assigned himself as my personal bodyguard. Not that I was exactly protesting the idea; it would be nice to have someone hanging around with a heightened sense of smell, incredible eyesight and superhearing abilities in case something should go awry. However, explaining to everyone else why he wasn't leaving my side might be a little trickier to get around.

A pensive expression drew Wren's features together as we drove through town. His left hand gripped the steering wheel tightly while his right rested just above my knee, gently stroking. "What's wrong?" I asked, studying his profile.

"I don't like our plan," he said ardently.

"You have a better idea?" I challenged. "And one that doesn't involve running away," I added. I couldn't do that to my father. He'd already been through enough heartache with my mother–there was no sense in twisting the knife of despair any deeper. This, in and of itself, was also why I couldn't tell him what was going on. I didn't want him to worry when there was absolutely nothing he could do to help.

"I just want you out of harm's way," he said, tightening his grip on the wheel. I watched his knuckles turn white as his skin expanded over the bones.

"I can handle this." I forced a smile of assurance, hoping it revealed strength in place of uncertainty. The truth was I'd never gone up against any form of evil, or had to use my magic to defend myself–except for last night being a first. I felt stronger now–unashamed of what I could do, but thinking of the way the Dark Witch's voice echoed in the trees was enough to get my skin crawling. I could hear the sharpness of it, the beguiling lure of her tone even now.

We were turning up the street in front of Annabelle's house, and my stomach flopped when he cut the engine. I knew her parents would be at church, and Caitlyn could sleep through a tornado siren–in fact–Caitlyn could sleep through the tornado itself, assuming it wouldn't lift her out of bed.

"You ready?" I turned to Wren, squeezing his hand. He shot me a piercing look and snorted. "We have to tell her, Wren, she's my best friend."

"I'm not playing a round of twenty questions," he said. "I'm not some bizarre science experiment that needs dissecting."

I nodded once, looking up into his eyes. For whatever reason, my mind flicked back to the conversation we'd shared about *Frankenstein*, and Wren's sympathy toward the monster. The realization clicked like the last puzzle piece fitting into place. He never asked for this life–yet here he was–part of it anyway. But Wren wasn't a monster. Even if he saw himself that way.

I looped my fingers through his as we walked up the drive, around the side of the house, and up to the back door. I reached for the key hidden behind the drain spout, and fished it into the brass lock. But Annabelle was already there, pulling the door open. There was a hard set to her jaw, her eyes were wide and shining with accusations I just knew she couldn't wait to hurl. She stretched her arm across the doorway, blocking our entrance.

"What gives?" I asked, narrowing my eyes.

"I was just wondering if tall, dark, and mysterious needed to be invited in?" She raised her eyebrows, shooting him a suspicious glance.

"He's not a vampire." I scowled. Beside me, Wren gave a derisive chuckle, jamming his hands into his pockets.

"Am I supposed to be relieved?" she asked, still blocking the entryway. "He looks pretty good for someone who was practically dead by the description you gave me on the phone last night."

"Step aside, would you?" I pushed by her, and led the way into her bedroom where I closed the door after everyone was inside. Annabelle was still glowering as she crossed her arms over her chest. She was wearing her yellow smiley-face pajamas, and the irony of her disgruntled attitude was not lost on me. I stifled a small giggle.

"What's so funny?"

"Nothing," I said, clearing my throat.

"You two better start explaining because I'm going out of my mind trying to figure out what could have happened, and my imagination is starting to derail." She lifted her hands, dramatically accentuating the gesture. "Not to mention, I didn't get an ounce of sleep last night."

Join the club, I thought. "Well, you better buckle up because I can almost guarantee that it's worse than whatever you've imagined."

"Should I sit down for this? I'm going to sit down," she decided at once, and plopped down onto her mattress, smoothing the hem of her shirt.

I took a deep breath, casting a nervous glance in Wren's direction. He stood beside me, a statuesque vision of ease. Better to just get it over with, I thought. "Wren is a werewolf," I blurted before I could stop myself. Wren rolled his eyes, but said nothing. Annabelle, to my surprise, remained expressionless. I gave her a minute to process.

"Go on," she said evenly.

I started from the beginning, explaining how my vision had altered and what had happened in the woods. I told her about the other wolves, and the Dark Witch and the tale that Niall had told me. Annabelle listened intently, nodding or shaking her head every now and then while I talked. Her face remained calm, like a carefully constructed porcelain mask. She sat there after I finished, gazing toward some far-off galaxy.

"Annabelle?"

She held up a finger. "I just need… one more minute."

Wren sighed, sinking back against the bedroom wall. I shot him a look. "Hey," he said, "I wasn't the one who thought this was a good idea."

"It's fine," Annabelle replied. "I'm fine."

"Your heart is racing like a hummingbird's," he told her.

"You can hear that?" She sounded amazed. "How good *is* your hearing?"

Now it was Wren's turn to shoot me a look, and in my mind, I heard him repeating, "*I'm not playing a round of twenty questions. I'm not some bizarre science experiment that needs dissecting.*"

"Look," I said, holding up my hands, "you both need to get over whatever hang-ups you have toward one another. It's ridiculous and juvenile. I care about you both, and I'm not here to play mediator. So just–be nice. We have a world to save and that means we have to work together."

"Fine," Annabelle said, "we'll call for a temporary reprieve."

"Fine," Wren agreed.

"Well if we're going to work together, we should probably know each other's strengths and weaknesses," Annabelle said.

Wren crossed his arms over his chest. "You first."

"I think quickly on my feet, and I'm a great problem-solver."

"And your weaknesses?" Wren lifted a trademark eyebrow.

"I'm human?" She shrugged. "Your turn."

"I don't like talking about myself."

"I'd call that an understatement," Annabelle snorted. "Come on, Wolf Boy–tell us a little about yourself. What makes you a viable asset to our team?"

His eyes were fixed on her like pointed daggers. His irises began to swirl with bright shades of neon yellow, glowing with agitation. I was sure that if he cracked a glimmer of a smile, his canine teeth would be exposed beneath his lips.

"Whoa," Annabelle breathed, staring at his eyes.

"Superhuman strength and speed, hearing, and sense of smell," I said, "are just a few of the basics." I reached out, wrapping my fingers around Wren's wrist to calm him. I thought it best to leave out the fact that he didn't have sparing patience, though I gathered that was just a Were thing.

"I don't suppose you have a strong aversion to silver?" Annabelle guessed.

"It's tolerable to be around so long as it doesn't touch me," he said.

"What happens if it does?"

"Then it burns," he said. "But I heal quickly."

"Fascinating. What about silver bullets?"

He made a small laughing sound, the deep rumble catching in his throat. "Survivable, as long as it doesn't hit me in the heart and I dig it out right away."

"Wolfsbane?"

"Extremely toxic," he answered.

"What about wooden stakes, crosses, or anything else of that caliber? Do they affect you in any way?"

He leaned forward from the wall, smiling wryly.

"Anna, he's not a vampire," I reminded her.

"But they are real, aren't they?" She was looking at me in a way that led me to believe she didn't want to know the answer. Knowing that your best friend was a witch was one thing–especially when you lived in a small town like Silver Mountain where virtually nothing exciting ever happened. It was like we were living in a snow globe. Sure, all those other things existed, but only outside the safety of our walls. But those walls were made of glass, and glass houses were breakable.

"The world is filled with more Supes than you can imagine," I answered softly.

"Fascinating," she repeated.

Silence settled over the room. As I watched Anna taking it all in, I wished, not for the first time, that I could have spared her from this part of my life. I remembered how good it felt to share who I was with her all those years ago, but a nine-year-old could never understand the repercussions of what the future would bring. Because of me, she would never be truly safe.

"I think that's enough for now," I said. "I need to change. I don't want Dad asking any questions about last night." I picked my track bag up off the bedroom floor and swung the strap around my shoulder. "Do you two think you can manage not to kill each other while I step out?"

"Now who's being juvenile," Annabelle retorted. Wren's lips

twitched. I ducked out of her bedroom and into the hall bathroom where I changed into a pair of clean jeans and a royal-blue thermal. It wasn't super chilly outside, but the sleeves would hide the scratches I'd received from tripping in the woods and getting tangled up in the underbrush.

I took a couple of minutes to freshen up before heading back to Annabelle's bedroom. I was about to turn the doorknob when I caught the tail-end of a conversation.

"–been headstrong for as long as we've been friends, but she needs someone to look out for her whether she wants to admit it or not," Annabelle was saying.

"You don't think I can be that for her?"

"All I'm saying is that you don't know her like I do. She's been through a lot, and I don't want to see her get hurt again. I know she comes across like she's this strong and capable person, but she's more fragile than she lets on."

"You should give her more credit," Wren said evenly. There was no malice in his voice, just honesty. "I get that you've been looking out for her since she shared her secret with you, and it's in your nature to protect her, but she *is* strong. And you should know that I'd *never* let anything happen to her."

Annabelle fell silent for a moment, and I imagined her sitting across from him, gazing into his eyes as she pursed her lips in thought. Annabelle was like a human-lie-detector. She had this way of looking at you–her eyes boring into the part of your brain that determined whether you were being truthful.

"This is all just… very weird," she decided.

"Yeah, well, you should be used to it by now, *Cat*."

"If you're going to keep calling me that, I'm going to start calling you *Dog*, or something as equally derogatory."

"Been called worse," he said.

"Oh, I have no doubt about that."

I decided that now was an appropriate time to let myself back in the room. "Still alive I see," I stated.

"Don't look so surprised," Annabelle said, lightly punching Wren in the arm. "He's not so bad if you can overlook the fleas and the scratching.

Not to mention the smell." She mimicked waving her hand in front of her nose.

"Hilarious," he retorted.

"So," Annabelle clapped her hands together, "what's the plan?"

"We're going to see Blaire," I told her. "Find out if she can help us track down the amulet or give us any leads on the Dark Witch's bloodline. We need to figure out why she's returned and how we can stop her."

"Good idea. Just let me get changed. Meet you in the kitchen?"

"Sure." Wren followed me down the hall, and into the kitchen where Caitlyn was standing with her back to us at the sink, filling a coffee pot with water in one hand, and had her cell pressed up against her ear with the other. She was wearing a satin pink robe, matching fuzzy pink slippers, and her hair pulled up in curlers.

"I don't care, Becky. If she doesn't cough up the money, then she can't do the event with us. The girls are tired of covering for her. Like, if you can't afford to do these events, then you don't need to be in the sorority." Caitlyn spun toward the coffee maker, but her eyes landed on Wren, widening. "Let me call you later. Yeah. Okay, bye." She put the phone down on the counter. "Quinn, hi," she said, smiling as though we'd totally caught her off guard. She reached up, straightening a curler that was sliding out of place.

"Hi Caitlyn."

"You just get in?" she asked, glancing from me to Wren.

"Oh. No," I lied. "We're just going out. We're waiting on Annabelle."

"Who's your friend?" she asked, still smiling in that flirtatious way girls do whenever they see something they like.

"Wren," he answered, his deep voice drawing her in that much more.

"Oh, it's nice to meet you. I'm Caitlyn." She reached across the island counter to shake his hand. "You must be the fast runner Quinn told me about?"

"He's still in high school, Caitlyn," Annabelle said as she sauntered down the hallway, slipping into her army-green jacket. "And spoken for."

"I wasn't–" She struggled to finish the sentence and a pretty crimson blush creeped over her porcelain skin. "I was just…" she gestured to the coffee pot, picked it up and then mumbled something inaudible as she poured the water in the back compartment. "Where are you going, anyway?"

"Town," Annabelle answered, "I'll be back before dinner."

"Good, it's your night to do the dishes." Caitlyn spun on her heel and strode off down the hall.

"If there's an art to getting under people's skin, I think you've mastered it," Wren told her.

"Wolf Boy made a funny, someone better alert the press."

I pressed my lips together to keep from laughing. Wren smirked, and wrapped his hand around mine as we headed for his car.

My breakfast settled like a weight in the bottom of my stomach when we pulled up in front of the Magic Shoppe. The two-story structure sat back from the sidewalk; a once proud roof slouched against the veteran brick. Nestled between Serendipity's and Snow Lily's, the Magic Shoppe was painted a deep, blueish-purple and surrounded by dozens of pink, tea rose bushes. I gazed up at the second story window, watching as some clouds rolled by, reflecting in the thin, mirrored glass.

"Shall we?" I slipped out of the car and started up the sidewalk. The crystal chimes sang when we walked in, gently pinging against the glass. A few customers looked up from display cases, and just as quickly glanced away.

Wren's eyes scanned the room, soaking in the detail in one swift motion. He lifted his face, and I could tell he was sampling the air, picking up scents I couldn't detect. Penny stepped from the back room with a couple of old books and sat them down at the counter before looking up. When she spotted me, her lips parted in surprise. She recovered quickly, and smiled.

"Well hello there," Penny said, "to what do I owe the pleasure, and again so soon?" She reached up, grasping the black stone that was threaded around her neck. It matched her gown and old-fashioned black corset.

"I was actually hoping to see Blaire." I pressed my lips into a smile, stepping up to the register. Penny's eyes swept up to meet Wren's face, keeping her expression unreadable. She glanced back at me, spotting the pendant that Blaire had given me. A dark cloud seemed to pass over her features in shadow. I watched her eyes click to the side, like she was working out a difficult equation in her head before clarity struck.

"Blaire isn't here, actually. She decided to visit the university today. I'll be sure to tell her you stopped by, I'm certain she'll be sorry to have missed you. Thanks for stopping in, though," she said dismissively.

"Sure," I said, feeling my eyes narrow in confusion. "See you around, Penny." Wren's hand gently gripped my upper arm, steering me back toward the exit with Annabelle trailing close behind.

"Okay, that was weird right?" I asked once we got back to Wren's car. The afternoon sun settled over my shoulders, chasing away the chill from the shop's atmosphere.

"Very un-Penny-like," Annabelle agreed.

"She was lying," Wren said. "There was someone else upstairs, I could smell them."

"So weird," Annabelle commented under her breath. Wren pretended not to hear her, but I could see the muscle tightening in his jaw.

"We don't know that she was lying about Blaire not being there," I said. "It could have been another family member, or anyone."

"Are you sure she's as reliable as you say?" Wren challenged further, hovering over top of me in a way that made me lean into the side of his car. He had the ability to loom without knowing he was.

"I've known her my whole life." I shrugged.

"Could it have been because of Wren?" Annabelle guessed.

"Not standing right here or anything," he said wryly.

"It's just an observation," Annabelle said. "Nothing personal."

"No, you're right," I said, "I noticed something there, too. It was like she was looking at us like she knew something we didn't."

"She's not a witch, right?" Wren asked.

"No." I shook my head.

"Then there's no way she could have known about us."

"Well," Annabelle sighed, "now what?"

"I don't know. Blaire was the only lead I had on tracking down that amulet."

"We can try again tomorrow after class," Annabelle suggested. "I mean, who knows? Maybe Penny will surprise us and actually give Blaire the message. Maybe she was busy and we were just misinterpreting the signs."

"That's a lot of maybes to bank on," Wren said, closing the door after we had slid into the car. He walked around the front of the hood, gliding into the driver's seat as he dug the key into the ignition.

"Could you do a locating spell?" Annabelle asked me.

"Nope, that only works on specific people, not objects."

"A lost and found spell?"

"Now you're just making things up." I eyed her over my shoulder, grinning at her attempt to lighten the mood. "It's okay," I tried forcing enthusiasm into my voice, "I don't think we're in any danger from the Dark Witch during the daylight hours."

"What makes you think that?" Wren lifted a customary eyebrow.

"Well, my mother once told me that the true face of evil could only take place under the cloak of shadow. If this witch is as evil as it gets, then she has no power in the sunlight. Nature always finds a balance," I said.

"Then how do you explain demi-demons and the Dark Witch's werewolf lackeys?" Annabelle asked skeptically.

"They still have their souls," I said. "They might have their toe dipped in the pool of evil, but that doesn't mean they're the true faces of what evil represents. To be evil, you must give your soul to the Darkness, turning your back on nature. There's no coming back from that."

"But that doesn't mean that you're not in danger," Wren reminded me, pulling away from the curb. "Especially with the other werewolves on the loose."

"So what do we do now?" Annabelle asked.

"Let's go to Jo's," I said. It was almost noon now, and I'd been up since dawn. If I couldn't talk with Blaire, I was going to need something to distract myself, and I felt like we all could benefit from a little normalcy.

"Great idea," Annabelle said, "I'm starving."

Jo's was packed. The regular lunch crowd shuffled in after the church services had ended, leaving us pressed to find an open table. The atmosphere was thick with the scent of cooking food, and the hum of mingled chattering. There was a small booth (meant for two) over by the window, but we managed to squeeze in. Wren sat beside me, his thigh pressing against mine beneath the table. He reached for the laminated menus in the metal holder, distributed them across the table.

"You know," Annabelle was saying as she scanned the menu, "I could probably check the antique shop to see if they've sold any old jewelry lately. If you could draw the amulet for me, I could show them a picture for reference."

"Even if they had, they'd never give out the name of the person they sold it to," I said. "Customer confidentiality."

"True, but at least we'd know whether or not the amulet was close."

"It would have to be, right?" Wren said. "Why else would she be *here* of all places? She'd have to return to the location she was summoned."

"It's not a bad idea, Anna, but, I think this particular piece of jewelry would have to be a family heirloom. We think that she could only be summoned by someone from her direct bloodline. Blood calling blood," I said quietly.

"Makes sense," Annabelle said, flipping over her menu. "It's just kind of scary to think that it could be anyone. I mean, we've known all of these people," she glanced around the room, "since we were kids. It's practically impossible to keep a secret around here."

"But not entirely impossible," I said, knowing firsthand that it could in fact be done. "I just don't get why it's happening *now*, though." My head was starting to ache from the layers of mystery that seemed to be multiplying. Every question I had was met with a speculated answer at best, usually resulting in more questions. They tangled in my head like the lines of a complicated road map, forking off in different directions, stretching down lanes that had no name.

I leaned my elbows against the table, reaching up to massage both my temples. "Are you all right?" Wren asked me. His right hand moved to the small of my back. When I looked up, I could see the concern coloring his eyes.

"I'm fine," I said, forcing a small grin, "just... tired."

"Hi there!" Nadine appeared beside us, a bright smile plastered to her face. "Sorry about the wait, y'all know how it gets on Sunday."

"Oh, no problem," I said.

"What can I get ya'?" She beamed as her ponytail bobbed behind her. She pulled a yellow writing pad from her apron pocket, holding a pen at the ready. We ran through our orders, and Nadine rushed to scribble them down. "All right," she said, "I'll get that right in for ya' so just yell if ya' need somethin'."

As she turned to scurry off, I peeked up at Wren who was only looking at me. I flicked my eyebrow upward, but he just grinned.

Annabelle reached for her coffee mug, misjudged the distance, and sent the mug tipping over the saucer. Wren reached out and steadied the cup before it could spill. Just a few droplets sloshed over the side, running down his knuckles.

"Damn," she breathed, "nice reflexes."

"Lucky for you," he replied, rising from the table. "Back in a minute." He nodded toward the bathroom.

Annabelle looked over her shoulder after he'd gone, blinked a couple of times and then shook it off. "He's..." She struggled to find a word.

"Extraordinary," I volunteered.

She tilted her head, rolling her eyes. "He's not so bad. Now that I actually know *what* he is. I suppose you'd like to hear that you were right about him not dealing for the devil."

"I don't need you to say that," I said, aimlessly stirring my teaspoon through my coffee. "I appreciate the way you think."

"Is that a polite way of saying my mind is abnormally freakish?" She smirked.

"Not at all," I told her. "You point out things that I wouldn't naturally think of, and challenge my assumptions. You don't just tell me what I want to hear, or agree with me to shut me up." I depended on her outlook. She had a way of keeping me level, encouraging me to look outside the box.

She snorted. "So I really am your Chloe Sullivan?"

"The real brain behind the operation." I grinned, and she laughed. "I am curious though. Is it weird, knowing that he's…"

"Not human?" she whispered. "Maybe it was at first, but I'm kind of pro at this whole, Supernatural thing. I've had years to get used to the idea that there are other *things* out there that challenge the laws of the universe."

"So you're okay with everything?" She did seem a lot better now, but one could never be too sure.

"Yeah I'm okay with it. I mean, my best friend is a witch for Pete's sake." She grinned at me, the right corner of her mouth tilting just a little higher than the other. "And Wren is completely bewitched by you– no pun intended. Just thought I'd also point out *that* particular observation. I don't think he even glanced at Nadine."

"He was probably making a conscious effort not to," I said.

"I don't know Quinn. He's awfully smitten."

"Which reminds me…" I thumped a palm across my forehead, reprimanding myself for being such a horrible friend. "I didn't even ask you how the dance went."

"You're excused," Annabelle said, "after all, you were kind of saving the world and stuff. Your mind has been a little preoccupied and rightfully so."

"So…" I prompted.

"It was incredible," she sighed. "Shawn only tripped over his feet like, twice, and he was a perfect gentleman."

"So was it the magical high school experience you were missing out on?" I teased.

"I'm glad I went, if that's what you're asking." She narrowed her eyes.

"Did our little Shawny put the moves on you?" I asked, wiggling my fingers across the table, to which, only caused her to throw a straw wrapper at me.

"He kissed me," she admitted.

I mockingly clutched my hands over my heart, sighing heavily, while Annabelle blushed at least three shades of pink.

Wren returned from the bathroom, catching the tail-end of our conversation as he squeezed in beside me. He didn't ask why we were laughing, but he lifted a trademark eyebrow, picking up his coffee mug.

"So," Annabelle said a moment later, "It's going to be kind of weird going to school tomorrow and trying to act like everything is normal. I mean, how do we pretend like there's not a spirit–or whatever–of a seventeenth century evil witch on the loose while we're just sitting there in trigonometry class?"

I looked up, running my fingertips across the rim of my coffee mug. I'd thought as much myself, but didn't see how we had much of a choice in the matter. "We can't let this fear rule our lives," I decided, "but, we definitely need to be prepared as much as possible. When we drop you off, I'm going to perform a protection spell around your house just to be safe," I told her. If the Dark Witch was somehow after me like Niall feared, I wanted to be one step ahead of her.

I'd seen enough superhero films to know that the villain always used the people the hero was closest to against him. I didn't want to give the Dark Witch an opportunity to use any of the people I loved as a bargaining chip to get to me.

"What about you?" Annabelle asked. "Who's going to protect you?" She looked up at Wren expectantly.

"That goes without saying," he told her. "I'm not leaving her side."

"Does that mean you're going to follow me into the bathroom, too?"

"If I have to." He grinned, thoroughly amused by the idea.

Annabelle snickered. "Good luck getting past her dad."

"I'll sleep in the bushes if it's a matter of making sure she stays safe."

The patio door opened in front of us, and Huck, Torrance, and Jamie walked in and spotted us. "Well look who it is. I guess we can call off the search party," Huck said sarcastically, clapping a big hand over Wren's shoulder.

"Oh leave them be," Torrance said, wrapping her palm around

Huck's bicep. Normally, I wouldn't think anything of it, but now I was all too aware of the affection laced within the gesture. "You could have called, though. We were worried." She looked at me as she said this.

"Sorry," I said, "cellphone died."

"That's what Anna told us." Torrance reached over, picking a fry from Annabelle's plate as Nadine returned with our lunch.

"I will stab you," Annabelle said, picking up her fork and pointing it at Torrance. Torrance only giggled.

"Did you guys see Hunter and Owen last night?"

"Well yeah." Torrance crossed her arms over her chest. "That's why we were so worried. He said you freaked out on him in the woods or something."

"I was just feeling sick," I quickly made up an excuse. "I didn't want him to have to watch me toss my cookies. That bourbon must have hit me the wrong way."

"Lightweight." Huck laughed, shaking his head.

"Guess so. Are y'all just waking up?" I asked, looking at Jamie. He was still wearing the same clothes I'd seen him in last night. His hair was rumpled, matching the miserable expression of his face.

"Jamie had a bad night," Huck said, confirming my suspicions. "He just can't seem to pass up a good challenge."

"Beer pong again?" I asked.

"Harper won," he admitted, "but at least I didn't spend the whole night in the bathroom." He winked.

"Never going to live that down, am I?" I shook my head.

"Your only shot at redemption is if you play me again," he said.

Beside me, Wren tensed. I wasn't entirely sure if it was because of Jamie and his flirting attempt, but I lifted my left hand, placing it on top of Wren's thigh. "I don't know how you can even think of drinking again after a night like that," I said to Jamie.

"I'm a man of many talents," he joked, "so what do you say–rematch?"

"I don't think so, Jamie."

"All right," he returned, "your loss."

"Well, we better find a table," Torrance said, "I think the alcohol has soaked clean through his brain. He needs sustenance." She grabbed his shoulders, steering him away from our table.

"See you tomorrow," I said, watching them go.

"Thanks for covering for us, Cat," Wren said, reaching for one of her fries.

"You're welcome," she said, "Now keep your paws off of my food." She reached for her plate, pulling it closer to her side of the table with a warning glare, to which Wren met with a lighthearted chuckle.

Chapter Fourteen
Father Knows Best

It was mid-afternoon when we pulled into my drive. My stomach twisted itself into anxious knots, coiling in my gut. Wren pulled the Pontiac off to the right-hand side of the drive, shaded beneath the large oak tree.

"You seem tense," Wren observed, looking over at me through those long, dark lashes of his. The sunlight streaming through the window caught the tips of them, making them gleam.

"Would you believe me if I told you that you were the first boy I'd ever brought home?" I pressed my lips together, furrowing my brows.

"Well, I'd hardly call myself a boy," he said, a slow smile tugging the corners of his mouth.

"You know what I mean," I said.

"Surely I'm not the first. Jamie seemed rather comfortable around you," his tone hardened a little.

"I've had my guy friends over, but no one that I cared about. At least, not the way I care about you."

His lips twitched. "So you care about me, do you?"

Admitting this made me vulnerable, especially for the short amount of time that I'd known him. But there was something about him that I sensed was different from the very beginning. It set him apart from anyone I'd ever known. I didn't know how to explain it, but I felt like I'd known him on some deeper plane–isolated from time or space–from a very long time ago.

"You know I do," I said softly.

Wren lifted his hand, cupping the side of my face in his palm while his thumb brushed the length of my jawbone. He leaned in, pressing a tender kiss to my forehead, sending a whole new kind of rush fluttering through my insides. I wanted to be alone with him, but responsibility echoed in my mind, knowing that my dad was probably aware of the strange car parked in the drive.

"We should go inside," I said with reluctance.

"You lead the way," he said, leaning across me to open my door.

The autumn wind brushed the hair back from my face, bringing with it the scent of crisp leaves and dying grass. Wren reached for my hand, twining his fingers with mine as we headed up the walkway. As I reached for the doorknob, I could hear the television humming through the door. Sunday was Dad's favorite day to lounge around eating junk food while watching football.

I fished my key into the lock, pushed the door open.

"Hey Quinny, how was your–" he stopped short, standing in the kitchen with surprise coloring his features when he discovered that I wasn't alone. "–weekend?"

"Hey Dad, you remember Wren." I gestured over my shoulder.

"Hi there." Dad recovered quickly, placing the bowl of popcorn down on the counter while he stepped forward to shake Wren's hand (only after wiping his buttery palms on his sweater, of course.)

"Sir," Wren greeted him politely.

"Are you coming from Annabelle's?" Dad asked me. I could tell he was trying to piece Wren into the picture–figure out how he fit in.

"Jo's, actually," I said. "Annabelle and I went out for lunch, and we ran into Wren. I invited him over to work on a French assignment, thought maybe he could stay for dinner. If it's okay with you," I added quickly, "that is?"

"Uh, sure," Dad said. "Wren, would you like anything to drink? I think we have some soda in the garage. Quinn doesn't drink the stuff, but I like to have it every now and then." He chuckled.

"Water is fine, thank you," Wren said.

"I should have known," Dad said, thumping a palm against his thigh.

"You athletes are pretty health-conscious."

"It wouldn't kill you to be a little *more* health-conscious." I poked my dad in the arm on my way into the kitchen. I headed for the cupboard beside the kitchen sink, and pulled a couple of glasses down. "Dad, do you have something?"

"I'm all set," he said, pointing to his drink on the coffee table. He picked up his bowl of popcorn and started for the living room. "Do you like the Panthers, Wren?"

"I'm not much of a football fan myself, but my dad likes them."

"Oh that's right; you said your father lived around here." Dad sank down into his recliner, spilling a few pieces of popcorn over the edge of the bowl. They tumbled under the recliner–lost forever in the furniture version of the Bermuda Triangle.

"Just up and around the bend, actually," Wren said.

"Who's your father?"

"Niall Whelan."

"Ah," Dad replied. His eyes widened and then narrowed as if he were thinking something over. "I think I know the place. Your grandfather built it, right?"

"He did, yeah."

"Nice cabin." Dad rubbed his mustache thoughtfully.

"Thank you. I'll be sure to tell him you said so."

Dad nodded, followed by an awkward moment of silence. He was staring into his bowl of popcorn, lost in thought.

"Well, my books are in my room so…" I motioned over my shoulder to the set of stairs–waiting. I'd never had a guy alone in my room, and wasn't sure how my father would handle this scenario. I knew he trusted me, but we'd never had a conversation that came close to broaching the subject of boys.

I could see his gears turning, knew he must have been picturing the layout of my room. I had a desk of course, but the only place to sit was my bed. My face grew warm just thinking of him thinking of *that*. I swallowed hard.

"Uh, keep the door open Quinny. Dinner in an hour." He nodded once, and turned his attention back to the game.

I pivoted on my heel, and Wren followed me up the stairs and into my room. The sound of the game was muffled through the ceiling. As casual as ever, Wren's eyes swept over my room, appraising the plum walls, the Florence and the Machine poster, and my book case that was stuffed to the brim.

"So," he said, "French project?" He lifted an eyebrow, shooting me a look.

"It was the best I could come up with on impulse." I shrugged, reaching up and running a hand through my hair. "Sorry."

"Tu es pardonné," he surprised me by responding in a flawless French accent. *You're forgiven*, he'd said.

I lifted my eyebrows. "Well you really are just full of surprises, aren't you?"

"I took three years in Washington," he said. "All the cool kids were taking Spanish, so I rebelled."

"Oh and I suppose that somehow made you uncool?" I narrowed my eyes in disbelief; Wren had a salient sort of presence. "I mean, rebels are kind of just trend-setters, aren't they?"

"You tell me." He grinned mischievously. He walked over to the far side of my bed, lowering himself against the pillows with his back pressed against the headboard. He held my gaze, tilting his head toward the open spot beside him.

"French project," I said, grabbing my school bag and emptied the contents out into the middle of the bed. The least we could do was *look* busy.

"Right." Wren cleared his throat, playing along. He reached for a notebook, flipped it open to a blank page and grabbed a pen. "You know I'll be able to hear if he so much as shifts in his chair, right?"

"I know, but–"

"–Your dad's opinion is important to you," Wren said.

I looked up, meeting his eyes. "He's all I have left."

Wren's expression softened. He reached out, his palm covering the back of my hand. He didn't have to say anything, I knew what he was thinking–could see it in his eyes. A few moments passed before he asked, "How does your dad handle you being what you are?"

"Well," I sucked in a breath. "He married my mom knowing she was a witch," I said, "but she passed away before my power of premonition manifested. He's never said it out loud, but I know that what I can do scares him."

"How old were you?" He leaned forward, propping himself up on an elbow. There was about six inches of space between our faces, and this close, the magnitude of his summer eyes took full effect.

"Thirteen," I answered. "I'd *just* turned thirteen actually. I remember I started getting these real intense headaches, but the doctors chocked it up to puberty–told me it was just a change in hormones." I shrugged. "Annabelle and I were actually at Skate Land when the first vision happened. There was this younger girl in front of me–just learning to skate for the first time. The place was jam-packed with a sea of people flowing at one speed going around the rink. I'm good at skating, but I was not prepared for that little girl to trip right in front of me. I didn't even have time to stop. I crashed into her and hit the floor hard. It was like a domino effect after that; a few others tripped and went down with us, but this little girl just started wailing full-blown crocodile tears. I looked around for her parents–hoping that they'd seen what happened, but the little girl was cradling her arm. I reached out to comfort her, but she'd scraped her elbow pretty bad and I didn't see." I dropped my gaze, absently picking at the chipped polish on my thumbnail.

"Then what happened?" Wren folded his hand over my knee.

"Then everything went black. Pain exploded behind my eyes, and I started seeing things. I didn't know what was happening to me, but I knew it was magic related. I've always been able to feel it–sense its presence. Anyway, I saw this man standing on a platform at a construction site. Do you remember when they built the new bank in town?"

"I wasn't here for that, but I remember when it happened," he said.

"Yeah, well, I saw the scaffolding equipment that was holding up his platform collapse. The newspapers said he fell eight feet and landed on his back. He broke his collarbone, shattered his right hip, and dislocated his shoulder. He has permanent nerve damage now.

"I didn't know what I was seeing when it happened, but when I read the report a week later in the paper I knew something was wrong with me. I shouldn't have been able to see that man's future. Stuff like that doesn't happen to normal people–and what's worse was I didn't do anything to stop it," I finished.

"Don't punish yourself for that. You couldn't have known what you were meant to do." Wren squeezed my hand. "That must have been terrifying–not knowing what was happening to you." His tone was soothing, soft and deep.

"Probably no more frightening than Changing into a wolf for the first time," I ventured.

"I've answered enough questions today," he said, "I want to hear about you."

"Take turns?" I suggested hopefully.

He sighed, and I could feel his breath on my face. It sent a shiver across my skin. "Fine," he agreed. "I wasn't afraid to Change."

"I should have guessed." I marveled at his dauntless mindset. If Wren were a work of art, he'd be constructed of iron. His cerebral awareness separated him from the frailty of a human mind. He may have been man, but he embodied the wolf.

"I knew it was coming though–spent my childhood watching my pack Change, and knew what to expect."

"How old were you?"

"Eleven," he answered. "My turn."

I pursed my lips together. Perhaps Weres matured faster than humans.

"Do you like being a witch?"

I blinked rapidly and bit the inside of my lip. "I guess there's no easing into this, is there?" I snickered.

"You don't have to answer if you're uncomfortable."

"It's not that," I said, folding my hands over his. "It's a good question." My mind retreated to the dark edges of regret. The image of Nathan and his wheelchair pulled me back there–those blue eyes, always haunting me. "I did hate my powers," I said finally. "There were a lot of moments in my life that I could have stopped something from happening, and I didn't. I was afraid, and my dad was afraid that I'd get hurt... I don't ever want to be that person again. I don't want to let fear rule my life and keep me from saving the innocent."

"You won't," Wren said. "You're not your mistakes."

I looked up at him then, feeling the guilt tightening around the edges of my heart. All those moments I'd wavered in the in-between of doing what was right, and trying to protect myself at the same time.

"I understand where you're coming from, but I can easily put myself in your father's shoes. If it was a question of your life or anyone else's, that's not even a decision I'd have to think about making." He reached out, fingers tucking a strand of hair behind my ear then lingering on my collarbone.

"You can't say that," I said softly, not meeting his eyes.

"I absolutely can say that."

"That's very selfish of you." The corner of my lips rose as he brought my chin up to meet his gaze.

"Yeah, well, I'm not a hero."

"Maybe there are no heroes." Maybe we all just try to do the best we can and that's enough, or it isn't. Maybe we just complicate things by drawing a straight line and deciding that one half is black and the other is white. What if there wasn't a line at all and life was just meant to be blurry?

"Your dad is coming to check on us," Wren whispered, slipping his hands out from under mine. He reached for my French textbook and flipped to a random page, positioning himself on the far edge of my bed as I scurried to find my notes.

Knowing that a seventeenth century evil witch was possibly after me seemed minuscule in comparison to the fact that the guy I had a crush on was currently perched on my bed, and my dad was coming to check on us. *Bring on the evil witch,* I thought. At least I wasn't powerless there.

"Hey, just checking to see how it's going?" Dad poked his head around the frame of my door. I watched his jaw clench as he scanned the books spread out over the comforter; dissecting the distance between us.

"Good," I said, pretending to scrawl out a sentence. "You need help with dinner?" I looked up, meeting his eyes.

"I'm thinking pizza," Dad said. "Easier cleanup. Wren–what toppings do you like?" Dad reached into his pocket and pulled out his cellphone.

"Anything is fine, sir, thank you."

"Quinny, the usual?" Dad asked. I nodded. "Okay, call you down when it's ready." He eyed the door as he turned–inspecting the two-inch margin between my wall and the doorknob. I rolled my eyes as he left.

"I'm going to have to work hard to earn his respect, aren't I?" Wren gathered.

"Well," I sighed, "I'm all he has, too."

He grinned slowly, slinking back against the headboard. "Lucky you're worth all the trouble."

"Quinn tells me you're a carpenter," Wren said, walking his plate to the kitchen sink. Dad behaved himself through dinner, mildly steering the conversation around cross-country and academics. He'd seemed a little put off about the fact that Wren hadn't applied to any colleges yet. I watched him stroking his mustache, rolling his crumpled napkin around in his hand while he listened. He was of course quick to mention that I'd applied to SMU for the environmental science program. It seemed strange, thinking of something so humanly normal when in fact, *things* were not.

"I am," Dad replied, "I learned everything I know from my father."

"You should show him the workshop," I suggested.

"I was thinking of taking a vocational class geared around something like that," Wren added. "I like the idea of working with my hands."

Dad's eyes swept up in approval. "Oh, well, that's a respectable path. Working with your hands has a way of keeping a man honest." He stood up from the table, brushing his hands across his jeans to shake off the crumbs. "It's a bit of a trek, but I'll show you around if you're interested."

"I'd like that, thank you."

We shrugged into our jackets at the back door, and headed for the patio. The trail was mostly uphill, and I could feel the ache in my calves as we pushed through the grassy terrain.

Wren reached for my hand, his palm wrapping around mine; I could feel the warmth of his touch–his thumb tracing soothing circles across the back of my hand. I glanced up at Dad who was pretending not to notice this. He tucked his hands into his jacket pockets, clearing his throat. "So, if I remember correctly, your father married Gabriella Mullen right after graduation."

"That's right," Wren said.

"She sure was a beauty," he complimented. "A lot of people thought they were crazy for getting married so young, but you know how it is with a small town, everyone knows everyone's business. They didn't keep their opinions to themselves."

"They were probably right not to. The marriage didn't last long." Wren couldn't hide the regret from his tone.

"I sure was sorry to hear about Niall losing his brother though. That must have been really hard on him." Dad reached for the doorknob of his shop, twisting. "The town hasn't always been... kind... to your family, but, I want you to know that your father was a good man."

"Thank you, sir, he still is."

Dad nodded, pushing the door open. I frowned, making a mental note to ask him what exactly he meant by that comment... perhaps there was still more to the story then Wren had let on.

Dad flipped on the light switch, encasing the room in a fluorescent brightness. He'd worked earlier that day–I could tell because there was still a haze of fine sawdust drifting about the air and woodchips littering the cement floor. His work station was covered in an ashen film and it smelled like home; that familiar scent of cedar and pine fusing in the air.

Wren whistled appreciatively, his eyes scanning the shop and all of Dad's tools and work stations. "This is top notch," he complimented.

"It's not state of the art or anything," Dad said, hooking his thumbs through his belt loops, "but it gets the job done."

Wren asked a question about one of the electric saws, and Dad jumped in, animatedly explaining this and that while Wren listened. I couldn't tell if he was putting on a show or if he was truly engaged in whatever Dad was saying, but I liked watching them interact. It felt important that Dad approved of Wren.

While they chatted, I took it upon myself to circle the shop. My rocking horse still sat in the far corner along with a small, circular table that held other childhood trinkets and memorabilia. I used to play there while Dad worked on the other side–his way of keeping an eye on me while Mom was at work. One of Mom's potion books was lying there, covered in dust, and as I ran my fingers across the surface, I remembered a conversation we'd shared.

I was around the age of eight or nine–Mom was braiding my hair one morning before school. I was sitting in front of the bureau mirror in her bedroom, aimlessly flipping through the book of herbs and spices for potion making. Her engagement ring kept catching the early morning sunlight, reflecting from the mirror and casting little slants of shimmering light against the hand-written pages. I don't know what made my young mind think it, but I remembered asking, "Mom, how did Dad react when you told him you were a witch?"

She looked up then, meeting my eyes in the mirror. She smiled at me distantly, as if she were reaching back to recall the memory. "Well," she began, "he was doubtful at first, but he'd already fallen in love with me. I got lucky, I suppose. Your father has a gentle spirit; he's open-minded so that helped."

"Was he ever afraid?" I wanted to know, thinking that someday I'd have to share my secret with someone who might be afraid of what I could do–afraid of what I was. I wanted to be prepared.

She thought for a moment, deciding how best to answer. "I don't think he was afraid of *me*," she said, "but I think he was afraid *for* me– afraid that he wouldn't be able to protect me if the wrong kind of danger found us."

I looked up into her eyes then, the soft, fern green eyes that matched my own. The corners of her mouth tilted down, an expression of concentration pulling her features together while she worked on my hair. With her full lips, light complexion, and willowy frame, I thought she looked like a fairy goddess. She was the picture of grace, but her storybook beauty gave rival to her unwavering strength.

I knew that if danger ever did find us, she'd confront it head on and conquer it without fear. She preached caution until she was blue in the face, but looking back now, I wondered if she ever recognized that strength within herself. The people I'd known to be the strongest, often didn't realize they were. Even in the face of absolute darkness, when the world threatened to drag them to their knees, strength found a way to prevail.

She wound the elastic band around the end of my braid as she finished, the palms of her hands settling over my shoulders. "You're a dreamer Quinny," she told me. "You'll find someone special who will cherish everything about you. He'll be your counterpart–a soul equally matched."

"What will he look like?" I asked dreamily, a smile tugging the corner of my mouth as my mother wrapped her arms around me. She lowered her face next to mine, looking at our reflections in the mirror.

"He'll be tall," she decided, "and very handsome. He'll be strong, and he'll always keep you safe." She smiled, and kissed my cheek. "Come on. Off to school now. Let's save our dreams for later."

"You're quiet," Wren observed. He was helping me clean up the kitchen while Dad retired to the living room–I think–to give us a little alone time. He seemed more at ease now that they'd bonded a little over tools and manly things in the workshop.

I looked up into his eyes, reaching for his hand as I put the towel down on the counter. "I'm just... thinking," I said.

"I'd love to know about what," he said, reaching out to tuck a stray piece of hair behind my ear. His thumb brushed the corner of my mouth tenderly, and on instinct I turned my face into his palm. I wanted to wrap my arms around him, tangle my fingertips through his hair...

"About you, mostly," I admitted.

"All good things I hope?" He grinned.

"Mmm." I nodded, pressing my hand to the back of his.

"I'm going to disappear for a little while," Wren said quietly, his voice was barely an octave above a murmur. "I won't be far from your house."

Ah yes, I'd almost forgotten. "The moon," I said just as quietly. I bit down on my bottom lip, watching as his eyes followed the movement; the amber hue darkening with longing. My heart sped up beneath my rib cage, fluttering anxiously. "I want to see you," I whispered, "I want to watch you Change." My head swirled with the notion, igniting with a spark of curiosity.

"I don't know if that's such a good idea," he said, caution laced through his tone. "The others will have to Change tonight, too. I won't risk putting you in danger."

"There are more of them then there are of *you*," I reminded him. "What if *I* don't want to risk putting your life in danger–yet again?"

His eyes narrowed into slits. "Don't be obstinate." There was a trace of irritation in his voice, but it only made me feel like I was one step closer to getting what I wanted.

I scrunched my eyebrows together, forcing a stern look. "You can't make me stay," I said deliberately, enunciating slowly, hoping my delivery would achieve the desired effect. "We can keep each other safe if we stay close together. Otherwise I'll worry the whole time you're gone, and believe me–I have an incredibly overactive imagination. It knows no limits." I pursed my lips.

The muscle in his jaw worked futilely over the bone as he clenched and un-clenched his teeth. His chest expanded as he drew in a lungful of air, exhaling through his nose; the breath leaving slowly.

"You'll be able to sense if something is wrong," I added. "You give me one nudge, and I promise I'll behave as you see fit."

He lifted his customary eyebrow.

"Wren... please."

He gathered my face in his hands, his thumbs brushing over my cheekbones as he gazed deep into my eyes. "What have you done to me, woman?" He tipped his forehead to mine, holding me close. I felt the breath tighten in my chest, constricting while he touched me. "Do you think you can sneak out without your father knowing?"

"More than likely," I said, heart hammering, "he's usually asleep by ten thirty. What time do you…" I let my voice trail off.

"I can Change at any time, but if I don't bring it on myself it will happen at midnight, regardless."

I grinned. "As do all things magical."

He rolled his eyes at the turn of a smile, pulling me into his arms. My head rested just below his chin, and I could smell the earthy aroma of him; the pine clinging to his clothes and on his skin in the most divine way.

"I'll be back at eleven," he said. "Meet me down by the steps, and dress warm."

"Okay," I breathed.

He sighed again, shaking his head. "I should head out. I'll need to run home and grab a few things if I'm going to be staying the night."

My stomach bottomed out, a coil of nerves and butterflies replacing my intestines. "You are?" I asked.

"Did you think I was joking about sleeping in the bushes?" The corner of his mouth twitched.

"Well, no, I just… I wasn't sure… how that was going to work? I mean, if you stayed with me… inside the house." *Goddess* I sounded like a puritan. Not that there was anything wrong with that–to each their own–but, I didn't want him to think me so juvenile… so… *innocent.*

He chuckled, the deep sound of it rumbling in his chest. "Do you want me to stay with you… inside the house?"

"Yes," I said, meaning it.

"Superhearing, remember?"

"Right." I nodded. "Okay."

He chuckled again. "I'll be back soon," he promised, and started walking for the living room. "Thank you for having me over Mr. Callaghan, I appreciate the tour of the workshop, too."

"Sure," Dad replied, hopping out of the recliner to shake his hand. "Don't be a stranger, Wren. It was nice talking with you."

"I'll be right back, Dad, I'm just going to say goodnight." I reached for the door handle, slipping out into the darkness to avoid the awkward look I was certain my dad was standing there giving. Wren followed me out, and I closed the door behind us. With the sun having set, the temperature had plummeted significantly. I crossed my arms over my chest, but Wren was already wrapping his arms around me to shield me from the cold.

"Thank you," I breathed into his chest.

"Dress warm," he reminded me. He leaned down, taking my chin in his hand and pressed a soft kiss against my lips. I closed my eyes and breathed in the scent of him, wanting more and knowing that I'd have to be patient. He kissed my forehead, and then he was gone beneath the moonlight.

I waited until his taillights disappeared from the drive before I headed back inside. The rush of warmth surrounded me, sending a shiver down my spine. Dad was in the kitchen, searching the cupboards for his usual after-dinner-snack.

"Have you seen the Oreos?" he asked, digging around in the wrong cabinet. I smiled, and opened the one below, handing him the package. "Ah, thanks."

"No problem," I said, turning for the stairs.

"Hey Quinn," Dad said, stopping me. I turned back to face him. "I know we haven't exactly discussed... boys..." he was struggling, and I was pressing my lips together in amusement. "But, if you're uh... dating... now, maybe we should set some ground rules or... something."

"Uh-huh?" I furrowed my brows, entirely curious to see where this was going.

"Well, are you... dating?"

"Maybe," I shrugged, "we haven't exactly had the dating conversation," I said truthfully. "But, I really like him." That seemed like a safe enough answer. I knew it wouldn't be smart to tell him that I felt like we belonged to one another. Even thinking it made me sound like a crazy person, but there something deeper at force here even if I didn't understand the semiotics yet.

"He seems like a nice guy," Dad offered, stroking his mustache in thought. "He seems to be pretty crazy about you."

I chewed the inside of my lip, unsure of how to reply. I opted for a subject change instead. "Earlier today, when you said that the townspeople haven't always been so kind to Wren's family... what exactly did you mean by that?"

"Oh," Dad sucked in a breath of air, exhaled slowly, "*that.*"

"Yes. *That.*" I flopped down on the couch, tucking my legs beneath me.

"Niall and I were in the same graduating class," Dad said. "He had a younger brother, Remy, who was always getting in trouble. He wasn't a bad guy per se, but he liked to test the limits." Dad sat down across from me, rubbing at his right temple as if it were somehow painful to recall the memories. "I don't think Niall and Remy's parents were much in the picture. From what I understand, they bolted and left Niall with all the responsibility of caring for his brother before he'd even graduated high school himself."

"That's awful," I said. Wren hadn't told me that.

"Niall was always... an observant guy–kind of like Wren in that regard. He was quiet, always there to cover for Remy or rescue him from trouble when he needed it, which was often. Then came senior year, and Gabriella moved to town. She was... a force of nature," Dad decided on the description, folding his hands across his lap. "Everyone noticed her. You couldn't help it."

I raised an eyebrow, understanding where Wren must have gotten his devastatingly good looks.

"She and Niall became an item rather quickly, and decided to get married right after graduation. Of course, the townsfolk had a *lot* to say about that, and they weren't shy about keeping their opinions to themselves, either.

"It wasn't until Remy died that things really got bad. I'd heard that Gabriella left Niall shortly after the funeral, that she'd run off with another man and took Wren with her. There was a lot of speculation that Gabriella had been running around on Niall for years, and there was talk that Wren might not even be his son."

"That's probably why Niall doesn't bother showing his face in town anymore," I said. "If people were saying such awful and untrue things about me and my family, then I probably wouldn't either." In fact, I sure as hell wouldn't still be living in the same town.

"Well... this is where it gets worse," Dad said, wringing his hands together. "People thought that Gabriella was having an affair with Remy... and when he died..." Dad was staring at the floor, unable to meet my gaze.

"They thought Niall killed Remy?" My eyes narrowed with cold, hard shock.

"He was put on trial for Remy's murder," Dad said, "yes."

Bile rose to the back of my throat as my stomach twisted in an awful wave of nausea. Wren told me about what Niall had to do to cover up the truth... how he'd been forced by pack law to murder a man to protect their secret. And in doing so, the townspeople had suspected him for the death of his brother.

I tried to imagine the torment and hell Niall must have put himself through, how much he must have suffered on so many different accounts.

"They found him innocent, of course. Niall didn't even own a gun."

I swallowed hard.

"A few weeks later they found a body in the woods. He had a bullet wound in his head, and a pistol in his hand. The bullets matched the ones they'd dug out of Remy during the autopsy. They just assumed the man must have killed himself–unable to live with the grief of having killed Remy," Dad finished.

I sat there; stunned. "I can't imagine having to go through something like that," I said meekly, my voice returning to me after a few moments of silence.

"Yeah, well, perhaps you should keep that to yourself... If Wren doesn't know, it's probably best to keep it that way."

I nodded.

We were silent for a few more minutes, both lost in our thoughts.

"So," Dad said, breaking the silence, "ground rules." I looked up, meeting his dark eyes. He was twiddling his thumbs, nervously chewing at the inside corner of his cheek. "You know... there are some things I wish your mother was around for." He gave a halfhearted, sad smile. "She'd probably know what to do better than I would, and, I'm sure you'd much rather be having this conversation with her."

I got up impulsively, moving to his side of the couch, and sat down beside him. I reached for his hands, folding my palms over the tops of his. "It's okay, Dad."

"You've never given me any reason not to trust you," he said finally, his voice tentative. "I'm aware that you're almost eighteen; so, let's just play this by ear, shall we? You're a smart girl."

"Sure," I said, nodding firmly.

"We'll just treat it the same way we've treated your friends—only, if he's here, I'd prefer that you kept your bedroom door *wide* open."

"Oh my goddess, Dad." I rolled my eyes toward the ceiling.

"Does that not sound reasonable?" His eyes grew wide as he said this, hands facing palm up on his lap.

"Yes," I said, pushing myself off the couch, "I'm taking a shower and I'm going to bed."

"Goodnight kiddo, I love you, I hope you know."

"I know." I pressed my lips into a small smile, reaching out and squeezing his shoulder. "I love you, too."

Chapter Fifteen
The Wolf in the Midnight Hour

I layered up after my shower, pulling on jeans and an old track hoodie that was buried in the back of my closet. The cuffs were ripped and held in place with safety-pins. Not exactly a glamorous look, but traipsing through the dark forest with a werewolf didn't exactly call for couture. I glanced at my alarm clock, making sure I had plenty of time to cast a protection spell. I moved the stack of books and blankets from the wooden trunk at the foot of the bed, and opened it. From inside, I pulled out one of my mother's grimoires, a stack of pillar candles, and a bundle of sage. I placed a candle at each representational point of the invisible pentagram, and sat cross-legged at the center of the circle on my bedroom floor.

"*Cuirim na heilimintí i bhfeidhm,*" I whispered, asking the elements to join me. "*Glaoim lasair an tine.* I call upon the flame of Fire." I closed my eyes, lifting my palms upward. I could feel the electric surge as the Fire element responded, licking at the flesh of my palm. I opened my eyes, watching as the swirling flames danced as if I'd captured the eye of a hurricane within a snow globe. It rolled obediently, waiting for my command. I closed my fingertips around the flames, pointing at the candle that represented Spirit. "Solas," I commanded, and the candle wick ignited with my orange-purple flame. I asked the same for the remaining candles, and once they were all ablaze, I lit the bundle of sage, fanning the smoke with an owl feather. I lifted my mother's grimoire, ready to recite the protection spell.

"In this night, I call upon the brightest light. By sun and moon, I summon thee; protect my home and hear my plea. I bind this spell with my blood–" I picked up the athame, pricking the tip of my thumb, and squeezing a few drops into the flame of the Spirit candle. "–so that no harm shall pass to those I love."

As I finished the spell, Air lifted its essence, blowing out the candles that signified the spells completion. I thanked each of the elements and let them depart.

The alarm on my nightstand was showing that it was a quarter till eleven. I packed my spell tools back in the trunk, and slipped into my hiking boots. Dad had gone to bed around ten, but I paused outside his closed door, holding my breath while I listened for the sounds of snoring. Relief fluttered through me at the sound. Fitting, I thought, that he still sawed logs in his sleep. Dad was a light sleeper, like me, so I crept as quietly as I could down the steps. I sent up a silent prayer, hoping that sleep would find him resting soundlessly on this night.

I shimmied into my jacket at the back door, slowly lifting the latch as it clicked open. I never paid much attention to the sounds things made during the day; they were just background noise, faded, like listening to the radio while you cleaned. But here in the dark, every sound came alive.

I waited on the other side of the door, my fingers still clamped around the handle. The sliding door had skimmed along its track with minimal sound, but to me it sounded as though a freight train came barreling down in its place. I stared though the glass, half expecting to see a light flicker in the stairwell.

And that's when a pair of hands gripped me firmly around the shoulders. I jumped clean out of my skin, opening my mouth with a scream rising in the back of my throat when a large palm closed over my mouth. I sucked in a gulp of air through my nose, breathing in the familiar smell of his skin. My eyes rolled back in my head with relief as I collapsed against his chest.

"It's me," he whispered, his voice warm against the side of my neck.

I wheeled on him, jamming a fist into his chest. "I could kill you," I breathed, dropping my forehead to his chest. I could feel the laughter bubbling there, catching short in his throat as his arms circled me. "How do you do that?" I asked incredulously.

"Do what?" he returned.

"Materialize," I said, "you're like permanently in stealth mode."

He leaned down, mouth at my ear again as he breathed, "I'm a predator, remember?" His lips twitched in an enticing sort of way, and he reached down to lace his fingers through mine. "Come on, before I regret this," he said, and I followed him down the patio steps, across the yard, and into the woods.

The wind didn't feel as forceful beneath the protection of the autumn canopy. The sky was cloudless, and the light from the full moon and silver stars pooled through the forest, casting beams of light that filtered through the leaves and bathed the ground in a brilliant bluish hue. The forest smelled wild, rich with the scent of dirt; like after a rainstorm, and crisp with the smell of decaying leaves. I breathed in a deep lungful, letting the scents stimulate my senses.

Wren lifted his face to the wind, sampling the air. I watched him with fascination as he closed his eyes, absorbing the forest. He opened them a moment later and they were glowing a vibrant yellow. They seemed larger, distinctly predatory.

"I never asked you, but, do you like being what you are?"

He thought for a moment before answering. "I've never known anything else," he replied. "But there have been times in my life that I wondered what it would be like to be normal; times when it would've been... *easier*, to not be what I am, but, I've never resented it."

"You make it look easy," I said, tucking my hands into the back pockets of my jeans as we walked; feet skimming over the leaves.

"Do I?" He snickered, finding amusement in my comment.

"You don't think so?" I glanced up at him from the side, watching the way the moonlight colored his skin. He was a creature of the night, and the Moon was bathing him in the embrace of her lustrous glow.

"My mind doesn't exactly function like a normal human's would. I think like a predator. I was made in the image of a wolf; made to be acutely aware of my surroundings. It can be exhausting–always being on guard."

"You can't turn it off?"

"Sometimes. When I'm with you, you have a way of making me want to forget everything, and at the same time, a way of making me feel so aware of everything because I'm overcome by an inherit need to protect you."

"So I'm a burden?" My voice dropped an octave.

"No, of course not," he said, reaching out to brush the hair back from my face. He pulled me into his arms, letting his thumb trace the contour of my jawbone. "You could never be a burden to me." His yellow eyes rested on mine, and I could feel the heat seeping through his skin.

"What does the Change feel like," I wondered, "is it painful?" We'd stopped walking about two hundred yards into the forest, and were standing in a small clearing. Lingering crickets were singing in the background. I stepped out of his arms and perched myself on a moss-covered log, tucking my hands in the pockets of my jacket.

"Every bone in my body has to rearrange itself, so yes, it is painful. I don't mind it though. The Change is like a double-edged sword. My body craves it, and when it comes it's like a sweet release." *It's difficult*, he'd told me, *to not become the wolf.* He stepped into the clearing, kicking out of his shoes.

For whatever absurd reason, with the rush of excitement my mind had totally skipped over the part where logic failed to fill in the blanks. Wren had to undress. I must have realized that somewhere in my subconscious, after all, he'd been naked–albeit covered in blood–last night when he Changed back to human form.

He stripped out of his jacket, tossing it over the branch of a nearby tree, and glanced back at me. "Are you blushing, Quinn?" A slow smile pulled the right corner of his mouth into a trademark smirk. *Could he see that well in the dark?* He peeled off his T-shirt, tossed it aside and started for the belt-buckle on his jeans.

I cleared my throat. "Of course not. I just… don't want you to feel like I'm staring." He'd kicked out of his jeans, knocking them to the side with his bare feet. "Aren't you cold?" I narrowed my eyes.

"Hardly," he replied, looping his thumbs into the waistband of his boxer-briefs.

My lips parted, my breathing halted–blood rushed to my ears, heating my face in a way that made me look away.

"Don't be shy," his tone was dripping with a tantalizing lure, dark and deep with a seductive edge. "Nothing you haven't seen before." He gave his boxers a shove, and I bit down on my lower lip a little harder than I'd meant to.

He was looking at me. Not in a way that made me feel shameful for seeing him this way, but in a way that made *me* feel like I was the one exposed. Compared to him, I was a soft, fragile shell composed only of flesh and blood, but Wren... he was something more complex; a labyrinth, unfathomably intricate.

His body came to life in the sheer darkness. He wore the midnight sky like a cloak of armor; the light from the moon haloing him in an ethereal, luminescent glow. He was the most beautiful being I'd ever seen... His eyes appeared as though they'd captured the essence of a summer lightning storm, and they were intently fixed on me.

"Still not afraid?" he asked softly, as if trying to decipher my expression of awe–mistaking it for apprehension.

"I'm not afraid."

He nodded once, and I caught a glimpse of muscle beginning to ripple under the surface of his skin. I watched his Adam's apple bobbing as he swallowed–his facial features shifting together in pain. He pulled his hands into fists; his body spasmed, twisting with convulsions that began the transformation.

I sat there, momentarily stunned by the sound his bones were making–the awful grind, popping and snapping of every bone in his body breaking and repositioning. His spine curved at an impossible angle, drawing his chest toward the sky as his muscles bunched and limbs twisted and curved.

I wanted to run to him. I wanted to throw my arms around him and protect him from the pain, but he'd barely let out a sound. I could only sit there, watching as a jolt passed through his forearms, causing the joints in his fingers to snap. Tendons bulged as a smattering of thick, black hair sprouted through the back of his hands. It spread quickly, springing from his arms and traveling across his chest. I followed the trail across his abdomen, watching with wonder as Wren fell to all fours.

Bones continued to crackle as they rearranged, his back legs stretching and bowing into the shape of a hock. His whole body seemed to shudder, spine jerking as his face began to shift. He lowered his head, eyes closing as a set of black ears pulled high on his head. His muzzle extended–jowls parting as sharply pointed canine teeth gleamed in the light of the silver moon.

Seconds seemed to slip into minutes as I lost track of time. His body gave one final tremor, and then I was standing face to face with a werewolf.

He was bigger than the average wolf; with his long slender legs, his head came up to my ribs. I reached out, tentatively at first, sliding my fingers through his onyx coat. His fur absorbed the moonlight, gleaming with a silver-blue gloss. Just as he was as a man, he was absolutely mesmerizing in his wolf form. I knelt beside him, spreading my fingers through his fur. He licked at my chin, and leaned against my side. "Can you understand me?" I whispered into his fur. He gave a grumble, nudging his head against mine–I took that to mean that he could. "What you are… it's incredible," I said, looking into his moon colored eyes. "I thought I knew magic, but…" I shook my head slowly, letting my words trail off; evaporating in the air.

The breeze picked up, and Wren lifted his muzzle–taking in the surrounding scents. His ears pricked curiously to the side, listening, until they shifted back to me. "All clear out there?" I asked.

He tilted his head–nodding–I presumed.

"I suppose I probably should have asked you before you lost the ability to talk, but, how long will you stay a wolf?"

He lifted his head, gazing at the moon.

"Until it sets?" I guessed.

He nodded again.

He knew better than I did, but I knew the moon's setting point had everything to do with the phase it was in, and the time varied. I stifled a yawn, covering my mouth with my hand.

Wren nudged my arm with his muzzle, whimpering a little. He looked down the path that led to my house, and then glanced up at me.

"I'm okay," I told him. Though I *was* tired; the events of the last couple of days had finally caught up with me. Exhaustion fell over me like a warm blanket, as if a fairy had doused me with a dram of sleeping powder.

Wren gave the small of my back a forceful nudge with his muzzle; a grumble of frustration catching in his throat. I could almost hear him repeating what I told him when I begged him to let me come along for the Change. *"You give me one nudge, and I promise I'll behave as you see fit."*

I rolled my eyes, pushing to my feet. "Okay, okay," I said with a sigh, moving to collect the clothing that he'd strewn through the clearing. I picked up his shirt and jacket from the tree branch, folding them over my arm, but when I turned to pick up his jeans–Wren was holding his boxers between his teeth. I snatched them out of his jaws, and shook my head. "You're just *so* hilarious," I retorted. I gathered up the rest of his belongings and followed him across the moon-bathed path.

He drifted through the forest like a shadow, camouflaged by the midnight sky. His footsteps didn't even register sound as he walked. His head lifted, testing the air; ears shifting like antennas in search of a signal. I followed behind him as he prowled through the forest, trying my best to keep up with his long, graceful strides. I felt bad for any of the animals that crossed his path–they'd never even see him coming. He was the perfect predator.

When we reached the edge of the forest, Wren slowed. He tested the air, scanning the premises with his superior night vision. After a moment, he broke through the tree line, loping over to the back deck as I followed him. I lost sight of him momentarily as he slipped beneath the steps and pulled a backpack out by the straps with his teeth.

I bent to unzip it, dumped his clothes into the bag and hauled it over my shoulder. My nerves skittered, pinging through my stomach as I reached for the door handle. Wren gave my hip a gentle nudge, letting me know the coast was clear. He walked in front of me, pausing at the bottom of the stairs while I locked the door behind us. The clock on the microwave read that it was nearly one in the morning. I clenched my teeth, holding my breath as I ascended the staircase. To my immediate relief, my father was still hard at work, sawing away at all those logs.

The vintage Edison lamp on the nightstand pushed out a soft, orange glow that encased my bedroom. In his wolf form, Wren looked out of place standing among the manmade furniture and artificial lighting. He had the look of summer lightning in his eyes; still silent and watchful, but wild and untamed–too magnificent to belong indoors. I reached for the stack of clothing I'd left on top of my dresser. "Make yourself at home," I whispered, "I'll be right back."

I slipped into the bathroom to change and brush my teeth. I scrubbed my face and studied my reflection in the mirror. There was a different light in my evergreen eyes–it reminded me of the way my mother looked before she performed a spell; confident and strong. I padded across the hall, backing into my bedroom so I could close the door with the slightest of sounds. But when I turned, I found Wren curled up on the left side of the bed; his giant wolf frame nearly taking up the majority of the mattress. I cocked my head to the side, smiling.

"I hope you know this isn't exactly what I had in mind when I pictured you staying the night," I told him, pulling back the lavender colored comforter and sliding in. The sheets felt cool against my skin. I reached out, resting my hand on the side of his face as he lowered his head closer to mine on the pillow. "I always wanted a dog though," I whispered. He grunted, showing disapproval at my selected terminology. "Kidding," I said, yawning.

No one would ever mistake him for a dog. His size alone was enough to give him away. It was amazing to me that there was magic out there capable of taking a man's body and turning into the majestic creature sitting before me. It didn't seem possible that the human body could do such a thing, but Wren was living proof that it could. It was the most beautiful form of magic I'd ever seen.

I dreamed of wolves running through the moonlit forest; the sound of their howling cries catching high in the treetops as they danced through the languid fog. I could almost feel the dirt and earth caked beneath the nails of their paws, and tasted the blood of a fresh kill on their tongue. My nostrils still burned with the sharp smells of the forest as I woke groggily. My back felt incredibly warm, like I'd fallen asleep pressed up against a radiator. My hair was gently gathered away from the side of my neck, and warm lips descended on the curve of my shoulder.

My eyes shot open, and I rolled to my back to see Wren propped up on his elbow, slightly hovering over me. "Still so jumpy," he whispered, his hand slipping to the side of my face until his fingertips were in my hair.

I licked my lips, relieved to find they still tasted of peppermint from my toothpaste. "What time is it?" I asked, my eyebrows knitting together. When had he turned back into a human, and how had I not woken up when he did? But then I remembered how quiet he could be–my silent shadow in the night.

"Just after two," he answered, "I slipped outside for a second to Change," he said. "I figured the sound of bones snapping would have woken your father."

"No kidding," I said, rolling to face him. "How did you manage to get out with the lack of opposable thumbs?"

"Careful," he said, nodding toward my pendant.

"Oh, sorry," I said, quickly taking it off and looping it over my bedpost. "I'll see about getting one in stainless steel or something."

"No," he shook his head, "silver is a precious metal; lunar exposure makes the charge more powerful. It's protecting you."

"But it's hurting you," I countered.

"We can work around it," he said, folding his hands around mine.

"I don't understand why silver would harm you if it's an element of the moon. You are what you are because of the Moon and Stars spell." I frowned, looking up into his eyes. They were still glowing, like the way an animal's eyes would if you shined a flashlight on them in the dark.

"It's like your magic," he said. "You get your power from nature, but if you abuse it there are consequences. Same goes for me. Everyone and everything has a weakness. The Great Moon gave us power and freedom, she's just making sure we don't let it go to our heads." He grinned.

For a minute we said nothing–just lay there gazing at one another in the soft lighting. Wren was running his fingertips through my hair, slowly, until they were grazing the skin of my bare shoulder, gliding down the curve of my back. The tenderness of his touch made me close my eyes, reveling in the sensation.

"Don't fall asleep," he said. There was a hint of desperation in his voice.

"I'm not," I promised. "It just feels… incredible," I decided on the word, "to have you touching me."

He pulled me closer then, pinning me against his bare chest. I bit down on my lower lip, tentatively reaching out to touch his skin. There was nothing soft about his body. He was covered in lean muscle, and my fingertips traced the indentation of his sternum, marveling at the sharp contours of his body.

"How's your side?" I asked, remembering the wound that had not yet healed yesterday. He lifted the sheet, letting me see the bruised skin. The wound had closed, much to my relief, but it still looked incredibly tender. I lightly brushed my fingertips over the new skin, knowing that it would soon be a scar.

I did something daring then, slipping my fingertips across his abdomen, exploring the hardness of his perfect stomach. A low moan caught in the back of his throat. He closed his eyes, his hand wrapping around my wrist. The heat coming off his body was smoldering. It mixed with the scent of his skin, tangling deliriously through my nostrils. I could feel him beneath the sheets, the firmness of him pressing against my thigh.

My heart was hammering in my chest. I knew he could hear the pounding of it, revealing just how much I wanted him. The fear of the unknown skirted through my subconscious, conflicting with my desire. Wren wrapped his arm behind my back, effortlessly lifting me so that I straddled his waist. His hands found the hem of my tank, pulling it over my head. For a minute he just looked at me, eyes swirling with the colors of the harvest moon as he ran his fingertips across my chest.

He pulled me to him, his mouth hungrily seeking mine. When he kissed me I felt like every cell in my body had come alive–my blood turning to liquid fire in my veins. He tasted electric. I wrapped my arms around his neck, tangling my hands in his hair and pinning myself as tightly as I could to his chest. I suddenly felt like I couldn't get close enough and the thought was making me ravenous with insanity. At that moment, every candle I had in my room burst into flame, shooting several inches into the air. I could feel my irises swirling with the reflection of their orange flicker.

His canine teeth had extended, and his fingertips were paused at the clasp of my bra. He was looking at me in wonder, like he wasn't afraid of what we were capable of. I knew that being with him was dangerous– *we*–were dangerous. The realization only excited me. My mother had once told me that I'd find someone special. He'd be my counterpart–a soul equally matched.

His thumb brushed against the corner of my lips; his eyes still latched to mine as desperation circled through. He was looking at me like he'd recognized me from long ago–like a soul calling a soul, everything he embodied was etched in my bones. I ached– excruciatingly–for our fingers to lace, for our bodies to intertwine. I couldn't deny the pull of our energy, the invisible force of it pushing us together.

"I need you," he breathed.

And I surrendered to him.

I drifted in and out of sleep with his arms securely wrapped around me. He pressed his lips to the tender place between my shoulder blades, sending a shiver trailing the length of my spine. I begged the night to hold the stars just a little longer. I wasn't ready for morning to come.

But morning did come.

The slant of light crept through my bedroom window, pooling on the floorboards. Wren was lightly tracing the curve of my hip, lying with his eyes still closed. Down the hall, my dad's alarm clock sounded, blasting a seventies tune from the FM radio. I heard the springs in his bed creak as he rolled to turn off the contraption, and pulled himself out of bed.

A wave of nervous jitters passed through my stomach. Dad wouldn't come in, I knew, but the thought that I had really done something so against my own moral code sank to the bottom of my gut like a leaded weight. I didn't regret it though–I knew I wouldn't regret it, either. Wren had stirred something ancient within my DNA. It didn't make sense, but somehow I knew that he was meant for me, as I was meant for him. It was like our souls had been around before.

"I should get up, show my face," I said, my features twisting contritely.

"Hurry back," he whispered.

I gave him a slow smile, and shifted out of bed with the sheet wrapped around me. I gathered up my clothing, and then checked the hall to make sure the coast was clear before dashing into the bathroom. Down below, I could hear my dad in the kitchen starting up the coffee pot. I showered, toweled off, and dressed in a pair of black jeans, and an ivory lace, flowing tunic. After brushing my teeth, I headed for the stairs. Dad was sitting at the kitchen table, reading the newspaper while sipping on a cup of coffee. His hair hadn't been combed yet, and a dark lock slipped across his forehead, dangling over his reading glasses.

"Morning," I said, reaching into the cabinet for a mug.

"Oh, hey, honey. I didn't hear you come down." He turned the page, engorged in whatever article he was reading.

"Did you sleep well?" I asked him.

"I slept like a log, actually," he said, and I pressed my lips into a thin line to keep from smiling.

"Good," I said. "It's rare that you get a decent night's sleep."

"How about you?" he asked.

"Oh. I slept all right," I lied. *Goddess* I hated lying, but I was finding more and more excuses to keep up with the trend. *They're harmless*, I told myself, *just little white lies.* "So," I said quickly, "what's on your agenda today?"

Dad reared back with an earth-shattering sneeze. "Excuse me," he said, sniffling. "I feel a little stuffy this morning."

"That's odd," I said. My dad never sneezed unless he was around animals.

"Anyway, I'm actually going to be at Jo's house today. She hired me to redo her wood floors." He sneezed again.

"Gesundheit," I said, pulling my brows together in a frown. "So you're working on her personal projects now, huh? I didn't think that was a service that Emmett Callaghan offered." I grinned mischievously.

"It's my slow season anyway," he countered innocently. He sneezed a third time, and the force of it sent the paper ruffling on the table. "Say, do we have any allergy pills up in the cupboard? I don't know what's going on with me."

And then it hit me.

Dad only sneezed when he was around *animals*. It was the sole reason why I'd never been allowed to have a pet. Wren had followed me into the house in his wolf form last night–which meant that my dad was allergic to *Wren!*

"Um, let me check," I said, hoping my voice hadn't wavered; my cheeks heated with a crimson blush from the awkward realization. I found a little bottle in the medicine cabinet and handed it to him. "You're in luck."

"Great," he said, "I'd hate to be sneezing my head off while I'm working at Jo's." He unscrewed the cap, shaking out a couple of pink pills.

"Is she going to be there?" I asked.

"For a little while, just before she heads into the restaurant."

"Dad... If you like her, I just want you to know it's okay with me." This time I held any trace of sarcasm out of my tone. I truly meant it.

He chuckled, and pushed out from the kitchen chair. "Thanks, I'll, uh, keep that in mind." He squeezed my shoulder before heading back up the stairs to change. I busied myself in the kitchen, filling my thermos and pulling leftovers together to take for lunch. A few minutes later my dad came back down the stairs; his hair was combed, and I could smell the subtle aroma of his aftershave as he shrugged into his jacket and hugged me goodbye.

"Have a good day," he said, slipping out the door.

I waited until his truck pulled out of the drive before I headed for my room. Wren was still lounging in my bed; one of his arms was propped behind his head as he lay there looking out the window. Goddess he was beautiful. Looking at him made me want to forget about the rest of the world and all my responsibilities. He turned his head; his tawny eyes seemed brighter this morning–clearer, somehow.

"Come here," he said, holding out his arms.

"We have school," I said weakly.

"I don't care." There was an aching plea to his voice, and I couldn't refuse it. I went to him, sitting on the edge of the bed as he pulled me into his arms. His fingers slipped through my hair, running the length of it until his hand was pressed to the middle of my back. "You smell nice," he said, inhaling deeply.

"You always smell a little like the forest," I admitted. My head was tucked beneath his chin, so I couldn't see his reaction.

"Is that a good thing?" he asked.

I nodded, tracing his collarbone with my fingertips. "Your scent is… wild," I decided. I pressed my lips to the hollow place on his throat, and I could feel the vibration from the pleasure he felt.

"Be careful," he warned, his voice was a husky growl. "You keep doing that and I'm going to take you again."

Excitement pulsed through my veins at the thought. I looked up into his eyes, tracing the curve of his jaw. "Tempting," I breathed.

He moved with lightning speed, sending a shock-wave through my system as he scooped me up and rolled me back onto the mattress. He hovered over me, a sly smile tilting the corners of his lips upward. He grasped both of my wrists in his hands, pinning them above my head in makeshift manacles. He lowered his head, bringing his mouth to mine with a gentle kiss. "Say you'll be mine and I'll let you up." He grinned, and I detected the playful tone in his voice.

"I thought I already was?"

"I want to hear you say it." He raised his eyebrows, eyes softening beneath them. He looked serious all of the sudden, like he really needed to hear my confession. This was the first time that I'd glimpsed anything other than confidence in his face–the first time he looked… vulnerable.

"I'm yours," I told him earnestly. Words like "always" and "forever" flitted across my mind, but I couldn't say them out loud. Words like that were easy to misuse and over use, I didn't want them to sound trite.

He kissed me again, and then helped me into a sitting position before climbing out of bed. My teeth raked across my bottom lip as I watched him walk to the closet and pull his backpack out. *Some people should just stay naked*, I thought as he shimmed into his clothing. Not that he was any less distracting with his clothes on…

Wren headed for the bathroom, and I pushed back my curtains, grabbing my amulet from the bedpost. There was a light frost on the ground, blanketing the fallen leaves and blades of grass with minuscule crystalline fragments. They glistened in the early morning sunlight, shimmering with a promise of the coming cold. The outside world was standing still; the quiet before the storm. I could almost smell it in the air–the icy pull of Darkness just looming beyond the trees.

A spark of pain shot through my temples. I winced, pushing my fingertips against the side of my head. A shadow crept across my eyes, and I could see the Hollow in my vision. The ground was rain-soaked, littered with golden leaves and russet needles. The colors faded, and the ground around me was saturated in thick, scarlet blood. It pooled across the ground, rising across my shoes. I could smell the iron stink of it, almost taste it in my mouth. I scurried backward, stumbling hard into the base of a tree trunk.

I fell forward on my knees, and pain shot through my legs as I hit my bedroom floor. Wren came running from the bathroom, sliding his arm around my shoulders as concern clouded his eyes. "What happened?" His voice was frantic.

"I don't know." My eyebrows pinched together, pain still humming through my forehead. "I saw something," I explained what I'd seen the best I could. "I've never had a vision without coming into contact with blood."

"Maybe your powers are growing," he said.

"I suppose it's possible." My teeth raked across my bottom lip, and goosebumps trailed across my arms. "I need to talk to Blaire, maybe she can help me figure out what all of this means."

"Hey," Wren pulled me against his chest, the warmth of his skin chasing away the chills, "don't be afraid. You're not alone, okay?"

I nodded, squeezing my eyes shut. With my ear pressed against his chest, I could feel and hear his heart beating; the steadiness of it easing my fear. I breathed evenly, in and out until I felt the ground become solid under my feet.

"You okay?"

"I'm okay," I answered.

"You want to try the Magic Shoppe again?"

"You don't mind?"

"Of course not." He helped me up from the floor, keeping his arms around my waist while the blood stopped pounding in my ears.

"I'll call Annabelle." I reached for my pocket, but Wren's hand wrapped around my wrist.

"I know you want to keep her in the loop because she's your best friend, but she's *human*," he reminded me, leveling his eyes with mine. "We don't know what we may be walking into, and she has no defenses."

"She'll be furious with me." I gnawed on the inside corner of my cheek, knowing full well what Annabelle's reaction would be when she learned that I had intentionally kept this from her. Still… I'd rather suffer the consequences of her hating me in place of something horrible happening to her.

"You're going to have to risk it," Wren said, pressing his lips together in a tight line. I could see the worry creasing his brows.

"I should at least inform Annabelle that I'm not going to be in class today," I said with a sigh. "She's going to ask why."

Wren moved his hands up my sides, palms curving around my arms until he gripped my shoulders. I could feel the pressure from each of his fingertips, the strength and stability burrowing into my skin. "Lie," he said evenly.

Chapter Sixteen
"My Face in Thine Eye,
Thine in Mine Appears"

Wren reached for my hand as we exited the car, his body visibly tensing as we headed up the sidewalk. I knew he was testing the air–deciphering the different scents that I couldn't pick up on. "Penny isn't here," he said as we reached the door. "Her scent is faded, but someone else is present."

"Blaire." I hoped. I rolled my fingers into a fist, raising my hand to knock on the door, but Wren stopped me, shifting me behind him. I rolled my eyes at his domineer protective instincts, but he was pointing toward the handle. I craned my head around his shoulder to get a better look and realized the door wasn't latched all the way. I looked up at Wren, a silent question drifting across my irises.

"Wait here," he instructed, giving the handle a little tug.

"Like hell," I retorted.

He gave me a hard look, and I could hear a growl of frustration building in the back of his throat. His eyes flashed with electricity and for a minute we just stood there, facing off as two determined knights on an invisible chess board, waiting for the other to relent. I shouldered in front of him, stepping across the threshold. He'd opened the door so quietly that the crystal chimes hadn't even been disturbed.

The shop itself hadn't been disrupted in any sense; Blaire's name began to take shape on my lips when she startled me, barreling around the corner with a spell rising in the space between us; a look of fury burning in her coal-blackened eyes. She was shouting in the ancient Gaelic tongue–a white, cloudy haze building in the palms of her hands. She reared back, flinging her energy-ball directly at Wren.

Adrenaline slammed through my chest as I cried out, "*No!*" I didn't think after that. I thrust my hands out in front of my body, and a cylindrical shape yielding a bright light pulsed in front of us, creating a makeshift barricade. The shield was iridescent, shimmering with the colors of spilled gasoline on pavement after a rainstorm. The colors swirled and spiraled, stretching out wide enough to protect myself and Wren from Blaire's spell. I watched as her energy-ball pinged off my shield, and went sailing toward the bookshelf. It exploded with a sizzling snap, sending books and torn pages raining down through the air.

"What the hell, Blaire?" I screeched, still pushing my shield out in front of us. Wren was half Changed beside me–crouched; his eyes churning with the colors of the harvest moon, and his teeth were visibly bared–jaw extended. A menacing snarl ripped through his throat.

"*Me!*" Blaire returned with an inconceivable tone. "Are you aware of the company yer keepin'?"

"What are you talking about?"

"He's one of them!" she accused, energy-balls rolling across her palms. "The shadows that come in the night–a servant of the Dark Witch!"

"You're wrong," I said.

"What's yer name, pup?" she demanded, jerking her chin in his direction. He only met her question with a deeper growl. She raised her arms, ready to fling her electric energy-balls.

"His name is Wren Whelan," I answered, afraid that I couldn't hold my shield much longer.

"Whelan," she repeated, "as in the descendant wolves of the Ossory bloodline?" Blaire lowered her hands, letting the energy-balls simmer out in her palms.

"Yes," I said.

"Well you can lower yer shield, lass. I've no intention of causing you or the wolf pup any harm."

"Don't do it," Wren hissed.

"I swear it on my coven's name, I mean you no harm. The Alderdice witches have sworn allegiance and protection to the wolves of the Ossory bloodline."

I glanced over, hoping that her declaration meant something to him because I could feel the control I had over the shield slipping. Wren finally gave a nod, and I lowered my hands.

"Where's Penny?" I asked.

Blaire's features crumpled then, a sincere look of worry flashing across her eyes. "I don't know." She shook her head. "She's been gone since yesterday, and I haven't been able to reach her on the cell. I'm worried. I think her disappearance may have something to do with the others..."

"The others?" I frowned. "You mean the other werewolves?"

"Yes."

Wren shifted beside me, his presence filling the room as he straightened.

"That's why we were looking for you," I said. "We wanted to talk to you about the Dark Witch. We came by yesterday, but Penny said you were gone... How do you know about all this, by the way?" I narrowed my eyes.

"I should be the one asking *you*," she said. She turned and walked over to the bookcase behind the counter–Penny's private collection. "Sorry about the spell. It was only a knockout spell; it wouldn't have done any permanent damage if it had hit you." She ran her index finger across the book titles on the second shelf, scanning the old, dusty leather-bounds.

"How did you know he was a werewolf?"

"Because of this," she said, holding up her right hand. Her ring finger was adorned by a bright, glowing aqua stone. The gem's surface rippled like water droplets on a lake. "It's a moonstone."

"Since when does moonstone look like that?" Traditional moonstone was more of a misty, bluish-white. And it certainly didn't ripple.

"When it's spelled to detect the immediate presence of werewolves," she answered with a crooked grin. "I've had it since I was a girl, and this is why." She pulled a big, brown leather book from the shelf with faded gold metallic lettering and placed it on the counter, facing us. *The Legend of Faoladh.* "My family was called to service by the White Witch during the Dark Ages. When she broke the curse and freed the wolves from the Dark Witch's slavery, we were sworn to help protect them. That's why I'm here," she explained. "My coven received word about the pack of werewolves that recently moved into the area, and they sent me to check it out."

I was sure my eyes were bulging out of their sockets. "How is that even possible?" I shook my head dubiously.

"How do *you* know about the werewolves?" she countered, resting her hands on her hips as her eyes narrowed.

I glanced up at Wren, catching the muscle in his jaw tensing. His eyes portrayed caution, mirroring the conflicted emotion in my own.

"You've heard the expression, I'm sure, but... your silence is deafening." Blaire's eyes shifted between our faces until they rested on Wren's, assessing. "You don't trust me," she decided. Wren's mouth twitched.

"She's an empath," I said, "she can read emotional auras."

"And yours is full of testosterone fueled rage, though you do a remarkably good job of keeping it in check." Blaire snorted. "W*erewolves.*"

"More to the point," I interrupted, "the others, haven't exactly been quiet about keeping their presence a secret and... I had a vision... involving the Dark Witch and her amulet," I said.

"I see," Blaire said enunciating slowly, "and how did you come about this vision of yours?"

"We were attacked a couple nights ago in the forest," I said. "I heard the Dark Witch's voice in the air, but, it was like she was only there in spirit. We think that someone has summoned her, or is at least trying to summon her. She sent the wolves on me, but, we were able to stop them." I looked up at Wren, wrapping my fingers around his wrist. "Wren was badly injured, and when I touched him..."

"You had a vision." Blaire was shaking her head slowly. "I need you to follow me. There's something you should see." She turned then, not even glancing over her shoulder to make sure we would follow her. I looked up at Wren, searching for strength. I needed his in place of my own. He took my hand and led me down the hallway, and we met her where the hallway came to a dead-end.

"*Oscailte*," she said, and before our eyes, the outline of a wooden door emerged. She reached for the handle and pushed it open to reveal a darkened set of stairs. *Great*, I thought, it probably led to a medieval dungeon with stone walls and ironclad cells. "It's my lair," Blaire informed us, noting the apprehension on my face.

"Why is it hidden?" I wondered.

"For protection of course," she answered simply.

We followed her down the creaking steps, and the air grew cooler–staler. Blaire flipped on a light switch, revealing quite the opposite of a dungeon. It was small, perhaps at one point used as a storage cellar for goods. Now, it contained several rows of thick, wooden shelves with glass Mason jars filled with herbs and various spices. The floors and walls were cement, save for an old red and gold Victorian rug that sat in the center of the room between a beige sofa and love-seat duo. There was a wooden trunk next to the sofa, and a whole wall of book-lined shelves. Blaire's "lair" was just a slightly refurbished basement.

Blaire knelt in front of the trunk, and pulled a large emerald-green book to the surface. Its cover was decorated by a metallic gold tree, encompassed by a brilliant display of Celtic knot-work. "This belonged to my mother, and her mother before her, and so on," Blaire said, brushing her fingers across the cover. "It traces back through a very long line of the Alderdice witches. We belong to the Aurora Coven–the Bringers of Light. It's been our job for nearly four hundred years to look after the Dark Witch's amulet, to make sure it doesn't fall into the hands of her bloodline... I take it you're familiar with the legend?"

"A little," Wren said, "my father told us the story of how the wolves of Ossory came to be freed by the White Witch during the Battle of the Dark Ages."

"Yes." Blaire nodded. "The legend tells us the White Witch vanquished the Dark One with the army of the freed wolves at her side. She gave Rionach the Dark–or more commonly known as the Dark Witch–a chance to repent, to seek nature's forgiveness and return to the rules that govern us by Light. But Rionach refused, and the White Witch was forced to destroy her." Blaire sat the book on the coffee table, and gestured for us to take a seat.

"Rionach the Dark left something very important behind," she said.

"The amulet?" I guessed.

"And a daughter."

"More specifically, a bloodline," Wren said, flicking his eyebrow upward.

Blaire chuckled. "You've actually got a bit of smarts in that pretty little wolf brain, don't you?" She snickered again. "Yes, a bloodline indeed. And only a direct descendant would be able to summon her back."

"How?" I felt the crease between my eyebrows deepen. "Your coven is protecting this amulet, right?"

"'Tis true," Blaire nodded, "Rionach can't return to her physical form without the amulet, but that doesn't mean her spirit can't be summoned. Rionach turned her back on nature and gave her soul over to the Darkness, so the same rules that govern you and I don't apply to her. Darkness has its own way, and it's allowing her to take shape in a spiritual sort of form. Just because she's not in physical form doesn't mean that she's not dangerous."

"Why hasn't your coven destroyed the amulet?" Wren asked.

"Don't you think we've tried? There's no spell on earth that can destroy it–at least none written by the laws of nature. That's why the White Witch left it in our charge, so that years after she'd died, someone would always know of the legend and prevent the Darkness from returning to its ultimate form."

I leaned forward, propping my elbows on my knees as I stared at the leather-bound volume between us. "But why now, and *here* of all places? You said your coven sent you here to check on the werewolves return, but you never mentioned how you found out about that in the first place." I looked up at her, waiting.

"Penny, of course," she answered. "Penny wasn't born a witch, but she's been kept in the loop as a sort of guardian to the coven. We needed someone on the outside to keep watch over Silver Mountain."

"Silver Mountain?" I raised my eyebrows.

"Silver Mountain is a metaphysical nexus for spiritual energies. It's a place of raw power, anchored by the positioning of the magnetic North and South Poles. The energy there is neither good nor bad, but it can be manipulated to go either way if someone knows the correct way to use it," she explained. "It's one of five places in the world. There's one in Ireland, where my coven hails from, Greenland contains another, and the remaining two are located in Africa and Brazil. All little places that no one ventures to on purpose, and all places that make up a representational point of a large-scale pentagram."

"Is there a guardian assigned to each post?" Wren asked.

"Yes." She grinned, pleased that at least one of us was catching on quickly.

"How do you know all this stuff?" I asked.

"I grew up learning it, everyone in the Aurora coven learns. It's part of our heritage, and honestly, I'm surprised you don't know." Blaire reached up to fiddle with the amulet around her neck. I recognized the trinity knot; three ornate loops weaving into an unbroken circle. An emerald stone was fastened to its center.

"What do you mean?"

"Well, I had my suspicions about you when we first met. I felt like I knew you somehow, but once you told me that you could do blood-magic, and then all this with the werewolves and the vision you had when you touched Wren's blood, everything just started to make sense. I hoped you'd have figured it out by now." She leaned forward, folding her hands in her lap. After a minute, she flipped through the grimoire and settled on a page that contained three family crests. She pointed to the one at the top–a green field against a white background. There were a couple of oak trees, and at the base of one of the trees sat a wolf. "This is the Callaghan coat of arms," she said.

My throat had gone dry, and I swallowed hard to force the moisture back through my esophagus.

"This–" she pointed to the one beside it–a white shield with two diagonal blue lines, slashed with diamond-shaped markings. The top of the shield had a red banner with three white *Fleur de Lis* symbols. She continued, "–is the Whelan family coat of arms–and just in case ya' didn't know, '*Whelan*' literally means '*wolf.*' This last one is the Alderdice coat of arms. The three of these crests represent the triquetra–the Trinity of Light. There's a prophecy written about the Trinity's reunion," she finished.

My insides began to twist, and the air in the room suddenly felt a little thinner. Wren must have detected the change of my heartbeat. He reached out, reassuringly resting his hand on the small of my back. A mixture of heat and blood rushed to my ears, vibrating in my eardrums. I saw what was in front of me, the three crests leaping at me from the page. How could it be that a Whelan, an Alderdice and a Callaghan all sat facing one another at this very moment, staring at something from the ancient past? My head was spinning, but somehow I forced myself to ask, "What is the Trinity?"

Unlike myself, Blaire seemed anew with a sense of clarity; her eyes sparkling. "After the Dark Witch fell in the final battle, Luiseach Callaghan (the White Witch) established the Trinity of Light in order to prevent the Darkness from returning. With Rionach's amulet unable to be destroyed, the White Witch bound herself to two others to form the powerful triquetra to vanquish the Darkness for generations to come. For without Light, there can be no Dark, and without the Dark, there can be no Light. Everything must have balance."

I swallowed hard, staring at her with a desperate sort of look in my eyes. She couldn't possibly be saying what I thought she was... Could she?

"Quinn, you're the direct descendant of Luiseach Callaghan–the Bringer of Light. She had a cousin, Aine Alderdice–the very first witch of the Aurora Coven. Luiseach was betrothed to Conan Whelan, she fell in love with him and they were married after the Battle of the Dark Ages. Don't you see?" Blaire was grinning wildly, pointing to the book with her red, manicured fingernail, "we're all connected. We're the descendants of the Original Trinity!"

The Original Trinity…

I sat there in complete stillness, listening to Blaire read off the ancient prophecy. Two witches and one werewolf from each of the ancient clans would be born anew with each passing generation. Their powers would be called forth should the Dark Witch ever return to physical form, and the three combined as one would ensure the balance of Light from Dark in the coming ages.

Ever since I was a young girl, part of me had always romanticized the idea of reincarnation–the idea that your soul would recycle at death, and be born again into a new physical form. I wanted to believe that I'd have memories of my past lives and use those experiences to help guide me in the next, but I didn't *remember* those other lives so much as I had an overwhelming understanding that what Blaire was saying was the truth. My soul–or at least part of my soul–had been around before. It was the reason why Wren was so achingly familiar to me, the reason we'd been so drawn to one another. We'd been finding each other for nearly four hundred years, and the thought both thrilled and frightened me to my core.

"So, you're saying that the three of us–our ancestors–have found each other before?" I asked incredulously when she'd first begun to explain the prophecy.

"In other lifetimes, yes," she said. "We were different people then, but because the Original Trinity bound themselves together, parts of their soul and powers have transferred through our bloodlines for many generations."

"But, we don't get to remember those other lives?" I narrowed my eyes.

"Not exactly, no." She shook her head. "The memories don't serve much purpose; we just get more of a feeling like when we're in the right place at the right time, or when you know something without knowing why."

"Like a strong case of deja vu?" Wren asked.

"Sort of," Blaire said, "it's how we know we're on the right track."

"So until today, you had absolutely no idea that you were a

descendant of the Original Trinity?" I leaned forward over the coffee table, already perched as far out on the edge of the couch as the cushion would allow.

"It's very complicated," she said exasperatedly. "The Trinity itself is a very complex concept. There are many witches in the Alderdice clan–in example, I have another sister, so it could have been either of us, or none at all. The Trinity has always protected itself–keeping the individuals veiled from evil so that our bloodline can't be wiped out. Typically, we can pass through each life cycle without ever being called to power, but it's different for the heir of the White Witch. Luiseach and Conan shared a much deeper bond. Their love was said to be stronger than any spell written by the laws of nature. Together, they conquered space and time. It was said that their souls would reunite with each rebirth, regardless if the Trinity was called forth or not."

I pinched the bridge of my nose between my eyes, squeezing them shut. Beside me, Wren shifted. I could feel the heat rolling off his skin and wondered what he was thinking right now but I was too afraid to look up into those expressive eyes of his.

"You had to know something was up when you had that vision of him," Blaire said. "You must have felt the connection. That's how it works right? Your visions show you something from the past pertaining to that specific person?"

"Yes, they do," I said. "I just wasn't really thinking about that. I... I thought Wren was dead." Even when Niall told me the story about of the Dark Witch, none of it had clicked. "I guess I just thought I'd been given the vision because Wren shared the bloodline with the wolves of Ossory."

"I'm honestly surprised your mother never told you," Blaire continued.

"What?" I blinked up at her. "What would by mother have to do with any of this?"

"It's complicated." Blaire's features scrunched together, creating a dark shadow below her brows that hooded her eyes even more.

"So you've said," I continued to push. The air around me grew warmer as she reached out to touch my arm and I could smell the subtle fragrance of jasmine and lavender. "Don't," I said, yanking my arm from her reach. She was manipulating the atmosphere–which meant that whatever news she had to deliver was going to be bad.

"Sorry, it's just… instinct." She cleared her throat, and interlocked her fingers. "Reincarnation for the White Witch is different than it is for the Whelan and Alderdice clans. You see, since Conan and Luiseach were bound to one another, it made it impossible for them to have an heir. It's not possible for other Supernaturals to carry the leanaí of werewolves… but the Trinity *must* have an heir." Her raptor-like eyes fell on mine, piercing through with careful precision.

"Leanaí?" I repeated

"It means children," she explained. "When your mother married into the Callaghan name, she would have been visited by the Earth Mother. She would've had to agree to carry the descendant of the White Witch, knowing what you'd become even before you were conceived. That's how it's been for decades," Blaire's voice was gentle as she finished; her eyes unblinking.

I could feel heat creeping up the back of my neck, pooling in my ears again. I cleared my throat, reaching up to toy with the pendant around my neck. "This is all… just a little much to take in. I'm just… I'm just going to get some air." I stood up from the couch then, and mechanically made my way to the top of the stairs and then out the back door to the shop. There was a picnic table there, the red paint chipped from years of elemental whiplash. I hoisted myself up by my arms, sitting on the surface of the table and letting my feet rest on the bench.

The forest was less than a hundred yards away, and Silver Mountain was peeking out from behind the tops of the tallest trees. I thought about walking in and letting the forest just swallow me whole. The air was cool, but I was numb enough not to feel it on my skin. I concentrated on my breathing, the natural pull of air through my lungs, and the slow and steady exhale of it through my nose. Somewhere between breaths my lips parted, and trails of hot tears began to stream down my cheeks. I didn't sob–wouldn't let myself cry out, but the rivulet of tears betrayed me anyway.

And then he was there, obscuring the sunlight as he took my face in his hands, and brushed the tears away with his thumbs.

"She never told me who I was," I said, voice breaking. "My whole life she tried to protect me, to warn me about what could happen if my secret ever got out, but I never knew the real reason... If she had only told me..." I let me voice trail off, slowly shaking my head.

"You wouldn't be any different than you are now," Wren said, forcing my chin up to meet his eyes. He tucked a loose strand of hair behind my ear, and tipped his forehead to meet mine. "None of us knew who we were."

"At least Blaire knew about the prophecy," I said derisively. "My mom should have been preparing me for what could happen."

"She probably wanted to give you as much of a normal life as she could," Wren said softly. "She wanted you to enjoy your childhood and to grow up without having to worry about something that may or may not come to pass. You heard what Blaire said. Sometimes the Trinity never gets called forth."

I nodded against his forehead, letting his words take root. He slid in beside me on the picnic table, wrapping a solid arm around me while his other hand gently pressed my head against his shoulder. We sat like that for some time, lost in thought. I wished I could ask my mom what had been going through her mind when the Earth Mother visited her. Why had she agreed to carry me? Was I even hers–or was I just a product of some magical seed? I looked just like her... I had to be hers.

"It's a lot of information to take in all at once," Wren said, breaking the silence, "but I meant what I told you this morning. Whatever the world throws in our direction, we'll handle it. I'll be with you every step of the way."

"As if you had any other choice," I said with a snort.

Wren pulled back then, his eyebrows furrowing as he looked deeply into my eyes. "We are not those people. I am not Conan and you are not Luiseach. Just because we carry their bloodline doesn't mean that we don't make our own choices."

"We were drawn to each other, Wren," I said plainly. "We've been making our way to one another for nearly four hundred years."

"So what?" Wren shrugged. "Most people spend their whole lives searching for their soulmate and never really knowing whether or not such a thing exists. And here you are complaining because you've found that it does." He cracked a glimmer of a smile as light began to dance across his eyes.

"I just want you to want me because *you* want to, not because the stars just happened to align in our favor. Out of all the people in the world, I want to know that if given the choice, you'd choose me."

He pressed his lips together, sighing with audible irritation. "If we've loved each other before, it wasn't because the stars aligned, and fate planted us in each other's path. See, the thing about a soulmate isn't that they're just destined to be together. You find that person–by divine intervention or not–and you become each other's strengths when weakness shows through. You challenge each other, and push each other because you'd rather go through life knowing that that person is going to stand by you on your best day, and hold your hand through your worst. We aren't just some perfect fit, Quinn. We're human beings capable of conjuring our own emotions, and making our own memories. And if somehow we've been lucky enough to find each other through different lifetimes then you should know… I'm glad it was you. If given the choice, I'd choose you over and over."

His mouth pressed to mine hard, forging his affirmation. I reached up, looping my arms around his neck to hold on from the sheer force of it. He kissed me like it was the first time and the last time all rolled into one single moment of transcendent rapture, and I knew… whatever the stars had called forth to make us, I no longer cared. I was his, and he was mine.

Chapter Seventeen
The Warning Signs

"Are you all right, lass?" Blaire asked once we'd returned to her lair.

Learning that you were a soul reincarnated from the White Witch was a lot to swallow, but there were more pressing things that needed our immediate attention. I'd have time to absorb the shock later. "I'm fine," I told her. "So what do we do now, I mean, how do we find Penny?"

"Have you tried a locating spell?" Wren asked.

"Of course I have," Blaire's features twisted into a scowl, "but she's being blocked, like someone is hiding her on purpose."

"It's the same with the other werewolves," Wren said. "My father and I have been tracking them, but whenever we get close the scent just disappears."

"The Chameleon Shield," I said aloud, "it's a cloaking spell. I remember seeing it in one of my mother's grimoires. It's like using a jamming signal on a GPS to keep someone from tracking you. Maybe the Dark Witch is using it somehow... Would she be strong enough to do that?" I looked up at Blaire.

"Not by herself." She shook her head.

"Someone is helping her, then." I bit the inside corner of my mouth, pursing my lips in thought. Wren was looking at me with an omniscient look in his eyes, waiting for me to catch on to what he'd already concluded. "What?"

"I think the both of you should be looking a little closer to home..."

he said, his deep voice rumbling with an accusation.

I narrowed my eyes. "You can't mean Penny?"

"Bollocks! She's a guardian," Blaire reminded him, the shock of his allegation registering in her tone. "Don't be saying things that aren't true."

"Why would the werewolves want anything to do with her?" he countered, raising a signature eyebrow. "You said yourself she's not a witch."

"No, but we *are*," Blaire gestured to herself and then me. "If the Dark Witch knows that we're part of the Trinity, she may be using Penny as collateral in attempt to lure us to her."

"Hmph." The gravelly sound caught in Wren's throat. "That's quite a stretch."

"But not impossible," I said.

"I can't find her on my own," Blaire said a beat later, "but perhaps if we link ourselves, the power of the Trinity will be enough."

"How does that work? I mean, can we do it ourselves or does someone have to do it for us?"

"In the days of old, a ritual was performed by the coven to bind the three together, but we haven't the time for that seeing as the coven is in Ireland. We can do the spell ourselves, but, we need to be at the center of the Nexus," Blaire said.

"And where might that be?" Wren asked.

"The Hollow," I answered, thinking of my sacred place in the forest—the place where my mother and I celebrated and where I frequently slipped to recharge my powers. Of course, I had been drawn to that place for a reason.

"You know the place?" Blaire seemed surprised.

"Just because I didn't know about any of this," I extended my arms above my head, gesturing to the opened books and legends surrounding us, "doesn't mean that I'm totally useless as a witch. I *can* detect the pull of energy." I knew without a doubt that the Hollow was a hot spot for natural energy. I could feel it circulating through the trees, stirring in the breeze. The very earth beneath my feet practically vibrated with its raw, electrical charge.

"I meant no offense," Blaire said with a shrug of her shoulders. "There is something that you should know, however..." She glanced up at me with hesitation. "If for some reason the Dark Witch doesn't yet know who we are, after we've linked ourselves together... there will be no guessin'."

"Good," I said straight-faced, "she should know we're coming for her. They should all know."

☾

I met up with Annabelle after practice had ended.

Wren agreed–with major reluctance–to go our separate ways for a couple of hours. He needed to fill his dad in on what we'd discovered, and I needed to warn Annabelle to stay away from the forest tonight. We'd decided to perform the ritual at the stroke of midnight so the spell would be at its strongest.

I grabbed Annabelle's sleeve as she came out of the locker room, catching her off guard. She jumped, clutching a hand to her chest and gave me a heartfelt glower. "Well don't you look incredibly rested for someone who is supposedly ill." She lifted her eyebrows, grimacing.

"I need to talk to you," I said quietly.

"Those of us who attended school today actually have homework to get to, so if you'll just excuse me." She started to walk away but I grabbed the hem of her shirt.

I had to admire her for standing her ground, even if I thought she was being unreasonably stubborn, but I'd never expect anything less from Annabelle. "Anna, it's important," I pleaded.

"Is it the truth this time?"

I sighed, leaning up against the painted cinder wall. "If I've ever intentionally held anything back from you it was only to keep you safe. You know I would never put your life in danger if I can help it."

"That decision isn't yours to make," she hissed.

"This isn't a game, Annabelle. We aren't little girls anymore where the biggest risk of exposure is me accidentally sending a campfire roaring up into the air. It's life and death. And you may not like it, or think that I'm being unfair to you, but do you have any idea what I would do if anything ever happened to you?" I reached out, sinking my fingers into her shoulder, gripping hard to get my point across. "I have already lost the most important person in my life; I couldn't handle losing you, too. It would break me, Annabelle, do you understand that?"

She fell silent, and her eyes began to soften.

"There's a reason Chloe Sullivan became Watchtower," I added, leveling my eyes with hers, knowing she'd understand my analogy. Chloe was the eyes and ears of the operation, holed-up in the tower overlooking the city where she could safely send all the superheroes on their secret missions.

She nodded, shifting on her hip. "So. Where were you this morning, really?"

"Let's go outside," I suggested. She followed me down the hall, and out the back door that led to the baseball fields. We walked to a small tree where a couple of empty picnic benches sat beneath the shade of the branches. Once I was positive we weren't in danger of being overheard, I told her everything that I'd learned from Blaire that morning. As I slowly and thoroughly reiterated the story, the meaning of the legend began to sink in even deeper. The history had long since been planted within my DNA, but it was starting to take root. I could feel it, the essence of it coiling through my veins and pumping with every beat of my heart.

When I finished, Annabelle's face was a perfect mask of composure, but I could tell she wasn't afraid. In fact, she hardly seemed surprised. Maybe I'd done enough over the years to spoil the chances of a "shock factor." She'd always been tough, but sitting here now, I wondered if perhaps she was also resilient.

"I told you that you were destined for great things." She met my eyes, lifting the corner of her mouth into a half smile.

"You understand why you can't be there tonight?" I said.

She nodded slowly. "I understand. I don't like it… but I understand. Blaire really thinks that the Dark Witch is using Penny to lure you out?"

"It's our best lead," I said.

"What will happen when you link yourselves together?" She looked over at me, her mask finally slipping enough to show me that she was worried.

"I don't know," I answered honestly.

"I mean… I'm not, like, going to lose you, or anything?" She was staring at her feet as she said it, avoiding my eyes now.

"Why would you think that?" My eyebrows laced together, creating a deep crease between my eyes.

"Because, Quinn, you're sort of this amazing, powerful being that's been called forth to stop the world from ending. I don't know where I fit in the picture anymore, or if there's even room for someone like me."

"Someone like you," I snorted. "You're my absolute best friend, and nothing that this world, or even the next has to say will stand in the way of that." I bumped her shoulder with mine. "We've a bond of our own."

"Right." She looked up and grinned. "Sisterhood."

"The deepest bond there is," I said.

"I don't know…" She shot me a questioning glance. "Finding your soulmate at seventeen seems pretty high on the charts."

I rolled my eyes. "It's kind of crazy, isn't it?"

"You know I'm not really into the whole sappy romance thing, but… I think anyone would just about give their life to find out who their soulmate is."

A jolt of static electricity snapped through my temples then. I closed my eyes, and saw russet leaves and pine needles blowing across the Hollow. *Not again*, I thought. A mass of thick blood rose up from the earth, covering the ground before me. I looked around this time, aware that this was some sort of premonition; the blood wasn't real and therefore couldn't hurt me. I was already in a vision; the damage had already been done. I stepped forward, slipping through the liquid mixture. Needles stuck to the bottom of my shoes, making it impossible to catch any kind of traction. I fell forward, and landed on my hands and knees. The blood splattered against my face, and I could feel the heat and smell the copper on my skin.

I tried to move but the blood was acting as an adhesive, keeping me planted to the ground as it congealed around me. *It's just a vision, it won't last forever.* I squeezed my eyes shut, willing myself to snap out of it. But when I opened my eyes, the body of a werewolf lay in front of me. There was a line of red smeared across its throat, staining its gray fur. I reached for the wolf, and the vision ended.

Annabelle was staring at me. Her eyebrows were pulled together, and her mouth was slightly parted. "Okay. What the hell was that?"

"What did you see?"

"I don't really know," she said, shaking her head. "Your head just sort of dropped like you'd passed out or something. Have you ever seen someone with narcolepsy? They're here talking or laughing one minute, and the next they're just transported right into sleep paralysis."

"I don't have narcolepsy," I snapped.

"Then *what* was that?"

"I don't know exactly. I started receiving visions just this morning, without ever coming into contact with blood."

"How is that possible?"

"I don't know." I shook my head. "Maybe my powers are growing." I explained to her what I'd seen in both visions, and let her roll it over in her mind.

"Probably a werewolf is going to die tonight?" she suggested. "It wasn't Wren in your vision, right?"

"No. He's," I bit my lip, looking up at her nervously. It was a bit awkward explaining to your best friend that you'd seen your boyfriend Changing into a werewolf. "His fur is black," I said finally, knowing that my cheeks were flushing.

She snorted. I shot her a look.

"Sorry," she said. "New territory."

"For all of us," I said.

"So, how *did* last night go?"

"Fine. It was a full moon, so he was a wolf half the night," I said with a shrug.

"And the other half?" She lifted an eyebrow, her mouth contorting deviously.

"He was human." I decided to play coy.

"Oh come on," she tipped her head back and laughed. "You can't honestly expect me to believe that nothing happened. He is your soulmate after all."

"Is that what you want to discuss right now when I've got a world to save?" My smile betrayed my tone.

"Fine," Annabelle rolled her eyes. "Don't tell me. I don't want to hear all that absurd, sentimental bullshit anyway."

I giggled, spreading my hands across my pant legs, watching as the tendons protruded beneath my skin. The wind was picking up, carrying the scent of rain with it. I looked up at the sky, noting the shape of the idle moving clouds and the color that was slowly darkening the Western Hemisphere.

"Are you okay, Quinn? I know this must have been a lot for you to take in all at once," she said softly.

"I'm not afraid, if that's what you mean," I said, and I meant it, "but it would have been nice if my mom would have told me what I was. Wren thinks she wanted me to have a fulfilling childhood, free of all future magical burdens 'that may or may not have come to pass.'" I quoted him.

"He's probably right, but I get where you're coming from. I mean, I'd want to know if I were secretly the Princess of Egypt or a descendant of Cleopatra or something. That knowledge bears a lot of weight, though."

"*So* not the same thing." I chuckled.

"Still."

"If I would have known about my heritage, I could have been practicing–preparing myself to be better at the craft, ya' know?"

"I'm not sure that really matters," Annabelle said after a moment. "You can't do anything to change the past anyway, so you might as well focus on the future. There's no doubt in my mind you'll know what to do when the time comes. So, let's get this evil bitch and vanquish her for real this time. I'm sure Satan has plenty of room for her somewhere within the nine circles of hell."

"Oh Anna," I laughed. "What would I ever do without you?"

Chapter Eighteen
The Light Bringers

"Are you ready?" Wren whispered against my ear. His breath was warm on my neck. The cool night air wrapped around me like a silk cloth, hugging the angles of my body. *Was I ready?* I didn't know. But I didn't have a choice in the matter so I laced my fingers with his, and headed for the forest. The Hollow was a good mile hike from my house, but I knew the trail by heart. I could probably make the trip blindfolded walking backwards through gale force winds. As we inched closer, the stronger the pull of energy became. I could feel the draw of it; the warmth of it inviting me in.

"Where's Niall?" I asked a few moments later.

"He's patrolling."

I nodded. I'd met up with Wren and Niall after walking Annabelle to her house. I wanted to see how Niall had taken the news, and make sure Wren was okay will the plans for tonight. Niall's beat-up Apache and Wren's Pontiac were sitting in the drive when the cabin finally came into view from the lane. I hadn't really noticed before, but there was a small garden peeking out from behind the cabin with a few rows of dried, golden stalks of corn and other various autumn vegetables. I remembered Wren telling me that Niall lived off the land, and the picture before me was proof.

Wren opened the front door as I raised my hand to knock. He greeted me with an easy smile; his body visibly relaxing in my presence.

"Please tell me you haven't been waiting there all afternoon?" I teased him.

He rolled his eyes. "I could sense you coming," he said, pulling me into his arms. I tucked my face into the crook of his neck, and breathed in the earthy scent of his skin. He smelled enticing, and I pressed my lips to the warm skin of his throat. "How did Annabelle take everything?" he asked.

"Surprisingly well," I answered, stepping into his kitchen. "She was upset that I lied to her, of course, but she seemed to understand why it had to be done."

Wren nodded, and led me into his living room where a large bay window sat within the western-most wall. He had a perfect view of the mountaintop, and the giant pines of the surrounding forest. The floors were wooden, adorned by a black-and-white Aztec rug and a dark leather couch. He sat down, and gently pulled me in next to him.

"How did Niall take it?" I wondered.

"He took it in stride," Wren said. "I think he feels responsible. He's worried the burden is too much for us to bear."

"It's not his fault," I said, thinking that Niall had been all-too acquainted with the familiar weight of burden from such a young age himself. Of course he wouldn't want his son to feel a fraction of the hardship that he'd faced in his lifetime. I thought his mindset was admirable. He was a hell of a better parent than his ex-wife for that reason alone. Wren was an adult, but Niall still wanted to protect him, which was an ocean's difference between he and Wren's mother.

"Are you going to tell your dad anything?"

I dropped my gaze, noting the contrast of the grass stain on my white shoelace. "I don't think so," I replied a beat later. "It's probably better that he doesn't know. Losing my mom almost killed him. I don't want him to worry about me when there's nothing he can do to help."

"You'll have to tell him eventually," Wren said, squeezing my hand.

"I know," I said, "but hopefully that will be after we've defeated the Darkness."

"I'm not sure it will ever end for people like us," Wren said, and I detected the hidden malice in his deep voice. "I don't think this is a onetime deal where we fight the battle of evil and that's that–assuming we even win."

I looked up at him, studying the doubt that so visibly flashed across the surface of his tawny colored eyes. It wasn't fear that made him uneasy. "Hey," I said, "we're going to be all right. Apparently, we were made for this." I tried to joke.

His mouth twitched, ever so slightly, and then Niall walked into the room. He was wearing a pair of faded jeans, and a plain T-shirt. His long hair was pulled back at the nape of his neck, trailing down his back in a gray braid. Niall's mouth pressed tightly together when he saw me, giving me a nod of his head in greeting. "Quinn."

"Hey, Niall," I returned, forcing a small smile. At that moment, I wished I had the ability to read minds. I wondered what he was really thinking behind those dark, omnipresent hooded eyes. I wanted to say something else, but 'I'm sorry I got your son involved in this ancient witch-hunt-thing that turns out we have no control over anyway– because hey! We're part of the Original Trinity, and it's our destiny to destroy the Darkness,' just didn't seem like the right thing to say at the time.

"I'd like to see you both, outside please." He turned from the living room and headed for the front door. I looked up at Wren, my eyebrows pulled together.

"Come on." Wren took my hand and led me out the front door, past their garden and over to a slow burning fire pit near the edge of the forest. As we got closer I could smell the smoke; it was different from any burning wood I'd ever smelled before, but in a good way. It was thick, but sweet smelling. The smoke coiled through the atmosphere in a sort of gray-colored rhythmic dance.

Niall was kneeling on the ground in front of the fire, unrolling a leather pouch that contained various handmade tools. He took out a large soft-brown, gray and white feather. "This is from a great horned owl," he told us, stroking the length of the feather. "In my culture, owl feathers are symbolic of great wisdom and protection. The feathers are sometimes worn as talismans to protect against evil spirits. The owl himself is a messenger of the night; a revered warrior." Niall gestured for us to sit, and we joined him around the base of the fire. "The wood in the fire is called pinion. My people believed that burning the wood would ward off evil, and give protection against impure witchcraft," he paused, studying both of us quietly. "You both have a dangerous journey ahead of you. Will you accept this gift of protection, and honor the Creator and the Earth Mother?" He was looking at me.

"Yes," I said, my voice barely registering in the air between us. Niall nodded once, closing his eyes. After a moment, he took up the owl feather, and began chanting in his Native tongue. With the feather, he fanned the smoke, using it to cleanse my spirit, giving me strength and protection. I didn't understand the words he was saying, but I could feel them channeling something inside my core. I closed my eyes and let the words and the smoke wash over me, and I felt my connection to the earth deepening. I pushed my fingertips into the grass beside me until I could feel the dirt beneath my nails. She rose up to meet me; a weapon at the ready.

I tried to hold onto that feeling as we walked through the forest with the moon on our backs. I wanted to feel the influential energy, and the power of it coursing through my veins. I wanted to be strong like the Earth.

A few minutes later we were breaking through the tree line of the Hollow, and Blaire was standing by the large boulder; her long onyx hair cascading down her back. She was wearing a floor-length black cotton dress with long sleeves. The silver-blue hue of the moon up above filtered down through the branches, haloing Blaire in an otherworldly glow. She was the real deal, I thought; the forest was ready to bend to her will. She looked up from the book, spotting us.

"Right on time," she said. "I've started the circle, but once it's been cast there's no breaking it until the spell has ended."

I nodded. There were five pillar candles spread wide on the forest's needle-coated floor, marking the five points of the pentagram. Each pillar was a different color, representations of the elements we would be invoking. The Spirit candle was purple, depicting spiritual power and energy. The blue pillar represented Water, for protection and focus. The red pillar represented Fire, for strength and survival. The green pillar represented Earth, for growth and grounding. And last, the yellow candle to represent Air for clarity and regeneration.

Wren and I joined Blaire at the center of the pentagram, and Blaire lifted her grimoire. "Hear us now, Great Mother," Blaire began, reading from the ancient text. "We come to thee in search of power that was gifted to the Trinity. We stand before you, ready for the honor and responsibility. What is done in evil's name, let it be undone, for we are the instruments of hallowed light, walkers in the sun. We are the Light Bringers. *Is iad na daoine a thugann solas duinn.*" Blaire sat the book at her feet, and picked up a gleaming, silver athame. "It's stainless steel." She said to Wren. "Repeat after me, and we'll finish casting the circle," she said. "We invoke the elements, please join us now. *Táimid ag plé leis na heilimintí, bí linn anois.*"

"*Táimid ag plé leis na heilimintí, bí linn anois,*" we repeated. I could feel Fire beginning to dance across my palm, the purple fury of it rolling, and waiting for my command. Beside me, Blaire was also holding a fireball in her hand. She looked at me, her mouth twisting into a grin as she nodded–knowing that I understood what came next. "*Solas,*" we commanded, and sent Fire jumping from our palms to the wicks of each pillar candle surrounding us.

"Now the hard part," Blaire said, unsheathing the athame. The smooth edge of the blade gleamed in the moonlight like liquid steel as she dragged it across the soft flesh of her left hand. A scarlet stream yawned across her torn skin, pooling in the center of her palm as thunder rumbled in the near distance.

"We better hurry this along," Wren said, lifting his face to the night sky.

"You're not afraid to get a little wet are ya' pup?" Blaire chuckled, and passed him the blade.

He glowered at her, quickly slicing the flesh of his right hand.

"You'll have to cut both of your palms I'm afraid," Blaire said to me. "I've got bandages for after."

I nodded, taking the athame from Wren.

"You'll be taking us with you this time," Blaire said, "whatever you see, we'll see, too. The Great Mother will show us the way. It's how she'll link us together."

I sucked in a sharp breath of air, feeling a bout of anxiety rake through my stomach and settle there like I'd swallowed a mouthful of lead. A seed of doubt began to take shape in my mind. *I didn't have to do this*, I thought. I could drop the blade and walk out of the circle, running away from responsibility. I could take heed to caution like my mother had always preached, and retreat into the fear I suddenly felt circulating through my insides. But then I remembered Nathan Reed and his icy blue eyes. I knew this wouldn't make up for what happened to him, but it was a chance to finally stand for something that was bigger than me. This was a chance for us to make a difference.

I felt Wren's hand wrap around my wrist then, and felt the warmth of his touch. I looked up at him and found the determination I was looking for written across the planes of his face. He was my other half–my counterpart, and I would find strength through him when weakness took hold of my bones and planted me in fear. I could stand there asking myself why destiny had chosen me, but maybe there wasn't a reason in all this–at least, not one that I could make sense of.

The only thing that made sense right now was Wren, and the touch of his fingertips as they wrapped around my wrist; the promise he made to me and for now, that was all I needed. I gripped the handle of the athame firmly, and pressed the tip of the blade into the flesh of my palm, wincing as the bite of it opened up my skin. A crimson flower bloomed in my palm; I quickly sliced the flesh of my other.

"And so the Trinity becomes one," Blaire said, holding her hand out to me. I nodded firmly, and reached for both of their hands with mine. When our palms met, a great burst of purple fire sparked high into the atmosphere from our pillars, and the wind began to roar around us sending leaves and pine needles swirling through the air. Above, I caught a glimpse of lighting obscuring the moon, but then there was the familiar pull that grabbed tightly to my ankles.

The ocean current was pulling us now, shifting and shimmering like the images on the ink-blot test until we were far pressed beneath the waves. My head was spinning, and the ache in my lungs forced me to let go of the others as I fought my way to the surface. My fingers broke through the surf and my lungs expanded with that glorious first gulp of air as I pulled myself up the hillside. Wren and Blaire were beside me, both panting and gasping for air.

The vision twisted us along her path, showing us a glimpse of three others before us standing beneath the light of the summer moon. Their hands were linked together–interlocked by a thread of ivory satin ribbon. A coven of witches in medieval garb were chanting before them in the ancient, Gaelic tongue. I looked at the woman in the middle, knowing in my core that she was the White Witch; *the Sword of Light*, I heard in my mind and for a moment, I swear her green eyes rested on mine. Her full lips tilted upward at the corners, hinting at a smile. Her hair was a golden honey color that fell in delicate waves below her shoulders. I could feel the power radiating from her being. Everything she represented was a part of me, and as the words of the witches roared high into the night, the spell bound the Original Trinity.

"Blood of my blood," the White Witch spoke only to me, "answer my call. For you alone have the power to walk the path of shadow and not turn from the Light. The others will try to help you, but you must walk this path alone."

"I don't understand," I said aloud, but the vision was already pushing us back. "Wait!" I pleaded, fighting against the force of wind.

"Seek the sun, when day takes up the false cloak of night," she left me with those parting words. The light was far too bright, pushing us back into the forest. The wind was still howling from the force of the coming storm.

But something else was wrong.

I could feel it under my feet, vibrating the very ground we stood on. The spiritual nexus–the place of pure, organic power was shifting beneath us, transforming with coils of blackened smoke that came inching out of the ground beyond our protective circle.

"She knows we're here," Blaire said beside me, studying the vapors that were snaking across the ground. They licked at our feet, but couldn't get through our circle; their tendrils caressing our invisible barrier, searching for a crack within the armor. I reached for Blaire's hand, watching the way the moonstone on her finger began to swirl with pulsing aqua light. *Werewolves.*

In the nearing distance, the call of the wolves rang high through the trees; the sound of their howls sent the hair on the back of my neck standing on end. In a matter of seconds, half a dozen wolves broke through the tree line, invading the Hollow with deep growls grating from their throats. Blaire and I called on Fire, and the element responded by igniting across our palms in a dazzling display of orange and purple globes of electricity.

"So," a female voice penetrated our circle, the ice of it melting down the backs of our necks, "the Trinity has been invoked once more. The White Witch has come out to play and she's brought her pet wolf and the empath along, too." A woman, probably in her mid-twenties stepped into the Hollow. She had a mane of thick, wild hair and eyes to match. There was something manic about the way she looked at us; her upper lip twitching at the corner, a sneer lining her mouth.

"Who are you?" I demanded.

"Someone who's come to deliver a message." The wolves inched closer, spreading out so they had us surrounded; trapping us like cornered cats. There was one wolf in particular that seemed to be more distracted than the others. I recognized the red coat, and as it got closer, saw that it was missing an eye. I'd hit him there with a fireball just days before, and I recalled the sound he made when the electricity snapped in his face.

"What have you done with Penny?" Blaire asked.

"Penny?" The woman cocked her head to the side; a movement that I thought was rather canine. As she stood there, I saw the muscle in her forearm begin to ripple. The Change was inching its way to the surface, and she was eager for the release.

Wren caught sight of this, too, and as I shifted my gaze to him I saw that his eyes were glowing electric yellow. His lips pulled back just enough to reveal the glistening dagger-like points of his canine teeth. His body was rigid, and half crouched in front of me as he stared down the encroaching werewolves.

"My aunt," Blaire said, "I know you have her."

"I don't know a Penny," the woman spoke slowly, "but I know another who's proven to be a great deal useful." She grinned, and her teeth extended into sharp little points. "You can come out now, Bram," she said in a sing-song tone.

Twigs snapped on the forest floor. There were sounds of a struggle, and then a mountain of a man stepped into the dim light and shoved Niall hard to his knees. His hands were pinned behind his back and a trickle of dark blood stained his temple, running the length of his jaw. Niall looked at me alone, and I felt my blood freezing over in my veins. It wasn't fear I saw on Niall's face–it was stone cold acceptance–as if he'd somehow known this was his fate all along.

An electric current snapped through my temples. I saw the gray wolf lying in front of me on the ground where Niall was now. The image sparked, and Niall took the wolf's place in my vision. I grit my teeth, fighting against the pain in my head.

A low, warning growl grated from the back of Wren's throat as he stared down the man who was pinning Niall to the ground. I'd never seen anyone remotely close to his size. He towered over the top of us, around the height of six-foot-six. He was as wide as he was tall, his body covered in great hunks of rippling muscle. His neck disappeared into his shoulders, and as my eyes moved upward, I saw that his face was distorted by two long scars that cut diagonally across his cheekbones. His eyes were black pits–hollow, mindless.

"Let him go," I said, stepping forward. Blaire reached out, wrapping her small palm around my wrist. She shot me a warning look. The circle, I remembered–if one of us stepped out, the protection shield would vanish. Thunder surged across the sky, and the tops of the trees swayed in the stormy wind. A bolt of lightning slashed across the midnight clouds, and with it came the first cold drops of rain. They hit the back of my neck and face with an icy spray that stole the air from my lungs.

"I don't think so, *White Witch*," the woman spat out the name like it was poison. "We've been sent by Rionach to deliver a message." She pulled a blade from her pocket and flung herself to Niall's side, she was holding the dagger against his throat before any of us could blink. "Every time you get in her way or try to stop her, she *will* kill someone you love," the woman said. "Let this be a warning to you." Her eyes were swimming with the cold current of yellow electricity, and the muscle of her arms contorted beneath her skin. "Kill the others," she commanded to the other werewolves, "but Rionach wants Quinn alive." And with those words, she slid the razor-sharp edge of the dagger across Niall's throat, and a smile of scarlet blood yawned across his flesh.

"*No!*" Adrenaline slammed through my body with all the force of a rising tempest. I ran forward, breaking through the circle as I sent my fireballs whirling for the woman. They exploded against her chest, sending her flying backwards through the air until she landed flat on her back. She rolled and bounced to her feet quickly, and began ripping out of her clothes with a scream as she brought on the wolf Change.

I slid to my knees in front of Niall, scooping his head into my arms and gently laying him against my lap. "I'm so sorry, I'm so sorry," I sobbed, and tears started pooling down both sides of my cheeks, blending with the rain that was soaking through our clothes. Lightning flashed across the sky, briefly lighting the scarlet necklace flooding his throat.

He looked up at me, and I could tell that his dark eyes were fading fast. His body was in between two worlds. "Take... care of him. Tell him... I love..."

"I will," I said, "I promise."

Blood trickled over the corner of Niall's mouth as he made a horrific gurgling sound. There was so much blood. It covered my clothes, and soaked into the earth below. His blood should have launched me into a vision, but there was nothing left to see of his future. His life was ending. My premonition had been a warning, I realized, and I'd been too blind to see it. Niall closed his eyes, exhaling his last breath on earth, and then he was gone.

Gone.

What a sad, final sounding word. I was still cradling his body when something hard slammed into me from the side, knocking the air from my chest. I crashed against the forest floor, feeling the ends of the dead pine needles pushing into my skin. I tried to catch myself with the palms of my hands, and felt the wounds reopening as they split even wider. I winced in pain, rolling to my side as I called on Fire. Flame ignited across my palm, spinning with white-hot energy. The red wolf was baring its teeth at me, close enough so that the light from my fireball obscured the true color of his single eye. I could see the firelight reflecting against his pupil. "You want to lose the other one?" My voice ripped through my throat with fury, and I flung my fireball in his direction.

He dodged it, flinging himself against me. His paws landed on my shoulders, pinning me against the ground as my head smacked against a rock. Pain screamed in my head, causing my vision to go black around the edges. The wolf's teeth were less than an inch away from my throat, but I pushed with all the strength I could muster against his neck, jamming my elbow into what I hoped was his larynx. Fire answered my silent call, and I blasted the wolf with my left hand. He yelped as my blast sparked against his face and he toppled from me.

Blaire pulled me up and sent another fireball whirling for a wolf that was running in our direction. The force of her blow knocked its feet out from under him, and he crashed hard into the base of a boulder.

"Where's Wren?"

"I'll wager he's in the mix," she said, gesturing to the wolves surrounding us. It didn't take me long to spot him. Even through the rain his onyx coat was gleaming with a blueish hue. He was fighting with a gray wolf, the sounds of their growls and cries ringing high into the night. "What happened to the big burly man?"

"No idea," I said, "but we need to get out of here."

"Here," Blaire said, extending her hand to me, "take my hand." I linked my hand with hers, and flung a fireball at a wolf with my other. "From shadow we call upon the flame of Light, warrior blood has been shed upon this darkened night. Hear our call across the sky, let the power of the witches' rise." Electricity snapped from her fingertips, pushing out a similar shield to the one I had conjured when I thought she'd been attacking Wren in the Magic Shoppe. "Push your shield out to Wren," she called to me over the roar of rushing wind and rain.

Before, the shield had been an automatic defense mechanism—something I pulled out of a hat when the need called for it. I didn't know how I'd done it, but I remembered the way I felt—overwhelmed by an innate need to save and protect Wren. I used that now to form my shield, and pushed it out in front of me until it joined with Blaire's and expanded across the land. It crawled across the blanket of pine needles, pushing out and enveloping Wren as he sank his teeth into the throat of another Were. The werewolf's body began to transform; bones and sinew popping and realigning in order to take the shape of a human man.

"Wren," I called out. "Stop!"

"Go to him," Blaire said, "I can hold this for a while longer."

I nodded once, and jogged across the Hollow. Blood was seeping from the man's throat, pooling on the needle-covered ground. Wren let go, but he was still crouched in front of him possessively and growling. I pressed my fingertips to the man's jugular, and detected a faint heartbeat. Wren turned, baring his teeth in my face. I jumped back, caught off guard by the hostility he was showing toward me.

"Wren, it's me," I said, tentatively reaching my hand for his coat.

"He's turned it off," Blaire said behind me. "The human part of his brain—he's turned it off."

"No." I blinked rapidly, searching for any sign that Wren was still in there. He was more than just the wolf, and I needed him to remember. I knew firsthand that grief could break a person entirely, but I couldn't let him go down that path. If I let him, even for a minute, I might never get him back. "Wren, it's me, it's Quinn. I need you to remember who you are," I said to him. "I know you can hear me. You once told me that it gets hard to separate the two halves, and I understand that, especially now. But I won't let you stay this way. This man," I looked down, watching as his chest slowly rose with a breath of air, "isn't dead. You didn't kill him because you are *not* a monster. Do you hear me?"

Wren didn't break eye contact with me, but at least he wasn't growling. His eyes were dilated, the pupils expanding wide over his yellow irises. His ears were shifted back on his head, but he was listening.

"I need you, Wren. I can't do this without you. Do you remember what you told me?" My voice quivered a little, and tears threatened to sting my eyes. "Whatever the world throws our way, we'll face it together. Do you remember? I choose you," I said in a whisper, "I choose you."

He closed his eyes then, and tossed his head back against the midnight sky, and howled. The low, haunting sound of it raked its way through my skin, and squeezed tightly around the corners of my heart. I reached for him, buried my face into the fur of his neck and wrapped my arms around him.

"You are mine," I reminded him.

Outside of the shield, some of the Weres had already run off. Most had been injured in the fight and were retreating to lick their wounds. But there were a few stragglers, still waiting just beyond the shield, baring their teeth.

The athame we had used in our Trinity ritual was lying on the ground, not even a foot out of my reach. I rose to my feet and snatched it up, fingers wrapping around the handle tightly. I knelt before the man at my feet, and placed the blade against his throat. "I have a message for the Dark Witch," I called out, making sure I had the remaining werewolves' attention. "Tell Rionach that we're coming for her, and if I see any of you come near someone I love–I swear to the Mother that I will kill you, but I'm saving Rionach for last." The wolves outside the barrier were growling but they had begun to back away. "The power of the nexus is ours to command, you are powerless here!" My voice echoed into the trees as another bolt of lightning snapped across the sky and collided with one of the pine trees.

The treetop caught fire, sending a cascade of sparks raining down as the branches bowed and snapped, and broke from its great trunk. The limbs came barreling down, and plummeted to the ground in front of us with a forceful sounding thud that continued to blaze with orange flame. The remaining wolves scattered then, vanishing through the tree line of the Hollow.

"Nice work," Blaire complemented.

"I didn't do that," I said.

"Sometimes the Earth Mother steps in when she's needed." Blaire lowered her shield so that it cloaked only the three of us, requiring less energy to keep it going.

"We need to get Niall out of here," I said softly, turning back toward his body. I shrugged out of my jacket, pulling the sleeves with some difficulty and looked at Wren. "I'm not going anywhere," I told him, "we'll do this together."

"I'll, uh, just turn around," Blaire said, and turned her back as she concentrated her energy on keeping the shield in place.

Wren rose, and I watched as the fur of his black coat began to retract. His bones began to pop, snapping and twisting as his limbs rearranged. It didn't take as long as the Change from man to wolf, but it looked equally as painful. When he finished, I flung my arms around his neck, and pressed myself as tightly as I could against his body. He was breathing heavy from the Change and streaked with mud and blood I prayed didn't belong to him.

His fingers looped through the back of my hair, and I winced as they brushed against a sore spot. When he pulled his hand away, his fingers were stained with my blood. "What happened?" he asked me.

"Landed on a rock, but I'm fine," I said, fingertips reaching for his face. I needed to look into his eyes. I needed the reassurance that everything was going to be all right... but it wasn't there. He was broken, I thought, seeing the forlorn look softening his features and pulling his brows together. "I'm so sorry, Wren."

He shifted his gaze then, sweeping over Niall's body on the forest floor. He reached for my jacket and tied it around his waist, walking over to his father. I started after him, but Blaire reached for my arm.

"Give him a moment," she suggested, pressing her lips together.

Wren knelt in front of Niall's body, placing a hand over his father's heart, and I felt mine break a little more.

"What are we going to do?" I wondered aloud. This wasn't a crime that we could report to the police.

"We have to leave him," Blaire said, and I wheeled on her with confusion lacing my brows together.

"What?"

"We can't place ourselves at the scene of the crime," she said regretfully. "This needs to look like a murder."

"It *was* a murder," I spat acidly.

"Yes, but not the kind we can report." She leveled her eyes with mine. "There are too many questions that we can't answer without giving ourselves away, and it's too dangerous to involve humans that way."

"She's right," Wren said. "If we report this now, the police are going to ask what we were doing up here during a storm in the middle of the night. The pieces that are missing will only point the finger in our direction."

"So what do we do?" I asked.

"I'll grab some camping gear and set up a tent and a deer stand not far from here in the morning. I'll tell the police that my dad went on a hunting trip last week, that he was supposed to be back days ago and hasn't come home."

"You'll be a person of interest." I shook my head.

"There could be worse things," he said coolly.

"The knife is still here," Blaire pointed out, "they could fingerprint it."

"Get rid of it," Wren said, his voice had turned to ice.

"Why?" I couldn't believe this!

"Say they find that Were," Wren wheeled on me, his face just an inch away from mine, "what do you think happens when they arrest a werewolf and she's trapped behind iron bars on the night of a full moon?" His eyes blinked back and forth between mine. "We can't stop the Change from coming," he said.

For a minute I thought, *good*, let them find out… but then I remembered that would only lead to much darker things. A discovery of any Supernatural in the wrong pair of human hands could be a death sentence. Fear would rule their ignorance, and we would end up science experiments–tortured in some horrible way. "So what then," I said finally, "Niall's murder just goes unsolved?"

"We'll know who did it." Wren pushed past me, bumping his shoulder into mine as he stormed out of the Hollow.

"Let him go," Blaire said. "His aura is fueled by an unhealthy amount of rage and agony right now. He's fighting it for your benefit, but he needs to let it out. I know you're worried about him, but he's a strong one. He'll get through this."

I chewed the inside corner of my lip, watching as his frame disappeared into the forest. The storm had passed, but the rain was still lightly sprinkling. I didn't realize how cold I'd gotten until my jaw started to quiver. How long had we been out here? The sky was just barely starting to lighten in the Eastern Hemisphere, awakening the sun.

"We can cast a protection spell around his body so that nothing happens until the police find him." Blaire's hand was on my shoulder, and she spoke softly. "Just in case the werewolves come back and get any ideas."

I nodded. "Yeah, okay."

Blaire retrieved her grimoire from behind a boulder. The pages were undamaged from the storm. Her book was spell protected, too. Smart, I thought. While she set to work casting the protection spell over Niall's body, I collected the pillar candles, and stuffed them in the backpack she'd brought them in. The athame was still lying beside the unconscious werewolf's body.

He looked like he was in his early twenties. He had sandy colored hair, and good bone structure. I knelt before him, and picked up the athame, studying the wounds on his body. They weren't as bad as the wounds that Wren had received when they'd left him for dead just a few nights before. He would heal soon. They all would. They might have won this fight, but the battle was far from over...

"Blaire," I said, "I have a really bad idea."

Chapter Nineteen
Out from the Ashes

Blaire and I carried the werewolf out of the forest. Her car was parked off to the side of the road just outside one of the park entrances. My muscles were screaming with the burning sensation of tension, but I was determined to get him back to the Magic Shoppe before he woke up. We loaded him into the backseat of her car, and tied an old blanket around his waist to cover up things I'd rather not have to look at.

We were quiet on the ride to the shop. Blaire blasted the heat to help dry our soaked clothing, but left the radio off. I needed the silence. I concentrated on the steady hum of the engine–the white noise–as we wound down the mountain pass. I didn't want to think about what we were doing. I wouldn't let myself question my choices because if I did, even for a second, there was a good chance that I'd have Blaire stop the car and leave the Were on the side of the road.

This wasn't me, or at least, it wasn't who I'd been.

It wasn't so long ago that my friends and I had been playing a round of twenty questions in between races at one of our cross-country meets. We always asked such off-the-wall, hypothetical questions that we thought would never come to pass. It was our way of getting inside each other's mindsets–really testing one another. Torrance always had the best questions. Her mind operated on a different wavelength.

"Let's say you were stranded on a deserted mass of land in the freezing cold where there wasn't any food, but you had your family pet with you… Would you starve, or eat little Muffin to survive?" she asked.

"That's sick, Tor," Harper told her, wrinkling her nose in disgust.

"That's the point," she said. "You don't know what you're capable of until you're actually put in a situation that tests you. You do things you're not proud of when your survival instincts kick in."

"So you're saying you'd actually eat your pet?" Jamie cocked an eyebrow.

Torrance shrugged. "I wouldn't want to, but humans are hardwired for survival… Starvation is painful beyond anything you can imagine. You probably start to hallucinate. I mean, there are actually studies on this stuff."

"I could never do that," Harper said, shaking her head.

"Quinn, what do you think?" Torrance was looking at me, waiting for my answer expectantly.

"I'll let you know if I'm ever in that situation," I answered, thinking I was taking the easy way out. I'd never owned a pet, but the idea of killing something you loved in order to save yourself seemed foreign to me. Not that I'd ever blame someone else for doing that in that particular situation. Survival was a funny sort of instinct that did strange things to the mind.

But now, I wondered if Torrance hadn't actually been on to something. At the moment, there wasn't anything in the whole world that I wouldn't do to protect those I loved. It helped that anger was fueling my resolve. I was infuriated that I had no control over what was happening to me–*to us.* None of us asked to be put in this situation, yet here we were anyway. I didn't feel like the deck was exactly stacked in my favor, but I had to play with the cards I'd been dealt regardless. So, I swallowed the conflicting emotions that were bouncing around my brain and hauled the werewolf into the Magic Shoppe.

"Shall we lug him into the basement?" Blaire asked once we'd gotten him through the door.

"Not unless we plan on letting him roll down the stairs," I panted. Luckily the werewolf wasn't a big man, but dead weight was dead weight.

"I'm not exactly against the idea." Blaire straightened, resting her hands on her hips. "There's a chair around the corner, we can fasten him in."

I nodded. "On three." We counted down, gathered what was left of our strength, and somehow managed to get the werewolf into the chair.

Blaire turned on a vintage, blue porcelain table lamp. She disappeared around the corner to the supply room and returned a moment later with bungee cables. "I'll grab the wolfsbane for precaution, you start securing those arms of his behind his back." She tossed me the cable and headed for the hidden lair.

Don't think, Quinn, just do, I told myself. I slipped around the back of the chair and worked on securing his wrists. Blaire returned a few seconds later with a jar of wolfsbane and a spell book. As I worked on tying his ankles to the chair legs, she began chanting in the Gaelic tongue. The bungee cables began to glitter with a silver sheen and I let go as they tightened.

"There's a spell for that?"

"There's still so much you've to learn," Blaire said, placing the book on the counter. The werewolf's head lolled against his chest, and I could tell he was starting to come to. His wounds had all but healed, leaving thin red lines and scratches across his skin.

"Get ready," I told her. I reached out, shaking the Were's bare shoulder. His eyes moved rapidly behind his eyelids and his lips parted. He blinked up at me, squinting against the lighting. His eyes widened, and his body tensed, flexing against the cables that bound his arms and legs to the chair. "There's no use fighting," I told him, "the bonds have been spelled to make sure you stay in your chair."

"Where am I?" His head snapped to the right, sweeping over the layout of the room and the shadows that blended into the walls.

"How about we start with your name," I countered.

The werewolf sneered, his lip curling upward. Even though he was the one tied to the chair, his smile was cocky. "I'm not telling you anything, so you might as well kill me."

"We don't want to kill you," I said evenly. "We just want some answers."

"Go to hell," the werewolf spat.

Blaire stepped forward then, pressing her hand against the werewolf's chest. Her palm was filled with wolfsbane, and the plant sizzled and snapped against his flesh. My stomach clenched as he ground his teeth, grunting in agony as silver vapor snaked up from his wound.

This wasn't humane. But then I reminded myself that he'd been trying to kill me and my friends. One of them had killed Niall. I forced myself to continue for his sake.

"What's your name?" I asked again.

"Garrett," he grunted. "My name is Garrett."

"This doesn't have to be difficult, Garrett," I told him. "We just want to know where Penny is. Do you know her?"

Blaire stepped back, and I saw the patch of blistered flesh on his chest. The wound was festering. "We know Penny," he growled.

"Where is she?" Blaire asked.

"She's probably halfway to Ireland by now, what's it to you?"

"Why would she be there?" Blaire narrowed her eyes.

"How should I know?"

"Because you're working for the Dark Witch aren't you?" I crossed my arms over my chest to keep them from shaking.

The werewolf snickered, rocking back in the chair in a way that made his chest puff out. I wanted nothing more than to wipe that little cocky grin off his face.

"Look, the rules are simple," I hissed. "You answer the questions and we'll let you go. It's as easy as that." I made myself take a step forward, squaring my shoulders. "We are not monsters."

Garrett snorted, flipping a lock of blond hair out of his eyes. "I don't know, looks like you're taking a walk on the dark side to me, White Witch, and it looks like you're enjoying it."

"This conversation is about as useless as a chocolate teapot," Blaire said, tossing her arms to her side in frustration.

"We're not monsters," I repeated.

"Says the girl who's got me tied to a chair." He sneered.

"Would you have cooperated otherwise?"

"Would you like to find out?"

"You said you know Penny, so what does the pack want with her?" I asked, ignoring his question.

"Like I said, you're going to have to kill me. I'm not telling you anything."

I glowered at him, but something from our vision quest popped to the foreground of my mind. It was what the White Witch had said to me before she sent us back to the forest. "*For you alone have the power to walk the path of shadow and not turn from the Light. The others will try to help you, but you must walk this path alone,*" she'd said. I still wasn't entirely sure what that meant, but I had a feeling that this was only the beginning. "We're not going to kill you." My voice was steady.

"Well then I think your plan is flawed. Don't get me wrong–I admire the little charade you have going on here, but I don't plan to play that nice. Who's to say I don't kill you the moment you untie me?"

"Me." I looked over by the bookcase where his deep voice had broken through. Wren was leaning in the doorway, his dark clothing blending in with the shadows. I didn't have to look at him to know what he was thinking; that it had been stupid and reckless of me to bring a werewolf here.

"Well, well, I thought I smelled rotting flesh. Didn't I kill you already?" Garrett snickered.

"I'm still very much alive," Wren said, hooking his thumbs through his belt loops. "And you would be dead if she hadn't saved your life." He jerked his head in my direction and I instantly felt my stomach coiling with knots. Had I known that this was the wolf who'd almost taken Wrens life, I'm not so sure I would have stopped Wren from ending his life. Maybe I should stop trying to convince myself that I wasn't a monster...

"I suppose I should be expressing my gratitude then." He looked up at me, a wry expression lining his lips.

"Just answer the question," Wren growled, leaning down so that he was eye-level with the werewolf. "Or *I* will kill you."

Garrett sighed. He stared off with Wren for a moment before deciding Wren was serious about his threat. He wasn't getting out of here unless he told us what we wanted to know. "Penny's working with the Dark Witch," he said pointedly. "She's helping her get the amulet back."

"That's a lie!" Blaire spat.

"It's not possible," I added. "The Dark Witch can only be summoned by her own bloodline and Penny isn't even a witch."

"She doesn't have to be a witch," Garrett informed us. "She just has to share the same bloodline as the Alderdice witches, and if I'm not mistaken, *Blaire*, that would be you. I mean, Penny *is* your aunt, right?"

"I don't understand." Blaire's eyebrows pinched together, creating a deep crease between her dark, raptor-like eyes.

"That was Rionach's insurance policy," Garrett said. "She was counting on the fact that none of you would be smart enough to figure it out," he paused. "Your coven has been keeping an eye on the original king's bloodline, but their daughter wasn't the king's true heir. Rionach screwed around with Aine Alderdice's husband. The bloodline that you needed to be keeping an eye on was your own." Garrett was wearing a smug expression, and Blaire's face went ashen pale.

"That can't be possible," she breathed out.

"Oh come on, you have to admit it's kind of poetic in a tragic way," Garrett went on. "The Trinity is supposed to be this pure, powerful force of light–and as it turns out, the bloodline is tinted with Darkness."

"The word is *tainted*, moron," Wren told him.

"Fuck off, grammar police."

"How did Penny find out about the link between the bloodlines?" I asked.

"No idea." Garrett shrugged.

"And where do the rest of you fit into this?" I wanted to know. "How many of you are there?"

"You saw for yourself tonight in the clearing," Garrett answered. "Penny came to us for help, she told us what the Dark Witch was after and we agreed to help."

"What's in it for you?"

"What's in it for anyone who agrees to follow the shadow?" he countered. "Power. Protection. A better life for our pack," he finished.

"And you actually believe you'll have that if Rionach returns to power?" I shook my head. "Are you not aware that she bound werewolves to their wolf skins permanently and made them do her bidding in the dark ages? She made them fight wars for her and the king, and forbid them from ever returning to their families. It was the White Witch who set them free so that they could Change when they wanted."

Something faltered in Garrett's expression then, like a light of realization flashing across his irises. "She wouldn't do that to us," he said, but his tone betrayed him, and the statement came out in the shape of a question.

"You've got it all wrong, Garrett. The Dark Witch gave her soul to the Darkness. The only being she's looking out for is herself–that, I can assure you. Whatever she's promised you is a lie." Garrett was shaking his head, anger knitted his deep-set brows together. "You could help us stop her," I said.

Garrett chuckled, leaning forward in the chair. "That's not going to happen."

I stared at him for a long moment, studying the colors in his icy eyes. I knew I had succeeded in planting a seed of doubt. I just hoped it was enough for him to do his research and discover the truth for himself. The pack had been tempted by the seduction of the darkest powers and the promises that Rionach had made. I remembered what that felt like from my vision. They were lost, and she'd found them, sinking her claws in and spreading the poison.

"So what now?" Garrett asked, breaking the silence.

"Tell me where the pack is staying," I said.

"Not a chance."

I gnawed on the inside of my lip and made an executive decision. Suffice to say enough damage had been done for one night. I was finally hitting that proverbial wall and doubted I'd get any more information. "Then you're free to go," I said.

"What?" Blaire jumped up from the couch with a handful of wolfsbane coiled in her fist. "He hasn't given us anything!"

"He's given us plenty," I said calmly, "and we're *not* monsters."

"What about Penny?" I could see the anguish in her eyes, knowing that she understood that we'd lost her but didn't want to admit it out loud. Wren reached out, wrapping his palm around her shoulder while I turned back to Garrett.

"Don't come after us," I warned him. "As long as you're working for Rionach you're our enemy, and I can promise that we're a lot stronger than all of you."

Garrett nodded, and I moved around the back of his chair to work on untying his ankles. Wren positioned himself in front of Garrett, letting him see the Change swirling in his irises while I untied his hands from behind his back. Blaire called on Fire, and two energy-balls were dancing across her palms, waiting at the ready.

As Garrett stood, Wren shoved him in the back to give him a little nudge toward the door. I followed close behind, ready in case he tried anything stupid. He didn't. When we reached the sidewalk, Garrett backed away slowly, acting as though he were as leery of us as we were of him.

"Despite what you may think, we're here to help if you change your mind," I said once he'd reached the end of the sidewalk.

The corner of his mouth raised into a smug grin. He snickered, and then vanished under the shadows. Wren and I stood there, gazing at the spot where he'd disappeared from. I was half expecting him to pop back out, only this time with the whole pack of werewolves at his side.

The breeze blew a couple of dead leaves across the rain-soaked sidewalk, and the sound startled me. Wren wrapped his arm around my shoulder and pulled me against his side. "He's gone," he assured me, and I tightened my hold around his waist, gazing up into his eyes. All the tension I had been holding seemed to melt when he had his arms around me. I breathed in the familiar scent of his neck, pressing my lips to the curve of his shoulder.

"Where did you go?" I breathed into the collar of his shirt.

"Running," he replied. "I'm sorry if I was–"

"–You have nothing to apologize for," I cut him off, reaching up to cup the side of his face in my palm.

"I shut you out," he said, his brows furrowing.

"No you didn't." I shook my head. "You did what you needed to do, and that doesn't require guilt or an explanation."

Wren tipped his forehead to mine, his fingertips slipping down the backs of my arms. "I don't know how to do this," he whispered, his breath warming my face. "I don't know what's going to happen…"

"It's okay," I said, holding his face in my hands. "We'll figure it out together."

We held on to one another as the sun broke over the horizon, climbing its way above the mountainside. Everything beyond our two bodies seemed intangible; it was all just a terrible nightmare, and we'd wake up from it if we just kept holding on. I wanted to believe that because I didn't want to face the reality of it all. But the facts were laid out before me now, like the missing pieces of a jigsaw puzzle just waiting to be linked into place.

Penny was helping the Dark Witch for reasons we couldn't possibly fathom, but I knew somehow we'd have to stop her from getting her hands on that amulet. The werewolves were another problem…

But then there was Niall.

Niall wasn't the first to die in my arms… but seeing someone leave this life wasn't something a person could ever get used to. Watching them take that final breath of air, and hear their final words… it was enough to shatter a soul. I remembered feeling helpless when my mother was taken from me. I remembered the sorrow and the way my body had gone numb to everything else. She'd suffered for so long, and I was so tired of seeing her in pain. I was almost relieved when the Creator took her home, only because it meant she could finally be at peace–free from pain.

I didn't feel that way about Niall. They'd killed him to make an example. Niall had been a warning. Hatred pulsed through my veins, boiling my blood at the thought of the woman who'd so heartlessly taken Niall's life.

Wren pulled back, just enough so that he could study my face. He must have felt my body go rigid in his arms. A single tear slipped from the corner of my eye, burning a trail of liquid fire down my cheek.

"Quinn?" His eyes blinked back and forth between mine.

"I was just thinking of something the White Witch said to me on our vision quest," I said.

"She spoke to you?" He narrowed his eyes.

"She said that I would have to travel a path of shadow alone, that only I would have the power to walk the path of Darkness and not turn from the Light... What do you think she meant by that?"

"I don't know," he replied after a short pause. His brows were still pulled together, veiling his eyes. "But you're not doing anything alone."

I nodded as he pulled me in against his chest, but a part of me wondered if I would really have a choice.

It didn't seem right that the sun was shining. I managed to sneak back into my room just before my dad's alarm sounded on his radio. I startled, clutching a hand to my heart as I collapsed against my bed. I could hear him shuffling down the hall, and as I looked down at my hands that were still stained in Niall's blood, hot tears threatened to spill from my eyes. I grit my teeth, keeping the sobs locked inside as I pulled my knees to my chest.

"You up, kiddo?" Dad knocked on my door.

My head snapped up. "I'm up," I called.

"Crazy storms we had last night, did you get any sleep?"

"Not much."

"Me either," he said. "Well, I'm going to get an early start; swing by Jo's after practice, okay?"

"Sure Dad, I love you."

"Love you, too."

There was a part of me that wanted to run to him and fling my arms around his neck like I had done when I was a little girl–scared of the make-believe monsters under the bed and in the closet. I wanted to tell him how much he meant to me, and that I was so grateful for all the sacrifices he'd made for our family. I wanted him to tell me, just one more time, that everything was going to be all right... But I knew it was better–safer–if he didn't know what was happening. I wasn't ready for him to learn the truth of what I was becoming. He'd protected me for all my life, and now, it was time for me to be the strong one.

I waited until his truck pulled out of the drive before forcing myself through the motions. I showered, scrubbed the blood from underneath my fingernails, and changed into clean clothing. I knew that Wren and Blaire were probably wrapping up the fabrication of the murder scene, and a fresh wave of nausea raked my gut just thinking about the deception. I hated that they'd gone without me, but I knew I needed to make an appearance for my dad if we really had a shot at making this thing believable. The police could never learn the truth about what happened.

Shortly after Garrett left us, Blaire made a call to her sister in Ireland to warn her about Penny. Whether or not Garrett had been telling the whole truth was still a mystery, but we thought it best to get the amulet moving just in case. Bryna agreed to warn the rest of the coven, and then she'd be on the next available flight to the States. In the meantime, we had a funeral to plan…

I slipped out into the cool morning air, watching the opaque frost of my breath billow out in front of me. I didn't call on it, but I felt the Spirit element reaching out to me, filling me with a renewed sense of vitality. Fire came next, the element I felt closest with, and filled my soul with determination. "Thank you," I whispered.

A beat later, Wren pulled the Pontiac into the lane, idling in front of the porch. As I climbed into the passenger's seat, I reached for his hand, entwining our fingers. Warmth spread between our two palms, and as I looked into his eyes and saw the tragedy of what we'd been through–I knew we were more than just our sorrow. Grit and iron flowed through our veins, our convictions making us stronger. Imminent danger was lurking on the horizon, but together we would face the Darkness.

"Are you ready?" Wren squeezed my hand. He looked at me like he was ready to take on the world, and so was I.

"I'm ready," I answered.

We were survivors, and something more–a force for good, and a beacon in the darkness. We were the Light Bringers.

Epilogue

```
Authorities found a local man's body in
the woods on Wednesday, September 27th in
Silver Mountain forest. Officials say the
man went by the name of Niall Whelan, who
had been a Silver Mountain resident for
over forty years. Police are investigating
the incident, but they believe that Whelan
was killed by a knife wound to the throat.
Whelan was reported missing by his son on
the morning of the 25th, announcing that
Whelan hadn't come back from a hunting
trip. Officials are still searching for
the murder weapon at this time.
```

I smoothed the paper across my desk, feeling the indentations of the wrinkles from where I'd crumpled it up the night before, and tossed it to my bedroom floor. Niall had deserved so much better, and the deadpan way in which the article had been written repulsed me to the point of inducing nausea. I cringed, reading it now, knowing full well that the police would never find the woman who did this or the murder weapon. Niall's death was our dirty little secret, and the guilt of it tightened around my heart.

"Quinn, we need to get a move on," Dad called from the bottom of the stairs. "I know you don't want to do this, honey, but Wren needs the support."

"Two more minutes," I called back, pushing up from my bureau. I checked my reflection in the mirror, and not even the makeup I was wearing could cover up the dark shadows that lined the hollow places beneath my eyes. My black dress was itchy; the fabric clung to my skin in all the wrong places. The last time I'd worn it had been to my mother's funeral, so I'd stuffed it in the back of my closet and there it had remained until today. I'd layered it with a pair of black tights, and black flats, and decided to pull my hair back into a ponytail. I looked like I'd stepped out of a Tim Burton film, or was auditioning for the *Corpse Bride*.

I tugged on my doorknob, and started down the hall. I'd all but gotten to the stairs when the pentagram pendant snapped from its chain, rolled down the front of my dress and continued on until it smacked into the wall at the very end of the hallway. When it hit, a blue spark caught in the space between my silver pendant and the wall. I frowned, bending slowly to retrieve it.

I had been seriously sleep deprived over the last week or so, but I knew magic when I saw it... I ran my fingers over the wall, wondering what could have caused the spark, and then I heard Blaire's voice in my mind when she led Wren and I to her lair. "Why is it hidden?" I asked her. "For protection," she'd told me.

There were some things that needed to remain hidden, and out of human reach for safety reasons. Magic was dangerous in the wrong hands. Lately, I couldn't stop thinking about my mother, and the fact that she knew what I was destined to become before she even had me... I needed answers, and she'd intentionally kept me in the dark. Until now, perhaps?

I rose slowly, holding the pendant in my palm while I touched the wall with my other. I could almost feel the energy pulsing behind the wall, and the excitement I felt crept up my spine and sucked the moisture from my throat. Could my mom have hidden a lair of her own?

"*Oscailte*," I whispered.

The End
...For Now...

Thank you so much for reading one of **Brittany Elise's** novels.
If you enjoyed our book, please check out our recommended title for your
next great read!

The Calling of the Trinity

The fate of the supernatural world lies in the hands of the Trinity. Now that
their powers have awakened, they're one step closer to putting an end to the
Darkness surrounding them. Or so they thought.

The death of Wren's father brings and unsolicited visit from the Alpha
Master of the Thornwood werewolf pack, and with it some troublesome
news. Wren is faced with a decision that could end his life if he doesn't choose
wisely.

A mysterious book hidden in a secret room just might have the answers
the Trinity is searching for. Perhaps with a little help from the past, a winged
guardian, and some new friends - the Trinity can persevere and rise against
the Darkness.